BLOOD-DRENCHED BEARD

BLOOD-DRENCHED BEARD

Daniel Galera

TRANSLATED BY
ALISON ENTREKIN

HAMISH HAMILTON
an imprint of
PENGUIN BOOKS

HAMISH HAMILTON

Published by the Penguin Group
Penguin Books Ltd, 80 Strand, London WC2R 0RL, England
Penguin Group (USA) Inc., 375 Hudson Street, New York, New York 10014, USA
Penguin Group (Canada), 90 Eglinton Avenue East, Suite 700, Toronto, Ontario, Canada M4P 2Y3
(a division of Pearson Penguin Canada Inc.)
Penguin Ireland, 25 St Stephen's Green, Dublin 2, Ireland (a division of Penguin Books Ltd)
Penguin Group (Australia), 707 Collins Street, Melbourne, Victoria 3008, Australia
(a division of Pearson Australia Group Pty Ltd)
Penguin Books India Pvt Ltd, 11 Community Centre, Panchsheel Park, New Delhi – 110 017, India
Penguin Group (NZ), 67 Apollo Drive, Rosedale, Auckland 0632, New Zealand
(a division of Pearson New Zealand Ltd)
Penguin Books (South Africa) (Pty) Ltd, Block D, Rosebank Office Park,
181 Jan Smuts Avenue, Parktown North, Gauteng 2193, South Africa

Penguin Books Ltd, Registered Offices: 80 Strand, London WC2R 0RL, England

www.penguin.com

First published 2014
001

MINISTÉRIO DA CULTURA
Fundação BIBLIOTECA NACIONAL

Obra publicada com o apoio do Ministério da Cultura do Brasil/
Fundação Biblioteca Nacional

HARDBACK ISBN: 978–0–241–14613–2
TRADE PAPERBACK ISBN: 978–0–241–14614–9

www.greenpenguin.co.uk

For DP

When my uncle died I was seventeen and knew him only from old photos. For some unfathomable reason, my parents used to say that he was the one who owed us a visit, and they refused to take me to the seaside to meet him. I was curious to know who he was, and once passed quite close to the town of Garopaba, in Santa Catarina, where he lived, but I ended up putting off visiting until later. When you're a teenager the rest of your life seems like an eternity and you imagine there'll be time for everything. News of his death took a while to reach my father, who was secluded in a cabin in the mountains of São Paulo, trying to finish his latest novel. My uncle had drowned trying to save a swimmer who fell from the rocks on Ferrugem Beach on a day of stormy seas and ten-foot waves exploding against the coast. The swimmer clung to the float he had given him and was rescued by other lifeguards. My uncle's body was never found. There was a symbolic funeral in Garopaba and we attended. My mother showed me the location of the first apartment he had lived in, though it has now been demolished. In old photos you can see the two-storey beige building with its roof terrace, right in front of the ocean, above the rocks. There weren't any tall buildings on the waterfront back then and the water was still good for swimming. The population of the original village, now heritage-listed, around which the town has grown, still partially made its living from fishing, which has since disappeared to give way to boat tours. We met his widow, a woman with very white skin covered in faded tattoos, and their two young children, a boy and a girl, both of whom had their mother's blue eyes. My cousins. There weren't many people at the funeral. My mother broke down crying, which I didn't understand, and later spent about half an hour gazing out to sea, talking to herself, or to someone. There were other people staring out to sea as if they were waiting for something and I had the strange impression that they were all thinking about my uncle, even though he had been described as a recluse whom few people knew well, a man from another era. I decided to film some interviews about him, and my parents allowed me to stay on in the town for a few days on my own. No one knew my uncle intimately but everyone seemed to have something to say about him. At the beginning of the previous decade he had opened a small studio, where he taught stretching and Pilates. Most people remembered him as a triathlon coach and it would appear that half a dozen state and national champions had trained with him at some point. During the summer season he would put his regular activities on hold to work as a lifeguard. He was the best. He trained volunteers every year. At dusk, after a twelve-hour shift rescuing swimmers, treating cases of sunstroke and jellyfish stings, and walking about under the brutal sun of a southern region devoid of an ozone layer, he was seen swimming alone out in the deep, oblivious to turbulent seas, downpours and sudden nightfall. He was a solitary man, but at some stage he had married this woman who had sprung from goodness knows where and built a little house on a dirt road that wound its way through the hills of Ambrósio. Everyone who remembers my uncle from the old days mentions a lame dog that swam like a dolphin and who accompanied him out into the deep. And here ends what we might refer to as the facts. The rest of the interviews were a kaleidoscope of overlapping rumours, legends and colourful stories. They said that he could stay underwater for ten minutes without coming up for air; that the dog who followed him high and low was immortal; that he had once taken on ten locals in a fist fight and won;

2

that he swam at night from beach to beach and was seen emerging from the sea in distant places; that he had killed people, which was why he was discreet and kept himself to himself; that he never turned away anyone who came to him for help; that he had inhabited those beaches forever and would continue to do so. More than one or two said they didn't believe he was really dead.

PART ONE

I

He sees a bulbous nose, shiny and pockmarked like tangerine peel. A strangely youthful mouth between a chin and cheeks covered in fine lines, slightly sagging skin. Clean-shaven. Large ears with even larger lobes that look as if their own weight has stretched them out. Irises the colour of watery coffee in the middle of lascivious, relaxed eyes. Three deep, horizontal furrows in his forehead, perfectly parallel and equidistant. Yellowing teeth. A thick crop of blond hair breaking in a single wave over his head and flowing down to the nape of his neck. His eyes take in every quadrant of this face in the space of a breath and he could swear he's never seen this person before in his life, but he knows it's his dad because no one else lives in this house on this property in Viamão and because lying on the floor next to the man in the armchair is the Blue Heeler bitch who has been his dad's companion for many years.

What's that face? asks his father.

It's an old joke. He gives his usual answer with the barest hint of a smile:

The only one I've got.

Now he notices his dad's clothes, the tailored dark grey slacks and blue shirt with long sleeves rolled up to the elbows, with sweaty patches under his arms and around his bulging belly, sandals that appear to have been chosen against his will, as if only the heat is stopping him from wearing leather shoes. He also sees a bottle of French cognac and a revolver on the little table next to his reclining chair.

Have a seat, says his dad, nodding at the white two-seater imitation-leather sofa.

It is early February and no matter what the thermometers say it feels like it's over a hundred degrees in and around Porto Alegre. When he arrived he saw that the two *ipê* trees that kept guard in front of the house were heavy with leaves and drooping in the still air. The last time he was here, back in the spring, their purple-and-yellow-flowered crowns were shivering in the cold wind. Still in the car, he passed the vines on the left side of the house and saw several bunches of tiny grapes. He imagined them transpiring sugar after months of dry weather and heat. The property hadn't changed at all in the last few months, it never did: it was a flat rectangle overgrown with grass beside the dirt road, with a small disused football pitch in its usual state of neglect, the annoying barking of Catfish, the other dog, the front door standing open.

Where's the pickup?

I sold it.

Why is there a revolver on the table?

It's a pistol.

Why is there a pistol on the table?

The sound of a motorbike going down the road is accompanied by Catfish's barking, as hoarse as an inveterate smoker shouting. His dad frowns. He can't stand the noisy, insolent mongrel and keeps it only out of a sense of duty. You can leave a kid, a brother, a father, definitely a wife, there are circumstances in which all of these things are justifiable, but you don't have the right to leave a dog after caring for it for a certain amount of time, his dad had once told him when he was still a boy and the whole family lived in Ipanema, in the south zone of

Porto Alegre, in a house that had also been home to half a dozen dogs at one stage or another. Dogs relinquish a part of their instinct for ever in order to live with humans and they can never fully recover it. A loyal dog is a crippled animal. It's a pact we can't undo. The dog can, though it's rare. But humans don't have the right, said his dad. And so Catfish's dry cough must be endured. That's what they're doing, his dad and Beta, the old dog lying next to him, a truly admirable, intelligent, circumspect animal, as strong and sturdy as a wild boar.

How's life, son?

Why the revolver? Pistol.

You look tired.

I am, a bit. I'm coaching a guy for the Ironman. A doctor. He's good. Great swimmer, and he's doing OK in the rest. He's got one of those bikes that weighs fifteen pounds, including the tyres. They cost about fifteen grand. He wants to enter next year and qualify for the world championship in three years max. He'll make it. But he's a fucking pain in the arse and I have to put up with him. I haven't had much sleep, but it's worth it. The pay's good. I'm still teaching swimming. I finally managed to get the bodywork done on my car. Good as new. It cost two grand. And last month I went to the coast, spent a week in Farol with Antônia. The redhead. Oh, wait, you never met her. Too late, we had a fight in Farol. And that's about it, Dad. Everything else is the same as always. What's that pistol doing there?

Tell me about the redhead. You got that weakness from me.

Dad.

I'll tell you what the pistol's doing there in a minute, OK? Jesus, *tchê*, can't you see I'm in the mood for a bit of a chat first?

Fine.

For fuck's sake.

Fine, I'm sorry.

9

Want a beer?

If you're having one.

I am.

His dad extracts his body from the soft armchair with some difficulty. The skin on his arms and neck has taken on a permanent ruddiness in the last few years, along with a rather fowl-like texture. His father used to kick a ball around with him and his older brother when they were teenagers, and frequented gyms on and off until he was forty-something, but since then, as if coinciding with his younger son's growing interest in all kinds of sports, he has become completely sedentary. He has always eaten and drunk like a horse, smoked cigarettes and cigars since he was sixteen, and indulged in cocaine and hallucinogens, so that it now takes some effort for him to haul his bones around. On his way to the kitchen, he passes the wall in the corridor where a dozen advertising awards hang, glass-framed certificates and brushed-metal plaques dating mostly from the 80s, when he was at the peak of his copywriting career. There are also a couple of trophies at the other end of the living room, on the mahogany top of a low display cabinet. Beta follows him on his journey to the fridge. She looks as old as her master, a living animal totem gliding silently behind him. His dad plodding past the reminders of a distant professional glory, the faithful animal at his heel, and the meaninglessness of the Sunday afternoon all induce an unsettled feeling in him that is as inexplicable as it is familiar, a feeling he sometimes gets when he sees someone fretting over a decision or tiny problem as if the whole house-of-cards meaning of life depended on it. He sees his dad at the limits of his endurance, dangerously close to giving up. The fridge door opens with a squeal of suction, glass clinks, and in seconds he and the dog are back, quicker to return than go.

Farol de Santa Marta is over near Laguna, isn't it?

Yep.

They twist the caps off their beers, the gas escapes with a derisive hiss, and they toast nothing in particular.

It's a shame I didn't get to the coast of Santa Catarina more often. Everyone used to go in the 70s. Your mother did before she met me. I was the one who started taking her down south, to Uruguay and so on. Those beaches have always disturbed me a little. My dad died up there, near Laguna, Imbituba. In Garopaba.

It takes him a few seconds to realize that his dad is talking about his own father, who died before he was born.

Granddad? You always said you didn't know how he died.

Did I?

Several times. You said you didn't know how or where he'd died.

Hmm. I may have. I think I did, actually.

Wasn't it true?

His dad thinks before answering. He doesn't appear to be stalling for time, rather, he is reasoning, digging around in memory, or just choosing his words.

No, it wasn't true. I know where he died, and I have a pretty good idea how. It was in Garopaba. That's why I never liked going to those parts much.

When?

It was in '69. He left the farm in Taquara in . . . '66. He must have wound up in Garopaba about a year later, lived there for around two years, something like that, until they killed him.

A short laugh erupts from his nose and the corner of his mouth. His dad looks at him and smiles too.

What the fuck, Dad? What do you mean, *killed him*?

You've got your granddad's smile, you know.

No. I don't know what his smile was like. I don't know what mine's like either. I forget.

His dad says that he and his granddad don't just resemble one another in their smiles, but in many other physical and behavioural traits. He says his dad had the same nose, narrower than his own. The wide face, the deep-set eyes. The same skin colour. The granddad's indigenous blood had skipped his son and come out in his grandson. Your athletic build, he says, that came from your granddad for sure. He was taller than you, about six foot. Back then no one practised sports like you do, but the way he chopped wood, tamed horses, tilled the soil, he'd have given today's triathletes a run for their money. That was my life too until I was twenty. Don't think I don't know what I'm talking about. I used to work on the land with Dad when I was young and I was impressed by his strength. Once we went looking for a lost sheep and we found it over near the fence, almost on the neighbour's side, in a bad way. About two miles from the house. I was wondering how we were going to get the pickup there to take it home, already imagining that Dad was going to send me to get a horse, but he hoisted the ewe on to his shoulders, as if it were hugging his neck, and started walking. A sheep like that weighs ninety to a hundred pounds and you remember what it's like out there: all hills and rocky ground. I was about seventeen and asked to help carry it, 'cause I wanted to help, but Dad said no, she's in place now. Taking her off and putting her back will just be more tiring. Let's keep walking, the important thing is to keep walking. I probably wouldn't have been able to bear that animal on my back for more than one or two minutes anyway. I was never scrawny, but you two are a different breed. You're even alike in your temperament. Your granddad was pretty quiet, like you. The silent, disciplined sort. He wasn't one for idle chatter, spoke only when he had to and was annoyed by people who didn't know when to shut up. But that's where the similarities end. You're gentle-natured, polite. Your granddad had a short fuse. Boy did my old man have a temper on him! He was famous for pulling out his knife over any little thing. He'd go to a dance and wind up in a brawl. To this day I don't know how he got into so many fights, because he didn't drink much, didn't smoke, didn't gamble and didn't mess around with other women. Your grandma almost always went out with him, and, it's funny, she didn't seem bothered by this violent side of his. She liked to listen to him play. He was one hell of a guitar player. She once told me he was the way he was because he had an artist's soul but had chosen the wrong life. She said he should have travelled the world playing music and letting out his philosophical sentiments – that was the expression she used, I remember clearly – instead of working the land and marrying her, but he had missed his true calling when he was very young and then it was too late, because he was a man of principles and changing his mind would have been a violation of those principles. That was her explanation for his short fuse, and it makes sense to me, though I never knew my dad well enough to be sure. All I know is that he was forever dealing out punches and whacking people with the broad side of his knife.

Did he ever kill anyone?

Not that I know of. Producing his knife rarely meant stabbing someone. He did it more to show off, I think. I don't remember him coming home hurt, either. Except that time he got shot.

Shot?

He was shot in the hand. I told you about that.

True. He lost his fingers, didn't he?

In one of these fights, he lunged at a guy and the guy fired his gun to give him a fright. The bullet grazed Dad's fingers. He lost a bit of two fingers, the little finger and the one next to it. On his left hand, the one he used for picking. A few weeks later he decided to take up

13

the guitar again and in no time he was playing just as well as he always had or better. Some people said he'd improved. I can't say. He developed a crazy picking technique for his *milongas*. I guess those two fingers don't make much difference. I don't know. They certainly didn't make any difference for him. What really did him in was when your grandma died of peritonitis. I was eighteen. Life was never the same again, not for me or him.

His dad pauses and takes a sip of beer.

Did you leave the farm after Grandma died?

No, we stayed on for a while longer. About two years. But everything started getting strange. Your granddad was really attached to your grandma. He was the most faithful man I've ever known. Unless he was really discreet, had secrets . . . but it was impossible in a place like that, a small town where everyone knows everything. The women used to fall in love with your granddad. A bold, strapping man, a guitar player. I know because I went to the dances and saw single and married women falling all over him. My mother used to talk about it with her friends too. He could have been the biggest Don Juan in the region and was insanely faithful. Blondes galore all wanting a bit, wives looking for some fun. I myself lived it up. And Dad would give me a piece of his mind. He said I was like a pig wallowing in mud. Ever seen a pig wallowing in mud? It's the picture of happiness. But your granddad's moral code was based on the essential, almost maniacal notion that a man had to find a woman who liked him and look after her for ever. We used to fight a lot because of it. I actually admired it in him when my mother was still alive, but after she died he maintained a ridiculous sense of fidelity that no longer served any purpose. It wasn't exactly mourning, because it wasn't long before he was back at the dances, livening up barbecues, playing the guitar and getting into fights. He took to drinking more too. The women were all over him like flies on meat and little by little he let his guard down to this one or that one, but in general he was mysteriously chaste. There was something there that I never understood and never will. We started growing apart, him and me. Not because of that, of course, though we didn't see eye to eye on how to deal with women. But we started to argue.

Was that when you came to Porto Alegre?

Yeah. I came in '65. I'd just turned twenty.

But why did you and Granddad argue?

Well . . . I don't really know how to explain it. But the main thing was that he thought I was lazy and a womanizer who didn't want anything out of life and wasn't even remotely interested in the farm, work or moral or religious institutions of any kind. And he was right, though he was a bit over the top in his assessment. I think he just got fed up and couldn't be bothered trying to set me straight. I wasn't really such a lost cause, but your granddad . . . anyway. One day I experienced his famous short fuse first hand. And the upshot was that he sent me away to Porto Alegre.

Did he hit you?

His dad doesn't answer.

OK, forget I asked.

We knocked each other about a bit, so to speak. Oh, what the fuck. At this stage in the game none of it matters any more. Suffice to say that he gave me a working over. And the next day he apologized but announced that he was sending me to Porto Alegre and that it would be better for me. I'd been to Porto Alegre several times before and knew right away that he was right. I felt big here right from the first day. I went to technical school. In a year and a half I'd opened a printer's shop over in Azenha. In three years I was making good money writing ads for shock absorbers, biscuits and residential lots. *Stylize*.

He chuckles.

15

The glasses for eyes with style. And worse.

OK. But Granddad was killed.

There's the thing. This is where the story gets a bit nebulous, and I heard most of it second hand. I'm not exactly sure what happened, and it may be that nothing specific prompted it, but about a year after I moved to the city your granddad left the farm. I only found out when I got a call from him. International. He was in Argentina. In some armpit of the world whose name I don't remember. He said he just wanted to travel around a bit, but at the end of the call he kind of let on that he had gone for good, that he'd keep in touch and that I shouldn't worry. I didn't. Not much. I remember thinking that if he ended up dying in a knife fight in some shithole, like the character in that Borges story 'The South', nothing could be more appropriate. Tragic, but appropriate. Anyway. I also thought there had to be a woman in the story, or at least there was a ninety-nine per cent chance of it, there's always a woman in these cases, and if there was it was a good thing. And over the course of the following year he called me three more times, if memory serves me. One time he was in Uruguaiana. The next he was in some town in Paraná. Then he disappeared for about six months and when he called again he was in a fishing village in Santa Catarina called Garopaba. And even though I don't remember exactly what he said, I remember sensing that something about him had changed. There was a youthful ring to his voice and some of what he said was nigh incomprehensible. His description of the place was incoherent. I just remember one detail: he said something about pumpkins and sharks. I thought my old man had lost it or, even harder to believe, that he'd started hanging out with hippies and got his head in a scramble with some kind of tea. But what he was saying was that he'd seen the fishermen catching sharks by throwing cooked pumpkin into the sea. The sharks would eat the pumpkin and that shit would ferment and swell up in their bellies until they exploded. And I said, Yeah right, Dad, great, take care, and he said bye and hung up.

Fuck.

He never called again and I started getting worried. One weekend a few months later, when I hadn't heard from him, I got on my bike, the Suzuki 50cc I had at the time, and went up to Garopaba. An eight-hour trip on Highway BR-101, against the wind. We're talking 1967. To get to Garopaba you had to travel about twelve miles on a dirt road, and in some places it was just sand, and all you saw along the way were half a dozen farmers' shacks, hills and vegetation. The people, when you actually saw someone, were all barefoot and for each motorbike or pickup there were five ox-drawn carts. The village didn't appear to have more than a thousand inhabitants and when you got to the beach you didn't see much more in the way of civilization than a white church on the hill and the fishermen's sheds and boats. The main village was clustered around the whaling station and, although I didn't see anything, they still hunted whales in those parts. They were starting to cobble the village's first streets and the new square had just been finished. There were cottages and smallholdings on the outskirts of the village and it was on one of these properties that I found your granddad, after asking around. Oh, Gaudério, said a local. So I went looking for Gaudério and discovered that your granddad had set himself up on a kind of miniature model of the old family farm, about five hundred yards from the beach. He had an old nag, a bunch of chickens, and a vegetable garden that took up most of the land. He got by doing odd jobs and was friendly with the fishermen. He also gathered palm leaves, which were used to fill mattresses. He'd dry the leaves in the sun, then sell them for processing. He'd slept in the fishing sheds until he found a house. I couldn't imagine my dad sleeping in a hammock, much less in a fishing shed with the waves hammering in his ears.

But it was nothing next to the spearfishing. The locals fished for grouper, octopus and I don't know what else, diving around the rocks, and even back then there were already groups coming from Rio de Janeiro and São Paulo for that kind of fishing. And your granddad told me that one day he'd gone out in a boat with one of these groups and they'd lent him one of those masks with a tube attached, a snorkel, flippers and a harpoon. He dived under and didn't come back up. A guy from São Paulo freaked out and jumped in to look for Dad's body at the bottom of the sea and found him down on the reefs at the exact moment that he was harpooning a grouper the size of a calf. And that was when they discovered that Gaudério was a born apneist. He knew how to swim, could cross a fast-flowing river without a problem, but he'd never suspected he had such a great lung capacity. You should have seen your granddad back then. In '67 he was forty-five or forty-six, or forty-seven, I've lost count, but it was something like that, and his health was incredible. He'd never smoked, turned up his nose at cigarettes, and was as hardy as a Crioulo horse. He'd always been strong, but he'd lost weight, and although the signs of ageing were all there, wrinkles, thinning grey hair, the marks of working on the land, all he needed was a little polishing up and he'd have been a seasoned athlete. He had a broad, solid chest. A few weeks before I arrived, a diver about the same age as him, an army officer, I think, had died of a pulmonary embolism trying to match Dad's diving record. I might be mistaken, as it's been a while since I heard the story, but it was something like four or five minutes under water.

So why did they kill him?

I'm getting there. Patience, *tchê*. I wanted to give you the context. Because it's a good story, isn't it? Oh yes. You should've seen him back then. It's not normal for someone to leave one environment and go somewhere really different and adapt like that.

Don't you have a photo of Granddad somewhere? You showed me one once.

Hmm. I don't know if I still have it. Do I? I do. I remember where it is. Want to see it?

Yeah. I don't remember his face, obviously. It'd be nice to look at the photo while you tell me the rest.

His dad disappears into the bedroom for a few minutes, beer in hand, and comes back holding an old photograph with scalloped edges. The black-and-white image shows a bearded man wrapped in a sheepskin, sitting on a bench beside a kitchen table, starting to raise the straw of a gourd of maté to his lips, looking kind of sideways at the camera, unhappy about being photographed. He is wearing leather boots, *bombacha* trousers, and a jumper with a pattern of squares on it. There is a supermarket calendar with a picture of Sugarloaf Mountain on the wall and the light is coming from up high, from louvre windows that are partially out of frame. There is nothing written on the back.

He gets up and goes to the bathroom. He compares the face in the photograph with the face in the mirror and feels a shiver run through him. From the nose up, the face in the photo is a darker and slightly older copy of the face in the mirror. The only difference worthy of note is his granddad's beard, but he feels like he is looking at a photograph of himself in spite of it.

I'd like to keep this photo, he says as he settles back on the sofa.

His dad nods.

I visited your granddad in Garopaba one more time and it was the last. It was in June, during the church fair, which is quite an event there. Music, dance performances, everyone stuffing their faces with fresh fish, and so on. One night a folk singer from Uruguaiana got up on stage, a big kid of about twenty-five, and your granddad took an immediate dislike to him. He said he knew the guy, he'd seen him play over near the border and he was crap. I remember liking him. He plucked at the strings vigorously, made deep-and-meaningful expressions as he played and told rehearsed jokes between songs. Dad thought he was a clown with a lot of technique and not much feeling. It wouldn't have gone any further, but after the show the singer was having some mulled wine at a stall and someone thought it would be nice to introduce them, seeing as they were both gauchos in baggy trousers. The guy took the singer by the arm and brought him over to Dad and the two of them quickly locked horns. I found out later that it was much more than a question of musical quality, but at first they pretended they didn't know each other out of respect for the guy who was so excited to introduce them. But the guy made the mistake of asking Dad point-blank if he'd liked the music and Dad was the sort who, if you asked, you got his honest opinion. His answer made the singer furious. They started to argue and Dad told him to turn his face away because his breath smelled like a dead pampas fox's arse. Several people heard him and laughed. The singer got nasty, of course, and then it wasn't long before Dad whipped out his knife. The singer let it go and that was the end of it, but the thing I remember was the reaction of the crowd that had gathered around. It wasn't just that they were curious about the fight. They were looking sideways at your granddad, whispering and shaking their heads. I realized that in the time between my visits they'd started to disapprove of him. I mean, nobody wants a bad-mannered, knife-wielding gaucho around. I told him to cool it, but it was useless with your granddad. He wasn't even aware of his own stupidity. The people here are scared of you, I told him. That's not good. You're going to get yourself into some serious trouble. I left and didn't hear from him for ages. At the time I was kind of stuck in Porto Alegre, working a lot, and it was also when I started seeing your mother. We went out for four years and she left me three times before we got married. But anyway, I didn't visit your granddad for quite a while, and several months later I got a call from a police chief in Laguna saying he'd been murdered. There had been a Sunday dance at some community hall, the kind where the whole town goes. When the dance is in full swing, the lights go off. When they come back on a minute later, there's a gaucho lying in the middle of the hall in a pool of blood, with dozens and dozens of stab wounds. Everyone killed him; that is, no one person killed him. The town killed him. That's what the police chief told me. Everyone was there, entire families, probably even the priest. They turned out the lights, no one saw a thing. The people weren't afraid of your granddad. They hated him.

They both take a swig of beer. His dad empties his bottle and looks at him, almost smiling.

Except that I don't believe that story.

Huh? Why not?

Because there was no body.

But wasn't it him lying there all cut up?

That's what they told me. But I never saw the body. When the police chief called me it had all been more or less wrapped up. They said it had taken weeks to track me down. They had gone looking for me in Taquara, as someone in Garopaba knew he was from there. They found someone who recognized Dad from their description and knew my name. By the time they called me, he'd already been buried.

Where?

There in Garopaba. In the little village cemetery. It's a stone with nothing written on it at the back of the cemetery.

Did you go there?

I did. I visited the grave and took care of some paperwork in Laguna. It was all very strange. I had the strongest feeling it wasn't him in that hole. The grass growing over the grave was pretty tall.

I remember thinking, I'll be damned if this here was dug the week before last. And I couldn't find anyone who could confirm the story. It was as if it hadn't happened. The story of the crime itself was plausible and the villagers' silence made sense, but the way I found out about it, what the police chief told me, that awful stone with no name on it . . . I was never really convinced. But, at any rate, whatever happened to your granddad, it was bound to happen. People meet the death they're due in most cases. He met his.

Have you ever thought about having the grave opened? There must be a legal way to go about it.

His dad glances away, annoyed. He sighs.

Listen. I've never told this story to anyone. Your mother doesn't know. If you ask her, she'll say your granddad disappeared, because that's what I told her. As far as I was concerned he really had disappeared. I left it at that. I didn't give it any more thought. If you think it's horrible, that's too bad. The way I was at that age, the life I had back then . . . it'd be hard to make you understand now.

I don't think it's horrible. Relax.

His dad fidgets in his armchair. Beta gets up and with a small lurch puts her front paws on her master's leg. He grabs and holds her face as if muzzling her, lowering his head to look her in the eye. When he lets go, she lies down next to the armchair again. It is one of many inscrutable rituals that are a part of his dad's relationship with the animal.

So why are you telling me this now?

You haven't read that short story by Borges that I mentioned earlier, have you?

No.

'The South'.

I haven't read anything by Borges.

Course you haven't, you read fuck all.

Dad. The pistol.

Right.

His dad opens the bottle of cognac, fills a small glass and downs it in one go. He doesn't offer him any. He picks up the pistol and examines it for a minute. He releases the magazine and clicks it back into place, as if to show that it isn't loaded. A single bead of sweat runs down his forehead, drawing attention to the fact that he is no longer sweating all over. A minute earlier, he was covered in sweat. He tucks the pistol into the waistband of his slacks and looks at him.

I'm going to kill myself tomorrow.

He thinks about what he's just heard for a good while, listening to his irregular breathing leaving his nostrils in short puffs. An immense tiredness weighs suddenly on his shoulders. He stuffs the photo of his granddad into his pocket, dries his hands on his Bermuda shorts, gets up and heads for the front door.

Come back here.

What for? What do you want me to do after hearing that kind of shit? Either you're serious and want me to convince you to change your mind, which would be the most fucked-up thing you've ever asked me to do, or you're having a laugh at my expense, which would be so pathetic that I don't even want to find out. Bye.

Come back here, damn it.

He comes to a halt by the door, looking back at the sad floor of pinkish clay tiles separated by stripes of cement, the lush fern trying to escape a pot hanging from the ceiling, the perennial atmosphere of cigar smoke that pervades the living room with its invisible consistency and sweet, strangely animal smell.

I'm not joking and I don't want you to convince me of anything. I'm just informing you of something that's going to happen.

Nothing's going to happen.

Look, understand this: it's inevitable. I made up my mind a few weeks ago in a moment of absolute lucidity. I'm tired. I'm fed up. I think it started with that haemorrhoid surgery. At my last check-up the doctor stared at my tests, then looked at me with a woeful expression as if he were disappointed in the whole human race. I got the impression he was going to quit my case like a lawyer. And he's right. I'm starting to get sick and I can't be bothered with it all. I can't taste my beer any more, cigars are bad for me but I can't stop, and I don't even feel like taking Viagra so I can fuck. I don't even miss fucking. Life's too long and I haven't got the patience for it. For someone who's had a life like mine, living beyond sixty is just being stubborn. I respect those who take it seriously, but I can't be bothered. I was happy until about two years ago and now I want to go. Anyone who thinks I'm wrong can live to a hundred if they want. Good luck to 'em. I've nothing against it.

What a load of rubbish.

Yeah. Forget it. I can't expect you to understand. We're too different. Don't bother, it'll be a waste of your time.

You know I won't let you do it, Dad, so why did you invite me over to tell me?

I know it's not fair. But I did it because I trust you, I know how strong you are. I called you because there's something I need to take care of first and I can't do it alone. Only my son can help me.

Why don't you call your other son? Who knows, he might even find the whole thing amusing. He'll write a book about it.

No, I need you. It's the most important thing I've ever had to ask anyone and I know I can count on you.

Give me that pistol now and I'll take care of it, whatever it is. OK? Are you done clowning around?

His dad laughs at his exasperation.

24

Tchê, kid . . . listen. What needs to be taken care of is because of the other thing.

The suicide.

That word makes it sound kind of gutless. I'm avoiding it. But go ahead and use it if you want.

What do I do now, Dad? Call the police? Have you committed? Go over there and take that gun away by force? Did you really think this would work?

It already has. It's as if it's already happened.

That's stupid. It's your choice. What if I make you change your mind?

It's not my choice. It'd be easier for me, and much easier for you, to see it as a choice. My decision doesn't lead to the fact, it's a part of the fact. It's just another way to die, kid. It took me a long time to come this far. Sit down again, son. Want another beer?

He walks quickly over to the sofa and sits down angrily.

Look, consider this: imagine what it'd be like if you or anyone else tried to stop me now. It'd be a pain in the arse. Me trying to act on my decision and you guys trying to stop me, goodness knows how, living with me, watching me, committing me to an institution, medicating me, your brother coming from São Paulo and your mother having to put up with me again. Who knows what you could do, but it'd be a nightmare for everyone involved. Do you see how crazy it'd be? There's nothing more ridiculous than someone trying to convince someone else. I've worked with persuasion my whole life and it's the worst cancer of human behaviour. No one should ever be convinced of anything. People know what they want and they know what they need. I know it because I've always been a specialist in persuasion and inventing needs, and that's why that wall there is covered in awards. Don't try to talk me out of it. If you convinced me not to kill myself, you'd leave me crippled, I'd live a few more

25

years, defeated, mutilated and sick, begging for mercy. This is serious. Don't try to persuade me. Persuading someone not to follow their heart is obscene, persuasion is obscene, we know what we need and no one can tell us what's best. What I'm going to do was decided a long time ago, before I even had the idea.

I expected more of you, Dad. More than this retarded drivel. I've never been able to play the victim, it makes me sick, and the person who taught me that was you. And now you're giving me this victim crap.

Well now I'm going to teach you something else: when you start shitting blood and can't get it up and wake up feeling fed up with life every goddamn day, you have a moral obligation to act like a victim. Write it down. Oh, don't give me a hard time, for fuck's sake. Have you grown balls all of a sudden? It's not you. You're the acquiescent sort, a bit of a pushover even. I've always told you that to your face. I've got you all worked out. I've warned you about so many things. And have I ever been wrong? Have I? I told you you'd lose your girlfriend the way you did. I told you the desperate would come to you your whole life. But you really are capable of thinking of the next person even though you can't remember anyone's face. And that's why you're better than me and your brother. I'm proud of it and I love you for it. And now I need you to stand by your old man.

Fuck, Dad.

His dad's eyes are red.

It's Beta.

What about Beta?

His dad waves at the front door and makes an almost inaudible sound. The dog gets up without hesitation and leaves the house.

You know how much I love that dog. We've got a real connection.

I'm not doing it.

Why not?

There's no way I can look after a dog right now. And anyway . . . fuck, I don't believe this. Sorry. I've got to go.

I don't want you to look after her. I want you to take her to Rolf, over in Belém Novo. After I've . . . done what I'm going to do. Ask him to give her an injection. I've done my homework, it's painless.

No, no.

She's already depressed. She knows. She'll waste away when she's on her own.

Do it yourself. You're the one who thinks he doesn't have any fucking choice. I do. I won't be a part of this.

I can't bring myself to, kid.

No, no.

You have to promise me.

Forget it, Dad. There's no way.

Promise.

I can't be a part of this.

Please.

No. It's not fair.

You're denying me my last wish.

It won't happen.

You'll do it. I know you will.

I will not. You're on your own. I can't. Sorry.

I know you'll do it. That's why you're here.

You're trying to persuade me. A few minutes ago that was obscene.

I'm not going to persuade you. I'm done. It's my last wish. I know you won't deny me it.

Miserable old man.

That's my name.

A very old memory comes to mind. The scene is incongruous and doesn't seem to deserve having been recorded in memory, much less

27

recalled at a moment like this. One morning before work, his dad was shaving in the bathroom with the door open and he, aged six or seven at the time, was watching him. After shaving, he washed his face with soap, lathering it up well, then rinsed it repeatedly. There was no more soap on his face by the second rinse, but he kept on splashing his face with water, four, five times. He asked his dad why he rinsed his face so many times if the soap was already gone by the second rinse and he answered as if it were the most obvious thing in the world: 'Cause it feels good.

My hand's shaking, Dad.

You're doing just fine. You're a superior human being.

Shut up.

Seriously, I'm really proud of you. No one else'd be able to do it.

I didn't say I would.

I could make you promise something much worse. To make up with your brother, for example.

I'll do it if you tell me all this is just a big joke. In a few hours I'll be giving him a hug. You can start organizing the barbecue.

Good try. But to be honest I couldn't care less. I wouldn't forgive him, if I were you.

Good to know.

Yeah, well, I don't mind saying it now. But I really do need you to spare the old girl. She's fifteen, but her breed can easily live more than twenty years. She's my life. Ever seen a depressed dog? If she's left here without me I'll take her suffering with me. Can I consider it promised?

OK.

Thanks.

No, it's not OK. I can't be a part of this.

Love you, kid.

I didn't say I would. I haven't accepted. Don't touch me.

I wasn't going to. I'm not moving.

The ocean finally appears at the end of the main avenue of the town, a cold blue sliver at the end of the stretch of tarmac glinting under the throbbing midday sun. It is his birthday. He drives in second gear with the windows down and the fan on to keep air moving through the car on the windless day, the muffled whir of the fan mingling with the shy drone of the 1.0-litre engine and Ben Harper music coming from the CD player, almost stopping at speed bumps so as not to scrape the underside of his overloaded car. In the boot and back seat of the small Ford Fiesta are two suitcases of clothing, a sound system that he is two instalments away from paying off, a twenty-nine-inch TV, his PlayStation 2, a camping backpack full of personal belongings, a carefully folded wool blanket and quilt, plastic bags containing trainers and shoes, CDs and some basic kitchen utensils. He has packed photo albums, a barbecue knife his dad gave him, with its armadillo-leather handle and steel blade that rusts now and then and needs to be cleaned with steel wool and greased with oil, his special rubber wetsuit for swimming, and an eight-by-ten-inch black-framed photograph registering his arrival in the Ironman Triathlon in Hawaii. A support attached to the boot with hooks and chains holds his white mountain bike, battered after a few years' use, an already-outdated model with a thick, heavy aluminium frame. Beta is asleep, curled up in the passenger seat, muscles softened by the hot sun, and lulled by five hours of driving on the highway. She sighs often, sniffs, sneezes from time to time, opens her eyes and closes them again without changing position.

He ate a toasted salami-and-cheese sandwich in Osório and a meat pasty at a petrol station near Jaguaruna, so he drives straight past the restaurants he sees along the way and instead pays attention to the estate agents with eye-catching signs dotted along the main avenue. They are all conveniently closed at this hour. He continues on in the light traffic towards the blue of the ocean, in the opposite direction to small groups of lethargic pedestrians in bathing suits, dazed by the sun, heading for restaurants or home, carrying folding chairs and beach bags. It has been over a week since Ash Wednesday took with it most of the tourists, and the few who have stayed behind or just arrived behave with the serenity of latecomers.

The main avenue ends in a curve to the right and turns into the seaside boulevard. He parks diagonally between other cars in the parking spaces facing the beach. The sun beats down on the Fiesta. He walks around the car and opens the passenger door. Beta raises her head but doesn't move. Just as on the other three stops he made during the journey, he has to pick her up and set her down on her feet on the ground before she decides to lap up the warm water he pours from a family-size plastic bottle into an empty ice-cream tub. He takes the last few swigs from the same bottle. He takes off his shirt and trainers, leaving on only his swimming trunks. He locks the car and heads down the cement ramp next to the Embarcação restaurant to the sand, carrying Beta. Groups of off-season tourists enjoy themselves on the spacious beach. He approaches a woman who is smoking and reading a book by herself under a beach umbrella. The book's cover is purple. Her knees are dark, her toenails are painted with pearly nail polish and she is wearing a delicate gold anklet. The beach umbrella is blue with an insurance-company logo on it and the sunlight that manages to pass through it gives her bare legs a green hue. He memorizes all this so he'll be able to remember her later.

Hi. Would you mind watching my dog for a bit?

She lifts up her sunglasses and gazes a moment at the animal in his arms.

Can't he walk?

She can walk, but she's a bit tired. If I could put her in the shade here, she'll just lie there until I get back.

OK, you can leave her. But I'm not chasing after her if she runs away.

She won't run away. And if she does, just let her go. I'll find her afterwards.

What's her name?

Beta.

He settles the dog in the shade of the beach umbrella and walks towards the water, feeling the cold, squishy sand on the soles of his feet. The bay is calm, ruffled by a weak southerly breeze that makes the small waves break with fine, almost foamless crests over a smooth, glassy surface. The clear, icy water wets his belly and he raises his arms in a reflex action. He plunges his hands into the water to wet his pulses and minimize the thermal shock, something he learned from his dad. It doesn't work, but he always does it anyway. On days like this the ocean resuscitates in him a childhood vision that miniaturizes everything. Tiny waves seen with his eyes at surface level are mythological tidal waves breaking over his head. The sinuous sand at the bottom is a scale model of a great desert where a crab's chitinous shell looks like the bones of some giant creature extinct many eras ago. Scraping his chest against the sandy seabed, holding his breath and with his eyes wide open, he sees the landscape of tiny dunes rippling out until they disappear in the opacity of the blue-green water. The vision is crystalline and silent and further up the sun refracts on the surface in shards of white flickering in a scramble of geometric patterns. Back at the surface, he swims out deep with long strokes, testing the resistance of the salt water. His muscles, aching with cold, slowly relax. When he stops swimming his body is warm and the ocean floor is already out of reach. He sees Coral Island on the horizon, with its white lighthouse almost indistinguishable in the distance, and much further away the south of Santa Catarina Island, with its hazy green mountains dissolving into the atmosphere. A seagull almost touches the water in a low flight towards Vigia Cove where, among a dozen fishing boats, a two-masted schooner with the name *Lendário* in large red letters on its white hull softly rocks near a wooden jetty. He turns his back to the ocean and looks at the beach. He has swum out further than he thought. He sees the row of fishermen's sheds facing the waves with their fronts of greyish wood or painted in soft tones, the beach promenade lined with bed and breakfasts and restaurants, the pine trees in the seaside camping ground being targeted by solitary swallows that appear from all directions, Siriú Hill, and, behind it, the creamy dunes of Siriú Beach extending for a few miles towards the cliffs that hide the tranquil Gamboa Beach. A world of gold, blue and green. The windscreens of the cars coming around the bend at the beginning of the seaside boulevard reflect the sunlight in flashes that blind him. Tired of the excess of light, he takes a deep breath and lets the air out little by little, letting his body sink vertically. He keeps his eyes open at the bottom as long as his lungs can bear it, feeling protected from everything. Then he holds his nose above water and moves his feet and hands just enough to float upright in an almost imperceptible rise and fall, his body already used to the temperature, experiencing the salty taste, mineral smell and sticky texture of the water. He doesn't notice the time passing and remembers to get out only when he starts to feel his forehead stinging in the sun.

When he approaches the woman, she is already defending herself.

You said to let her go, that I didn't have to do anything. You said she'd stay put. She took off. I tried to call you but you were too far out, she rants. There is a smooth depression in the sand in the place where the dog was.

Which way did she go?

That way.

He thanks her and takes off running over the firm sand towards Siriú. He passes a kiosk with half a dozen thatched umbrellas protecting obese men and women, the unmanned lifeguard post, a platform built on top of a knoll with exercise bars. He keeps running until he sees the dog in front of the lookout in the camping ground, drinking the water trickling from a cement pipe. He kneels next to her and strokes her vigorously, pulling her ears back. The dog pants with her wet tongue hanging out and appears to be smiling, as all dogs do when they are hot. There you are, he says in a reprimanding tone of voice. Rather than a problem, Beta's solo walk is a welcome sign of her old energy and initiative. She follows him back to the car but she stops several times and needs to be called again. He calls her by her name in a dry, commanding voice, as his father used to.

That afternoon he starts house-hunting. He visits three estate agents and gets just one contact. The agents say there are no year-long rentals in the town. One of them even seems angry about it. People here don't rent for the whole year, only for long weekends and the tourist season. We're trying to change this culture. Garopaba is going to grow a lot over the next few years. People are coming here to live.

33

Property owners want to charge an arm and a leg in the summer and not think about the matter for the rest of the year. You won't find anything.

He gives up on the estate agents and drives around the streets near the beach, looking for rental signs and marking the addresses on a map of the town. Contrary to what the agents say, many landlords are willing to discuss year-round rentals. One of the houses he sees is on Rua dos Pescadores, in the heart of the original fishing village, separated from the beach only by the fishermen's sheds. The varnished brick façade has two windows with cream shutters and practically juts out over the beaten-earth pavement and cobbled street, where barefoot children, dark from the sun and scantily clothed, are holding a penalty shoot-out with a torn, deflated ball. There is a faint smell of fish and sewage in the air. Over the murmuring of the waves he can hear an old man guffawing, pool cues clacking and women whispering on the side veranda of the house across the way.

The owner of the house, Ricardo, is a nervous Argentinian who seems to switch off at regular intervals as if he doesn't want to stop thinking about some urgent problem. He looks to be in his early forties and has watery eyes and grey stubble on his chin. They walk down the driveway to the back of the house, where the entrance is. An outdoor grill made of scorched bricks piled up on the ground looks like it was built many summers ago. The patio is all cement and gravel. The floor and walls of the veranda are covered with horrible whitish tiles that remind him of cold and death. The house is neat and tidy on the inside but too dark, even with the windows open. The noises of the calm afternoon reverberate in the rooms and suggest the infernal symphony of busier days.

Ricardo doesn't interfere or explain anything, just accompanies him through the house. He seems impatient. As they leave, Ricardo

34

asks in a lazy mix of Spanish and Portuguese why he is moving to Garopaba. He says he just wants to live near the beach, and the Argentinian replies that yes, of course, everyone wants to live near the beach, but why does *he* want to live near the beach? Naturally hard-wired not to trust Argentinians, like so many Brazilians from the south, he ignores the question. After locking the door, Ricardo asks if he surfs. He says he doesn't. He asks if he wants to learn to surf. He says he doesn't. He asks if he intends to open a business. It's not in his immediate plans. The Argentinian gives him a good once-over.

Then the problem is woman.

What?

People come to surf or to forget woman, *solo eso*.

I just want to live near the beach.

Sí, sí. Of course.

How long have you lived here?

Almost ten years.

And why did you come here?

To forget woman.

Did you?

No. You rent the house?

No. I think it's too dark.

Dark. True. Well, good luck.

He parks the car in the Hotel Garopaba garage and pays the employees an extra thirty reais not to see the dog. He lies on the bed as it grows dark outside. His nap is interrupted twice by phone calls, which he tries to keep as short as possible because his mobile is from Porto Alegre and the roaming charges are devouring his credit. His friends are calling to wish him happy birthday and to give their condolences after his father's death, unaware that he doesn't live in Porto Alegre any more and that he left without telling many people, a detail that he himself omits because he knows he still doesn't have any answers or patience for the questions they might ask.

He wakes up hungry and feeling as if he has been inside for too long. He leaves the dog in the room with some dog food and water and heads out on foot to look for a restaurant. He takes the map with him to mark the locations of relevant places and people, a preventive measure against the pathological forgetfulness he has had since he was a child. He passes two bars offering steak-and-cheese sand-wiches, then a buffet with hot meals and ice creams. A pizza parlour on the main avenue has a special all-you-can-eat price that night. The attractive round wooden tables are almost all taken and three wait-resses glide calmly past, serving the customers, who are colourfully lit by hanging oriental lanterns in the shapes of vases and stars. He picks a table for two in the outside area, near the pavement, the seat for which is a comfortable sofa with its back to the wall. The waitress who serves him is a tall brunette with skin peeling from too much sun, pouting lips and shoulder-length curly hair. Knowing that her hair alone is probably enough to recognize her by, he nevertheless focuses on her oval face and slanting eyes. Sometimes he wonders if women in general are as beautiful to other men as they are to him, inwardly suspecting that his incapacity to remember any human face for more than a few minutes gives them extra appeal that others might think was just his eyes playing tricks on him. Because beauty is fleeting, he has learned to see it everywhere. This woman, how-ever, must be beautiful to everyone. She is used to being looked at like this and returns his stare with a combination of politeness and tiredness, activating a perfunctory smile. With the rising inflections typical of small-town Santa Catarina, contaminated with sarcasm or incredulity, she asks if he wants the all-you-can-eat.

Are the pizzas the same as the ones on the menu?

What do you mean?

Do they use the same ingredients as they do on the pizzas on the à la carte menu? Or is the cheese on the all-you-can-eat ones not as good?

She lets out a hearty laugh, changing to co-conspirator with surprising ease.

Just between you and me, the cheese isn't as good.

OK. I won't be having the all-you-can-eat, then. It's my birthday. I'll have a half-margherita, half-pepperoni, please.

Well now. It's your birthday. Happy birthday!

She chews on some gum that was hidden in a corner of her mouth.

And a beer.

She finishes taking his order and leaves. It is a while before she returns with his beer. He focuses on her face again.

You should wear your hair up.

Come again?

It's beautiful down. But I can imagine it up. Do you ever wear it like that?

Sometimes.

The way it is now it hides your face a bit.

Sometimes hiding's a part of the game.

She leaves bashfully and he quickly downs his beer with satisfaction.

Later he strolls, belly full, down the main avenue and through the cross streets, marking on his map a café, a hardware shop, a launderette and a Uruguayan grill, until he realizes that many of the establishments are transitory and open and close with the summer season. Taking a look around, he sees that many have already closed after Carnival and some of the windows are covered with brown paper or cardboard. A handwritten sign in an ice-cream-parlour window says that it will continue operating during the winter on another street. Everything that isn't summer is winter. A sign on the launderette door says it will reopen only in December. A bookshop, a corner shop and several boutiques selling women's clothes appear to still be in operation but have already closed for the day, and an internet café is turning out the last few clients from its computer terminals. People are still drinking beers in snack bars and there is a hot-dog stand in the supermarket car park with clients sitting on little plastic stools on the pavement. There is a European-style pub called Al Capone. Adolescents smoke and shout on the lawns of the empty summer-rental houses. He returns along the main avenue and stops just before the seaside boulevard at the Bauru Tchê, a snack bar operating out of a trailer with a tarpaulin covering half a dozen metal tables. He takes a seat and orders a beer. A small TV over the counter is showing a documentary about Pantera on MTV. Phil Anselmo is banging the mike against his forehead until he bleeds and Dimebag Darrell is soloing. A drunk of indeterminate age and a fat teenager are glued to the programme. At another table an old man and two youths in baseball caps who look like locals are drinking beer. The old man is talking, relaxed in his chair, while the youths listen.

Ninety per cent of the world's evil is the rich guy paying for the poor guy to do it, he says. The young men nod in agreement.

A boy of about ten, the snack-bar owner's son, comes to clean his table even though it doesn't need it. He wipes it down with ostensive efficiency, removing the bottle and putting it back when he is done.

He thanks him. The boy says, You're welcome, and races back to the counter.

The kid begs to work, says his father at the counter. I've never seen anything like it.

The accent of the old man at the next table is hard to understand and the blaring Pantera video clips don't help, but now he is saying that the Department of Public Prosecution owes him two million reais. His two listeners nod.

The boy comes back and looks at him.

Heard the one about the pool table?

No.

Leave him alone, says his father without taking his eyes off the money he is counting.

What's green on top, has four paws, and if it falls on your head it'll kill you?

A pool table?

How did you know? the boy hollers and dashes back behind the counter, cackling with laughter.

Leave him alone, repeats his father.

He has two beers while joking with the boy, eavesdropping on the conversation at the next table and watching people going past on the pavement. On the TV, Dimebag Darrell is shot dead on stage by a crazy fan. He is a little tipsy when he gets up to leave. He pays the manager, a friendly, tired-looking man with deep bags under his eyes and stubble growing on his chin.

My family used to own Rua da Praia in Porto Alegre, the old man is telling the youths in baseball caps as he leaves. I've got the deed to prove it. The youths nod.

He walks along the seaside towards the fishing village and the hotel. The waves make a crashing sound like breaking tree trunks.

He carries a flip-flop in each hand and feels the wet sand on his feet. The idea that the day is ending disturbs him. Behind Vigia Hill, speckled with the lights of houses and lamp posts, looms precisely the emptiness that he came here to look for. It's too early to find it. He has fantasized about a long or even infinite search and it is frustrating to be reminded so soon of that which he would rather keep pretending not to know, that the feeling of emptiness he yearns for is dormant inside him, that he takes it with him wherever he goes. It's like a surprise party announced in advance or a joke that is explained before it is told. He remembers the boy in the bar's joke. He hadn't laughed at the time, but now he does so, absurdly.

The dog has eaten her food and drunk all of her water. He refills her water dish while she watches him from her favourite towel on the sticky tiled floor of the hotel room. He brushes his teeth and throws himself on to the bed, wearing only his underwear. The room smells of cement and fabric softener. He listens to the waves breaking two hundred yards away. He hears motorbikes at high speed and the prevailing silence.

He gets up again and pulls on jeans, trainers and a clean T-shirt. The clock on the beach promenade says that it is just past midnight. He walks quickly to the pizza parlour. Two tables are still occupied by customers who are smoking and dawdling over their last few drinks. The employees are clustered in the small interior of the restaurant, impatient, staring outside and biting their nails. He looks for the curly hair, the tallest waitress. He should have asked her her name. There are lots of curls here. In his memory, her face is now an almost abstract caricature of watery brushstrokes. But he recognizes her from her posture. She is outside, further back, half hidden in the penumbra of the small gallery of closed shops, trying to pack up a folding table. Something isn't snapping into place. He approaches her timidly. There is nothing left of the momentary impulsiveness of customer-chatting-up-waitress. He thought she was beautiful the first time around, and this fact remains, but the content of her beauty was lost and is now recovered. He gazes at her as if for the first time. She smiles when she sees him. Everyone can tell when they're recognized, but he has refined this ability more than most out of sheer necessity. An expression of recognition may contain everything he needs to know.

Hey. Want to do something when you get off work? Want to go out for a beer?

She thinks for a moment, as she finally manages to fold up the table.

There's a little party today over at the Pico.

Pico.

Pico do Surf, don't you know it?

No. I got here today. I don't know anything.

Over in Rosa. I said I'd meet some girlfriends there. But I haven't got a lift.

I've got a car. Want a lift?

Her name is Dália and she asks him to come back for her in half an hour. He runs back to the hotel, takes a quick shower and heads for the adjacent car park. He stands there a moment, staring at the car still piled high with his belongings. He takes out the other suitcase of clothes, the TV, the bag containing his PlayStation, a box of documents and everything else of any value that can be seen and takes it all into the hotel room. He has to make three trips. Beta is asleep and doesn't wake up. He is running late and sweating by the time he turns the key in the ignition. The car smells of dog.

Dália is smoking in front of the closed pizza parlour, accompanied by a young man in a baseball cap and surf shorts.

41

Is he coming too? I don't think there's enough room in the back.

She opens the door, gets in and says the guy was just keeping her company until he got there. He has already forgotten her face again. He isn't able to get a proper look at her in the short instant of a peck of greeting on the cheek and now she is looking straight ahead, revealing only her profile.

I need to swing by my place quickly, OK? To get changed. If you don't mind?

She guides him through roughly paved back streets that lead to the town's older districts. Enormous dogs and swift cyclists move through these nocturnal streets that have only the occasional lamp post. Everything is dark, with the exception of a few taverns. The houses are asleep and the hills surround the town with their imposing shapes. The radio is playing reggae music at a low volume. She talks about her routine at the pizza parlour and he explains that the junk in the back seat is part of his move from Porto Alegre. They turn on to a dirt road and then a trail of tyre tracks through the grass. A street light illuminates old tree trunks and the fronts of four or five houses. She points at one of them and he parks.

Wait here, OK? I'll be right back.

She takes almost an hour. He waits without getting out of the car, investigating the radio stations. He knows how to wait.

Dália reappears smelling of vanilla-scented perfume and wearing jeans, light-blue sandals, a black top with almost invisible straps, and a necklace with a silver sun pendant. Her hair is strangled by a white elastic band on top of her head, sprouting over it like black coral. Her lips are shiny.

Let me see you, he says, and she turns to face him.

Along the way she asks to stop at the petrol station. She re-emerges from the corner shop with a beer and a bar of chocolate. He accepts the sip and the bite she offers him. The road is empty and she likes to talk. She is twenty-two, was born and raised in Caçador, where a lot of tomatoes are grown, until she was a teenager, and intends to move to Florianópolis in July to study Naturology at university. She isn't particularly interested in the fact that he is a PE teacher but enthusiastically approves of his move to Garopaba.

You'll be happy here. Everyone's happy here. This place is so beautiful. I'm really happy here. Can I smoke a joint in your car?

She lights up and offers it to him. He takes a few puffs and starts feeling afraid of other cars' headlights.

They arrive at the Pico do Surf along a potholed sandy road flanked by ditches. He tries to remember the route he has just taken and can't. It takes him a while to park his Fiesta without falling into the crater between the road and a vacant lot. There is a palisade around the nightclub, which throbs with bass notes and emits blasts of strobe lights. Some people are drinking beer outside, leaning against the cars. There is a short queue at the entrance. The girls are all wearing high heels, short skirts and tops falling off their shoulders and alternate between nervous glances and fits of laughter. The guys are wearing Bermuda shorts and some are in flip-flops. They all look like surfers and surfers' girlfriends. Dália says she's going to get them both in for free but in the end the doorman only lets her in and he has to pay the entry fee of twenty reais. They climb a staircase carved into the sloping terrain and cross a garden with large wooden tables and a pool table. The dance floor is dark and the music very loud. The hypnotic and rather disturbing hip hop music has an immediate depressing effect on him. They go to buy some beers at the bar in the corner and Dália disappears as soon as he turns his back to her.

43

He loses sight of her for long enough to forget her face and only identifies her much later by her necklace, as she dances in a circle of people. She hugs him when he approaches and introduces him to her friends, but then she moves away again, dancing with a can of energy drink in her hand. He tries to dance but can't get into the mood. He hovers nearby, stationary. A guy with short peroxide-blond hair soon appears and talks insistently in her ear. Dália looks uncomfortable but stays there listening and answering back for a time that seems never-ending. He thinks about the car poorly parked beside a ditch with his belongings in view on the back seat. He forgot to take out the radio. Someone's going to break the window and steal my radio, he thinks. He buys another beer. He feels as if he's been listening to the same song since he arrived. Dália's pulled-back hair reappears in front of him and she complains about the guy she was talking to. Her warm breath, mint-scented from her sugarless chewing gum, has a calming effect. Jesus, that guy's totally clueless, she says. Stay here with me and he won't bother you, he says. She wraps her long, agitated arms around him, dancing, and asks if he wants an E, because she's just had one. A friend is selling them for thirty reais a pop. Her sweat is visible on her collarbone and trapezius muscle. He touches her neck with his nose and inhales the sour smell of her skin mixed with her sweet perfume. She says, I'll be right back, and disappears again. He considers taking some Ecstasy too, something he hasn't done since his college years, and letting it dictate whatever happens for the rest of the night, partly because he still believes that she is his for tonight, and partly because he feels too lazy to take the initiative. When he runs into her again a little later she is listening to the guy with peroxide-blond hair again. The darkness swallows not only people's faces, but also their bodies, gestures, clothes and accessories, almost completely eliminating any possibility of recognition. A short, blonde photographer is circulating through the party, taking photos. Groups of friends pose with their arms around one another and smile as they poke out their tongues and make a V sign with their fingers. The photographer comes over and sets off two flashes in his face. He thinks again about his car, the dog at the hotel, the house he hopes to find and rent tomorrow. He goes over to Dália, excuses himself to the guy with peroxide-blond hair, and says he is leaving. They are close to a speaker and have to shout to be heard. You can't leave now, she says, placing her hand on his chest. I'm going! he shouts. I don't like it here and I'm going house-hunting first thing in the morning. But I need a lift back, she says, a little irritated. Then it's now. What the fuck, man! she protests. Fine, go then. I'll figure something out later. You're so boring. Without thinking he plunges his fingers into her hair, at the nape of her neck, forcefully working them into her taut hair, feeling the roughness of her roots and the resistance of her scalp. He holds her head by her hair in front of his. She stares at him with bulging eyes, not understanding what he is doing, and he doesn't know what he is doing either, but it feels good and she seems to like it too, in spite of everything. It might be the Ecstasy. He kisses her on the face and lets her go. She sort of smiles. The guy with the peroxide-blond hair shoves him away and he takes advantage of the momentum to move towards the exit with decisive footsteps, laughing to himself.

He asks the bouncer at the entrance for instructions on how to get back to Garopaba by car. He drives drunk, tense, and starts to hiccup. He drives down the empty highway and crosses the dead town. The hiccups still haven't stopped by the time he enters the hotel room. He gets a surprise when he walks in. The dog is sitting on the bed. Beta, Beta, Beta, he repeats affectionately, hugging her tight. She is warm and submissive and her soft hide slides over her muscles. He inhales her salty smell with pleasure and finally lets her go. She remains sitting near the pillow. He only notices that he has stopped hiccuping when he is brushing his teeth.

Before lying down, he looks for his mobile phone to see what time it is and finds a missed call from his mother.* There is also a birthday

* *He came. He got there before me. He just left. I've never seen your brother like that, he looked terrified. He was afraid of running into you, of course. He spent ages over by the coffin. [. . .] Of course he didn't cry, your brother doesn't cry, you know what he's like. All he asked was if I knew what time you were coming and if she was coming with you. I told him she wasn't coming, but he doesn't have a problem with her. It's you he doesn't want to see. He told me he couldn't stay. He said, if I do, I'll plant one on him when I see him. And I told him, Your father's lying there dead. Stop being a child, you're almost thirty-three years old, do it for your dad, he'd want you two to make up, but your brother just laughed. [. . .] I don't know why, I've never understood, but your father and him always had something that was theirs alone. Go figure. He had Beta in the car with him. [. . .] I have no idea, Dante. [. . .] I also think it's really weird, but I'm afraid to ask. Your father left a note . . . he left the house to me and some money for you kids. We're going to read his will tomorrow. He didn't have anything else, it's incredible. He blew everything. And now it'll be a while because there's all the bureaucracy – [. . .] Nothing. Oh, there's also a private pension plan, which will go to you two. It's a decent sum of money. He wrote, about the house, Do what you want with it, Sônia, but I know you're going to sell it and split the money between the princes. That's what I'll do, of course. It's been so long since I loved that man and we fought so much afterwards that I can't remember what it was like any more. But your brother stayed for about fifteen minutes, spoke to Uncle Natal, to Golias, who's over there . . . he's the only one of your father's old pals that I can stand too. He spoke to that woman there who I don't know. Was she his girlfriend? [. . .] I knew it. Just look at that tart's face, all stretched out. [. . .] A whole bunch of them are going to show up, there'll be venom flying everywhere and they're going to treat me as if I was some parched old prune.*

[. . .] What? [. . .] He didn't do anything else. He came, looked in the coffin and left. [. . .] No, darling. Come to think of it, he did say that he'd have to talk to me some

text message from her. *No matter how much I curse you I love you son. A mother has no choice, has she? Happy birthday darling. I hope you got there OK. Take care. Mother.* It's four o'clock in the morning. He types an answer and sends it. *Thanks. I got here fine. Love u too.*

A coal-coloured dog slumbers in the ethereal blue of a fishing net coiled up on the lawn in the square. The sun strikes the grey stairs up

---

other time because he was moving. He's leaving Porto Alegre. [. . .] I don't know yet. He just wanted to leave. Except for the minute he spent over at the coffin, he spent the whole time looking at the gate and then he came and said, I've got to go, I'd better go, then he hugged me and left. [. . .] But I tried! It's your father's wake, I said, stop being a child, it's going to be horrible for me, for you, but he upped and left. I think he only came for my sake, if he didn't people would give me a hard time. He just stayed long enough to be seen, but what good was it, leaving like he did? Family was never our speciality. Only you, darling. I was able to introduce him to Ronaldo, I'm going to introduce you too in a minute, he's gone to park the car somewhere else, he was afraid of getting a fine, there are parking meters. [. . .] Yes, I'm happy. [. . .] Do you think so? I'm old, that's what I am. [. . .] Just because I'm your mother. But it may be. We look better when we're at peace with ourselves. It's a tragedy what your father did, but we had been so distant for such a long time. I thought he'd die of a heart attack or something like that at some point, after all, he never looked after himself, as you know, but something like this . . . at his age. Why do it at sixty-four? And in such a horrible way, he could have . . . [. . .] Yes, we'll never know. Now he's gone. [. . .] Yes.

[. . .] I agree, darling. [. . .] Yes, you're right. [. . .] No, leave your brother in peace. It'll be worse. Let him be. He doesn't want to see you. If he didn't want to see you today, he doesn't want to see you ever again. [. . .] I think so too, but that's how he is. I think you suffer more than he does, darling. [. . .] Yes, I know. But let's not talk about it now, OK? Come here, let your mother give you a kiss. [. . .] They let you pay for the service in four instalments. This funeral parlour is good. We'll put it all down on paper afterwards. Look, here comes Ronaldo. I'm so happy with him. You have to come and visit us. [. . .] Yes, it's near Assis Brasil. São Paulo isn't so far. It's just a hop, skip and a jump. You should come more often. OK? Come and visit your mother more. Ronaldo, this is my eldest.

47

the hill to the parish church face-on. The short, steep cobbled street next to the church passes a boat shed and a prefabricated wooden house. He waves at the tanned old lady basking in the sun on the veranda in a colourful beach chair. A salty north-easterly rustles the trees and waves. Vast clouds advance in formation from the sea to the continent like an army in a trance. The street curves to the left and passes in front of a small eighteenth-century building with peeling white walls and freshly painted cobalt-blue window frames. A craft shop exhibits striped rugs, miniature ships and wicker baskets piled up in the doorway and windows. A group of hyperactive children in blue-and-white school uniforms passes in the opposite direction, led by a tense teacher. The street continues towards Vigia Point, passing summer homes perched on the hill. He slowly surveys the sweeping view of the ruffled ocean and the beaches and hills stretching around in a big curve to what he imagines to be the distant Guarda do Embaú Beach. He walks slowly so Beta can keep up. When she decides to stop once and for all, he fastens the leash to her collar and urges her on with little tugs. On the tiny Preguiça Beach he sees parents sunbathing as they watch their children playing on the stretch of sand protected from the wind. Washed-up bits of algae, tree branches and molluscs form fans on the ochre sand and give off a pungent smell. He nods at the bathers as he passes and takes a trail that starts at the rocks. His feet sink into the warm salt water hidden under the prickly grass. The houses here are immense palaces with glass fronts, solar panels and ample wooden verandas jutting out over land that has been radically reworked by landscapers. At Vigia Point a megalomaniacal mansion leaves little room for pedestrians and on the other side of the low wire fence a hysterical toy poodle wildly dashes back and forth, squeaking like a bat, while a woman in the house yells at it to come inside. Beta completely ignores the fellow member of her species. Cloud shadows slide across the frothy sea and he imagines the fish believing the shadows to be the clouds themselves. He walks along, jumping over rocks, until he comes to a series of corroded metal girders sticking out of a concrete base. The sharp skeleton of a mysterious structure has long been disfigured by the sea breeze and its crusts of orangey rust give it a deadly look. From here he can see all of Garopaba Beach head-on. Beta watches water bugs darting through the rocks at the tideline.

He is almost back at the church when he notices a small handwritten rental sign on the wall of one of the old blocks of apartments built by the fishermen on the slope between the street and the sea. On the other side of the gate all he sees is a long, narrow staircase following the wall down to the base of the two-storey construction and ending at a footpath around the rocks, some ten or so feet from the waves. He dials the number on his mobile and asks the man who answers if the apartment is for rent. In an instant the man appears out of one of the nearby houses. He is short and tanned and looks as if he is amused by something, but he isn't. The apartment is the ground-floor one, right in front of the rocks. The man takes a padlock off the gate and they head down to the bottom of the stairs, passing the entrance to the upstairs apartment. Under the stairs, in the damp space between two neighbouring buildings, is a brown door. They enter a small living room with an adjoining open kitchen. The furniture is limited to two beaten-up sofas and a rectangular wooden table. It is much colder inside than outside. There is a predictable smell of mildew. The short guy tinkers with the latch on the living-room window and opens the shutters after a few jolts, revealing a view of the entire bay of Garopaba, the fishing sheds and the old whaling boats anchored offshore. Right in front of the window is a flight of cement steps from the footpath down to a large, smooth rock that the bigger waves are covering with spray but which is probably dry when the sea is calm. On top of the rock is a large blue tarpaulin protecting what appears to be a fishing net. The guy shows him the bedroom, which has a double bed, the bathroom and the kitchen, with a small outside laundry area, but he doesn't really care. He'd decided he wanted to live there when he saw the shutters opening.

I want to rent this apartment. Will you rent it to me for a year?

You'll have to talk to my mother.

Do you go through an estate agent?

You'll have to talk to my mother. She's the one who handles the place.

His mother, Cecina, lives two houses up the street. Her veranda projects over the slope and is surrounded by the tops of lime and *pitanga* trees that are rooted several yards downhill. Cecina invites him into an impeccably arranged living room with ocean views and asks him to take a seat on a leather sofa. There is a beautiful collection of Marajoara ceramic vases on the coffee table. Cecina's face is lovely, wide and round with narrow eyes and slightly puffy eyelids. After they sit she remains silent and appears to be trying unsuccessfully to stifle the flicker of an indulgent smile. She has the poise of a priestess waiting for a disciple who has come to her to pour out his soul. He tells her that he wants to spend a year living in the ground-floor apartment. She explains in a soft, sibilant voice that she rents it out only in the high season and that the most she can do outside of that season is rent it on a monthly basis, renewing it month by month if both parties are still interested, until November at the latest, when the high season starts. She would lose money if she accepted an annual price because the prices are five times higher over the summer and she has regular customers who come back every year. He proposes that she calculate how much she would make in the high season, add it to the monthly rent for the rest of the year, divide it all by twelve and tell him the price. He is willing to pay. He assures her that she won't lose any money. She tells him that she has had too many problems renting out apartments in the low season to people like him who show up alone or to couples or friends who want to spend the winter living in front of the beach. People leave without paying, she says. I don't have any way to go after them afterwards. He suggests that they draw up a contract and have it notarized as a guarantee. She laughs heartily and says she doesn't bother with contracts. Contracts are no good to me. What am I going to do with a contract? Waste my time chasing after people? And even if I find them, am I going to sue them? Lose my peace of mind over the whole thing? He proposes a monthly price that, multiplied by twelve, is equivalent to almost all of his savings. This time she doesn't answer right away. She sits there reflecting, still with a somewhat indulgent smile on her lips. She asks what he does. He says he is a PE teacher. She asks what he has come to do in Garopaba. He says he wants to live in front of the beach. She asks if he intends to work and settle there. He says yes. That he wants to teach, that he has future plans to rent a professional space and maybe even, if everything works out, open a gym. He says he is an athlete and intends to train too. Ocean swimming is his favourite thing and her apartment is five yards from the swimming pool of his dreams. Cecina says that the year before two friends rented the same place for a year. They were surfers and wanted to surf and settle in Garopaba and open a bed and breakfast. They disappeared four months later, with the rent in arrears, leaving the apartment completely trashed. They broke furniture and walls. There was marijuana smoke coming from the apartment all day long. The neighbours heard fights and shouting almost every day. They were homosexuals, nothing against that, and drug-users. They started hanging out with the druggies who dealt and smoked in front of the building and they did lots of drugs and broke everything and then ran off without paying. Everyone comes here saying the same thing, she says softly. I just want to live in front of the beach. I just want to surf. I just want to think about life. I just want to enjoy nature. I just want to write a book. I just want to fish. I just want to forget a girl. I just want to find the love of my life. I just want to be alone. I just want a little peace and quiet. I just want to start over. And then people fight, get depressed, break things, drink too much, shout, have orgies, do drugs and disappear without paying, or kill themselves. It's tough, she says. We never know who to trust, and it's a shame. I don't know you. To be honest, I'm planning to renovate the apartment in April. I need to fix it up during the year so I can receive visitors in the high season. So I can't rent it out.

I don't do drugs. I don't cause problems. I'm going to live by myself with my dog, and I'm the quiet sort.

I know. But I'm going to fix up the apartment.

He thanks her for her time, says goodbye and leaves.

He has lunch at the cheapest restaurant he can find, goes back to the hotel and lies on the bed. He casually reads the entire last edition of *Runner's World*, which features yet another article on the interminable debate about the benefits of stretching before and after running, and then lies on the mattress with his eyes open, immersed in extensive calculations and daydreaming.

Late that afternoon he pulls on trainers, shorts and a polyamide T-shirt and goes for a jog on the beach. He leaves Beta in the hotel room. He runs along the beach from end to end four times, with long strides. The bathers have gone and few people are outside due to the strong wind. A fisherman pedals past on a bicycle with supermarket bags hanging from the handlebars. A tall woman strolls by with a young boy, drinking maté and swinging a Thermos. An elderly couple walks along hand in hand, the varicose veins of their ankles in the water. He doesn't know anyone because he has just arrived, but they all look his way and make some kind of acknowledgement. Near the fishing village he sees a group of children and teenagers playing football between two sets of goalposts marked with flip-flops. There are no lines to mark the field and no clear criteria for differentiating between the teams. They are all playing barefoot and the girls dribble the ball and attack with notable skill and physical force. Some are wearing only bikinis, sweating and obstinate, their tangled hair flapping in the wind as they fearlessly clash with their male opponents and fight for the ball with an energy bordering on violence.

He finishes his run in front of the fishing sheds and from there he can see the front of Cecina's apartment, with its cream façade and two windows with brown shutters. He can see boats and fishermen in the dark insides of the fishing sheds. The fishermen follow him with their eyes and respond to his waves with economical gestures. Instead of returning to the hotel, he climbs the partially collapsed steps at the end of the beach, takes the footpath around the rocks and passes in front of the apartment. He stands there a while looking at the closed windows, then sits on one of the last steps of the cement stairs leading down to the rocks. Seagulls take off and allow themselves to be lifted up by gusts of wind. He rests. A motorboat enters the bay and anchors. A dinghy comes to fetch its two crew members. He gets up and goes to knock on Cecina's door.

She laughs to see him again so soon, dishevelled from his run and with his face covered in a fine crust of salt.

What if I pay all of it up front?

All what?

The rent. The whole year. The price I told you earlier, except all at once. Today. I can give you a cheque with today's date on it.

She laughs, presses her hand to her mouth, glances inside the house and shakes her head.

Ai, ai, ai.

If I leave or break things it's already paid for. You won't be running any risks.

You're crazy.

He laughs along with her.

I'm not crazy, Cecina. I really want to live there and I think this way everyone will be happy.

He returns that night with the cheque. She calls her son, not the short one who showed him the apartment, but another one, to examine it, then hands him the keys.

The next morning he parks his Fiesta out in the open in the car park at the top of the building, by the gate, and carries his belongings down the steps in a long operation that goes on almost until midday. The steps are very narrow and the low railing is an invitation to fall. He transports one thing at a time. He leaves the inside of the house as it is, not seeing any need to rearrange furniture or do any additional decorating. He goes to the grocery shop in the fishing village and buys bathroom and kitchen products, coffee, bread, fruit, yoghurt, honey, granola, chocolate, two packets of pasta and some ready-made sauce. It isn't the first time he has slept to the sounds of the sea, but this time they aren't a distant murmur, a background noise. The ocean breathes in his ear. He hears each wave crashing against the rocks, the fizzing of the foam and splashes. Gulls, or at least what he imagines are gulls, let out guttural cries like cats on heat in the middle of the night and sound like they are locked in bloody battle. He is awakened before sunrise by the growl of the fishing boats' diesel motors. The yellow light coming through the slats in the shutters is from a lamp post almost directly in front of the apartment. The busy fishermen shout incomprehensible things at one another at an absurd volume until their voices disappear into the rumble of the ocean along with the motors.

He falls asleep again and wakes a little later to the sound of voices engaged in animated debate. After urinating and splashing cold water on his face he opens the shutters, dampened by the sea breeze, and sees a boat anchored right in front of the apartment. Several fishermen are perched on the rocks and footpath. He watches the scene from the window for a few minutes. The night wind has died down and the sea is smooth and opaque. The water looks hot. A black power cable trails from the back of the boat, suspended over the water, and is wrapped around the trunk of a tree right in front of his building. One of the men is in the boat, another is sitting on the stairs, and the rest are standing around the white fishing net heaped up on the rock. Slowly the fishermen make eye contact with him and nod their heads.

He goes inside and makes some coffee. He is sitting at the table eating a sandwich when there is a knock at the door.

Hey, champ. The boss wants to know if we can plug this in here.

The man's bottom teeth are rotten and he has a long rodent's face. He raises a cigarette to his lips with thick, cracked fingers that get thinner at the tips and end in ragged nails. With his other hand he is holding up a plug with two rusted pins and a clump of black electrical tape holding it together. It is the other end of the power cable trailing from the boat.

It's for the soldering gun, says the man when he sees him hesitate. We're fixing the boat's motor over there.

OK, you can use that socket there.

Thanks, champ. You're a good man.

In a moment the soldering gun goes into action somewhere in the innards of the boat, a white whaler with decorative yellow-and-red stripes called *Poeta*. It must be about forty feet long. Sparks fly from an opening in the deck while the vessel softly rolls from side to side. He leaves the apartment and goes to watch the activity from the footpath. The men on dry land make fun of one another and joke about money. The man who knocked at his door, who looks like a beaver with a long face, is the one who talks the most and someone calls him Marcelo. It is hard to decipher much of what they say, but he understands that one of them, a fat man who is watching the scene from a certain distance and may be the owner of the boat, has just received an army pension. The others are asking him for money jokingly.

Gimme a hundred bucks.

Haven't got anything.

Don't you feel sorry for me? I can't even afford a packet of biscuits.

That's your problem.

The man who was welding the motor appears on deck and shouts that the soldering gun has stopped working. The others start to examine the cable, looking for the problem. There is a patch on part of the cable and one of the fishermen takes to it with his pocketknife. In the meantime the boat has drifted closer to the rocks and the cable that was previously suspended above the water has lost height and is almost completely submerged. The whole situation looks risky, not to say insane.

Do you want me to unplug it?

No, champ, thanks, but it won't be necessary.

The fisherman somehow manages to re-establish the electrical current by fiddling with his pocketknife in the cable. The soldering gun starts droning and spraying sparks again in the bowels of the boat. The job is quick. Marcelo pulls the plug from the socket and tosses the rolled-up power cable to the man on board. The man takes the cable, collects up his tools, jumps from the whaler into a rowboat and joins the other men on the rock. He turns out to be the owner of the whaler and is burly, with a sparse beard, curly hair and impassive facial expression. He introduces himself as Jeremias. He thanks him for the use of his socket with a handshake and says that tonight they are going to sail south, looking for a school of croakers that was sighted in Itapirubá, and that they'll bring him some croakers the next morning to return the favour.

Jeremias and another fisherman use the rowboat to take one corner of the fishing net to the deck of the whaler. The net is attached to a crank-operated reel and with the help of this mechanism they begin to transfer it from the top of the rock to the whaler.

He offers the fishermen water, coffee and sandwiches but they don't want anything. He asks how long the net is. Marcelo says it is two thousand fathoms but he doesn't know what that is in yards. A young man with blue eyes who has been quiet until now says that it's about one and a half miles. It's a small net. They often use nets that are three miles long or more. They get enthused and start telling the newcomer stories. Last year this boat came back up to its eyes in water. Eleven tons of croakers. It was riding so low that water was washing over the top of it and they had to bail it out with buckets. They all hold their cheap cigarettes with the tips of their fingers and when they aren't taking a puff they keep their hands behind their backs as if they want to hide the fact that they smoke. They are wearing faded sweatshirts and rubber boots or worn-out trainers.

You live there? Marcelo asks with a jerk of his head.

I moved in yesterday.

You surf?

No.

What happened then? Get divorced?

I just wanted to live by the beach.

Right you are. Life's good here. This place is beautiful.

It is.

It's peaceful. To see the ocean in the morning.

It's priceless.

Everyone here is really nice. Did you know no one's ever been killed here in Garopaba?

Never?

Lots of folk have died, of course, but there have never been any murders! It's really laid-back. There's almost no violence.

I don't believe no one's ever been murdered here.

Marcelo doesn't answer. The tiny waves tickle the still air.

I heard my granddad died here.

What was his name?

People used to call him Gaudério.

No one says anything in a way that says a lot. He decides to carry on.

The story I heard is that he was murdered here.

Here? How? I don't think so.

But that's what my dad said.

They called him Gaudério, did they? Gauchos are pretty common in these parts.

The blue-eyed young man's lips curve up in a private smile and he continues staring out to sea.

My granddad used to go spearfishing for grouper. Ever heard of him?

Marcelo raises his eyebrows and turns his head theatrically from side to side. He is squatting at the top of the stairs like a bird on a perch, hugging his knees with one arm and smoking with the other. He stares deliberately straight ahead and keeps quiet. The conversation runs dry and everyone looks more concentrated than necessary on whatever it is that they are doing. A couple of tourists glides between the boats on kayaks, the man stopping every so often for the woman to catch up. A cloud covers the sun. The weather is beginning to turn.

You from Porto Alegre? Marcelo breaks the silence.

Yep.

Porto Alegre is really violent.

True.

I lived there for two years. Long time ago. I know it well.

Yeah? What did you do there?

A bit of this, a bit of that. Do you know Bar João?

The one over on Osvaldo?

That's the one. It was wild. That was my haunt.

It's not there any more. They tore it down.

Really? Well there you go. I used to drink jaguar milk there. They also had cachaça with a brick in it. There was a guy who used to drink it. The place was full of crazies. And a few bad folk too.

I used to live in Porto Alegre too, says the oldest of the group. He is a thin, wrinkled man with enormous ears with tufts of white hair growing out of them. I spent ten years there. Back then I worked in a bar. Remember the trams? Did you ever see a tram in Porto Alegre? Right, you're too young for trams. They got rid of the trams in '71. There were trams going up and down Cristóvão Colombo and several other streets. You could go all over the place on them. They auctioned them off and the owner of the bar I worked at bought one.

He took off the front of the carriage with a blowtorch and stuck it on the front of the bar. The place was small. It fit perfectly. Know the place?

No. I think I was a kid.

The old guy doesn't continue his story. There is an anticlimactic silence. The owner of the whaler is still on board winding up the net with the crank.

Jeremias!

The fisherman raises his head.

Ever heard of a guy who lived here in the 60s called Gaudério?

Gaudério?

He was my granddad. I'm trying to find someone who knew him.

Mustn't be from my time, says Jeremias, without taking his eyes off the net. Try talking to someone who's been around longer. Lots of folk pass through here. Most end up being forgotten.

Marcelo tosses his cigarette butt into the water and gets up.

I'm off.

Jeremias finishes winding up the net minutes later and they all get on the whaler. The motor coughs out puffs of grey smoke. The boat advances with its propeller gurgling to a point further out and is anchored. The smell of fuel hangs in the air.

He goes inside. Beta is prostrate, in the same position as the day before, lying on her favourite towel, and, as is often the case, he can't tell if she is asleep or awake. She breathes very slowly and needs a lot of encouragement to go out for walks. He sets her dishes of water and food in the outside laundry area, which at least forces her to get up to eat.

He gets his wallet from a drawer in the kitchen cupboard. Among his documents and bank cards is a recent passport-size photograph of himself, one of those neutral, bureaucratic photographs whose only function is facial recognition. He is in the habit of carrying this kind of photo around so he can remember his own face, since the photos on his driver's licence and ID card are too small and too out of date, respectively, for this purpose. He takes the photo out of its plastic envelope. He goes into the bedroom, opens his backpack of personal belongings and takes out his most cherished photo album, the one that serves almost as a catalogue of the faces of the greatest sentimental importance to him. He finds the photograph of his grandfather that his father gave him and compares it to his passport photo. Then he goes into the bathroom and holds the photo of his grandfather next to the mirror.

He looks back and forth at his grandfather's face and his own reflection. He runs his hand over the beard that he has been growing ever since he spoke to his father for the last time. He finds a pair of blunt, slightly rusty scissors in the cutlery drawer and, with some difficulty, cuts his grandfather's portrait down to the size of an ID card and places it in the same plastic envelope in his wallet where he has kept his own picture until now.

3

The village cemetery is located on a square plot of land between two summer homes. Behind it is an abandoned smallholding covered in emerald-green grass and, further back, Silveira Hill, with a winding dirt driveway announcing a future housing development. The incandescent green of the vegetation makes it look as though it's about to catch fire under the sun. The graves are blocks of cement, bare or covered with tiles or flagstones, almost devoid of adornment. Here and there is a silver angel statuette or a cross decorated with gold paint or colourful stones. Not many graves have photographs on them and most of the flowers are plastic. He tries to walk through the middle of the cemetery but can't. The graves are so close together that the few available passages turn out to be dead ends. The labyrinthine layout forces him to jump over graves and lean against them as he looks for a way through. More than once he has to retreat and find another path. At times there isn't even enough space to manoeuvre and turn around. He tries using the edges of the cemetery, but the graves touch the wall. They appear to have been repositioned throughout the years so that more bodies could be buried there until every possible space has been used and all that is left are a few holes and furrows, like a faulty puzzle. He spends a long time trying to get to the back of the cemetery, where, craning his neck, he can see the oldest and simplest graves, among which are some small, worn gravestones atop mounds of soil covered with clover and other weeds. From afar, two or three of these gravestones appear not to have any inscriptions. He trips over a grave that is no more than a little fence of bricks and falls on to another bigger one, smashing a vase of plastic flowers. He picks up the flowers and tries to rearrange them as best he can on the dark slab of imitation marble covering the grave. He looks around for a gravedigger but doesn't see anyone.

The sun is almost setting behind the hills in the neighbourhood of Ambrósio and everything in the bay dozes under the rosy light. He pulls on his Speedos, gets his swimming goggles out of a backpack and takes the stairs down to Baú Rock, feeling the roughness of the cement and warm stone on the unaccustomed soles of his feet. Boats and flocks of gulls bob up and down on the shiny water and the ocean's vapours instantly unblock his nasal passages. He jumps carefully from the rock, so as not to cut his feet on the tiny barnacles, and his body is annulled by his own reflection, shattering the water's filmy surface. His feet disappear with a swallowing noise and concentric circles ripple out for a few yards before he reappears much further along, near an anchored boat, and starts swimming out to the deep. He swims following the coast, happy with the freedom of the cold, salty, endless pool, a little wary of the growing darkness and the probable proximity of some marine animal. It is almost night when he leaves the water. He is relieved, still a little giddy from the effort and musing over everything he thought about while swimming. He has decided to sell his car.

The waning moon is rising behind the hill when he gets his map of the town and heads for Nestor Petrol Station. He talks to the manager and, in exchange for a commission of three hundred reais, leaves the Fiesta parked next to a flower bed at the entrance to the petrol station with a for-sale sign printed out in an internet café and taped to the window. The market value of the car is fifteen thousand but he offers it for fourteen. He buys a can of guarana soda in the corner shop and asks the girl at the cash register about gyms in the town. There are three main ones. He marks them all on his map. Academia Swell is opening a new heated indoor semi-Olympic pool, the first in the region.

With Beta on her leash, he walks the six blocks from the petrol station to Bauru Tchê and orders a cheese-and-chicken-heart sand-wich. This time the owner of the trailer strikes up a conversation and introduces himself. His name is Renato. Three girls are drinking beer at a table and the TV on the counter is showing the eight o'clock soap opera.

Who's the mutt? shouts Renato.

My dog. Beta. She was my dad's, but now she's mine.

Didn't he want her any more?

He passed away.

Oh, pardon me. Sorry to hear it.

It's OK.

Renato asks where he is living and ruminates on his answer as if he really doesn't care much. The subject is redundant and people come and go from these seaside dwellings year after year. Register-ing who comes and who goes is like talking about the weather, which is what he does next.

It rained all summer. Then March comes along and it's all fine and dandy, sun every day, no wind. It's not fair.

His wife prepares the sandwich on a hotplate behind the counter, wearing an apron and a hairnet. They are going to close the snack bar in two weeks' time. He says this year wasn't very good. There won't be much left after he's paid the rent. He plans to return to Cachoeirinha, where his home is.

Hey there.

The person who says this is one of the girls sitting at the next table and the voice is familiar. It is the tallest of the three who is looking at him. Her curly hair is down and he had memorized it on top of her head. It would be silly to pretend that he has only just noticed her, as she is sitting right in front of him at the next table, and it would be equally ridiculous to try to make her understand, under the circumstances, that only her voice or some more complex form of interaction could have revealed her identity to him. It is an explanation that he has learned to give a little further down the track, when he has had more contact with a person. People tend not to believe him straight up and the bad first impression can almost never be undone.

Dália.

He pronounces her name in a cautious, almost interrogative tone. It is inappropriate but he can't avoid it in these situations.

I wasn't going to say anything, man, but you're pretending not to see me so brazenly that I couldn't keep quiet.

Sorry. My mind was elsewhere.

Well, then your mind's always elsewhere, because I passed you on the beach yesterday and you acted as if you didn't see me then either.

He could say his mind is always elsewhere or apologize a second time, but neither solution is satisfactory, the first because it is a lie, the second because it is unfair. Until a few years ago, he was always apologizing for not recognizing people, it was part of his routine, but he started feeling silly and stopped. The forgetting isn't his fault. The only thing he can do is keep quiet in the face of people's indignation and wait to see what happens next. He has learned that most people can't stand not being recognized. There are some who rise above the momentary awkwardness, who don't take themselves so seriously that they are truly offended, and joke about it, and even make an effort to situate him and provide him with the context of their previous encounters even though they aren't aware of his handicap. And there are some who take offence and end the conversation, even going as far as never speaking to him again or paying him any kind of attention.

Come join us, says Dália.

He moves to the empty chair at their table. The boy brings him his sandwich, playing his waiter role ceremoniously. The girls talk as he eats. He tries to participate in the conversation between one bite and another. One of the friends, Neide, is thin and quiet. She lives in town, worked the summer in a little bikini shop and doesn't know what she is going to do for the rest of the year. The other one, Graziela, is plump, an attention grabber, and is only there on holidays. She is heading back to Porto Alegre in a few days to continue her Law degree. Compared to Dália, neither of them is attractive. He never has conflicting impressions about a woman's face on different occasions. A beautiful woman will be beautiful each time. For those who remember, it isn't always so.

After half a dozen bottles have crossed the table the four of them pay the bill and walk down the pavement to the beach. Graziela rolls a joint and they smoke it. The sand is already cold and the sea breeze relieves the sting and lassitude of a scalding-hot day.

March is the best month, says Neide.

It's the month for those who live here, says Dália. The best is left for those who worked all summer long.

How amazing a day was that? says Graziela slowly. I wish I could stay another two weeks. I wish I could stay for ever.

The perfection of the month of March is a fertile and ongoing topic of conversation. The dog sprawls on the cool sand but at a given moment gets up and stands in front of him with her tongue hanging out, panting.

I think she's hungry.

Girls, there's a party at Bar da Cachoeira today. Shall we?

Let's go!

Dália asks if he can give them a lift.

He isn't at all partial to the idea of getting his car from the petrol station but he says yes. Before he does, though, he has to take the dog home.

Have you found a place already? Whereabouts?

He points at the right-hand corner of the beach.

Over there at the foot of the hill. In front of the lamp post. With the brown windows.

We'll wait for you here, says Graziela, lighting a cigarette.

He stands and picks up Beta's leash. He waits a second and looks at Dália. She gives him a sleepy smile, eyes half shut from the marijuana.

OK. I'll be back soon.

He takes a few steps and turns.

Want to come keep me company?

Dália gets up immediately.

Sure. I think I need to use the bathroom. May I?

Grazi and Neide give them suspicious looks.

We'll be right back, girls.

Yeah.

Don't be long.

Dália is wearing a colourful ankle-length skirt that flutters rhythmically around her long legs. The circular movements of the hem allow him to see only the tips of her long feet clad in pink plastic sandals, with burgundy toenails. Her sleeveless white lace blouse shows off her narrow waist and broad hips. She isn't wearing the silver necklace today but she has on a pair of spiral earrings, two delicate metallic structures that manage to find room under her mane of curly hair. The lamp posts on the beach promenade project bright, orangey light over the sand. It is like walking through an empty stadium ready for a rock concert at night. Their long shadows drag their heads through the calm sea.

What are you looking at?

Your earrings.

She fiddles with them.

Did you manage to get back from the party that night?

Jesus. I was really out of it. I can hardly remember a thing. But it was OK, a guy gave me a lift.

That dickhead with dyed-blond hair?

Don't remind me. I hooked up with him once and he thinks he can just rock up talking shit and it's going to happen again whenever he wants.

Next time I won't let him bother you.

Tough guy. The worst part is that I hooked up with him again.

He raises his eyebrows and doesn't say anything.

Why did you leave?

I was a bit worried about the car. And to be honest I haven't got much patience for parties.

You left me there alone. You didn't feel sorry for me. Not nice.

So I passed you on the beach yesterday, did I?

You did, and you pretended not to see me.

When?

Yesterday afternoon. You were running. I was with Pablo.

68

Who's Pablo?

My son.

I didn't know you had a son.

Didn't I tell you? Pablito, my love. I did so tell you.

No, you didn't. How old is he?

Six.

I didn't know you had a son. But that kind of explains it. If you had been alone I think I would have recognized you. By your hair.

Man, you're really weird.

The stream that runs into the sea in front of the row of fishing sheds is too wide to jump over. Near the old stone bridge, a footbridge has been improvised with a plank. He touches Dália's arm and nods to indicate where to cross.

I'm going to tell you something, Dália. But you have to take it seriously, OK?

OK.

But let's cross this plank first.

He goes in front with the dog and holds out his hand to Dália just before he gets to the other side. She lifts up her skirt a little and takes his hand. She crosses the plank with a single step.

I'm incapable of recognizing faces. That's why I didn't realize it was you on the beach. Or in the bar tonight.

That's no excuse for ignoring someone you've known for two or three days. It means you couldn't care less about them.

Listen. I can't recognize any face. It's a neurological disorder.

She stops and stares at him.

Take a good look at my face, she says, pointing at it. Can't you see it? Can't you see my mouth, nose, eyes? Is that it?

I can see it. But I won't remember it. My brain doesn't retain it. I have brain damage right in the part that recognizes human faces. If you leave my sight I'll forget your face in five minutes, or ten, or half an hour with a lot of luck. It's inevitable.

I've never heard of it.

It's very rare.

She stares at him for another instant then starts walking again.

Don't you believe me?

You said you were serious, so I'm taking you seriously. But if you're messing with me. . . the sooner I know the better. A moment from now is going to be too late.

I'm serious.

The fishing sheds are all closed. They pass a young couple heading in the opposite direction, coming back from the rocks, listening to electronic music weakly amplified on a mobile phone.

So you'll never be able to recognize me? If I want to talk to you I have to go up to you and say, Hi, I'm Dália, remember me? Waving my hands and all? She opens her eyes wide and makes a funny smile, gesticulating as she talks.

No, of course not. There are lots of things besides a person's face. The voice almost always helps. And the context. I know you're the tallest girl in the pizza parlour. If I go there while you're working I'll know who you are immediately. Sometimes it's an item of clothing that the person wears a lot and I memorize it. A way of walking. I always have to be on the lookout for things that can identify a person, besides their face. I scan the details. In your case the first things I noticed were your height and your hair. The better I know someone, the easier it is to recognize them. But it's always a little complicated. Yesterday on the beach, for example, it would have been almost impossible because you were with your son and I didn't know you had a son.

I'll introduce you to him as soon as I get a chance.

Please do.

They reach the crumbling stairs that lead to the footpath around the rocks. He lets her go first and follows, pulling Beta along by her leash. There is a strong smell of sewage around the winding stairs. Dália hunches up and hops on the spot a few times.

I need to go.

As soon as he unlocks the door she hurries to the bathroom. He puts out dog food and water for Beta and leaves her eating in the tiny laundry area. He gets a can of beer from the fridge and opens the living-room shutters. Dália doesn't take long. He hears the flush, then the door opens and she comes out talking.

OK, but tell me, how did it happen to you?

Perinatal anoxia.

Well, of course. It had to be perinatal whatyamacallit.

At birth. I wasn't breathing when I was born and it caused brain damage. I've had it since I was a baby.

Oh, how awful.

No, it isn't awful. It's just a bit of a drag sometimes. People generally refuse to believe it exists. Hardly anyone is OK about it, like you.

Hey, remember me? she jokes, batting her eyelids, as she comes over and takes the beer can from him. Don't tell me you've forgotten me!

Exactly.

She leans on the windowsill beside him.

Why don't you put some music on?

I burned out my sound system. The voltage here is two hundred and twenty.

Silly. Anyway, we need to go and get the girls and see if this party's any good. Your car's at the petrol station?

71

Yep.

Did you leave it there to have it washed?

I left it there to sell it.

Who's going to give me lifts now?

He doesn't answer.

I can't really be bothered going to this party, to be honest.

What about your son's dad, where's he?

A young man in a baseball cap and no shirt comes along the footpath with a panting white-and-yellow pit bull on a leash, its large mouth open in a crocodile smile. They take the stairs down to the rocks.

He went back to Criciúma. He's from there. He moved here with me a few years ago, but then we had a fight and he left.

Do you get along OK?

Yeah, pretty good. Pablo loves him. He goes to spend a few days with John twice a month. We treat each other well. Pablo is what matters.

His name's John?

Yeah.

Is he American?

No. He's from Criciúma.

The young man lets the pit bull off its leash and throws a plastic bottle half filled with water into the sea. The dog studies the edge of the rock for a moment and launches itself after its toy. The young man lights a cigarette and watches the dog swim.

Does he give you child support or something like that?

She swallows her beer quickly and gives a short, explosive laugh, before answering scornfully.

All he does is smoke pot. But no, to be fair, he gives me some money when he can. But he hasn't got a thing. He's a lazy-arse, that one.

Do you live on your own with Pablo?

No, I live with my mother. She helps me. She moved here when we broke up and she lives with me. Tell me, do you recognize your own face in the mirror?

I don't know if I want to talk about it any more.

The pit bull comes out of the water with the bottle in its mouth. The man wrests it from the dog's jaws and throws it again, several yards out. The dog dives in.

No, I don't recognize my own face in the mirror. And there's no point staring at photos. When I wake up the next morning I've already forgotten it.

That must be really crazy. What if you shave or cut your hair? Does it change anything?

No. But my mother always told me I look better without a beard. I trust her.

And do you know if someone is good-looking, if they're sad, angry, that kind of thing?

Yes. I can tell if I'm looking at the person. I see emotions normally. I know if someone's ugly or good-looking, young or old. No problem. But I forget their actual face. I remembered that you were gorgeous. So, it's nice to see you again.

She bumps him with her shoulder.

You did not. You're just saying that.

They stand there for a while, watching the pit bull's workout, which seems interminable. He turns his head and sees that Beta has made herself comfortable on her towel at the other end of the living room, next to the front door.

Sometimes I think the dog's watching me.

What?

Nothing, it's silly.

So if I spent the night here you wouldn't recognize my face in the morning?

Honestly? No.

You're the only person in the world with a good excuse for it.

She leaves her empty can on the windowsill and turns to him.

Are you really sure you wouldn't?

It's never happened.

Not even if it was a really, really good night?

I don't want to give you false hopes, Dália.

Where would we be without false hopes?

He wakes up without opening his eyes. There is the heat, the smell and a clear memory of all of the things for which a face, and even sight itself, is unnecessary. Weight is one of his favourite sensations. He'd be able to identify her at once if she lay on him the next morning or in a year's time. It wouldn't matter. And the way a body moves. If it is in intimate contact with his, if he can hold it firmly with both hands at its diverse points of articulation and in this manner read its voluntary and involuntary movements, soft and brusque, repeated or not, he can forever retain a tactile image that can tell him much more than any visual stimuli about how the person draws back and lets go, asks and refuses, approaches and retreats. Dália has protruding collarbones, wide hips and full, muscular legs. Wiry hair and slightly bitter sweat like weak coffee. Milk-and-sugar breath. The way she uses her teeth. The bodily self-consciousness typical of beautiful women restricts her movements. A collection of little embarrass-ments and inhibitions that fade somewhat, as the half-light in the musty room reveals more and more. Her reserve gives way to a certain submission. The difference is subtle. He'll remember every-thing. The darkened bedroom and the kitchen light filtering through

74

the open door. Her feet twitching when he tried to kiss them. Tension in her whole body that took a while to yield. She digs her nails in lightly, gives little punches. When her hand holds something her fingertips press alternately as if trying to remember how to play a tune on the piano. Maybe she plays piano or played it when she was little. It is moving to think about a person's repertoire of caresses. Why they touch others this way or that. It comes from so many places. The things we imagine must feel good, the things we've been told feel good, the things we've had done to us and liked, the things that are involuntary, the things that are our way of giving pleasure, full stop. She comes almost in silence or, come to think of it, in total silence. And with her eyes closed. Not a peep. He can hear the waves. He won't forget a single detail of it. He will still be able to recall it several months or years from now and it will only remind him of her. He catalogues with renewed amazement the countless ways in which the world can be unveiled by his senses. Nothing but faces are lost. Dália sleeping soundlessly by his side, emanating heat, her buttocks pressed against his hip, her back against his left shoulder, the waves almost hitting the window. He'll remember everything.

Academia Swell is located at the bottom of Silveira Hill, a short distance before the steep and winding road gouged into the hillside that provides access to the beach on the other side. Just inside the gate is a small structure made of thick planks of wood, which houses a snack bar with round wooden tables. He peers through the door and sees the waitress behind the counter, a girl with indigenous features and straight black hair. She explains the way to reception in Spanish. He walks down the driveway past a long, tall building with exposed brick walls and an asbestos roof, which, judging from the dimensions and fogged-up windows, must house the recently opened heated swimming pool. He opens the glass door at the back of the complex and enters reception. To his left is a large weights room. Half a dozen gym-goers are straining their muscles on outdated equipment. There are vases of plants everywhere and colourful reproductions of what he thinks are Hindu gods hanging on grubby walls, creatures with female or pachydermal features and a slightly arrogant serenity plastered across their happy, erotic faces, some blue-skinned with several plump arms and thin fingers holding tridents and other ritualistic objects. The afternoon light tinges the walls and metal equipment with a golden colour and the mild March temperatures make air conditioning unnecessary. It is an atypical gym environment, more reminiscent of a religious temple in which physical exercise is a ritual practised as a means of attaining enlightenment. Hidden loudspeakers are playing reggae at a low volume, which sounds out of place. The blonde sitting behind the counter wishes him good afternoon.

Hi. I hear you've opened a pool.

She gives him a photocopied pamphlet with the opening hours and prices of the gym and swimming pool.

Do you know if they need a swimming instructor?

You'll have to talk to Saucepan.

Saucepan?

The owner.

They smile at each other.

And where's Saucepan?

He should be here in about half an hour. Or you can come back at night and talk to his partner.

She stifles a smile and looks at him. She is a little chubby with a freckled face, deep lines from too much sun exposure, and a round nose. He hears explosive noises coming from the pool, as if someone were beating the surface of the water with a spade. Both of the receptionist's arms are covered in colourful tattoos. There is a Japanese-style wave, a tribal bracelet, a dolphin. He chuckles.

Am I going to have to guess the partner's name?

He's got a nickname too. Try.

I've got something in mind but I'm afraid it might be wrong.

Spatula.

No way.

Yes way. Spatula's the one who comes at night.

The two of them laugh silently and look at one another as if they know each other well and have a plan to get revenge on someone. It is a pleasant feeling that appears to have sprung from nowhere.

OK, I'll wait for Saucepan.*

OK.

---

* Yeah, he taught here until six weeks ago. He started in 2004 and was here for almost three years. [. . .] No, he's very professional, you can be sure of that. Keeps to himself. But very professional. Does he want to teach there? But what's he doing in Garopaba? [. . .] He told me he was leaving Porto Alegre but he didn't say where he was going. He gave me a month's notice. His dad killed himself at the beginning of the year. [. . .] Pretty heavy shit. But tell me, what's your new pool like? [. . .] Fuckin' amazing? Have you bought lane lines yet? Milton's got a supplier in Florianópolis. He called me here once, said his price is good. I'll email you the guy's contact details afterwards. [. . .] You've got to get word out there, otherwise people won't come. Maybe you could have unstructured morning sessions for people who want to do longer swims. Think of something to get the athletes in. [. . .] Yep, to make money you've got to offer lessons at set times. Have they asked you to heat the water? [. . .] Eighty degrees? Hahaha. You're crazy, man. They're going to ask you to heat it every day. You'll have to raise the temperature. [. . .] Doesn't make any difference, you'll have to bump it up. First it'll be an old guy who won't get in the water, then a mother who doesn't want her kid to get cold, then everyone'll be wanting warm water. People want warm water. I keep it at eighty-six but I tell people it's eighty-two. [. . .] Look, like I said, he's very professional.

Can I take a look at the pool?
Yes.

_____

He knows a lot. He was the one who coached Pérsio in 2007, when he won practically everything. And he's a good athlete too. He did the Ironman in Hawaii. He did well in the qualifier but didn't do a good time in the event itself. He had some kind of meltdown halfway through. You know, the kind of guy who doesn't have much of a competitive spirit? He does better times in training than in competition. But he's an awesome swimmer. Best style I've ever seen. [. . .] He keeps to himself. I had a problem with him once but I ended up keeping him because the students asked me to. We were changing our approach to lessons to make them more fun. We started implementing games and music and stuff. It's where things are going nowadays. And there was this whole recycling process for the instructors to make the lessons more interesting. Today they're all on friendlier terms with the students. We encouraged it. We paid for them all to do a course in playful sports instruction, which is our approach here. It's important in keeping enrolments up and really boosted our number of students. Music pumping, rankings, everything turns into a game. But at the time I had a problem with him 'cause he refused to take the course. He told me to my face that he thought it was bullshit. And that put me in a difficult spot 'cause I couldn't make an exception just for him. I ended up confronting him and he told me he was a swimming instructor, not a clown. Things got heated and I had to fire him. [. . .] But less than a week later students started coming to management asking about him, asking for him to come back. I made up an excuse, 'cause at that stage it didn't really matter, but the next month we found out that four or five students had left because of him. [. . .] They wanted lessons with him and no one else. And then the whole story got out and lots of people took his side. We discovered they absolutely loved him, but no one here in management had any idea 'cause you'd see the guy teaching and he was always kind of scowling, correcting everyone all the time. He's a bit harsh. [. . .] Yeah, it was funny. Watching him from a distance, it looked like he never talked to anyone, that he was just there to do his job. I thought everyone hated the guy. Then a student of ours came along, Tatanka – [. . .] You know Tatanka? True, he surfs, he's always around, true. So anyway, Tatanka told me that thanks to him he discovered that he swam all wrong. He'd been here for years and no instructor had ever corrected him properly, then he showed up and gave him two months of technique and Tatanka's times dropped way down and he made it to the podium in

78

What's your name?

Débora.

The poolroom looks much smaller from the inside than the outside and is filled with white steam and the strong smell of chlorine and clay tiles. He breathes in the warm, moist, slightly caustic air. It feels like home to him. In indoor-pool areas he always remembers the sessions he had with a nebulizer to treat a brief bout of bronchitis when he was a child: the green plastic mask, the noisy little machine like a small pool pump, his mother looking on approvingly as she oversaw things. The semi-Olympic pool is the narrowest he has ever seen, with only three lanes demarcated with lines of navy-blue tiles and still without floating lane dividers. There is a swimmer at each end. Both are finding it hard to breathe properly in the choppy water. The swimmer on the left is older and fatter and wearing a yellow snorkel, goggles and flippers. He is the one responsible for the explosive sounds he had heard earlier. The man raises his right arm

---

the Torres Swim. There were also some girls who told Maíra, another instructor of ours, that they only swam at our gym because of him. They liked his presence. [. . .] That's what they said. They liked his presence. Whatever the fuck that's supposed to mean. [. . .] He broke up with a girl about two years ago. I think he's more of a doer than a talker. [. . .] Right. Something like that. [. . .] Anyway, the upshot is that I went and asked him to come back. He did, there were no hard feelings, he stayed another two years, until the month before last. We make fun of him because he doesn't remember people's faces. Did he tell you that? [. . .] Ask him, it's no bullshit, he's got a really rare memory problem. I think it has something to do with the way he comes across. [. . .] You'll have to see if he fits the profile of what you're looking for. People here really liked him. I'm the one who didn't really get along with him . . . he doesn't open up much. I don't really hit it off with people like that. But here's the thing, Saucepan. The guy's good. Always up to date. A fucking good instructor, seriously. You can count on it. And don't forget: warm water and music pumping.

completely out of the water, very slowly, as if trying to project his hand as far as possible from his body, holds it out of the water for a moment, then brings it down with supersonic speed, like the arm of a catapult, slamming it into the surface of the pool with a deafening bang and splashing water several yards away. His left arm doesn't even leave the water properly and makes an atrophied movement that generates zero propulsion. If it weren't for the flippers on his feet, the guy would barely leave the spot. The world's swimming pools are full of these comical, extreme cases that can rarely be remedied. The swimmer on the right is younger and swims well. His rhythm is firm and he takes a breath every four strokes, but his legs are scissor-kicking and his right arm is coming down a little too far to the side. He turns swiftly and fluidly, surfaces quickly, crosses the pool again and stops at the edge, panting, consulting his watch to count the interval before his next sprint. Twenty seconds. He is doing a set of one-hundred-metre sprints and he does each in ninety seconds, some in eighty-eight, eighty-seven. As he watches the man swim he can't help but count the seconds in his head. Swimmer's tic. Over the years his inner clock has become precise, almost infallible.

A barber by the name of Zé calls about his Ford Fiesta early one Friday afternoon. They meet at the petrol station. Zé looks under the bonnet, inspects the engine and says he can pay that day. They go straight to Laguna in the car itself to transfer the ownership of the vehicle and arrange for the deposit. The whole operation takes less than two hours and soon they are back in Garopaba. They park in front of the barber's shop. He hands the new owner the car key and orders a Coke at the bar adjoining the barber's. Zé offers him a shave.

Thanks, but I'm letting it grow.

Want a trim?

A what?

A trim? Trim your beard. Tidy it up.

But tidy it up how? Cut it shorter?

Haven't you ever trimmed your beard?

I've never grown it before.

A drunk with a shaved head who is drinking beer alone at the counter slurs something incomprehensible and stares into space. His moist eyes shine in his puffy red face.

How long have you been growing it? Three months?

Two and a half.

You need to trim it. So it'll grow right.

Nah, don't worry about it.

It's for free.

But what're you going to do?

I'll just shorten it a little with the scissors and shape it here at your neck and here on your face.

Zé points to where he intends to shape it. He is a man of almost seventy, short and grey-haired with sun-ravaged skin. Zé appears to be laughing inwardly and he realizes that other locals have given him the same impression.

OK, you can shape it then, but don't take any length off it.

The operation takes some time. The reclining barber's chair is in the centre of the modest shop and a window lets in the glare from outside. There is a wooden bench under the window, a small chest of drawers and a square mirror in an orange plastic frame hanging on the wall. There are no work tools in sight. Zé comes back from the adjoining bathroom with a bowl of warm water and a traditional razor, applies a warm towel to his face and takes it off only when it starts to cool. Zé applies lather to his neck and cheeks with a shaving brush and passes the razor fastidiously, with long intervals between strokes. He gazes out the window as Zé works. The drunk from the bar stumbles through the door and across the street. He gets into the cabin of a white flatbed truck parked on the other side, starts the engine and drives off.

You living in Garopaba?

Yeah, I moved here not long ago.

Do you surf?

No. I just swim.

What did you come here for?

To live. I didn't come to surf or to run away from something. Isn't that what they say everyone comes here for?

If someone said it, it wasn't me. I don't know anything.

Next Monday I start teaching swimming at the gym.

But do you swim in the sea?

Yes.

Careful, 'cause the mullet season is about to start. The fishermen are going to force you out of the water.

So they told me.

When he is done with the razor, Zé dries his face with a towel and wets his own hands with a rose-coloured cologne that reeks of alcohol.

Know how we tell if someone's a gaucho? asks Zé, nodding at the footrest. If their feet shake, they're a gaucho.

So let's see.

The cologne stings his neck but his feet don't shake.

You're not a real gaucho.

Zé returns the chair to its normal position and goes into the bathroom.

He gets up and looks at his face in the mirror. He sees the careful contours and his slightly red skin from the razor. It is hard for him to notice any difference since he doesn't really remember what he looked like before.

Stay for a beer? Zé says, coming out of the bathroom.

I've got to go. How much do I owe you?

I said it was on the house.

So you did. It looks good, thanks. Look after my car well. If you have any problems in the first few days, let me know. Have a good weekend.

Want a lift?

Thanks, but I'll walk. My place is over by the beach.

If you want to buy land here I've got three lots in Siriú.

I'll keep it in mind.

He shakes the barber's hand and leaves. The sun is almost setting behind the hills and a cool breeze is blowing towards the ocean. He takes a few steps, turns around and goes back into the barber's shop.

Zé. Are you originally from Garopaba?

Yep.

Have you always lived here?

Almost always. I lived in São Paulo for a few years.

In the late 60s my granddad lived here for a while. They used to call him Gaudério. Ever heard of him?

Gaudério, Gaudério . . .

Zé is silent for a while then turns and heads into the bar saying he is going to get his wife. His wife is wearing an orthopaedic collar around her neck and asks who he is and why he wants information about his grandfather. He says he is just investigating a family story, out of curiosity. She asks if he's been asking around about his grandfather and when he says yes, that he has asked a few people, she wants to know who. Zé's wife doesn't smile but she doesn't give off any aggression either. She seems to be studying him, even turning her head a little to the side, in spite of the collar. Sometimes he has the urgent feeling that he should memorize for all time the faces of certain people that don't mean anything to him and who he will probably never see again in his life: a pharmacy attendant, someone's cousin who goes to a party and is only passing through town, another patient sitting in the dentist's waiting room, and this urge is never justified in the future, at the end of the day, or at least he doesn't remember it ever having been justified, but when it arises it feels imperative, as is the case now, looking at this woman with her neck immobilized and without any distinguishing facial or physical characteristic, a woman made not to be remembered or even imagined. He decides to lie. He doesn't remember who he asked. Just one or two people he didn't know in the fishing village. She doesn't say anything else and disappears again through the back door of the bar, allowing him a glimpse of a living room with a threadbare sofa and blue walls. The bar is suddenly dark. Night has fallen. Zé leans both arms on the counter and lowers his voice.

Don't worry about her. I remember Gaudério.

Did you know him?

No, I just remember him. He lived on a small property near the parish church, over where the residential subdivision is now. I wasn't even twenty when he passed through here. He once gave my brother some money to fix his bike, a brown Barra Forte that he used to ride.

What's your brother's name?

Dilmar.

Any chance I could talk to him?

No. He passed away.

Is it true my granddad was murdered here?

I don't know. But don't go around asking that kind of thing.

Why not?

Because you don't talk about that kind of thing. It doesn't matter if it happened or not. People don't know certain things after some time has passed because they don't want to. Do you follow?

He stares at Zé for a moment, then nods.

You're a good kid. Let it go. And come back here to shave that beard off when you get tired of it.

Will do.

Take care.

Thanks, you too.

Now I know why I thought I knew you from somewhere.

What do you mean?

You really look like Gaudério.

Yeah, I know.

The penny will drop for some people. It probably already has.

No one remembers him. It's as if he never existed.

There are some who'll remember. If they want to. To remember you have to want to.

But why wouldn't people here want to remember him?

It doesn't matter. Just remember what I told you.

Thanks for your concern. But I think I need to get to the bottom of this.

This place is blessed. So much beauty everywhere you look. Right, gaucho? A person can be really happy here.

4

The cold nights torture the summer with a slow death. Dália rests her cup of coffee on her legs, which are extended on the small canvas sofa in the living room, as she stares through the window at the crystalline surface of a lazy sea that looks as if it is stretching, like them, waiting for the sun to come up and warm it. He is sitting on the fabric sofa pushed up against the opposite wall, but the room is so small that they could touch hands if they held out their arms. He looks at Dália in profile, her curly hair, delicate features in a broad face, the up-turned crest of her top lip backlit by the light from outside. He enjoys in silence the pleasure of being in the presence of such a beautiful woman. He maps the circumstances that put her there as if they were of his own doing. Outside, local children run past laughing euphor-ically and shouting, wearing only bathing suits, carrying pieces of wood and primitive fishing rods, packets of biscuits and colourful plastic buckets, and staring unashamedly through the window into the apartment. The sky is blue but he can somehow tell it is going to rain later. Several weeks in Garopaba have enabled him to make this kind of intuitive meteorological reading based on signs that he still can't put a finger on: the direction of the wind, the humidity inside the apartment, the behaviour of the birds, the background noise of the ocean. Dália uses her big toe to turn on the tiny televi-sion set on the chest of drawers near the window, and says she wants to watch the morning cartoons. A popular talk-show host appears on the screen and he warns her that the TV will turn itself off in a minute at the most, which is exactly what happens. It has been like this since his second week in the apartment and Cecina explained that it is a common problem caused by the same salty ocean air that has already started to rust the barbecue knife that he got as a present from his father and to cover all surfaces with a slippery film that corrodes all kinds of metal at an alarming speed no matter what anyone does to protect them. The door is open and he hears Beta's firm footsteps, as her long nails rasp on the cement outside and then the beige-tiled floor of the living room. He snaps his fingers, whistles and calls her, almost simultaneously, because he isn't really sure how she likes to be called now that his father's familiar gestures are no longer there for her. In the last few days she has responded to his calls more enthusiastically and accompanies him on walks without the need of a leash. He likes the responsibility of looking after her, the objective simplicity of his mission to cheer her up and keep her alive. She comes over and he pats her head, runs his hand over the short, thick fur on her back, which is a dark blue-grey spattered with rust-coloured spots.

Scratch the back of her head, says Dália. She likes it.

How do you know? My dad didn't do that.

Beta, Beta, come here.

The dog immediately goes over to Dália. Dália grabs her by the skin at the scruff of her neck and holds her up in the air, a manoeuvre that to him seems violent, inappropriate for an adult animal.

Don't do that. You'll hurt her.

It doesn't hurt. You don't know dogs.

Dália sits Beta on her thighs.

That's how her mother used to carry her when she was a puppy, wasn't it, Beta? Tell him, girl.

87

She vigorously rubs the back of the dog's head, grabbing the loose skin there and massaging it with her fingertips. Beta curves her neck forward and closes her eyes.

See? All dogs love it. They remember their mothers when you rub them here.

His mobile rings. He goes to get it from the kitchen counter.

Guess who.

Hello, Mother. Not exactly quantum physics.

He goes outside to take the call. It is a replay of all of their recent conversations. It starts with a few practical questions about probate, the inheritance, debts, and what to do with one of his father's belongings, and soon progresses to her asking him to go to Porto Alegre for something and comparing him to his older brother in some way, always favouring the latter and accompanied by a failed attempt to hide what she really thinks. He tries to let it go but ends up protesting and there is a joint effort to quickly finish the conversation so as not to end it in a really unpleasant way. Before hanging up she asks if he intends to come home for Mother's Day. He is irritated by the word choice of *come home* and she says it's just an expression and that he doesn't need to get worked up. He says he isn't worked up and really doesn't feel that way. A better description for what he feels would be tired. He says he still doesn't know and will think about it and let her know closer to the date. Right after he hangs up he realizes that this will be the first time she won't be taken out for lunch on Mother's Day. The person who has fulfilled this function in recent years is him. He almost calls her back.

Are you OK?

Yes.

Do you get along well with her?

Pretty much.

Must be hard for her to be left alone there.

She's fine. My dad left her some things in his will and she's mediating between me and my brother, because I don't speak to him. She's in good health for her age, and her boyfriend's well off. His family owns a notary's office. At any rate, the son who really matters to her is the other one. I was just the one who was available recently. She'll soon get used to it.

But she and your dad were divorced, weren't they?

Yes.

Why aren't you speaking to your brother?

It's not worth talking about. My family doesn't make any sense.

He dumps the mobile phone on the table and sits on the floor next to her sofa. She caresses the back of his neck with her long nails.

Do you think he likes this too, Beta?

He sighs and feels his body slowly soften under the waves of pleasure radiating from the top of his back to the tips of his toes.

I was wondering if I could ask you a favour, says Dália.

She says she has taken a second job and starting next week she'll be working in a beachwear shop every afternoon in the nearby town of Imbituba. A friend of hers who lives in Silveira is a bank manager there and can give her a lift home every day in time for her evening shift at the pizza parlour. She needs the extra money so she can move to Florianópolis and go to university, a plan she has had to put off until next year. Her mother has diabetes and has a hard time walking and she needs someone to pick up Pablo from school and take him home every afternoon, which she will no longer have time to do.

Of course I can.

I pick him up by bike. He's used to it. He sits on the bar or the rack. He likes it. But if it's too much of a hassle, don't worry. It's just that I don't have anyone else I can ask at the moment.

Something about the circumstances of the moment moves him. The dog seems happy and at peace for the first time since his father's death. Dália is entrusting him with the care of her son, whom he hasn't even met. Maybe it is the urgency with which she is seeking to plant her flag in his life, maybe he just wants to be on his own and is feeling momentarily needy, maybe deep down she doesn't feel right for him: he doesn't have a precise diagnosis, but he has a strong feeling that the nascent intimacy between them has just now begun to end. He hopes he is wrong. And at the same time there is a comforting inner coherency in the way in which they have already irreversibly affected each other's lives. Something good has already installed itself and is protected, and it will last even if these mornings cease today.

I'll pick him up. No problem.

Just until I find someone else. I didn't want to have to ask you.

I'll pick him up for as long as you need. Don't worry about it. But it's probably a good idea that I meet the kid first.

We'll arrange it tomorrow. I'll call you. How are you going to recognize him at school?

There's always a way. Let me meet him first.

He's got big ears.

I'll figure it out.

OK.

I'll put a bike seat on for him.

Don't worry about it. He sits on the bar. He never . . .

She trails off without finishing her sentence. Outside, the *Lendário* blows its long, shrill whistle once, twice, while tourists hurry down the path outside his window. They are couples and small families trying to make the most of the schooner tours during the last few warm weekends of the season. The knowledge that this is a beautiful,

90

sunny Saturday morning before an afternoon of rain in late March is written in their eyes and their reverent attitude before the schooner. He kneels next to the sofa Dália is on and kisses her. The bitter coffee tastes nice in her saliva. They shoo away the dog, close the living-room shutters, take off their clothes and are soon in the bedroom. The rumble of the diesel engine passes through the walls, the whistle sounds again and the schooner takes off. A cloud covers the sun behind the closed shutters and the room slowly darkens. With him on top, Dália comes without a sound and a tear slides out of each eye. She rolls over and sniffs.

Shit.

You OK?

No, I'm not. If I were moaning like a whore, it'd mean I'm OK.

The cloud uncovers the sun. Dália rolls back and places her hand on his chest.

Just pretend I didn't say anything.

It takes about ten minutes pedalling slowly to get from the Pinguirito Municipal School, where Pablo is in the first grade, to Dália's house, but today he takes a detour past the Gelomel ice-cream parlour before handing the boy over to Dália's mother, who had a foot amputated a few months ago as a result of a diabetic ulcer. She always invites him in for some cake and juice. Sometimes he accepts the invitation. Dália's mother likes him. She claims to be something of a witch and says she dreamed about him before they even met in person, perhaps influenced by the things Dália had already told her about him.* At

---

* *I appeared in a corridor, unmoving and suspended in the air, and I couldn't feel my own body. I could see my body but it was as if it didn't belong to me. Then on my right I saw a room with a large table made of dark wood and four chairs, two on each side,*

each visit she adds some details to the dream, things she has remembered or new interpretations she has made. He has already told her he doesn't believe in such things but she doesn't seem to care. Sometimes he gets the impression that she makes up her dreams on the spot.

He is still riding down the main avenue to the ice-cream parlour when he passes a corner block in front of the supermarket and hears a shout and a loud thud. Two men are demolishing the wall of a semi-destroyed kiosk with kicks and an enormous sledgehammer. He has never paid the place much attention but is sure the kiosk was

---

with a window at one end. The room was very white, with dark floorboards and a very high ceiling. It was night and I saw you sitting with your back to me, in black trousers and a shirt, with your hair recently cut, and clean-shaven. You looked behind you as if you could feel my presence but couldn't see me. In the dream I was afraid of being discovered, because I knew that shortly I was going to witness something important. Then, at the same time, a man appeared sitting in front of you and another standing on the left. The man sitting in front of you was a stranger and I didn't know what you were talking about, because you were communicating telepathically. But the man on the left was communicating with me telepathically and told me that he was your brother and your guardian. At that moment, my astral body very quickly went up a staircase on the right to a corridor and an intuitive force made me find an envelope hidden in a crack in the wall. The envelope had a wad of banknotes and a kind of dossier that said who you were. It had everything about you. The dossier said that you are a mysterious creature who has already lived many lives and knows it. When I returned to the room you had disappeared along with the two men. At this moment I was immediately transported to another scenario: a rotting wooden deck outside the house that was falling to pieces. I saw a marshy lake surrounded by forest. An unknown woman, tall, brunette, passed me without a word, entered the murky water and vanished. Then I woke up and the first thing I thought was that you were a vampire. I don't think you're going to admit it, you may not even be aware of it, but there's a reason why you don't know it or deny it and one day I'm going to explain it all to you.

intact yesterday. The bold, dark-skinned man holding the sledge-hammer has a pear-shaped body, with a pot belly, short arms and no shoulders. He waves at Pablo.

Hey Pablito! Go Grêmio!

The boy raises a fist and shouts, Grêmio!

They arrive at the ice-cream parlour. He leans the bike against the glass door and unbuckles Pablo from the bike seat.

Who was the man with the sledgehammer?

Bonobo.

Booboo?

No, Bo-nooo-bo!

At the ice-cream counter, Pablo fills his bowl with balls of coconut, grape and chocolate-chip ice cream. To top it off, jelly teeth and a good dose of condensed milk. According to his mother he can put whatever he wants in his bowl as long as he doesn't overdo it on the quantity. It can't cost more than five reais. Pablo is an easy child to deal with, at least as far as he is concerned. He doesn't complain about anything and doesn't make extravagant requests. Dália says that sometimes he is stubborn and hyperactive and she thinks he might be bipolar or something of the sort. He never recognizes Pablo among the dozens of children in the schoolyard, but Pablo always gets his backpack and comes running over. All he has to do is wait a little.

Pablo pulls out of his SpongeBob backpack the swimming goggles that he gave him as a present the day they met. He has been the Goggles Guy ever since. Pablo puts on his goggles and attacks the ice cream. There are milk teeth alongside half-grown adult teeth in his mouth, smeared with melted ice cream.

So, Pablito. Are you going to learn to swim now?

No.

I'll teach you.

OK.

You can use your goggles to protect your eyes when we ride on the bike. They're for that too.

OK.

He takes an alternative route through back streets and drops Pablo home. He doesn't stay for juice or cake today. He doesn't want to know why he is a vampire. On the way back he passes the corner where the two men were trying to demolish the kiosk wall. Now they are trying to get an ice-cream freezer on to the back of a pickup. It isn't working. The shoulderless man who had waved at Pablo turns his head and shouts.

Hey, mate! We need a hand here. Quick, quick!

He brakes the bike and surveys the scene. Two walls of the kiosk have been brought down with the sledgehammer. There are shards of glass everywhere, pieces of brick, crumbling cement, iron bars, a wooden door and window frames and all manner of debris lying around. At one end of the property, next to the wall of the neighbouring house, is the abandoned carcass of an old beige VW Beetle destroyed by rust and exposure to the elements.

A dozen crumpled beer cans are scattered about the crushed grass that looks like it has been trampled by hordes of holidaymakers during the summer. Near the kiosk is a half-full bottle of Smirnoff Vanilla Vodka. The tendons in the men's necks are bulging and the freezer is slipping from their hands. He dumps the bike on the ground and runs to help them.

Over here, says Bonobo. We need to get this freezer on the back but it's a bitch. Give us a hand 'cause it's about to fall.

Afternoon, says the other man. He looks a little older. He has a dyed-black pompadour, a small chin, yellow teeth and a sunburned face with deep wrinkles and grooves. Hoop earrings in both ears. He is wearing blue-and-black-checked surf shorts and a filthy pink polo shirt drenched with sweat.

This is Altair, says Bonobo as he helps lift the freezer. After a few more pushes and adjustments it is safely positioned in the back of the pickup.

Thanks for the hand, mate. I saw you giving Pablito a lift on your bike. You hooking up with Dália?

Yeah.

Cool.

But where are you from? asks Altair. You're new around here, aren't you?

He explains that he moved there not long ago and tells them the whole story. The two men listen without hearing. They are out of breath, exhausted, addled from the alcohol and the physical exertion. The faded, stained and torn yellow T-shirt that Bonobo is wearing, with black sleeves and yellow stripes, is a Grêmio Football Club jersey. No one remembers this shirt, he says with pride. It's the goalkeeper's. It was worn by Gomes and Sidmar in '91.

He is wearing a necklace of wrinkled brown beads that look like nuts, and covering his legs is an item of clothing of indeterminate colour that could be long shorts or short trousers.

So, what are you guys doing?

Knockin' down the kiosk, says Altair.

Yeah, but why?

Altair has to return the property by two o'clock tomorrow afternoon, says Bonobo. Without the kiosk. It's in the lease.

Between swigs straight from the bottle of Smirnoff Vanilla, they explain that Altair leased the land in the middle of the previous year to open a business during the summer months. He built the kiosk with money from a small bank loan and the sale of a motorbike. His friends helped him build it. It took longer than planned and wasn't ready until after Christmas, when the tourists had already arrived, and suddenly he found himself with a debt and an empty kiosk on one of the best corners in Garopaba at the peak of the busy season. He quickly arranged for a visit from a Kibon Ice Cream representative and a few days later he was given the freezer on consignment. By New Year's Eve he had a dozen surfboards made by a shaper friend of his on display. By the second week of January the kiosk also had a stand of trinkets and costume jewellery made by a well-known itinerant hippie couple who come to town every summer, three small tables for customers to sit at and a well-stocked Skol Beer fridge, and a table where Lisandra, a voluptuous young masseuse from Goiás who had been in Garopaba for three years, provided massotherapy, chiropractic, lymphatic drainage and reiki at any time of the day or night. At night the kiosk began to host bands playing samba, *pagode*, reggae and Brazilian pop music. The samba sessions were especially lively and went on into the small hours with people occupying the vacant lot around the kiosk and spilling over on to the pavements and even into the middle of the street, which forced the police to put in the occasional appearance and stop the fun. On 22 January, Altair organized a luau to celebrate the first full moon of the year on the sands of Ferrugem Beach and attracted hundreds of summer tourists thirsty for beer, refreshing cocktails, massages and drugs, which he also arranged for them. He sold all the surfboards at gringo prices. Everything sold like hot cakes: the ice creams, the wire-and-resin earrings, the coconut-shell bracelets, the beer, the kiwi caipirinhas, Lisandra's famous hands with her almost erotic sessions of do-in, the LSD and the E. It became a sales outlet for tickets to all the major parties of the season. Before January was over he had already raised enough money to pay for the lease of the land. Before mid-February he had paid off his loan too. He doesn't want to say how much he profited but he indicates that he won't need to work until next summer and that he is going to buy a new motorbike, much better than the last one. Now, at the end of April, he needs to return the land in the same state as when he leased it. The owner isn't interested in the kiosk.

But why don't you pay someone to demolish it?

I don't want to spend money on it.

Altair knows his shit, says Bonobo, setting down the bottle of vodka and picking up the sledgehammer. This guy knows his shit. He takes three steps back, lifts the sledgehammer over his head to his back and, with a frighteningly ample movement that explores the limit of his short reach, hurls it with all his might at one of the walls that are still standing. Not a single piece comes loose, it doesn't even make a crack, but the wall vibrates and fragments of dry paint and cement fly everywhere with a dry thud that echoes in his head and slides down his throat to his stomach. Bonobo gives it another few blows, lets out a crazy laugh and does a little dance. Then he offers him the sledgehammer.

Have a go, mate. It's really cool.

He hits the wall with all his might. The impact travels up his arms and sends a tremor down his spine. He experiences a deep pleasure transferring so much energy in a single blow to the pile of bricks and mortar, and the structure appears to cede a little.

Awesome, isn't it? Give it a few more tries.

By nightfall they have brought down another wall and are working on the last one, alternating between blows with the sledgehammer and kicks. They have finished the bottle of Smirnoff Vanilla and take turns going to the nearest tavern to get cans of cold beer, which they guzzle down. Altair and Bonobo have been at it since daybreak and midday, respectively, and are showing alarming signs of tiredness. Altair falls asleep sitting up for about half an hour, snoring, but wakes with a start, takes a swig from a can of warm beer that is within reach, gets up, asks for the sledgehammer and attacks the wall again. Bonobo looks catatonic from time to time, staring straight ahead, but returns to action within one or two minutes. The sky is full of stars and the air is warm. The three of them talk little and pass the sledgehammer back and forth at regular intervals that, to anyone observing them from the entrance to the supermarket or the hot-dog stand on the opposite corner, look carefully measured and synchronized. A well-oiled team with a method.

Bonobo tells him that he is from the South Zone of Porto Alegre but many years ago he moved to Rosa Beach, where he opened a bed and breakfast.

It's just before Canto do Mar. You know it? The small bed and breakfast on the left. Last year I opened a café too.

Altair falls asleep again, this time lying on the gravelly ground, hugging the sledgehammer, his head resting on a backpack. A third of the last wall is still standing but they are too tired. He and Bonobo pool the change in their pockets and go to the tavern to get their last few cans of beer. They return and drink them sitting down, leaning against the remaining section of wall. Exhaustion instals a feeling of companionship in them. Before he realizes it, he is talking about his dad's suicide and the dog he decided to adopt. Bonobo listens, nodding his head the whole time, wanting him to be sure he is listening and understanding.

That's heavy shit. But why did you decide to come here?

He wonders if he should tell him the truth. Altair is snoring. He gives Bonobo a good look and decides that he likes him. He tells him that his grandfather disappeared or was murdered in the town in the late 60s. Bonobo doesn't understand why anyone would want to go digging up that kind of story but is moved when he tells him about his father's death. His own father, he explains, lives in Porto Alegre and is very ill.

I think about visiting him all the time, you know.

So go.

Yeah, I really should one of these days.

Do it.

To be honest, I keep putting it off 'cause the bastard left my mother to bring us up on her own and never had much to say for himself. I also don't like going back to Porto Alegre much. I had some pretty hard times down there.

But he's family. Go. If he dies you'll regret that you didn't go.

Bonobo has scars on his face. Marks that are fading with time. Vestiges of stitches in his eyebrow, spots on his full lips. The movements of his misproportioned body are harmonious and remind him, improbably, of a dancer. Even now, drunk and exhausted, he appears to have everything under control. He stares into his empty can, burps and tosses it on to the grass with the others.

Damned beer's gone.

Who's going to drive this pickup?

Altair.

He can't even breathe properly, look at him.

I'd have another beer.

Me too.

Bonobo gets up and riffles through Altair's pockets.

Try the backpack.

The backpack's mine. There's no money in it.

We can go back to my place. I've got beer. And cachaça.

Bonobo shakes Altair violently. Altair gets up on to his knees, where he stays for a time with a twisted expression on his face, as if everything he sees is unfamiliar and disgusting, then finally he stands up and starts walking in circles and talking to himself, excited about something or other. They leave everything as it is and walk down the main avenue towards the ocean. Bonobo and Altair wave to a few acquaintances, stop to chat here and there and sometimes introduce their new friend. They look like a trio of peaceful madmen or happy zombies at the end of a long journey to the beach. Bonobo improvises dance steps that make him think of Michael Jackson dancing samba. Altair eggs him on and claps, like the straight man in a comedy duo.

When they pass the pizza parlour he identifies Dália, who is swiping a credit card through a hand-held terminal at a table on the patio. Their eyes meet but she pretends she hasn't seen him. After the machine has printed out the receipts she comes out to the pavement. He affectionately pulls her to him by the apron and tries to give her a kiss.

Hey, I'm working.

Oops.

You look disgusting. What's going on? You reek of alcohol. Did you pick up Pablito?

Yep. I took him for an ice cream and he's at home, safe and sound.

Dália, my princess! cries Bonobo.

Where'd you find these two bums?

We were demolishing a kiosk.

Dália, my love!

She gives Bonobo a look that says 'not now'. Customers sitting at the outside tables turn and glare at them disapprovingly. Altair is swaying in silence in the middle of the road, facing the sea, almost falling, as if sent into a trance by a song that only he can hear. A delivery man on a motorbike swerves to miss him, honking.

We're going to my place to drink some more.

I don't want to know about it. For heaven's sake, be careful.

Don't worry, everything's OK.

I've got to work, bye.

Farewell, Princess Dália! shouts Bonobo.

She ignores Bonobo and warns him again. Be careful.

They pass in front of the Bauru Tchê. The TV is on and there are no customers. The owner, Renato, is leaning against the counter and looks depressed. He greets the trio and asks if they are going to have a beer. They say they haven't got any money. They pass the Embarcação restaurant and walk down the cement ramp from the beach promenade to the sand. The calm, waveless sea looks more like a dark lake. A small group of children is playing in the water, stirring up the green glow of luminescent seaweed. Near the fishing sheds, Altair wades out until he is knee-deep in the water and stands there staring at the ominous horizon, ignoring his companions' pleas to come back, and then suddenly vomits. He takes a step back after each heave to avoid the floating emissions of his stomach, then wades back out of the water and runs to catch up with them. The gulls standing in the sand aren't flustered by the passing trio and the orange rings of their eyes shine intensely as they blink non-stop. They climb the stairs to Baú Rock cursing the disgusting smell and take the footpath up to his apartment.

Beta bounds over to greet him when he opens the door. He kneels and ruffles her fur. He wonders if he forgot to feed her but he sees that her bowl is still full of dog food. There are half a dozen beers in his fridge. Altair says he is done drinking but changes his mind that very instant and goes into the kitchen to help himself to a beer.

When he opens the window, Bonobo stops clowning around and admires the view in silence. Altair suggests he put on some music but his radio isn't working. They go into his room to play *Winning Eleven*. They run out of beer and the bottle of cachaça is summoned. Altair begs to play *God of War II*, gets permission, and takes over the controller. They leave him playing and go back into the living room. Bonobo climbs on to the window ledge and says he misses smoking. He asks for a cigarette but no one smokes. I haven't put a cigarette in my mouth for three years, he says, but I'd smoke one now. Beta starts barking at Bonobo. After a dozen barks she stops with the same lack of motive with which she started, licks her teeth, looks around as if she is positively surprised at herself and sits on the carpet. Bonobo says that she is happy and he agrees. They are slurring their words and leaving sentences half-finished. He hears what he intends to say clearly in his head but his mouth deforms the words as he utters them. They sit in silence for a long while, forgetting the cachaça, just gazing at the dark ocean and the lit beach and listening to the epic soundtrack and violent sound effects of the video game in the bedroom. He has the feeling that this moment will last indefinitely, that nothing else will happen, as if the world has reached a kind of final state in the insignificant scene he is living out. Bonobo asks in a low, circumspect voice if he has noticed the thing too. What thing? he asks. Haven't you noticed *anything* different? asks Bonobo, holding up his index finger like an antenna and looking sideways as if concentrating on some very subtle phenomenon. He pays attention but doesn't notice anything besides the murmuring of the waves, the throbbing of his temples and the room spinning under the effect of the alcohol. Then suddenly it comes to him. The most revolting thing he has ever smelled in his life, an almost viscous stench of concentrated methane that makes him gag in the middle of an attempt to shout a swear word. Bonobo hoots with laughter, gets down from the window ledge with an incomplete somersault, takes a swig of cachaça and does a little dance holding the bottle and hollering, Radioactive Fart! Let's get outta here! Life's short and the night's a babe!

He escapes to the bathroom, pees and washes his face, trying to recover from the effect of the nauseating gas.

You're rotten inside, Bonobo.

I am and so what? Let's go party.

He laughs until he realizes that Bonobo is serious.

There's a party over at Rosa that must be starting to warm up about now. A sushi bar near my bed and breakfast is closing for the season. Let's go back to the kiosk and get my car.

You've got a car?

Yep. Let's go. Get Altair.

They discover that Altair has passed out holding the video game controller. He is half sitting, half lying between the wall and the brown-tiled floor with the game stuck on a screen saying Continue? They try to rouse him without success. They pour a glass of water over his head and Bonobo slaps him about the face a few times. Altair doesn't show any sign of waking up. They decide to leave him in the apartment, lying on his side on the rug in the bedroom, with the spare key placed conspicuously on the table in the living room. He changes his T-shirt and locks the windows while Bonobo tries to contact people on his mobile phone. Some girls I know said they were going, he says. The girls aren't answering the phone, but another acquaintance picks up and says that people are arriving. The party is starting to heat up. He lets Beta out and locks the door from the outside. They head quickly down the footpath and over the sand. This time the gulls standing around skitter towards the water and some take flight. Bonobo glances over his shoulder.

Did you see that your dog got out? She's following us.

No fucking way am I leaving her locked in there with Altair.

It is already past midnight and the streets are deserted. They walk along the central reservation down the middle of the avenue to what is left of Altair's kiosk. Bonobo crosses the property, kicking empty beer cans aside and hopping about.

What are you doing, you retard? Where's your car?

Bonobo goes over to the old VW Beetle carcass and starts jiggling the door handle.

No way.

What?

Is *that* your car?

Yep. Meet Lockjaw.

That thing there? I thought it was scrap metal.

She's a *mean* machine. Just be careful getting in.

Bonobo manages to open the door on the driver's side and climbs in. He walks around and tries to open the door on the passenger's side in the narrow space between the car and the wall. The corroded door handle needs to be pressed in a very specific way for the mechanism to work. The car is covered in fractal rust patterns and peeling beige paint. It has a large roof rack capable of holding a small boat. There are holes and jagged edges everywhere. The tyres are crooked, bald and half flat. He climbs in carefully, trying not to cut himself. All that is left of the passenger seat is a frame of iron rods covered with old cushions and a piece of folded cardboard. The back support of soft foam is relatively intact. On the dashboard is a gilded sitting Buddha with a smile at the corner of its mouth and enormous earlobes dangling over its shoulders. He whistles to Beta. She comes around the car and jumps on to his lap. He strokes her, praises her for being a good girl and settles her on the back seat, which is covered with a

Grêmio Football Club sarong. He sees the car battery sitting behind the driver's seat amid a baroque tangle of electrical wires. Bonobo turns the key in the ignition. The engine chortles.

It takes a while to start, but once it does, it doesn't die, says Bonobo.

On the fourth try, the engine starts. Bonobo steps on the accelerator and revs it scandalously until he hears a couple of explosions in the exhaust pipe.

Can you get me my eyepatch from the glove box?

Your *what*?

My eyepatch.

He opens the glove box and fishes an eyepatch made of cloth and black elastic out of a jumble of used tissues, business cards, bars of wax, condoms, a filthy rag and a pair of broken sunglasses. Bonobo takes the eyepatch and adjusts it over his right eye.

It's to stop me seeing double.

Only then does he put the car in first gear. It moves forward. The grass and debris from the kiosk scrape its undercarriage. He feels as if he is riding inside the engine itself. They take the state highway out of Garopaba. A car passes them going in the opposite direction and the lit-up tarmac looms beneath his feet through a hole in the floor. Bonobo zigzags a little but considering his degree of intoxication and the state of the vehicle his driving is actually quite comforting, focused, at a moderate speed, his sight limited by the absurd eyepatch. He is hunched so far over the small steering wheel that his simian nose almost touches the windscreen. Figures such as cows or cyclists come to life in a flash and go back to being spectres in almost the same instant. They turn left on to the road to Rosa Beach. The Beetle needs to halt almost completely before he can drive it over speed bumps. The stone-paved streets give way to steep dirt roads. The car's clutch doesn't disengage automatically. To deal with the problem, Bonobo has tied a length of blue clothes line between the pedal and the door handle. The operation to take his left hand off the steering wheel and tug on the clothes line at the exact moment after each gear change is complicated and requires a certain amount of skill and timing. In more complex manoeuvres Bonobo looks like a puppeteer manipulating a prop car.

The party is on the deck of the sushi bar and there is hardly anyone there. A hip-hop duo is rapping in the corner of a veranda that has been made into a dance floor. The music is really bad and there are eight men and two women dancing and talking on the veranda. He takes a look out back and finds a meticulously designed Japanese garden with rock arrangements, a fountain, a lake inhabited by a small gang of carp, and a stream. Three girls are drinking in silence at a table in the garden. That's the extent of the party. He orders a beer and is given a warm can. He is hungry but there is no sign of food. Bonobo orders a mojito and goes to talk to someone on the dance floor.

He goes back to the Beetle parked near the entrance and lets Beta out. He returns with her to the restaurant and sits in an armchair on the front veranda. Dirty glasses and empty cans left on the tables indicate that a lot of people have already been there and gone. Beta sits next to the armchair and he stares into the surrounding vegetation to forget the monotonous vocals of the rappers, who don't seem to have the energy to keep up with their rhymes. His mobile phone rings. It is Laila, a former student from Porto Alegre who is now his friend. He doesn't find out why she is calling so late because the roaming charges gobble up his credit in seconds.

In his mind he starts putting together the training session he is going to give his students in the pool tomorrow. Meanwhile, two men walk on to the veranda talking in low voices, with furtive gestures, their heads hunched down between their shoulders, and it is a while before they notice he is there. They stop talking when they realize they have company. One of them has peroxide-blond hair and he is almost certain it is the guy who was with Dália at the Pico do Surf the night they met. Peroxide-blond hair is common around here, but the guy gives him a long stare. He begins to feel threatened.

Do we know each other?

The blond guy just stares at him and doesn't answer. He is younger than him, twenty-something, and has obviously been snorting all night. He looks for some other feature to help identify him in the future. He has a shark tattoo covering one whole side of his left calf. The two friends abort whatever they have gone there to do and go back into the restaurant.

He waits a few minutes and goes to look for Bonobo. There is no sign of him. There is no sign of almost anyone. The three girls in the garden have disappeared. The rappers have stopped singing and are talking to the few survivors gathered around the DJ. He leaves the restaurant and sees Lockjaw still parked in the same spot. He puts Beta in the car, closes the door and goes to the bathroom. When he walks out he bumps into Bonobo in the corridor. He is accompanied by two girls.

Where you been? slurs Bonobo, completely off his face but still standing, an experienced drunk. I've been looking for you for ages. This is Liz, a really good friend of mine, and this here is Ju.

Bonobo and Ju are in the middle of a conversation dripping with terms such as 'soul', 'impermanence' and 'vanity'. Liz looks like she is just along for the ride, accompanying her friend. Neither of them seems drunk and he isn't really sure what's going on but senses that it must be obvious.

Bonobo's bed and breakfast is near the sushi bar and in a few minutes Bonobo's Beetle and the girls' red Parati are driving up a steep, narrow driveway between bamboo fences that leads to a well-tended property with a large two-storey building and two smaller cabanas behind it, all built with a combination of bricks, mortar and wooden logs, with green Portuguese roof tiles and glassed-in verandas. A sign over the front door says BONOBO'S BED AND BREAKFAST and on the adjoining building with French windows another sign says BONOBO'S CAFÉ. He climbs out of the Beetle with difficulty. He scratches his forearm on a rusty corner of the door and tries to remember when he had his last tetanus shot.

Bonobo opens the door and tells them all to make themselves at home but asks that they try not to make too much noise because there are guests in one of the upstairs rooms. Downstairs is the reception desk with a cosy sitting room and access to the kitchen, a guest breakfast room and another room with an engraved wooden sign on the door saying BONOBO'S BEDROOM. It isn't long before Bonobo and Ju go into his room. Ju is from Brasília and has large breasts and that is all he has had time to find out about her.

In the reception area, he sits on a small, comfortable sofa, while Liz sits in the armchair next to him. Liz is a native of Garopaba. She has recently had highlights put in her brown hair and has an athletic body and a slightly masculine face. There is zero attraction. They chat at a calm, tired pace, listening to the reggae music that Bonobo has put on at a low volume in the background. They are songs about the beauty of the moment, the importance of freedom, the need for awareness, about stars and love and the ocean waves. Liz's full name is Elizete and she hates it. She says there is a whole generation of girls in Garopaba of her age with names that end in 'ete', just as her and her girlfriends' mothers and grandmothers have names that end in 'ina', which are so much simpler and sweeter and sound like parents' terms of endearment for their daughters: names like Delfina, Jovina, Celina, Ondina, Etelvina, Clarina, Angelina, Antonina, Vivina, Santina, and the more common ones like Carolina and Regina. But now it is the era of the Elizetes, Claudetes and Marizetes, with their rather stunted sound. She muses, I wonder why? If I have a daughter I'm going to call her Marina, or Sabrina, or Florentina, what do you think? He thinks she is right. Her voice is soft and sibilant like that of other locals he has spoken to, including Cecina. Maybe it is a characteristic of Azoreans. After the music stops they hear only the silence of the night and gusts of intermittent wind rustling the trees and the bamboo thickets. Occasionally the low murmur of a halting conversation comes from Bonobo's room. Beta has fallen asleep on a knitted rug. Liz wants to know something about him and he talks about swimming, triathlons, how he competed in the Ironman in Hawaii some years ago, and she seems only partially interested but still interested enough. It's almost as if they were intimate and were having one of those conversations that people have before they fall asleep together. I don't have the build to really compete properly, he says. I've got small feet. Liz murmurs things so he'll know she is listening and he keeps talking. Time flows at the pace that it should always flow, he thinks. A slowness in keeping with his inner discourse. They hear a short moan from Ju, the bed banging against the wall or the floor, then a longer moan, which she tries to muffle unsuccessfully. It goes on for a few minutes. When the door opens, Ju walks out fully dressed and perfectly composed and tells her friend that she needs to go because she has to get up early the next morning. The Parati drives off and the girls crank up the radio. The beat of the electronic music fades into the distance.

Bonobo comes back from the kitchen with two bottles of Heineken and says, Peace to all beings. They clink their green bottlenecks.

Isn't that what the Buddhists say?

Yep, I'm a Buddhist.

He laughs.

What's so funny?

You don't strike me as a Buddhist.

What's a Buddhist supposed to be like?

I don't know. But you don't strike me as one.

Don't talk crap.

Don't you have to take a vow of chastity, stop drinking, that kind of thing?

Not exactly.

Bonobo says he started becoming familiar with Buddhism in the late 90s, flirting on ICQ with a girl from Curitiba who followed the religion. Ideas such as compassion, non-attachment and impermanence were new to him. It all made sense right from the start. His eyes light up as he tells the story. Sometimes he stops talking and meditates on what he has just said, nodding his head lightly. He is convinced that if that girl hadn't been open to his silly online advances and spent night after night explaining samsara, karma and the law of moral causation to him, he probably would have killed someone or been killed himself. Or both. Bonobo invited her to Porto Alegre and she went. She travelled by bus and stayed in a dive near the bus station. She wanted to go to Garagem Hermética, a nightclub that other online friends of hers frequented. They went together. They saw a band from Esteio that played Smiths covers and they had a hell of a night. The girl brought him several books as a present and convinced him to learn English. Eva was her name.

The girl studied Physics, man. Physics. A nerdy weirdo and totally introverted but an angel in human form. A being of light. We visited the Três Coroas Temple together and it became a second home to me. I worked as a labourer there and went on several retreats. I wanted to live there but the lamas wouldn't let me. They said I wasn't ready. And they were right. I wasn't ready for that. Eva never came back again but we kept in touch online and used to send each other photocopies of philosophical and Buddhist texts in the post. She died of leukaemia in 2003.

Sorry to hear it. That must have been hard to deal with.

A rooster crows once, twice, three times.

It was. But life goes on. Didn't you like Liz?

She seemed nice. But there was no chemistry.

Chemistry? What sissy talk. Liz is a wild thing, all you had to do was make a move.

I'm tired as fuck.

Uncle Bonobo spoon-fed you and you –

I'm really drunk.

– give me this shit about –

I stink. We're revolting.

– *chemistry*. C'mon now. You left the girl high and dry.

She'll get over it. What about Ju?

I was teaching her some stuff.

Did she achieve nirvana?

Actually, it's serious. Ju's in a really fucked-up cycle of suffering. Her marriage broke up and she can't accept it. She needed to talk a little. I think she's starting to understand the question of imperman-ence and it's helping. I suggested that she visit Lama Palden over in Encantada. But come with me, I want to show you something.

He follows Bonobo into his room. There is a monstrous ball of pillows, sheets, blankets and items of dirty clothing on the mattress of his double bed. The floor is hidden under a layer of underwear, towels, T-shirts, shorts and a long black wetsuit. The reigning fragrance is one of rancid human secretions, incense and wet clothes forgotten in a plastic bag. Two incense sticks are filling the room with a light haze. On one wall are posters of Led Zeppelin and a Buddhist divinity with writing in Tibetan. The desk is completely covered with a printer, an old laptop, a small LCD TV, a jumble of papers, bottles, cans, used glasses, a full bottle of tequila and a picture frame with a black-and-white photograph of what looks like a Chinese man in braces pointing a revolver at his own head. A shelf on the wall is curved under the weight of a few dozen books.

See over there?

What?

Leaning against the wall.

The sandboard?

No, next to the cupboard.

The rifle?

Bonobo leaps over the bed and picks up a weapon.

It's a speargun. Come here.

How do I enter?

You can step on the clothes.

He walks around the bed and takes the speargun. He has never held one before. Bonobo shows him how to load the galvanized steel spear in the bands of rubber and ready the spool.

You mentioned that your granddad used to go spearfishing here. I remembered that I had this speargun and never use it. I tried to fish with it a few times but I can't stay underwater for long. You can have it.

Fuck, these things are expensive. I can't accept it.

Stop being such a girl. It's a present from a man to a man. Catch some groupers so we can cook up a *moqueca*.

They shake hands firmly and Bonobo gives him a kind of sideways hug while patting him on the shoulder, staring seriously into his eyes. To escape the unexpected and slightly disturbing familiarity he glances around for something to change the focus. A red T-shirt catches his attention among the dirty clothes.

Aren't you a Grêmio supporter?

Obviously, says Bonobo.

So what's that Internacional T-shirt doing on the floor there?

It takes Bonobo a moment to locate the item in the mess.

Ah, that's for the chicks to wear.

You ask Inter supporters to wear that T-shirt?

Yep.

And do they?

Most do. Some Grêmio supporters do too if you know how to ask. There's this humiliation thing that some of them like. An Inter chick with a mouth full of cock, nothing better.

They sit in the bedroom and continue drinking. It's still dark out but two little birds are engaged in a twittering duel.

I won't even be able to sleep, says Bonobo. The girl who makes breakfast called in to say she's not coming today. Shit. I forgot to buy fruit.

Since you're religious, let me ask you something. Let's say that a famous writer writes something that he never publishes, but he gives the manuscript to a trusted friend, his best friend, and asks him never to publish it. The writer dies. The friend reads the manuscript and discovers that it's a masterpiece. So he shows it to an editor, the editor publishes it and everyone agrees that it's a masterpiece and the writer becomes even more respected after his death.

OK. What about it?

Is what his friend did wrong? Did he betray the writer?

I don't follow. Do you have a writer friend?

No. Fuck. Hold on.

What's it got to do with religion?

Wait. I'm going to change the question.

Bonobo's mobile phone beeps but he doesn't get up to check the message.

The only thing I don't get is why the writer left the manuscript with the guy if he didn't want to publish it. Why didn't he just burn it?

No, forget the writer. Let's say that a guy has a father who's really attached to his dog. *Really* attached. He's had the dog since it was a pup and he loves it more than people, more than his wife and kids. The father decides to kill himself and asks his son to have the dog put down after he's dead, because he doesn't have the courage to do it himself and he knows the dog will suffer without him. He manages to convince his son to do it and makes him promise. The son does, more or less. The father kills himself but the son doesn't take the dog to the vet to have it put down. He keeps the dog and decides to look after it.

Was that what happened to you?

It's just a random example that I made up.

Ah. Right. I get it.

Bonobo hiccups and burps inwardly.

What do you think?

I think the dad's a prick.

OK, but that's not the question. Do you think the son betrayed him?

If the son made a promise and didn't keep it then he betrayed him, didn't he? Just like the friend who publishes the masterpiece against the writer's wishes.

And what does a Buddhist think of it?

Bonobo laughs.

Look, I can't speak for all Buddhists, but if you want to know my opinion, the betrayal is what matters the least in this story. What does matter is the result of his decision. How are the person's actions going to impact on everyone involved? After the dog's owner kills himself it doesn't make much difference to him what happens to the dog, right? He doesn't exist any more, at least not in this life. What matters now is how breaking the promise will affect the son's and the dog's lives and the lives of everyone directly or indirectly involved. Whether it increases or decreases people's overall suffering.

No, but it's just that —

Let's suppose, purely as a completely hypothetical exercise of the imagination, that the dog in this story is the dog sleeping over there on the rug. She looks well fed. Her coat's shiny. She's even got some flesh on her. She's sleeping now, but when she was awake she struck me as perky and proud. I'd even go as far as to say that she's belonged to you since she was born. And I get the impression that her company is good for you too. If she were the dog in your story then I'd say that only good things had come of the broken promise. In which case, it's all good.

But even so it's a betrayal. And I don't see how it can be ignored. It doesn't matter that the father is dead. A promise was broken and it's never going to stop being part of the story. Maybe it'd be better if the dog were dead. The son wouldn't even know what life would have been like with the dog but he'd know he'd fulfilled his father's last wish. These things matter. Don't they?

Bonobo thinks a little.

Yeah. It's never easy.

Because it doesn't make any difference that the father is dead and doesn't exist any more and has no way of knowing he was betrayed. Understand? It's a betrayal. The thing is there. For ever.

I understand. I don't agree, but I understand. I don't know what to tell you, sorry.

Bonobo picks up the speargun and starts winding up the spool.

About three years ago a curious thing happened here in Garopaba. A guy used to go spearfishing with his son almost every week. One day they were snorkelling off the coast between Ferrugem and Silveira beaches at a place called Saco da Cobra. The guy dived down really deep and at some point saw a giant grouper hiding. The water was very clear that day and with several yards of visibility. The fish was monstrous, a size you don't see any more, and just stared at him from inside its hole, moving its jaw. The following week he went diving at the same spot and found the fish in the same hole. He decided to harpoon it at any cost. He became obsessed with it and couldn't think about anything else. Whenever the conditions were right he and his son went out in the boat. But the hole was too deep and the grouper was flighty. Sometimes it didn't appear and when it did it just wouldn't let itself be harpooned. No other diver had seen the fish with his own eyes, they had only heard about it. A few weeks later he went out with his son again to fish. He went down the first time without any equipment. He surfaced a few minutes later and told his son he had found the fish. He put on all of his equipment, got his speargun and went down again. And he didn't come back.

Bonobo places the spear in the gun and aims at the kitchen.

When his son realized something was wrong he tried to go and help his dad but couldn't get down that far. He left and came back with the coastguard and divers. They went down and found the guy's body with his arm tangled in the cord of the speargun and the spear through the grouper's tail. The fish was alive, but maimed. The spear had pierced its spine. The guy had tried to pull the fish until he blacked out and drowned tied to it. They took them out of the water together. They say it was the biggest grouper ever caught in Garopaba. It weighed over a hundred and eighty pounds.

What made you remember that now?

Still sitting on the sofa, Bonobo twists around and points the speargun at one of the armchairs.

It's like a fable. The guy and the grouper were connected in some way, like you and the dog. We can't understand why exactly, we can't see the whole path that the two beings have travelled to that point. But things like that make you think, don't they? It can't just be chance. There's a whole history of many rebirths that has brought the two beings to a situation like that.

Nonsense. Are you talking about reincarnation?

Bonobo fires at the backrest of the armchair but misses and the spear hits the wall behind it with a sharp crack.

Fuck! Careful with that shit.

It's not reincarnation, it's rebirth. It has more to do with the propagation of states of mind through time. What you understand to be your *mind*, which is really an illusion, also continues acting in the world after your physical death and comes back to manifest itself. They're cycles. The mind continues on, mixes, recombines and re-emerges.

But my mind isn't *mine*, man. You just said so yourself. How can I say that some part of me will be reborn sometime in the future? It doesn't make sense. It's just things mixing and recombining.

So we have a materialist swimmer. In which case I think it's funny that you're so worried about what your dead father would think about what you have or haven't done with his dog. Since death is death. I mean, if that's how it is, why worry? Why not be selfish and wild and live it up as much as possible until you die a little desperate?

'Cause it's important. 'Cause only an arsehole wouldn't care. Death isn't an excuse to be an arsehole.

We have an existentialist-materialist swimmer.

You making fun of me?

No. I'm still a bit drunk. So are you. Go on.

I don't know if I agree with this idea of yours that I can know what the best decision is based only on the amount of suffering that it does or doesn't cause. Suffering isn't always an indicator of what is best or worst. Sometimes the right thing to do causes suffering. Suffering is bad, but it's a part of life.

Now try to decide the right thing to do based on those principles. Good luck.

Bonobo stands and goes to check the messages on his mobile.

Altair texted me. He left your place and is back at the kiosk to finish knocking it down.

Shit, I've just remembered I left my bike there.

I've got to buy things for breakfast. I can give you a lift in Lockjaw.

Nah, I'll find my own way back.

I insist. It'll be my good deed for the day. My debt is big, swimmer. I've got an overdraft, credit cards covering credit cards, loans, money in my underpants, everything. I'll be paying it off for many lifetimes. Besides, the road's beautiful this time of day.

Before the long weekend in early May he comes across a week-old edition of a local newspaper with news of a murder stamped across the front page. It says that the body of a sixteen-year-old girl from Praia da Pinheira has been found in some vegetation near Highway BR-101, just north of Paulo Lopes, a few miles past the turn-off to Garopaba. Her eyes and lips are missing and there are clear signs of strangulation, the probable cause of death. The forensic expert suspects or wants to believe that the mutilations on the victim's face were made after death, and the missing body parts have not been found. She wasn't wearing a blouse but it still hasn't been confirmed if there was any sexual violence. There is also considerable evidence that she was dragged, leading the police to believe that she was murdered elsewhere, probably in an area of dense vegetation and rocks, then moved by one or more people who couldn't or didn't want to carry her and dragged her instead. The story was published two days after the discovery of the body. A photograph shows the victim covered with a small, light-coloured blanket or sheet. All that can be seen of her are her hands with bent fingers, wrists and part of her arms, up by her head like a baby in a crib. When he looks at the photo, he suddenly imagines the girl's face under the blanket or sheet like a hideous flashback in a horror movie, and the image haunts him for a few days. Experts have discarded the theory that her eyes and lips were eaten by an animal because of the precision of the wounds: almost clinical incisions, made with a sharp object. The girl told her parents that she was going camping with friends at a waterfall in the region and her friends actually did go camping but said she hadn't shown up at the agreed time and place so they had gone without her. The police are working on the hypothesis of a revenge crime but stress that they are still examining all of the evidence and anything is possible. The story doesn't go into any more detail.

The newspaper was lying on a bench in the gym dressing room as if someone had left it in their backpack and relieved themselves of it days later without going to the trouble of putting it in the rubbish bin. It strikes him as odd that no one at the gym, at the beach, at Pablo's school, in restaurants, bars, or the internet café, that not even Cecina or Renato or Dália, or the grocer or the fishermen, has mentioned such a heinous crime, something that happened so close to their beautiful, happy little coastal town; a town that appears to have been abandoned for good by the tourists, at least until next summer, and now looks more like a pavilion of closed shops and empty houses, entire blocks deserted except for the very occasional visit of a caretaker to trim a tree. The sudden emptying of the town, the arrival of the cold weather, the brutal murder of a teenage girl not far from there, nothing that he finds worthy of note seems to worry the locals. They talk about how this year's mullet season is going to be an even bigger disaster than the last, and the population in general concerns itself with what to do with the money earned during a tourist season that has been well and truly left behind and already feels like a distant memory, a time when they worked so hard amid so many people from elsewhere that they barely managed to see one another and talk to their own friends and family, months spent less like residents and more like the employees of an enormous convention centre in the midst of a mega-event. In the streets people are also talking about a municipal election that won't take place until September. He has the impression that everyone is merely hoping to rest up and breeze through the cold, sunny days during which nothing will happen. They say the calm will bring boredom and sadness and that the cold and solitude will resuscitate all the familiar ghosts of the season and some unfamiliar ones too, but they say it as if it's still a long way off and there is plenty of time to prepare for it.

PART TWO

5

In the first few days of May he sees something that he will later suspect was a dream. It is a muggy afternoon and, since Pablo has gone to spend the long weekend with his dad in Criciúma and Dália has gone with her mother to Caçador, he gets on his bike after his shift at the pool and rides to Ferrugem Beach, where he hopes to find some good waves for bodysurfing. The beach is empty and its coppery sands are warm and still scarred from the last influx of tourists. The Bar do Zado is open as always but there are no customers, not even the occasional surfer or pot smoker contemplating the waves from one of the wooden tables. An adolescent tends the bar while watching a game of European football on the TV on the wall, and later, still glued to the screen, now for the UFC, will say he saw nothing. The sky is overcast and someone in one of the houses or bed and breakfasts behind the dunes is trying to drill through something very tough, perhaps a tile. An early fog is covering part of the sand and a smell of decomposing sea creatures hangs in the air. He leans his bike and backpack against the wooden wall of the bar and heads down to the water's edge. The water is freezing cold but he enters nonetheless. He swims out to the sandbar in a few strokes, then wades into the water on the other side and dives in again, swimming vigorously to where the waves are breaking. His lungs fill in desperation and squeeze every bit of air out of their alveoli in reaction to the freezing temperature. His skin burns, his head throbs and his body just won't warm up. Afraid of taking a bad turn, he catches the first wave back to the sandbar and gets out. The transition from the icy water to the warm air perks him up and he decides to walk until he is dry. The fog disappears as he walks along the beach and is there again when he reaches Índio Hill, at the end, and looks back. The mouth of Encantada Lagoon is silted up with sand, so he is able to walk across it to Barra Beach, which he also walks end to end, and returns. He sits on the sand and stares out to sea, then lies down and shuts his eyes.

He gets up a while later, not really sure if he dozed off or not. Something important has changed in the atmosphere but it is hard to tell what. The clouds have grown thicker and the dusk is colourless. The fog has disappeared. He looks at the horizon and feels a chill run down his spine. A terrifying storm is gathering out at sea. Dark clouds rise up like mountains advancing towards the beach, an ominous wall that extends along almost the entire visible horizon, but something about it doesn't seem right. The storm moves and doesn't move at the same time. It changes shape but the transition from one state to the other can't be perceived. The more he looks the more unsure he is that they are storm clouds. There is no lightning or thunder. The dark mountain range is mirrored by the horizon and deformed here and there as it compresses and stretches. Its shapes appear both close and blurred by the distance. They are somewhat holographic. If they are as close as they look, he'll be engulfed by a typhoon before he can run to shelter. If they are as distant as they also look, they must be of gigantic, other-worldly dimensions. He thinks he might be watching a tidal wave roll in. The effect of an apocalyptic meteorite in the heart of the Atlantic. The end of the world approaching in silence. He is hypnotized as he watches the phenomenon change shape, float, always looking like it is arriving without drawing any closer. Shortly before nightfall the vision begins to fade and disappears uneventfully.

Students start showing up in the afternoon at the pool. Some are surfers and tend to have poor technique but excellent fitness, good students to work with as long as they accept that there is room for improvement. This is the case with Jander, a short, stocky, bald guy of about forty who is always sunburned and owns a roadside pet shop and kennel in Palhocinha famous for housing some of the town's most beloved dogs when their owners are away. Jander surfs, swims, runs and rides a bike regularly, but without any supervision or method. His incredible endurance is wasted with an ungainly swimming style and his first few lessons are devoted to trying to make his reddish body turn less in the water and to better synchronize his arms and legs. There is a strapping young Rastafarian surfer named Amós, but he is always off his face and refuses to take any advice. He stops, listens, agrees and then ignores all instructions. His impermeable hair doesn't fit in his swimming cap but Saucepan's orders are to turn a blind eye. He uses up all of his energy in the first two or three sprints of each set and then straggles through the rest of the session, breathless, swallowing water, swimming slower and slower and with ever-more visible suffering. On the third week, a pair of introverted teenage twin girls enrols, Rayanne and Tayanne, who arrive together, swim bureaucratically with identical black bathing suits on very white, almost identical bodies, and leave together. He tells them about his problem with faces because they suffer from the inverse problem of not being immediately recognized by most people. He thinks it is funny but they don't. Two students are triathletes. One is professional, swims like a missile and comes with his pre-prepared session written in blue pen on a small white piece of paper that he always leaves stuck to a tile on the edge of the pool when he goes. He doesn't ask for or need his attention. The other one is a rheumatologist who has seen better days as an athlete. He always brings giant hand paddles that he insists on using every session despite the fact that they are the obvious cause of his constant shoulder pain, probably tears in his supraspinatus tendons. But he's the doctor. There are two students who can barely stay afloat. One is a corpulent, hairy, bearded man who likes to clown around and showed up on the first day laughing and asking if he could swim in his tracksuit. He calls himself Tracksuit Man and gets a laugh from the twins when he announces his Special Weapon, the Dive Bomb, before leaping into the pool as dramatically as possible. The other one is Tiago, a polite, shy, hard-working seventeen-year-old with a severe case of gynaecomastia. His favourite student so far is Ivana, a friendly, plump little woman in her early fifties. At first Ivana struck him as the sedentary sort but she has proved to be an experienced and dedicated swimmer. She occasionally participates in the Santa Catarina short-distance swim circuit and is interested in training for longer distances. She is a public prosecutor and works in the Garopaba Courthouse. She is one of those people for whom swimming is not a means to an end such as losing weight, curing a disease or winning medals, rather, it is as much a part of her life as working, eating and sleeping. She is someone who can't not swim. In that, they are the same. Swimming for them is a special relationship with the world, the kind of thing that those who understand it don't need to talk about. Ivana swings her shoulders in an odd way and he recognizes her by her walk.

At times he isn't sure of the identity of a new student. Sometimes someone comes in just to look at the pool or ask for information and he thinks it's a student he knows. Instead of explaining his problem, he prefers to let people think he is forgetful, strange, absent-minded.

Some think he is a misanthrope. But in that small, three-lane pool with his handful of students, misunderstandings are rare and short-lived and there are no hard feelings. He likes meeting new people, starting a whole set of social relations from scratch. He ignores faces and learns to recognize people by their attitudes, problems, stories, clothes, gestures, voices, the way they swim, the progress they make in the water. Their characteristics congeal to form a diagram that he can evoke and study in his free time. Each person has a recognizable pattern that he can situate on an imaginary panel with a little sign underneath saying: MY STUDENTS. He keeps many such pictures in his head. His picture of Academia Swell also includes Débora, who insists she is going to teach him to surf, and Saucepan, who, as well as being a partner in the gym, also works as a *pizzaiolo* at a gourmet pizzeria at the entrance to the town, a jovial sort with a shaved head and well-defined muscles who is an enthusiastic spokesman for his undertakings day and night and puts in an appearance at every social event in town. His partner in the gym, Spatula, is an international kite surfer who spends much of his time abroad. Sometimes Spatula comes to swim in the pool at night, after he has already left. Débora assures him that they have already met at some point but he doesn't remember. Spatula sent a message to say that he doesn't want any dogs on the gym premises but Saucepan doesn't mind having Beta lying on the cement floor in front of reception or being patted by students on the lawn near the front gate. He has told Débora to tell Spatula that if there really is a problem, to come and speak to him directly instead of sending messages through others.

Prohibited by the fishermen from swimming in the ocean since 1 May, which marked the beginning of the mullet-fishing season, he swims in the pool before lunch or runs on the beach or dirt roads of

Ambrósio and Siriú, passing rural properties overshadowed by fig trees, pigs running loose and smooth dunes criss-crossed with the marks of sandboards. One cold morning he witnesses the first big mullet haul of the year on the tiny Preguiça Beach. Dolphins follow the shoals, displaying their dorsal fins and leaping joyfully, guiding the boat as it moves in on its prey. Two dozen fishermen surrounded by a flurry of gulls drag in the nets teeming with plump, terrified fish with straight rows of silvery scales and bellies gleaming like molten lead, which are piled up on the sand until they form an inert mountain, working their gills in vain as they wait for death. A shirtless young fisherman has 'Joseane, Tainá and Marina, The Stars of My Life' tattooed across his back. A drunk with white whiskers and bulging eyes pulls in the net, in a trance. An older fisherman oversees the work with a disdainful air born of decades of experience at sea. They all take the job very seriously, and don't crack jokes or chat, limiting conversation to practical interjections. Cats and dogs prance around the nets and the more experienced ones grapple with the heads of the smaller fish discarded by the humans. The local dogs treat Beta with hostility and she has already learned to keep her distance from them. He helps the fishermen pull in the net and is given two fresh mullet, which he cleans on the rocks using his father's knife. He sets aside two steaks to pan-fry with a little olive oil and lime and freezes the rest. Later that afternoon, after picking up Pablo from school and leaving him with Dália's mother, he returns home to find four launches moored in front of the fishing sheds near the remains of an almost eleven-ton haul. People are finishing loading the fish into two small refrigerated trucks in white plastic tubs. Locals cart off their quota of fish hooked over their fingers by the gills or in plastic supermarket bags. In spite of the large quantity of mullet caught this day the fishermen are pessimistic and fear the worst season in years. Some blame the temperature, others the huge amount of rain in Patos Lagoon. The street lighting comes on and there is a soft red glow in the west behind the hills where the sun has set. A sudden silence settles over the bay after everyone has gone and for a while the only sound is the waves, until someone decides to play electronic music from the open boot of a car parked on the waterfront.

The fishermen don't talk much to him. Everyone he has tried to talk to about his grandfather's death now ignores him. Some watch him with hostile looks as he walks through the village centre, while others greet him with an exaggerated friendliness. At times he worries that he is being paranoid. He isn't really sure who is who and has stopped asking questions because he is starting to feel scared.

Often, through the shutters, he overhears the conversations of fishermen or kids who come to smoke pot or sell drugs on the stairs next to Baú Rock. The fishermen's topics of conversation are as infinite as they are unfathomable. Disputes over the division of the mullet catch, insults and effrontery, village gossip.

Another day, returning from one of his morning runs to Siriú, he stops for a swim and a stretch near the Embarcação restaurant and sees a woman stretching by the wooden fence next to the ramp down to the beach. He approaches her and asks if she minds if he gives her a suggestion. From close up he sees that she has slightly Asian-looking eyes and milky-white skin behind her rosy cheeks. She is covered in sweat from head to toe. She has no dissonant features and he doesn't find anything that might help him recognize her in the future. She is stretching the backs of her legs and he teaches her to point her supporting leg forward and straighten her torso, holding the toe of the leg she is stretching with both hands, which she is able to do without any difficulty once he has shown her how. She recognizes that she is stretching the muscle differently now. Her name is Sara and she is a pharmacist. She works in one of the town's many pharmacy chains. She mentions her husband, who is a dentist. They both graduated a few years ago in Porto Alegre and have been in Garopaba since the previous year, motivated by the dream that brings so many dentists, pharmacists, physiotherapists, doctors, lawyers, engineers and small-business owners here from capital cities: to be an independent professional living a simple life by the sea, surfing and sunbathing every week, earning less but happy, with space in the garden and on the sand to let their Belgian shepherds, Labradors and future off-spring run free. Sara started running when she moved there but is already thinking of giving up because she is experiencing strong, chronic pain in her shins. She shows him where it hurts. When he presses on the sides of her tibia she shrieks and flinches. It appears to be a fairly serious case of shin splints and he offers to give her some strengthening exercises to do at the gym. And it would be a good idea to ice the region and rest up for at least two weeks. She thanks him and leaves in a brand-new economy car parked on the waterfront, which greets its owner with a shrill beep. Two days later a woman strikes up a conversation with him at the gym but he only recognizes her about five minutes later when she mentions the pain in her shins. He teaches her to stretch and strengthen her lower leg muscles with exercises. Because she attends another gym closer to her house they arrange to meet and exchange phone numbers. He agrees to be her running coach three times a week starting the next week in front of the Embarcação, bright and early. She has a friend who also runs and is interested in working with a coach. She suggests that they start putting together a running group.

Some mornings he forgets any modest ambition he may have and doesn't know how he ended up there. He thinks that deep down there is nothing to uncover or understand no matter what. Mornings like the cloudy one when he sits for a while outside the window with the dog beside him and watches a furious north-easterly whip up the water, which is somewhere between blue and green, with no shine, as if seen through a polarizing filter. The waves explode on the rocks in fans of meringue-white spray and the thick drops wet his feet and give off a perfume of salt and sulphur. Then the wind turns without warning. Its invisible force reconfigures the entire landscape in moments. Blowing from the south, it stretches the ocean's agitated surface towards the horizon as if smoothing a crumpled sheet over a bed. The silence contains something of the tension of the previous moment. The water becomes smooth and glossy and the waves form long, gentle rows that break near the beach, lifting up crests of vapour against the sunlight that has just appeared out of nowhere. The film-like surface slides over the waves in the opposite direction. The ocean recedes, the exposed strip of beach grows and the temperature drops a little. The sun comes out and encourages a group of kids to go swimming in front of the rock. The four boys, wearing shorts and no T-shirts, quickly dive into the water. They jump off the wharf and swim near the rocks, swearing at one another. The two girls are about twelve or thirteen and walk over the rocks with ease. One is wearing a bikini and the other, in a white dress with a triangular-shaped hem, has an upturned nose and high forehead. They take red lollipops out of a bag and sit on the rock. The one in the white dress turns her head and briefly looks at him for the first and last time with honest disinterest, at once emanating a precocious sexuality and the profound boredom that prevents her from using it. The boys splash water on them and try to pull them in. They tolerate it as if it were no more than a fleeting interruption and quickly return to their lollipops and monosyllabic conversation. Then the girl in the dress stands and climbs down to a larger rock at the water's edge. The tame waves wash over her feet. She stares at the sea and the boys playing in the water as if joining them were an inevitability, an implicit obligation of her female existence. The white dress is removed with resignation, folded and carefully placed on a rock. She turns and looks at her friend. In agreement, the two of them go to meet their destiny. They enter the water at the same time in lookalike black bikinis and are immediately surrounded by the boys. They get water splashed in their faces and are grabbed and dunked mercilessly. The boys fall about laughing and the girls resist but end up laughing too, the same way that adults laugh when they feel like children. From where he is, he can see the eyes of the girl who was wearing the white dress lit by the reflected sunlight and notices that they are exactly the same colour as the ocean that day, the same coppery green and the same translucence that, in the case of the sea, allows him to see pieces of seaweed and little clouds of sand hovering at the bottom. In her case he can't tell. They are big eyes. He can see them well in spite of the fact that she never looks at him, just as horses and birds watch you without ever looking at you.

The Mailer Circus arrives in town in the third week of May. A car drives around town endlessly announcing its presence from a loud-speaker and posters appear on lamp posts and supermarket bulletin boards. Dália has been complaining that she hasn't seen much of him and that he no longer answers her messages, so, to show that he is making an effort, he offers to take her and Pablito to the Saturday-night show. There is also an element of personal curiosity in it. As a child and teenager, he was taken by his mother to see a few plays and dance productions and his father took him to the Expointer cattle shows, to see the depressed Simba Safári animals and the noisy stock-car races at the Tarumã Speedway, and once or twice a year he'd watch Van Damme or *The Lion King* at the cinema, but he never went to the circus. He stops off at Delvina's grocery shop on Saturday afternoon to pick up three bonus vouchers that reduce the price of adult tickets to five reais and children's ones to three. The piece of porous paper in black and magenta with the face of a clown in the centre promises The Brother Show, Flying Trapeze Artists, Beautiful Girls, Clowns, Jugglers, Aerial Silk, Contortionists, Los Bacaras (International Attraction), Globe of Death with 3 Motorbikes, Spiderman Live and Crazy Taxi. The moon is shining in the cool night sky and the popcorn stands trail the aromas of caramel and butter through the air. He meets Dália and Pablito in the main square, in front of the post office. Dália has the night off work and is smiling, beside herself with excitement. She gazes at everything with unbridled fascination. She appears to have suddenly forgotten that she was feeling ignored by him, but scolds him nevertheless for not having accepted her friendship request on Facebook, a sign of disrespect. He hasn't logged on to Facebook for three months. People are converging towards the large, circular blue-and-yellow big top that has gone up on the block of land behind the municipal health clinic. Pablito wants to see the lion. The circus doesn't have a lion but he answers mysteriously so as not to dash the boy's hopes. Do you really think there'll be a lion? Yes, Mama said so! cries Pablo, jumping up and down. And a bullet-man! We'll see, we'll see, he says. Dália tells him not to worry because the kid'll love it all, he likes everything and couldn't care less about promises, maybe it's even a problem, she thinks he might have ADD, do you think he's got ADD? They say you've got to treat it from a young age. Her hand brushes his arm as they walk and he doesn't know if he should hold her hand in front of other people, in front of her son. He is afraid of violating the local codes of social conduct. He is the Goggles Guy. Dália is wearing high heels and shorts. Her calves glisten with moisturizer. He has never seen her so made up. He feels like kissing her but stifles the urge. The back of a pink truck has been converted into a ticket booth and a splendid young woman with glitter on her cheeks, glossy lips and a blue butterfly mask painted around her eyes takes his bonus vouchers and money and hands him tickets through the little window. She must be one of the Beautiful Girls. Two boys of about sixteen dressed up as clowns are planted at the entrance not doing anything, in neutral, watching the audience arrive. They pass through a corridor of stalls selling toffee apples, candyfloss, hot dogs, popcorn and churros and arrive in an open space with chemical toilets, trailers, and old cars in a dreadful state. There is a first-generation Chevrolet Opala, a V W Beetle, a good old Ford Belina, a Chevrolet Caravan and an incredible beaten-up red Volkswagen Passat from the 70s, proud to still exist. The ropes holding up the food tent have been tied to the chassis of an old brick-coloured Scania 110 truck that itself looks like an exotic animal with rounded, elephantine contours. Dália wants a toffee apple and Pablito wants candyfloss. He orders a churro for himself. A short time later, beneath circus tents, a huge white horse and three llamas looking rather tense about all the activity chew on things and contribute to the omnipresent stench of manure and quadrupeds. It is almost time for the show and they hurry into the main tent. They choose a place amid hundreds of plastic chairs arranged in a semicircle around the ring, which has a bulky purple-and-silver curtain. Dália takes off her jacket, sways her shoulders, left bare by a strapless blouse, and hums the chorus of the romantic country song playing over the loudspeaker. Families are attending the show all together: adults with grandparents and rows of children all holding hands in tow, young mothers with babies. The family groups are counterbalanced by gangs of hyper adolescents messing with anything that moves. Boys with gel-sculpted quiffs, jeans with zippers all over them and watches borrowed from their dads strut around girls with wet hair, daring little dresses and six-inch platform clogs. A recording says: Ladies and gentlemen, welcome to the fabulous Mailer Circus. The opening song has been taken from some American film studio's jingle. The curtains open. The spectacle begins with the International Attraction: Los Bacaras. The three trapeze artists in gold-sequined costumes scale a mast performing choreography to the simultaneous narration of a ringmaster who treats the performers as non-human, if not slightly subhuman. They greet the audience . . . like this! he cries as the three artists stretch out their bodies parallel to the ground, which isn't at all easy to do from a muscular point of view but doesn't get a rise from the crowd. But right after this three clowns come in wearing braces and enormous colourful shoes, giant blazers with buttons the size of compact discs and skull masks from a popular TV show. In a matter of seconds the audience has been won over by the stylized violence of old cartoons and the lewd jokes of Saturday-night television. When the house gets messy you can call a cleaner, when a girl gets married, she thinks about the wiener! The children's laughter is constant and explodes with each new joke. Some laugh so hard they cry. The ringmaster announces the jugglers. A man comes in throwing batons into the air while a dancer gyrates around him. The soundtrack of the number is a fast Eurodance song and Dália closes her eyes, raises her arms and starts dancing in her seat. Fuuuuuck, this is awesome! she shouts, and only now does he realize that she is high. What are you on? Acid, she says with an ecstatic smile. Then she goes serious and opens her eyes wide as if trying to sober up. He is irritated but doesn't say anything now. He is overcome by the conviction that he needs to end the relationship without delay, preferably tonight. He won't be able to take an interest in her life. He won't be able to be patient with her. He doesn't think he'll truly be able to love her, or at least not for very long. He admires her tenacity and finds comfort in her beauty but they don't have much else to offer one another beyond what they already have. He doesn't like this fascination with parties, drugs. Any day now, and it won't be long, he'll end up hating himself. He grabs her hair from behind, from the roots, like he did at the party the night they met. Dália likes it. She raises her head and purrs, half-smiling, spaced out. Pablito is glued to the show. Five batons . . . Perfect! says the ringmaster just as the juggler drops one. The man picks up the baton and tries again. He looks bored rather than focused. It's the artist seeking perfection! says the ringmaster. The audience grows tense, in total silence, and breaks into applause when the juggler succeeds. Pablito claps slowly and looks at him. Do you really think it's a good idea to take acid when you go out with your kid? She shrugs it off. It's OK, she says, looking at him as if it is obvious, as if everyone alive has already taken acid and knows it's no problem, for Christ's sake. The juggler makes another mistake, this time with the balls. Oh no! It's very difficult, almost impossible! But he seeks perfection! Then on comes Jardel, the Bird Man, who leaps and twirls from elastic ropes hanging from the roof to the sound of New Age music. A human whirlwind! It is every man's dream to fly through the sky! Stéfany, the Aerial Silk specialist, appears in a tight red vinyl bodysuit with gold detailing. She shakes her bleached ponytail and winds and unwinds herself in the silk several feet above the ground, simulating falls that make the audience gasp. The clowns come back on and announce the NASA Special Attraction, a Secret Super Machine! A tiny car made from the front and back of a Fiat 147 welded together is the centrepiece of several misadventures and gives the audience a number of frights involving bangs, smoke and a radiator

136

that squirts water. In the interval Pablito asks to see the animals again. Dália goes to the bathroom and he takes the boy to the animal tents. There they find a weary ostrich and a camel that at first looks like an odd-shaped lump in the half-light, but suddenly clambers up when they approach the fence and gives them an expectant stare, perhaps thinking he is about to be fed. Pablito is transfixed by the large creature with two mounds wobbling on its back and a curved, jowly neck. Stinky, isn't it? he says to Pablito, holding his nose. Do you know what those things on its back are called? Humps. It stores water in them so it can survive in the desert. An old drunk also walks over and stands there staring at the camel, who grows bored of the humans and goes for a walk around the pen, its hooves squelching percussively in the soft earth. For some reason the camel starts sniffing the tail of a horse that is minding its own business in the neighbouring pen and the horse quickly bucks, just missing the camel's face and hitting the aluminium bars between them with a loud clang. Pablito doubles over with laughter. Crazy animal, says the old drunk, shaking his head and leaving. Dália appears and takes her excited son up very close to the camel. He notices a difference in her behaviour. She is trying hard not to seem high. As they go to buy Pablito a soft drink she says, So that's it, is it? Aren't you going to talk to me any more today? Then she says she's sorry and says that he is right, that it was irresponsible of her. She kisses him and takes his hand in front of Pablito. He glances around. He isn't sure if they are being watched and, to be honest, he isn't sure why he is worried about it. What's wrong? Do you hate me? Or are you anxious because you don't recognize anyone? He says it's nothing. The show continues after the interval. Dália notices that the stagehands who set up and take down the set for almost all of the numbers are Los Bacaras. She suspects that they are all from the same family. Raíza performs her act on the hoops and, as soon as she has left the stage, the camel comes in and stands in the middle of the ring for almost a minute, fouling up the air with the pungent smell of wet wool and tobacco, until it is introduced as The Dromedary. It is accompanied by two trainers and a tiny pony that immediately starts galloping around the ring, jumping obstacles as if it has been lobotomized and chemically stimulated for the mission. The camel does nothing, it's just there to be looked at. The clowns come back on and ask people in the audience to pretend to toss something into the air. They pretend to catch the object in a bucket with a metallic clang. One of the clowns points at Pablo and Dália encourages him to collaborate. He pretends to throw something and the clown starts backing away to catch the imaginary projectile and trips over his colleague, who has slyly bent down for this purpose. It all works. The audience loves the clowns. When they exit at the next interval he pulls Dália to him and whispers in her ear. Remember the guy with dyed-blond hair from the Pico do Surf? What about him? Did he have a shark tattoo on his leg? What kind of question is that? she says, looking at him, offended. Nothing, it's just that I think I saw him giving me a dirty look the other day, but I wasn't sure if it was him. I need to know if he's got a tattoo. I think so, says Dália. A shark on his shin, right? I think he does. The African Show starts. Two strongmen and four beautiful women come on in stereotypical African tribal costumes with tiger and leopard prints. Only one of the performers is black. Don't mess with that guy, says Dália. You hear? It's not worth it. One of the girls has a blue butterfly painted around her eyes and he figures that she is the girl from the ticket booth. She is half naked in her skimpy costume. He fantasizes he is screwing her on the hood of the red Passat. I won't, I just want to know when he's around. Another three men enter the ring, all white. The ringmaster says that the act won a competition on a popular Sunday variety show. The group dances and performs complex acrobatics that wow the audience. At some point the tribal music gives way to a Caribbean rhythm. The teenagers next to them think the human pyramid is funny and tell one another that the performers are all sitting on each other's dicks. When the African Show ends, the long set-up for the Globe of Death begins. The clowns invite the children into the ring and it is quickly invaded by a swarm of little people, jumping about and shouting as if possessed, not knowing where to direct their energy. Pablito goes too and stands there waiting for the clown to ask him his name over the microphone. Dália gets a little nervous because Los Bacaras are positioning the large metal globe in the ring while the clowns are interacting with the children and it looks dangerous. But everything goes smoothly. The children are removed from the ring and ten-year-old Jonatan, a precocious talent, appears and does his first few turns inside the globe on his miniature motorbike to the sound of 'Sweet Child o'Mine'. The lights in the tent are dimmed for the last number. The motorbike engines blast people's eardrums while sparks and spotlights provide a pyrotechnical show. The ringmaster warns of the risks of the performance in a rumbling voice. Exhaust pipes backfire, all of the lights suddenly go out and the girls in the audience squeal. One by one the motorbikes enter the Globe of Death and ride around with what seems like impossible daring, avoiding crashes by inches. The audience is spellbound by the action as if it were high on the smell of burned fuel. The whole thing really does evoke death as a concrete threat. No one thinks about anything else until the show is over.

Later, at her home, Dália puts Pablo to bed and they watch TV. Assuming that the effect of the acid has passed, he gets ready to have a talk with her, but right then she tugs on his hand and says, My mother isn't here, let's go into my room. Pablo won't wake up, come on. But he just sits there. He says that he doesn't want to continue the relationship and prefers to be on his own. Idiot, she says, once she has assimilated the information. How can you tell me something like that when I'm high on acid? She gives him a look of profound disappointment and is near tears as she says, Today of all days? After an awesome night? Did it have to be today? He doesn't know what to say. When is the right time? After a fight? In the middle of the week, when she is busy holding down two jobs? There's no such thing as the right time. The right time is before things get bad, isn't it? No, it isn't! she almost shouts. It's supposed to get bad first, you idiot. Today of all days? And why? Tell me why. She calms down, sighs, strokes his face, shakes her head. Go home and we'll talk later. Please. He gets up and starts to leave. But why? she keeps asking uselessly. Why? I just want to understand why.

Every three or four days he goes to the internet café on the main square and checks his emails. His in-box is always overflowing with new messages but generally only two or three are of any interest. A message from the lawyer about a little problem with the probate process. Another from his mother saying that she and her boyfriend are thinking about coming to spend a weekend in Garopaba. He answers that they can stay with him if they want. A former classmate from university is getting married. He replies that he won't be able to attend the wedding, congratulates him and uses his credit card to purchase a bread maker from the couple's gift list on a department store site. Then he reads the four messages in the email list created by Sara for the running group. They have decided that lessons will start at seven instead of seven thirty so that Denise, Sara's friend who has joined the group, will have time to run and make it to work on time. He answers with an OK. There is also a private message from Sara saying that they need to talk about the price of the lessons because everyone is asking. He answers that they can discuss it in person another time. Some messages are from previous weeks. Condolences from someone who only just found out that his father died, invitations to compete in triathlons, races and open-water swimming competitions sent by organizers or people who don't know he has moved to Garopaba. He recalls that Dália told him off for not answering his Facebook messages. He types in his user name and password and enters the site for the first time in three months. He thinks the layout may have changed. There are dozens of friend requests and his face in his profile picture is beardless. He scans the names and accepts requests from Dália Jakobczinski, Débora Busatto, who he presumes to be the receptionist from the gym, and Breno Wolff, a friend who swam for União. These are the ones he is able to recognize by name. Then he clicks on the requests from mysterious faces one by one and takes a look at their walls in search of clues. He watches a new Coldplay clip that has just been posted by a blonde whose name doesn't mean anything to him. He looks at the YouTube suggestions and watches a few more videos. A baby laughing, a clip by a new band called Little Joy, a really impressive compilation of the best moments in professional tennis in 2007. Almost all of the terminals around him are occupied by people who are hunched over, engrossed, wearing large head-phones. Diagonally opposite him a foreign gentleman in glasses is in the middle of a tense conversation with someone on Skype, shouting emphatically in English and pausing at length to listen to the replies as he holds the arm of the microphone between his thumb and forefinger and keeps his face almost glued to the computer screen, gazing into the depths of a black screen covered in icons. The connection is slow and he suddenly realizes he has spent more than half an hour watching half a dozen videos. He returns to Facebook and remembers to check his personal messages. Four are from Dália.* He scrolls down the list of messages a little further and finds one sent by Viviane two weeks earlier. He takes his hand off the mouse and stares at the screen. Then he clicks on the message and reads it.† He suddenly

---

* *(1) i want you to masturbate every day thinking of me. promise! i spend the whole day with the taste of your skin in my mouth and feeling your hands on me. i'm feeling something that won't go away. this has never happened to me before. (2) i tried to erase my last message, sorry, how embarrassing. did you read it? am i going to see you today? ps.: Pablo loves the goggles!! why don't you teach him to swim? (3) check out the clip of that song we heard yesterday that you liked, by the guy from red hot: https://www.youtube.com/watch?v=4v9CfE90Sts&feature=youtube_gdata_player (4) aren't you going to answer me???*
† *Hey. I thought a lot before writing to you because the last time I called you, when I heard about your dad, you made it clear that you didn't want to hear from us. You can ignore this message if you like, as you have the others, and I'm sorry if I'm being pushy. But I suspect you're like that so people will come to you, because you don't want to talk first, you know? If I'm wrong, I'm just going to make things worse, but . . . I've decided to take the risk.*

I only just found out that you're in Garopaba. Your mother told me you gave up the apartment and sold everything. I remember you always said you wanted to do something like that one day, to go and live by the beach. I hope things are going well for you. I imagine you hitting the water bright and early, then sitting on a rock to warm up in the sun. Are you surfing? I always thought you should surf. Sometimes it's only life's jolts and bumps that make us take the plunge and act on our dreams. I only wish you well and always will. You know that (even though you don't want to hear it, but you know it, don't you?). Your mother said you talk to her, but you hardly speak to anyone else in Porto Alegre and didn't tell anyone where you were going. Of all the people I know, you're the one who most has his demons under control, but I'm sure they're there inside you because I've seen them. I know I fed them and I'm really sorry for it. Solitude wears people down and I'd hate to see them take hold of you while you're there alone, not knowing anyone. Though you like it, don't you? Or maybe you've already met a whole bunch of people and are dating a local and this idiot here is worrying for nothing. I know you're not a child, but I can't help but worry and it's been tormenting me.

needs to catch his breath and realizes with a fright that he forgot to breathe when he was trying to decide if he should answer it or not. He takes the mouse again and, clicking quickly, searches his

---

You probably think it's a bit selfish of me to be writing to you like this, to relieve my guilt. But I've always thought that you see our story in a very simplistic way. It's complicated and we need to face it sooner or later if we want to make peace with life.

Ever since your dad died, Dante hasn't been well. I think he misses you more than ever now. He'll never admit it to you. He never wanted to do you any harm and suffered as much as we did. Maybe more even. You were able to forgive me. Couldn't you find it in yourself to forgive him too? Now that a bit of time has passed, now that your dad's gone? I don't really know what you still feel about all this, but I want to ask you not to write off the idea of forgiving him too. He tries to play the tough guy, but he has to. Both of you want to be tougher than the other. Think about it, put your heart into it. If it really isn't possible, fine. But if it is . . . it would be good for you both.

As for me, I'm enjoying São Paulo more and more. Apart from my job as a children's book editor, I now have a newspaper column about books. The thing I miss the most is the Guaíba, with that horizon, a place where I can gaze out into the distance when I'm upset. It's a bit complicated for your brother because he works from home and the city's cultural life is a temptation for him. But he's OK, besides drinking too much, in my opinion. He's writing a new book. I don't know what it's about. I told him to write about us but he said he'll never do it. I know it's not for my sake, because he knows I don't mind. It can only be out of consideration for you. Did you really keep Beta?

I'll never forget when you introduced me to your dad, remember? He puffed up like a priest and said, 'Kids, love isn't an easy thing and shouldn't be treated as such. Just try to be nice to each other. Amen.' I think he hated me in the end. He never joked around with me ever again. He must have thought I was a whore. But I'll always remember him affectionately.

I don't want to treat something that isn't easy as if it were. Until not long ago I used to dream I had fish hooks caught in my throat and now I feel them when I'm awake. But that's precisely why I believe we should do everything we can to ease the burden. I miss you. Stay in touch. And take care. Love, Viv.

143

account settings and closes his profile down, ignoring the automatic message saying that his friends are going to miss him.

It is raining heavily on Monday morning and the members of the running group text him to say they aren't coming. He goes back to bed and sleeps a little longer. He wakes up with the dog lying next to him and gently shoos her away. She climbs back on to the bed again. His dad never used to allow her on beds and sofas and it is curious that she has started now. He lets her stay there for a while, stroking her back. He falls asleep again and doesn't wake up until almost noon. He walks to the supermarket in the rain and buys a pound of liver, which he fries up and eats with some leftover pasta and tomato sauce. He gives a slice to Beta, who takes a few seconds to believe she has been given something other than dry dog food. He gets dressed for the gym. Before he leaves the dog barks three times for no reason and looks like she is waiting for a reply. Do you want out? Want to stay? he asks. She decides she wants out when he starts to close the door and comes running behind his bicycle. The old dog's energy never fails to surprise him. She lags behind somewhat but always catches up and flops to the ground to rest whenever she gets the chance. Sometimes she disappears for minutes or hours but is always near by when he returns home.

The cold has already frightened some of his students away from the pool. The Rastafarian and the rheumatologist didn't last the first month. Others are still going strong. Tiago has visibly lost weight, learned to do flip turns and can already maintain regular times in his sets of fifty and one hundred metres. The twins are starting to loosen up and today they show him a dance they have rehearsed. They gyrate, twist their wrists and flick their hair around by the edge of the pool as Tina Turner's 'Proud Mary' plays on one of their mobile phones. As soon as they enter the water they become serious again and swim with their characteristic stoicism. Every time he sees them, he has to ask which of them is Rayanne and which is Tayanne. They try to trick him but he figures it out as soon as they start swimming, because they kick their legs differently. Tayanne bends her knees too much and can't point her toes, which is why she tends to be left behind by her sister. Late in the afternoon he manages to convince Ivana to learn to swim butterfly, which a doctor forbade her to do many years ago because of her swayback. If they take it slowly he doesn't think she'll have any problems.

He eats a piece of orange cake while talking to Mila, the Chilean from the snack bar, and goes to pick up Pablito from school as always. The clouds have lifted somewhat and he can see the moon on the wane. He stands there waiting for the boy to run up to him at the gate but he doesn't. After a few minutes a teacher notices and walks over. Dália has already picked him up. He calls her.

I clocked off early in Imbituba and went to get him. I didn't have any choice. I still haven't worked out what to do.

But, Dália, I can keep picking him up.

Yeah, right. Listen here. You can't go around playing with my son's expectations. Or my feelings. Don't you get these things? What are you doing there? You haven't called me or said anything. I don't understand you. You –

It's no problem, Dália. We can be friends, can't we?

She sighs into the receiver.

I can pick him up.

She thinks for a few seconds.

OK. Just until I find another solution.

6

The police station is a low, square building surrounded by wire fences; there is an unoccupied grey-and-white police car out front. It is almost night and an amber light is shining through the louvre windows. He enters expecting to find a sordid, messy little room but the inside is clean and organized. There are no papers in sight and the cupboards and filing cabinets look empty and untouched, like display pieces in an office-furniture shop. Posters of campaigns to fight crack and violence against women share space on the walls with road and geographical maps of the region. At one of the three desks a policeman in a khaki uniform is half slouched in his chair, staring at a computer screen and fiddling with the mouse. He turns to greet him. The policeman is a tall man, wiry and muscular with powerful bones that seem to beg an even bigger body. His jaw and ears are enormous and make the other parts of his head look small in comparison. He sits in the chair in front of the policeman and explains why he is there, hesitating a little before each sentence.

I moved here not long ago. I'm living in a little apartment over in the corner of the village, next to Baú Rock, which I rented from Cecina and . . . To be honest, I'm not here about a problem of any sort. I'm actually curious about something that happened a long time ago. My granddad lived here in Garopaba in the late 60s. And he was killed here. I think he was buried in the town, but I'm not sure. His nickname was Gaudério.

Gaudério.

Yep.

And he was killed here.

Apparently so.

When exactly?

In '69.

In 1969?

Yep.

The police officer stares at him expressionlessly.

What I'd like to know is if there is a police record of it somewhere. Some kind of report. Apparently the police chief came out from Laguna at the time.

From Laguna?

Yep.

Gaudério.

Yep.

What did you come here for?

What do you mean?

You said you moved here not long ago. What for?

The officer is leaning back in his chair but his arms are so long they reach the table. His relaxed wrists are slightly contorted like the hands of someone with arthritis.

I didn't come here for anything. I wanted to live on the beach. I'm a PE teacher. But what's that got to do with it?

Back then there wasn't a police station in Garopaba, says the officer. If there was any kind of inquiry, the files would be in Laguna. But I doubt it. That was a long time ago. I'm from here, born and bred, my parents and grandparents and great-grandparents are from here and I've never heard of him. People remember the ones who die.

I've asked some of the older locals.

I know.

You know?

Yep. I know.

Well then. There are people who remember my granddad. But no one remembers his death.

If no one remembers, then it didn't happen.

I just want to be sure.

The officer's enormous twisted hands come to life. He straightens his fingers then clasps them together. He lowers his head a little and stares at him.

You won't find anything here from back then. Maybe in Laguna.

There is some shouting outside that rises in volume before bursting through the door. The officer leans back and looks over his shoulder, on guard. Two other officers come in violently dragging a young man in handcuffs. Behind them comes a pale, blond man of about fifty, fat from the waist up and thin from the waist down, who is gesticulating non-stop and shouting things in a foreign language. The hulking, big-eared police officer excuses himself, gets up slowly and goes to give the newly arrived problem his attention.

What's going on?

One of the officers who has just arrived, a short man whose uniform sits loosely on his body, says they caught the young man breaking into the German's house. The blond man, who must be the German, bellows in protest in a tongue that isn't German or any other foreign language, rather, a truncated form of Portuguese with an almost incomprehensible accent. He shouts that it is the third time the thief has broken into his house, holding up three fingers. This time he saw the intruder coming into his garden, so he hid in his own garage and took the young man by surprise with a blow to the head.

Günther waited in the garage and *wham*, he says, simulating the gesture of a baseball player.

The other police officer says they found the man tied to a beam in the garage by his feet, hanging upside down. The German continues narrating the story at the top of his lungs and gesticulating. The officers start to interrogate the young man, whose hair at the back of his head is drenched with blood. Realizing that the officers are no longer listening, Günther turns to him.

Three times! he cries, exasperated. I tell police *three times*! I have thief's *address*! Everyone knows him!

Günther is wearing leather sandals, a pair of battered cargo jeans and a blue Pepsi T-shirt. He has very blue eyes and a white beard cut close to his red face. He says that the man broke his window twice in the last few weeks to steal a blender and a pair of running shoes.

They steal small things to smoke crack! Blow to the head! *Wham!* You can't be afraid of the delinquent!

Günther grabs his arm forcefully and starts telling him how he came to Rio de Janeiro to look for his daughter, who had been kidnapped by her Brazilian mother. He had been warned that Brazil was very dangerous and stayed locked in his hotel room for four days eating nothing but peanuts and drinking only soft drinks. He ran out of peanuts and was forced to go downstairs and find a tavern where he could get something to eat. He ordered some fries and a delinquent tried to take them. Günther stabbed him in the hand with his fork and everyone stood around watching. No one else bothered him. Since then he's never been afraid.

The police officers have begun beating up the young man in a corner of the police station. Günther's face twists in horror. He shouts at them to stop and, seeing that it isn't enough, lunges at the officers, who are trampling the kid, who can't be any more than eighteen years old and is curled up on the floor saying he is sorry. The officers try to immobilize Günther and stop the suspect from getting away at the same time. Tables are dragged about and the bottle is knocked off the water cooler. He watches the pandemonium until the German is brought under control. The young man is sitting on the ground protecting his head with his hands. The officer looks surprised when he realizes he is still there.

Can I help you with anything else?

No. Thank you for your time.

Good evening.

Ah. One more thing. A girl was killed in Paulo Lopes a few weeks ago. Strangled. Her face was mutilated. Do you know which case I mean?

Yep. They caught the guy.

Did they? Who was it?

A neighbour. I don't remember his name. He's locked up. Why?

I read about it in the paper and just remembered it. Just curious.

He confessed. An acquaintance of the family. He'd already been seen with the daughter.

Did he say why he killed her like that?

Apparently he was in love with her. She wasn't interested.

Is he normal, or a whacko?

The officer looks like he is about to laugh and shrugs.

He thanks him and leaves with his bike and Beta.

He returns home on foot, pushing his bike through the streets skirting Capivaras Lagoon. The light from the lamp posts gives an oily yellow hue to the carpet of water moss that covers almost the entire surface of the polluted lagoon. A cloud of mosquitoes hovers over a small rotting warehouse. Huge dogs start to emerge from the vegetation on an empty lot and he hooks his finger under Beta's collar as a precaution. Several members of the pack are purebreds, Rottweilers, German shepherds or mixed breeds in which he recognizes the features of Collies and Labradors. They are all filthy and lean, with tongues hanging out, fur bristling with sweat and cold, trotting through the night with no apparent destiny as if following a ghostly leader. They are a common sight in the town, large dogs abandoned by holidaymakers who live hundreds of miles away. They seem haunted, as if they can't fully stifle the instinct to search for home.

He notices that his front door isn't locked, which is something he doesn't usually forget to do. From the door he can see almost the entire apartment and at first glance there doesn't appear to be any sign of forced entry. He looks at the position of the cushions on the sofas, the pamphlets on the table, the two magazines on the counter next to his dirty dishes. His wetsuit, which is worth hundreds of reais and is, perhaps, the item of greatest interest to a thief, is still hanging on the clothes line in the laundry area. The folder where he keeps four hundred US dollars and eight hundred reais in cash, among magnetic bank cards and personal documents, remains under the cutlery tray in a kitchen drawer. He locks the door from the inside, keeps the shutters closed, sets out food and water for the dog and goes to have a shower.

Later he sits on the sofa for a while, looking at his mobile phone. He tops up his credits with a recharge voucher and dials a number.

Gonçalo?

His old school friend starts in with the usual interrogation about why he felt compelled to move to the coast out of the blue but he quickly cuts him off. He asks Gonçalo if he is still working as a reporter for the newspaper *Zero Hora*. He says he is looking for any information at all about his grandfather's death and tells him everything he knows: the year, the story about the unsolved murder at the dance, the jumbled details that his dad told him about his move to Garopaba in the late 60s.

Man, are you really OK?

Listen, Gonça. Dad came here at the time and said he'd spoken to a police chief from Laguna who had supposedly come to look into the matter. But the folk here know fuck all and no one at the police station is going to help me. The subject is taboo here and I still don't get why.

That's going to be tricky. Didn't your father have a death certificate?

No.

If that's really what happened and a police chief actually did go to oversee the case, he must have started an inquest. But imagine the guy arriving, in 1969, in a fishing village that had just become a separate municipality, to deal with a murder without a culprit. To deal with a case of community justice. The only neutral witnesses were most likely hippies and they were probably licking the sand, high on mushrooms. Or maybe the guy didn't even start an inquest, or didn't go to the trouble of finding a culprit. It was the people's justice, period. That kind of thing used to happen a lot in small towns and still does. And even if he did conduct an inquest, I bet it's sitting in some dead archive somewhere.

OK, but is there a way to find out?

Look, I'll talk to a friend of mine, a source in the Department of Justice. Maybe he'll have a suggestion. I'll get back to you, OK?

He washes the three days' worth of dirty dishes piled up in the sink and then looks for something to eat. He hasn't been shopping in days and doesn't find anything nourishing in the kitchen except for a packet of peeled shrimp in the freezer. He thaws it and cooks the shrimp in salted water for a few minutes. He squeezes lime over them and eats them with the remains of a packet of biscuits. He is doing the dishes again when his mobile rings.

Hey, Gonça.

Hi. I talked to the guy.

What'd he say?

It's like this, mate. Let's suppose it really was a police chief from Laguna. The guy may have started an inquest or not. If he did, he may have named a suspect or not. Sometimes there is no one to name, or sometimes an agreement is struck because there are important people involved, that kind of thing. OK? At any rate, the police chief has to refer the inquest to the Department of Justice. The judge sends it to a public prosecutor even if there are no suspects. When there is a suspect the prosecutor seeks an indictment. When there isn't a suspect he can either ask the investigators for further information or request that the case be archived, which is most likely in this nobody-knows, nobody-saw-it kind of crime. It's the judge who makes the final decision.

Right. So you think it must have been archived straight off, then?

It's most likely. If there was an inquest. So let's consider this hypothesis. The guy had it archived. In 1969. So what happens forty years later? What matters now is that the case has two destinations. One copy has to go to the civil police archives. After twenty years the statute of limitations expires and if no one has reopened it, the police send it to the state public archive. Right?

Right.

And another copy goes to the state court.

So all I have to do is go to those archives?

In theory, yes, but here's the thing. The archives should be kept for ever, but in some cases the states get authorization to have them incinerated because they take up a shitload of space. You'll have to see what the story is in Santa Catarina. The upshot is that if there was an inquest and if it was correctly archived and if it hasn't been incinerated or lost in the last forty years, you might find it – if you're lucky and you look properly and talk to the right people.

Right. And . . . ?

That's it.

OK.

Did you get it all?

I didn't get anything, to be honest.

What part?

I dunno, I've already forgotten everything. I don't know how you memorize all that crap. You're a journalist. I'm dumb. Any chance you could email it to me?

Fuck, man.

Sorry. It's the state archive, right? Civil police.

Look . . .

Gonçalo thinks for a moment on the other end of the line.

Look, leave it with me. I know how to talk to these people. I'm snowed under covering the traffic department scandal here – have you seen what's going on? They siphoned off forty-fucking-four million. It's blowing up in the governor's face – but as soon as I have a minute to breathe I'll make a few calls and try to get something for you.

Great. Thanks. Thanks a lot, Gonça.

No problem. You've done me lots of favours. It's my pleasure. I think I might even owe you money.

You don't owe me anything.

I'm going to visit you there one of these days.

Do. Bring the girls.

Man, Valéria's so big. You won't believe it. And you should see her typing on a keyboard. It's frightening.

Is she, what, seven now?

Six. But she's like a little grown-up. She only acts like a kid when it's convenient. What about you? I heard about your dad. That was pretty heavy shit. I didn't find out until ages afterwards. I'm really sorry.

Thanks. Everything's fine. It was fucked up, but it's over. You still swimming?

Me? Fuck no. Just smoking like a chimney and drinking non-stop. It's over for me.

No it isn't. You just can't allow yourself to fold, Gonça.

It's too late for me. How're you doing?

I'm great. I'm working at a gym here, I can swim in the ocean whenever I want and I can keep to myself. I really want to see this thing with my granddad through.

But is there any special reason why you want to dredge it all up?

As he thinks about his reply he looks at Beta, who is asleep on the living-room rug, kicking her back paw, perhaps struggling to remain in a dream.

There is. But I don't know how to explain it.

Did your dad ask you to?

No. Or maybe he did ask without asking. You know? Or maybe I just decided I had to know and now I have to know.

OK. Don't sweat. We'll find something.

Thanks, Gonça.

I'll call you as soon as I've got something to tell. Take care there, swimmer.

You too.

The running group now has four members. The other three were brought by Sara. Denise, her best friend from the pharmacy, is over-weight but has a lot of willpower and is immune to tiredness. Clóvis wears glasses and seems like an intellectual sort. He doesn't know how to explain what he does for a living but he has a state-of-the-art watch with a heart-rate monitor and a GPS that costs several hundred dollars. Celma is a slender, middle-aged woman who runs a home bakery business specializing in banana-and-muesli pies and delivers her wares to her customers by bicycle. They all meet three times a week in front of the Embarcação restaurant at seven in the morning with still-sleepy bodies and tight muscles. Sara always gets out of her car in the same way. She activates her car alarm and approaches the group with a focused, studied air, as if she cannot forget that she has an important part to play on a stage. By the time she has walked down the ramp she is already in character. She loosens up, laughs with her eyes and shakes her ponytail, clapping her hands and encouraging the group. Shall we go, then? Let's shake a tail feather?

Clóvis says he woke up with a dwarf clinging to each leg. He grumbles that today isn't going to be easy. He coordinates his students' stretching and Sara shows off her brand-new Asics running shoes filled with cushioning gel.

How're your shins, Sara?

Much better!

She squats down and massages the muscles along her bones as he taught her.

They're better, but they still hurt a bit.

Are you doing your exercises at the gym?

Yep.

Let's take it slowly. You're going to use this here today.

He shows her a watch with a heart-rate monitor and explains how she should position the chest strap right under her breasts.

Your mission today is to control your heart rate. Let's keep it at a hundred and forty, OK? If it drops below that you pick up the pace, if it passes it you reduce it.

Can you give me a hand?

She shows him the strap. It appears to be in the right place.

What's the problem?

Is this the right height?

He pushes it up a quarter of an inch.

There.

The ocean is choppy. Much of the sky is covered in clouds but orange streaks indicate that the sun has just risen behind the hill. An enormous catamaran is anchored about five hundred yards from the beach with its sails down and its mast conducting the rise and fall of the waves. The group sets out running along the sand, slowly. Sara's watch beeps. Her heart rate is already one hundred and fifty-five, and they slow their pace. Clóvis takes off ahead of the group. He lets him go. At the end of the beach they take the road to Siriú, which has a short paved section and then is all dirt road and sand. A kid shoos chickens from the patio of a roadside hut. Every two or three minutes a car or motorbike goes past and he insists that they all run single file along the edge of the road and keep an eye out on bends. Sara finds her pace and Denise accompanies her, puffing loudly. Clóvis has left them all behind and Celma, who has yet to build up her endurance, has started to tire. He tells the girls to go ahead and stays with Celma, alternating between running and walking. Celma says it is a blessing to live there and to be able to go for an early-morning jog in such a beautiful place. She says that God made her go through a lot before she arrived here. He encourages her and she tells him her whole life story.

When they get back Sara is sporting the flaming-red cheeks that are her trademark. Her face is covered in sweat and visibly giving off steam. She says that her husband, the dentist, wants to have a barbecue at their place and the group is invited. Then she takes his arm and pulls him aside as if she wants to tell him a secret.

We still haven't settled one thing.

What?

How you're going to charge for the lessons.

I'm still not sure. We'll talk about it later.

But don't you have a price?

I'm going to think about it. We'll talk about it later.

It's just that it's been almost a month and they want to know how much they're going to have to pay.

Don't worry about it. We'll talk about it later.

She looks frustrated but lets it go for the time being.

After the students have gone he gets the backpack he left hidden behind the wall of a house and puts his running shorts, T-shirt and shoes in it, leaving on the swimming trunks he is wearing underneath. He gets his goggles and heads out for a swim. The water is cold but bearable. The wind is blowing hard enough to whip up the waves and he heads through the choppy sea towards the catamaran, planning to swim around it, return to the beach and repeat the circuit until he is tired. He doesn't want to swim to Preguiça Beach, as it might anger the fishermen, who are still exercising their right to exclusive access to the bay during the mullet season.

As he approaches the catamaran he hears warning cries. Puffing and with fogged-up goggles, he raises his head out of the water and sees two crew members in the stern shouting and waving their arms. He takes off his goggles and looks around, trying to see or hear a boat coming in his direction or perhaps a porpoise or goodness knows what. One of the men in the catamaran beckons him over and points at something in the back of the boat. He swims over cautiously and as he gets a little closer he is able to see over the top of the waves. An animal is glistening on the stern platform. It is a large, round seal, its fur mottled with patches of light and dark grey. The men are laughing, enchanted by the awkward, whiskered mammal swaying back and forth from flipper to flipper. He stops a few yards from the boat. One of the men says that it was there when they woke up and isn't showing any sign of wanting to leave. They think it is hungry and the other man goes into the cabin for a minute and comes back out with a small fish. The seal takes a look at the fish that the man is shaking over its head, gives two short, loud, nasal grunts that sound like pure mockery and, after a dramatic pause, flips effortlessly into the sea and slips beneath the water without a splash. They look at each other, not knowing what to say. He asks who the catamaran belongs to and the men start to explain that they are just looking after the boat. The owner, a guy from São Paulo who is sailing around the world, stopped there to see to something in Garopaba. The seal leaps out of the water with a somersault worthy of a gymnast and lands in the same position as before on the stern platform. It has a large fish in its mouth, at least three times bigger than the one offered by its hosts. The fish flaps about until the seal tires of showing off and devours it.

That same afternoon he is explaining to the twins how to do a drill to extend their strokes when a woman appears at the entrance to the pool and runs towards him with a worried face and flailing arms.

Your dog's been run over.

He doesn't recognize her.

It can't be mine, he says. My dog's here.

I saw it! she shouts in exasperation. It was right in front of me, over on the avenue.

159

He strains to recognize her. She is a slender woman in her early forties, with veins like tree roots running down her arms to her hands.

It isn't possible, Beta's lying at the entrance to the gym, he says with an impatience that sounds affected to his own ears. She always waits outside reception or with Mila in the snack bar.

He takes two steps towards the door but realizes he doesn't know where he is going, so he stops and hesitates. The twins take in the scene wide-eyed. They look more identical than ever. He is sweating in the warm air, pungent with the smell of chlorine. The woman grabs his arm.

Come on, let's go. The man who hit her took her to Greice's. That's where you should go.

Do I know you?

Before he has even finished saying it, he knows it was a mistake. He hasn't rushed in with a question like this in a long time.

What? Are you nuts?

He stares hard at the woman's face, glances at her sandals, her green-and-gold sarong with Indian patterns, the blouse without any distinguishing characteristic, earrings, hair, teeth. Nothing.

She places her hand on his face and gives him a maternal look. As if he were a sick child.

Stay calm. I'll come with you, come on.

He follows her, breathing quickly. His vision has tunnelled and outside of it everything is blurry and no longer of interest.

It's me, Celma, your student, she says, glancing at him.

I know, sorry. I'm a bit confused.

So this is what Celma's face looks like. They ran together earlier that morning. She told him much of her life story. He apologizes again. She shakes her head as if to say she doesn't mind.

As he leaves the pool building he can't help but look in the places where Beta normally spends her time. Débora says she hasn't seen her. Celma loses her patience.

I'm telling you, your dog's over at Greice's! Get down there before she dies! Do you want me to take you there? If not, I'm going home.

Who's Greice?

The vet over in Palhocinha. The guy said he was going to leave her there.

They pass through the front gate of the gym. Celma climbs on to her bicycle and turns to fiddle with something in the wicker basket lashed to the bike rack with bungee cords.

How is she?

Celma presses her lips together and sighs.

He ran right over her. He got her good.

But is she alive?

I don't know. She was in a bad way. But he stopped the car and asked where there was a vet. Lúcia from the coffee shop told him to take her to Greice and explained where it is. He went to pick her up and she tried to bite him. Someone gave him a hand and they managed to get her in the car and the guy sped off.

It's the clinic over by the highway, isn't it? The one with the greenish sign.

That's the one. Near the fire station. Want to take my bike?

But before she can finish, he thanks her and sprints away. He runs three blocks to the main avenue, where he turns left and almost collides with a cyclist riding down the bike lane with a surfboard under his arm. He runs in his T-shirt, Speedos and flip-flops. When the strap of one of the flip-flops breaks he slows down, kicks them off his feet in a kind of clumsy dance step and keeps running. The soles of his feet pound the cracked tarmac and hard sand at the shoulder of the road. He passes a shop selling Indian decorations and one of the many pizza parlours that closed right after Carnival. In the swamp on the right side of the road, which extends for several miles to the hills, a column of grey smoke is rising from a fire. He hears the crackling of burning bamboo and sees pink tongues of fire in his peripheral vision. There is no time to look now. His breathing is becoming more laboured. The vegetation along the side of the road stinks of carrion. He stares straight ahead as he runs with long strides, his feet stinging from the friction, and wonders why he is running to the vet's, why he didn't take Celma's bike, why he didn't ask for a lift or, better, why he didn't take his own bicycle, which was where he always left it back at the gym. Idiot. He approaches the turn-off to Ferrugem Beach. At the back of his throat he detects the zincy taste of being out of breath. He runs until he sees the green sign saying PET VIDA.

The young man in reception is startled when he bursts in, or was already startled.

Did someone bring in a dog that's been run over?

The man doesn't say anything and just looks at him. It is a common reaction in these parts. People sometimes look surprised that they have been spoken to, as if addressing someone in words were the most peculiar thing.

My dog was run over and someone told me she was here.

The man jolts out of his stupor and says yes, the dog is here. He says he's going to talk to the vet and tells him to wait there. He returns and says that she's in the consulting room and will be out to see him in a minute.

Can I go in to talk to her?

No. She'll be right out.

The man still looks nervous, as if he were being tested.

Is the man who brought her in still here?

He's gone. He waited a while, then left.

Was it someone from here? Was he a local?

The man shrugs. His ears have no outside folds, as if someone had cut off their edges when he was a child in an act of insane cruelty. The veterinary clinic's reception area is actually a fully stocked pet shop. Tall piles of bags of dry dog and cat food take up most of the small space and the strong smell unearths childhood memories, visits to stables and agricultural fairs with his father. Once, when he was barely a teenager and the whole family still lived in the house in Ipanema, he ate dog food just to see what it was like. The floury taste and gritty texture come back to him. He used to feel sorry for the dogs who had to eat it. He sees a poster on the wall with illustrations of every dog breed in the world and fading photos of what appear to be members of several generations of beagles from the same family. A poster about vaccination. On the glass door is a large sticker with a drawing of a cow munching on grass that says ANIMALS ARE FRIENDS, NOT FOOD. Plastic dog houses, padded pet beds, collars and multicoloured shampoos. He hears a small animal yelping at the back of the clinic.

A blonde woman in a white coat appears in reception.

Are you the owner of the dog?

There is a smear of blood near the waist of the coat.

Yes.

You know she was hit by a car, don't you?

Yes. Where is she?

In the consulting room. I've just stabilized her. Please, let's go into my office because I need to explain a few things to you.

They sit facing one another at her desk. On top of it is a portrait of her next to her husband, a stout, bald man. He reminds him of his student Jander, who owns a pet shop.

Are you Jander's wife, by any chance?

Yes. Do you know him?

He's my student at the swimming pool.

Oh, so you're his instructor?

He says yes with a little smile and takes a deep breath. He rests his forehead in his hand with his elbow propped on the edge of the desk.

The vet explains that Beta has a fractured humerus and a lumbar spine injury, probably with a complete fracture of vertebra L6 or L7, which means that she will probably be paralysed. The vet's tone of voice is funereal. She may also have a fractured pelvis. In addition to her abrasions, which are ugly. In a case like this, she says, we need to offer the owner the option of euthanasia.

I don't want to put her down. Try to save her.

Of course you don't. But think about it a little.

Can't you operate?

I can. But even if she survives, it is almost certain that she'll never walk again. And no matter how much you love your pet you should give some thought to what things will be like afterwards. She may suffer a lot, she won't be easy to care for, she'll need a trolley in order to walk.

So there's a chance she might walk again?

It's almost impossible. I'm sorry.

Can I see her?

It's better if you don't. In general we don't allow it. You think you want to see her but you don't. Believe me.

I don't have a problem with these things.

Even if you're a doctor or a vet, it doesn't matter. It's not a question of being used to seeing blood. You don't want to. It's better if you talk to me. Trust me, I've seen this before.

Sweat drips from his chin. He is still breathing heavily. He remembers that he is in a T-shirt and Speedos, barefoot.

Excuse the state I'm in. I ran here from the gym.

Don't worry. Look, forgive me for insisting. I'm really sorry and I know that you love your dog a lot, but I need to emphasize that it would be best —

Your name's Greice, isn't it?

Yes.

Greice, I understand. But I need to see her before I decide. I won't leave without seeing her.

She stares at him for a moment.

Come with me, then.

There isn't much in the operating room: a wall cabinet, a support trolley, plastic tubes, cotton wool, not a surgical instrument in sight. In the centre, on an aluminium table under an operating light with four bulbs, is his father's dog.

I've cleaned and sedated her. But like I told you, she's badly hurt. You'll get a shock.

He walks over and looks at the dog.

Then he approaches the vet, who stayed in the doorway, and talks to her in a low voice close to her face.

Do everything you can, Greice. It doesn't matter how long it takes. I don't care how much it costs. I'll pay more than normal if necessary. I'll pay whatever you think is fair. If you need to take her somewhere else, let's do it. Do whatever you can for her to survive and to get as well as possible.

You understand that she's going to be paralysed? That there's no guarantee that she's going to walk?

Yes.

The surgery costs around two thousand reais. But it might end up costing more.

That's fine. The price doesn't matter.

Leave your contact information with William in reception. Mobile phone and everything. I'll call you as soon as I've got some news. And she'll need to stay in the clinic for at least thirty days. That'll cost you too.

OK. Do everything you can.

I promise you I will.

Thanks.

He gives William his contact details and walks back into Garopaba.

The news has spread through the gym. Mila hugs him and kisses his neck. He feels the satiny skin of the Chilean descended from Mapuche Indians on his. She strokes his hair with her hand and offers him a slice of wholemeal chocolate cake. She says he is pale and looks weak. Débora is signing up some new clients but straightens up in her chair and asks how the dog is with pity written all over her face. She tells him to go home as it's almost time anyway and Saucepan is watching his students in the swimming pool. He thinks about calling his mother as he gets changed in the dressing room but decides not to. To her, Beta is just a dog, if not to say a kind of enemy, and he realizes how absurd it is to be jealous of a dog and a dead man, even if not entirely without cause. When he told his mother that he had decided to look after Beta after his father's suicide, she shook her head, unable to understand. If it were up to her, she would have pressured someone in the neighbourhood to take her in. But her son keeping the dog? It was a kind of offence.

He arrives early to pick up Pablo from school. When the children get out, Pablo appears accompanied by a teacher. He lost the fingernail of his index finger in a game. He is sporting an oversized bandage on the finger, a thick wad of gauze held down with plasters. The teacher strokes his hair.

He had to go to the health clinic, didn't you, Pablito?

Yep.

And what did the doctor say?

The nail will grow back, says Pablo with a sideways glance, paying attention to something else.

He puts Pablo in the bike seat.

Ready?

Ready!

Can you hold on properly with your finger like that?

Yep.

Did it hurt a lot?

Yep.

He continues asking questions the whole way and Pablo answers them as succinctly and directly as possible and with an honesty that still hasn't been contaminated by sarcasm or irony. When they get to Dália's mother's house, she asks if he has read the last email she sent him. He confesses that he hasn't yet.

I had another vision with you in it. Or a dream, if you prefer. This time it was really strange. I want to know what you think.

I promise I'll read it as soon as possible.

On his way home he stops in front of the pizza parlour on the main avenue. He identifies Dália by her height and exuberant curls. She is in a meeting with other employees at the counter of the bar and signals through the window for him to wait a minute. As she walks out, she makes a funny face with twisted lips and squinting eyes.

Hi, you wooking for me?

I'm looking for a really pretty girl who works here.

She lets the funny expression go and he discovers her face all over again. How many times has it been now? Thirty? Fifty?

Hey there, sexy. Your beard's getting long.

Letting nature follow its course.

Been breaking many hearts?

I just came to say hi and tell you that Pablito's at home. He managed to lose the fingernail of his index finger playing hide-and-seek, but he's taking it in his stride as always. They took him to the clinic and he's got a huge bandage, but everything's OK.

Oooh. My poor baby. I'll give him a call now. Thanks for letting me know. Actually, it's good that you stopped by. I need to talk to you. As of next week you won't need to pick him up. I'm quitting this job. I'm just going to work in the shop and I can pick him up when I get back from Imbituba.

I see. Changes. Some kind of problem?

No, but I don't need two jobs any more. I make more money there. And I don't have to work nights. Thanks for helping me out. You're an arsehole but you're an angel too.

That's what folks used to say to my dad. But with him it was the opposite: You're an angel, but you're an arsehole. And I recognize that sparkle in your eye.

I'm seeing someone.

Already?

She gives him the finger.

I knew it. You're looking very smug. Someone from here?

From Florianópolis. He's fifty but he isn't as square as you.

What does he do?

He's a contractor. He's working on that project to widen the highway. What's the face for? Everyone makes that face when I tell them his age. Why?

Did I make a face? I don't think I made a face.

Fine.

I don't see anything wrong with it. I don't even know the guy. Maybe you're the one who's worrying too much about what other people think.

She doesn't answer but her gaze is reconfigured. Now it is a look of farewell in which he can tell that she isn't saying goodbye to him, because they'll still see each other around, but to another world identical to this one except that in it they are still together, in love and have lasted the distance, a world imagined in detail and nurtured for a time, which she is just now letting go of. A great sadness overcomes him. He suddenly wants her again. It is as if her attachment to that other world has leaped out of her body and into his like an invading spirit. Maybe he is feeling exactly what she was feeling a minute earlier.

What's wrong? asks Dália.

He feels like crying. Truth be told, he'll never know what she was feeling. He could have asked her. She'd have told him. He clears his throat and tells her that Beta was run over earlier that afternoon.

Oh, how awful. Is she going to be OK?

She's in a bad way. But she'll pull through.

Are you OK?

Yeah. I'm fine.

The other waiters start bringing the tables outside and Dália has to get to work.

The waves hit Baú Rock with a thud followed by an effervescent hiss. He mashes up a tin of tuna with mayonnaise, slices a tomato and makes sandwiches. He can smell the dog in the apartment and sees her short bluish hairs on the ground and her empty dish abandoned on the damp cement under the clothes line.

Suddenly there is nothing to do or to think about and in this hiatus he glimpses how and where he is going to die. The vision doesn't come to him in detail. It is less a scene and more a combination of indistinct circumstances that fit into a clear pattern. It isn't the first time he has fantasized about his own death. He is always doing it and is pretty sure everyone else does too. But this time it is different. He tears a page out of the old diary that he uses as a notebook, fishes a pen out from between the fruit dish and a pile of magazines, jots down a few lines, dates it and signs underneath. His heart is beating fast. He opens a can of beer and calls Bonobo.

Want to come over for a beer?

Sure, sounds good. I've got a few things to sort out here at the bed and breakfast first. I'll be about an hour. I actually need to talk to you about something. I need a favour and you might be able to help me.

The night suddenly turns hotter and coaxes hungry mosquitoes out of wherever it is that they hole up in the cold weather. He sprays insecticide everywhere, overdoes it and has to go outside as he lets the apartment air out.

Bonobo shows up about two hours later with a twelve-pack of beer and a salami that he peels and slices slowly with a small pocket-knife. He says he is going to pray for Beta to recover fully.

He hands Bonobo the folded page from the diary and waits as he reads what is written on it.

What the fuck is this?

I want you to sign it too and put it away somewhere. Somewhere safe. Don't lose it.

What makes you think you're going to drown here in Garopaba?

You don't have to take it seriously. Just put it somewhere safe.

Sorry, mate, but I'm not signing this. Do you want to kill yourself in the ocean? Why did you sign this? What's this paper going to prove? I don't get it.

Relax. It's just something I think is going to happen. Not any time soon. It's still a long way off.

If you really believe what's written here you'll end up setting the thing in motion. Tear it up.

If it does happen like that there'll be no way to know if it happened because I said it would or if I said it would because it was going to happen.

Bonobo hands back the piece of paper.

I don't want to hang on to this crap. Tear it up.

A few beers later, Bonobo asks for a loan. They're already a little drunk and through the window silent flashes of lightning can be seen in the darkness of the ocean. He is surprised by the request. He thought the bed and breakfast was doing well. It does pretty well, says Bonobo. It'd be more than enough if I only had to support myself here. He tells him that he sends money a few times a year to his sick father and his unmarried sister who is always ill and can barely run her day-care centre. He says that, truth be told, he's always had more luck than common sense with the bed and breakfast. It's as easy to lose money there as it is to make it and he's not a business-minded administrator like his ex-partner, who he had a fight with two years after they'd gone into business together because the guy had started selling marijuana and coke at the bed and breakfast, and then crack, until one day they ended up in a fist fight and he gave the guy a lot of money to disappear, which he promised to do but didn't because he continued dealing in the area until he was shot in the head by a rival in Encantada. And now he owes money to the lumber dealer, the accountant and the bank.

How much do you need?

To get out of the worst of it, about three grand. Three and a half.

Get the pen on the table there and write down your account number on a piece of paper. I'll transfer it to you tomorrow.

Man, it doesn't have to be the whole lot. There are some other people I can ask too. I've got a friend over in Silveira who's given me a loan before.

I've still got most of the money from the sale of the car. Pay me back when you can.

You're going to spend a fortune on vet bills. Seriously, it doesn't have to be everything. If you can just loan me some of it, it's already a huge favour.

If I'm saying I can, I can. No sweat.

Bonobo writes his account number on a blank page of the diary.

Now take that same pen, sign this paper and put it somewhere safe.

Bonobo reads what is written on the piece of paper again.

Man, you're the most disturbed individual I've ever met. I admire you.

He signs the paper, folds it three times and tucks it inside his battered canvas wallet with a Velcro fastening.

All I have to do is hang on to it?

Yep. Keep it safe. Don't lose it.

A yellow cat climbs on to the window ledge and peers through the open glass. It looks surprised to find two men in the apartment. It stares at the humans and the humans stare back until it decides it's in the wrong place and disappears into the darkness with a leap.

What do you do when you're here alone?

I cook a little. Sometimes I play a video game.

What about Dália?

We broke up.

Fuck. Right before winter. What happened?

I don't know. I just lost interest.

She's a really awesome chick but she's a bit of a space cadet.

No, she isn't. She's actually got her shit together.

That's the thing with relationships. We don't get to choose when they happen. They come and go on the wind of karma. When you least expect it, another one'll appear. Just be careful with these local girls: they're easy to knock up.

The locals have already got it in for me 'cause I keep asking questions about my grandfather's death. If I get involved with one of their daughters, I'll meet the same end that he did.

Want to rewrite what you put on that piece of paper?

He doesn't answer and the two of them sit there smiling for a while in silence.

Hey, do you play poker?

I've played a few times. But it's been ages.

We're going to play poker over at the bed and breakfast. I'm trying to organize it with the gang again. Altair plays, and Diego from the petrol station, and some guys from Rosa too. It's awesome. But you've got to be prepared, 'cause the rounds take time. We play geriatric-nappy poker. Everyone has to bring a packet of nappies.

Come again?

Geriatric nappies. That way no one needs to stop the game to take a piss.

You can't be serious. That's deranged.

We've played for more than twenty-four hours non-stop.

What if someone needs to crap?

In that case, fine. They get up and go. But no one takes a dump in the middle of a game of poker, do they? You drop your boulders before the game. It's a question of professionalism. You've got to take it seriously. I'll let you know the next time we're going to play. Get prepared.

When the twelve empty cans are sitting on the table, Bonobo says goodbye with a complex handshake that involves touching fists, patting one another on the chest with the backs of their hands and cracking their fingers. Then he hugs him.

Thanks for the money. You're a lifesaver.

No problem. That's what friends are for.

I'll pay you back soon.

Don't sweat. When you can.

Try not to isolate yourself too much here.

Don't worry.

I worry about you a bit.

Fuck off, Bonobo. Go home.

Later, after Lockjaw's engine has laughed and started and the noise of the car has disappeared into the distance and the fishermen's dogs have stopped barking and rattling their chains, he opens one of his backpacks in the closet and takes out a photo album. He sits on the floor and flicks through it. There are photos of his father, his mother, Dante and Viviane. He takes out a photo of his older brother and compares it to one of himself to see once more how different they are. His brother takes after their mother. He looks at photos of his first girlfriend and his favourite cousin, Melissa, who lives in Australia and hasn't been in touch in months. Photos of a few university friends. Fellow triathletes. He looks at the images and tries to guess who is in them. He is actually capable of getting his brother wrong, or even his parents in some cases, but he has memorized most of the photos in the album, which he considers his most important album, a catalogue of his family, social circle and love life. He gazes at a photo of five sweaty athletes in the early-afternoon sun posing side by side on their racing bikes with Lami Beach in the background and the corner of a fruit stand on the right, each of them holding a different piece of fruit: Maísa with a bunch of bananas, Renato with a slice of watermelon, Breno with a pineapple, himself with an orange skewered on the end of a kitchen knife, and Pedro on the right with some pink grapes. It was one of the group's last workouts before the Ironman in Hawaii. The people's names are handwritten on the backs of the photos, at the bottom or right across the picture itself. 'FATHER'. 'MOTHER'. 'PARENTS'. 'DANTE'. 'VIVIANE', 'ME AND VIVIANE'. 'VIVIANE (2ND ON RIGHT) AND FRIENDS'. 'TRAVELLING SALESMEN CLUB: RENATO, ME, BRENO, MAÍSA, SANDRA, LEILA' hugging by a poolside and 'PEDRO' with an arrow pointing at a smiling face in the pool. There are three portraits of himself, all labelled 'ME'.

Thousands of people flock to the main square on the second Wednesday in June, on a freezing cold night, for the opening of the XIth Garopaba Church Fair with a Gian & Giovani concert. The country-music duo's songs have been playing non-stop on the local radio stations and a five-year-old girl is now singing one at the top of her lungs while swaying on her father's dancing shoulders. The square itself has disappeared beneath the crowd, the small stage, the main stage with its green, red and blue spotlights and the dozens of stalls selling arts and crafts, drinks, pine seeds, mulled wine and endless sweet and savoury snacks. The air is filled with the smells of caramel, spices, baked mullet, fried foods, cigarettes, wet earth, minty colognes and trampled grass. The whole town has turned out. Younger children climb the trees and sit there with their little legs dangling like rotten branches to watch the concert from above the mass of teenage gangs, hand-holding couples and families advancing as a solid block. Everyone seems eager to see and be seen in the ant colony of the community in celebration, seeking a promised and greatly desired social catharsis. Some people are wearing their best dresses and suits. Heavy earrings and gold watches flash in the dark. Politicians, the disabled, doctors, police officers, fishermen, athletes, couples with prams, tramps, tourists. The town's crazies are all there, mellowed by the chaos. There are also the bored, those who can't sleep because of the noise and those who glance around with looks of disapproval or incomprehension. Everyone.

He walks alone holding a cup of mulled wine. He takes short, quick sips, partly because he is anxious about being in the middle of a bunch of people he knows whose faces he cannot recognize and partly because the icy night air cools the steaming mixture of sweet wine, sugar, cachaça and cloves in a matter of minutes. One of the singers – he isn't sure if it is Gian or Giovani – asks those who are in love to raise their hands and shout between one song and another. Everyone is in love. He watches the children playing on the plastic slide in the playground and riding around in the cabins of a tiny Ferris wheel as their parents look on and take pictures. Some parents smile and talk to their children, while others are lost in thought. Each cabin of the miniature Ferris wheel is a small, closed plastic cage, each cage is a different colour and the children inside them either look frightened, about to fall asleep or, improbable as it may seem, self-conscious about where they are. Other children leap about wildly on trampolines and scamper like rodents through the passages and labyrinths of complex inflatable structures, screeching with laughter and shouting as they chase and flee from one another.

Someone calls his name and he turns cautiously, afraid he won't recognize the person. It is the twins, Tayanne and Rayanne, who are with their parents and another family of friends to whom he is introduced as the girls' swimming instructor. They have to speak up to be heard over the loud music, clamour of voices and revving motorbikes. Gian and Giovani finish the concert and invite two girls from the audience up on to the stage with everyone watching. The girls are allowed to kiss the artists and are presented with Gian & Giovani towels. The group decides to get something to eat and he accompanies them through the food-stall circuit. There are hot dogs, steak rolls, sandwiches made with Lebanese bread, appetizing servings of French fries and grilled sausage. The Pastoral Care for Children stall is selling fried pastries and skewers of meat. He buys some coconut sweets from the Association of Parents and Friends of the Disabled stall. And there is still the entire dessert sector with fried coconut shavings coated in brown sugar, coconut flans, chocolate fudge balls, coconut fudge balls, cakes, star fruit, passion-fruit or apple compotes, hand-made chocolates with nuts and wine and a hugely popular delicacy known as 'coconut delight'.

At some point in the evening he catches sight of a silhouette without shoulders that can only belong to Bonobo. He is wearing red tracksuit bottoms and a white ski jacket and is drinking mulled wine with Altair and a bald guy who looks like a surfer. They are standing next to the small stage where, they tell him, a local street-dance group is about to perform. You're going to be blown away by all the hotties, says Altair, who is sporting a shiny leather jacket and smoking a clove cigarette, puffing sweet-smelling smoke through his nostrils. The dance group performs an aggressive, eroticized dance that combines the aesthetics of tango with cinematically choreographed street-gang clashes in a *mise en scène* replete with simulated fights, seduction and caresses, set to the sound of techno music. The dancers are wearing black-and-red skirts with slits up the side, fishnet stockings, jackets with flowers in the lapels and hats. The girls really are beautiful, the men have athletic builds, the dance is vigorous and acrobatic and the crowd applauds enthusiastically.

After the performance, the four of them head to a side street where the League of Women Against Cancer has set up a Mullet Feast tent.

The fresh fish are baked over hot coals and served on clay roof shingles. A colourful buffet of side dishes is arranged on a real boat. They order two mullet and drink a few cans of beer while sitting at the plastic tables. The live performances end and the tourists start returning to the vans and enormous buses that brought them there from all over the state.

The next morning he goes to check on Beta at the veterinary clinic. The operation went well but Greice won't allow visits yet and promises to call him when the time is right. He runs with the group on the beach early on the Friday morning, teaches swimming at the pool in the afternoon, picks up Pablo from school for the last time and makes an online bank transfer to Bonobo from the internet café. He spends Thursday and Friday nights at home in bed listening to the noise and music from the fair blending with the rhythmic wash of the waves under his window until well after midnight.

The fair heats up again on the Saturday night. He watches the interminable coming and going of groups of adolescents with their dramas, crushes and scheming. In the blink of an eye, they oscillate between laughter and seriousness, between being full of attitude and staring off into space. Couples in love walk along, light and serene, rubbing faces and exchanging body heat, looking proud. Those who aren't quite as in love are resigned, carrying out a necessary ritual, and there are also those who look as if they have been forced together and are merely fulfilling an obligation. Some parade their partners like trophies, proud to be holding hands, or have their arm around the shoulder of someone who anyone can see doesn't desire them or just tolerates them. There is hatred between some couples. Most of the single men are adult fishermen and old men in dress clothes. They are wearing tailored trousers and jumpers or even suits and hats.

They walk with their heads up. They have earned the right to their air of authority. For older members of the community, the church fair is a pompous occasion and they appear to be inspecting the habits of the younger generations. They drink at the counters of beverage stands or wander about, not really understanding what is going on. They don't look flustered. Nothing would surprise them at this stage.

The first Saturday attraction on the small stage is a funny educational play with an ecological theme. Three actors dressed in black bodysuits act out dialogues and make jokes about deforestation, global warming and the hole in the ozone layer – which really isn't a problem because all we have to do is wear SPF 349 on our bodies and 686 on our faces, right everyone? – as well as pesticides and the hormones used in animal husbandry, which, according to the script, make men impotent and cause girls to menstruate at the age of nine. Night is falling. In the Little Miss pageant, ten girls of nine or ten represent their schools. One by one they parade quickly before three judges, one of them the parish priest, and then pose for the audience. They are wearing country costumes with checked dresses, frills and bows in their hair. Some are shy and awkward, while others try to strut like adult models, with burlesque results. The presenter asks each of them if they have something to say and they state their names, ages and the full names of their schools, which in some cases are quite hard to pronounce, and explain why they like to study there. Some have memorized texts that talk about their communities or neighbourhoods but those who improvise get more applause, especially when they get confused and look vulnerable. The littlest of all freezes up completely, forgets the speech she has learned off by heart and gapes at the audience. She sways this way and that with a little smile plastered across her face until she is removed from the stage to the sound of great applause. The winner is from Pinguirito School, which Pablo attends. She parades again and is given an indecipher-able gift. Then the Teen Miss is chosen. There are only three contenders, all of whom have broad hips, heavy make-up and hair straightened with a flat iron. The Areias do Macacu Community rep-resentative is by far the prettiest but the Garopaba Radio candidate, the preppiest, wins. They are all given enormous bouquets, almost as big as themselves. An area is cleared in front of the stage for a ribbon-dance performance by a group of elderly people. The men and women dressed in typical country clothes sing and dance while holding the ends of colourful ribbons tied to a central post and the choreography follows commands in verse given over a microphone by a singer. They change partners, reverse the direction of the wheel and weave the ribbons together in a complex pattern. He thinks it is beautiful but the audience that is pouring into the square grows impa-tient and starts making a noise. The two beauty queens were invited to watch the ribbon dance but only the Little Miss stayed and has been forgotten up on the stage by herself for twenty minutes, stand-ing there in the cold, without anything to do. He is approached by someone who calls him 'teacher'. He suspects it is Ivana and confirms it when she jokes about the difficulty of the previous day's training session. Ivana is with her husband and they make small talk during two belly-dancing performances. Male members of the audience jos-tle for a position in front of the stage. The second dancer is representing the goddess Lakshmi but the presenter can't pronounce the name. He gives up after a few tries and just repeats that she is doing the 'dance of the goddess'. The schedule of performances on the small stage ends and Ivana and her husband say goodbye and go off to do something else. The main stage lights up for the Garopaba Talent Show. He is already drinking his third cup of mulled wine and decides to get a sandwich. In the queue he recognizes Tracksuit Man from the tuft of hair escaping over the top of his shirt. He didn't last more than a few weeks in the pool but he says he is doing Pilates and loving it. They soon run out of things to talk about and he excuses himself to go and watch the rest of the talent show. When he joins the crowd again a local soft-metal band called Random Reflections is wrapping up its short performance with a wall of distorted electric guitar music and drum rolls. Immediately afterwards a girl who can't be any more than ten years of age gets up on stage and plays a song by Sérgio Reis on the accordion with surprising skill and sings in a high-pitched, melodious voice. The crowd claps enthusiastically.

The third-to-last attraction of the evening, before the *pagode* music band and the much-awaited sentimental pop duo Claus & Vanessa, is the folk singer Índio Mascarenhas. The man who climbs on to the stage must be in his early sixties. He is wearing black *bombacha* trousers, brown boots, a red handkerchief and a gaucho hat. Even from afar his indigenous features and solid jaw are striking. A diagonal beam of light exposes his deep wrinkles, like scars. There is an abundance of cartilage in his broad, pockmarked nose and ears. His skin is the colour of wood and looks like it is wood. There is no band, just the man and his guitar. Instead of singing he launches into an interminable speech about his journey as an artist.

I play a different kind of music, from my part of the country, Uruguaiana. Round here, you folk listen to music with more of a dancy feel to it. Forgive me but I'm more of a savage. My hat is different to yours, the brim is broader. Across the road from my house is a church, with a bar on one side and a whorehouse on the other, and I feel happy in all three places.

The audience in the square isn't very enthusiastic about Índio Mascarenhas and starts to disperse. Some teenagers start to curse him. But he is drawn to the figure of the singer and moves closer to the stage. The sob story goes on for several minutes and is self-centered and narcissistic, but it is also sincere and filled with a touching *naïveté*. The man claims to be tough but seems fragile and exposed. There is an ancestral purity about him. His repetitive speech doesn't come to any kind of conclusion but he is suddenly satisfied and starts to play. His amped-up guitar is out of tune and the volume is much higher than it should be, which distorts the sound and makes the amplifiers crackle. Índio Mascarenhas never plucks his instrument. He just strums the strings with a quick, percussive beat that never stops while the fingers of his left hand get tangled in chords that barely sustain the melody. His voice is deep and beautiful but nothing extraordinary. It is his attitude and way of playing that are hypnotic. His father used to have a lot of old records of folk music and he grew up listening to gaucho classics, but this rustic, somewhat improvised sound is different.

After finishing his first song, as he receives a mixture of applause and booing from the remaining audience, Mascarenhas looks into the crowd and suddenly gives a start, a look of surprise on his face. The singer squints at him, then opens his eyes wide and raises his eyebrows as if he has just seen a ghost.

After the show he sees Mascarenhas leaning on the counter of a drink stand and walks over. At close range the singer reeks of sour sweat and it makes him feel dizzy. The singer is drinking cachaça out of a plastic cup. His wide-brimmed hat is on the counter and his thick hair, a mixture of black and white, is greasy and stuck to his scalp. By his side is a girl of about thirteen with black hair tied up in a ponytail, big, inquisitive eyes and indigenous features. He is talking to a short man who is also wearing *bombachas* and a brown leather jacket over a long-sleeved shirt. When he sees him approaching, Mascarenhas looks him up and down and goes back to talking to the short man in an attempt to pretend he didn't recognize him earlier. Nevertheless, he stops in front of the singer and greets him. Mascarenhas's reply is accompanied by a gust of bad breath that could knock a man down and his olfactory aggression brings back a detail of his last conversation with his father. The intervening decades apparently haven't diminished the problem at all. To make things worse, Mascarenhas is smoking a hand-rolled cigarette and chewing on handfuls of peanuts from a bowl on the counter.

I really liked your show, he says, holding out his hand.

The singer receives the compliment with his massive, rock-hard hand and smiles.

Thanks, kid.

Without further ado, in his warm voice made hoarse by an incessant regime of boiling-hot maté and hand-rolled cigarettes, Mascarenhas goes straight to the point.

Kid, you look just like a guy I met here in Garopaba many years ago.

Índio's been coming to play here since the 60s, says the short man. This guy here's got stories to tell!

Man, did you give me a fright, Mascarenhas goes on. I thought you were a ghost.

Did you think I was Gaudério?

Mascarenhas frowns and turns his head to one side theatrically. Whoa, he says, and then is unable to say anything else and eats another handful of peanuts.

I'm his grandson. My dad told me about when you met. You guys had a run-in, didn't you?

We did. A run-in, yep, we did. Well, I'll be. It's been a long time. This fair was no more than two stalls and a low stage in the church hall.

The girl tugs on Mascarenhas's sleeve.

What's up, my princess? Hey, this is my daughter. Noeli. She's a bit skittish. She's travelling with her dad, ain't ya? What do you want, my little swamp rose?

The girl asks her dad for some money to go and buy a toffee apple on the other side of the square. The short man jumps in, takes a wad of notes from the pocket of his *bombachas* and gives the girl five reais. She thanks him timidly and leaves holding the notes with both hands.

Go around the outside where there ain't as many people! the singer shouts. The crowd has been growing constantly since the beginning of the *pagode* concert.

What an adorable girl, says the short guy.

The kid's never left Bagé before, says Mascarenhas. She used to complain, All you do is travel, Dad! So come with me, then, I told her. Now she's been to Toledo, Cascavel, Pomerode. Today she swam in the cold ocean and tomorrow we're going to Bom Jesus and then Amaral Ferrador. After that we have to go back 'cause she's got school.

Índio plays all over Brazil, says the short guy. He played in the Amazon at the beginning of the year, didn't you?

Yep.

We used to play together down in Uruguaiana in the 1970s.

Yep. Homero here was my partner and now he's my manager in Garopaba. One of us moved up in life and the other one's still an artist. I'm going to die a poor old folk singer.

You were going to tell me about Gaudério.

Gaudério. So you're his grandson, are you?

Yes.

Mascarenhas takes a deep drag on his cigarette, making sparks fly, then blows the smoke through his mouth and nose.

Well, I'll be darned. After everything I've seen, the devil still manages to give me a fright. Amazing. Will you accept a drink of cachaça?

Of course.

184

He takes a sip of the cloudy yellow cachaça. Índio Mascarenhas pushes a shirtsleeve up over his elbow, revealing brown skin like cured leather. He shows him a sinuous scar of about two or three inches that ends in a dark keloid in the middle of his arm. Talking loudly in order to be heard over the music and subjecting him to pungent doses of the fragrance that his grandfather once defined as the smell of a dead pampas fox's arse, Mascarenhas says that it is where Gaudério's knife nicked him at the fair forty years ago. It was an ugly fight and the only reason someone wasn't killed was because they were quickly pulled apart.

Gaudério was a charming sort who scared folk, if that makes any sense, says the singer. I was young then and stood up for myself when I had to, but your granddad really spooked me even though he was much older than me. We'd had a run-in before at a dance in a town near the border, I'm not sure which, but I think it might have been Sant'Ana do Livramento. He thought I was competing with him for a girl, but it was all in his head. I didn't take much notice of him the first time. I'd seen even wilder horses around, but the second time, here in this square, it was different. He was a different man, he seemed possessed. It's hard to describe. I think he'd lost his mind. What do you know about your granddad, kid?

Not much. Just what my dad told me and what you're telling me now. I never met him. He disappeared before I was born. Apparently he was killed here.

I'll be darned. You really look like him. I think he was taller. But you're the bastard all over again. His spitting image.

He takes the photograph of his granddad out of his wallet and hands it to Mascarenhas. The singer flicks his cigarette butt on to the grass before taking it carefully with the tips of his fingers. A tambourine solo mixes with a noisy round of fireworks.

That's him all right. A bit different, but I'll never forget that face. Different how?

I'm not sure. You meet half a dozen individuals in your life who make such a strong impression on you that you never forget them. People who give you the creeps. It's like there's something evil in them, but it's an evil that's only evil in the eyes of mankind, not in the eyes of nature. I remember another man like that who I met a few years back after I sang at a rodeo in São Jerônimo. Know where that is? Down around Pântano Grande, Charqueadas . . . The day after the rodeo I went to see some steers that a guy there wanted to sell to a friend of mine. The place was quite far out, in the hills. The man there said he had something to show me, a man who lived in a hut at the bottom of the valley. We rode down a craggy slope on horseback and down at the bottom was this hut made of stone and clay, really old and beaten, almost falling apart, and in it lived an old man, hard to say exactly how old, with really wrinkled, dark skin, white hair down to his shoulders like this . . . he lived there without anything. Just a teapot and a dagger. He slept with his pigs. But the man had some money hidden somewhere near by. I don't know if it was a fortune, but it was a lot for the old guy to have buried. He had a son who had his eye on the money, a son who'd gone to the city and was waiting for his old man to die so he could get his hands on the cash, but the guy didn't want anything to do with his son. He said he was a good-for-nothing and never wanted to set eyes on him again. He said the son had threatened to kill him and he'd been waiting for the son of a bitch to show up there for months. He had one of those turn-of-the-century derringers, falling to pieces, this big. He showed us the weapon. Rusted through. You could see it couldn't fire a bullet any more. It looked pretty sad, but the guy slept clutching his pistol, waiting for God knows how long for a showdown with his son, living there like a wild animal. And there was something in his eye, deep in his little eyes, that you could barely see. He had small, closed, deep-set eyes, but they gave off a fury that sent shivers down your spine. And your granddad gave me the same impression. Not the first time we met. Just the second, here in Garopaba. He'd changed. Don't ask me what it was. It's the night of the world. The kind of thing that gives me nightmares.

And do you know what happened to him?

To Gaudério?

To the old man in the hut.

He died hugging his derringer and was eaten by his pigs.

Fuck.

The son found his body but didn't find his money. How about that?

And what about my granddad? Did you ever hear of him again?

I never saw him again after our fight. The next time I came here I thought it was strange that there was no sign of him. It wasn't just that he'd disappeared. No one talked about him. No one remembered. But it couldn't be true 'cause he was well known. People were lying. I don't know why. I asked, Where's that son of a bitch that sliced my arm open? I don't know who you're talking about. Gaudério. Did he leave town? Kick the bucket? I don't know who he is, they all said. When you brought the subject up, folks would suddenly go quiet.

Dad said he was killed at a dance. Someone turned out the lights and they stabbed him to death.

Really?

That's what they told Dad at the time. He'd caused so much trouble they decided to get rid of him. And they did it in such a way that no one would ever know who did it. Maybe that's why to this day everyone pretends that nothing happened.

Makes sense. I didn't know about that. Did you, Homero?

Nope. I've lived here for twenty-five years and it's the first time I've heard this story. But this place is full of legends. There's even the ghost of a whale here.

But that kind of explains it, muses Mascarenhas. That could well be what happened. Especially since –

He stops.

Especially since what?

I don't know if it's worth mentioning because I'm not sure if it happened. But someone must have told me back then or I wouldn't have remembered it just now. It's not the kind of thing you dream up. They said Gaudério had killed a girl.

Really? Someone from here?

I don't know. It was just something that someone said. I understood that it was a young girl. She'd been found dead and people were saying that he'd done it.

How was she killed?

Kid, I told you, I really don't know. I don't even know if it's true. But I don't think your granddad was just a thorn in the side of a few people. He may well have done something bad and had it coming and that's how they settled the score. At the dance. But don't take my word for it. I might be wrong. That's the problem with booze. You get old and can't remember things.

He sits there thinking about it and can't say anything else. He had imagined his grandfather many ways but not as a killer, much less as a psychopath. The idea doesn't sit well in his mind, his body rejects it.

A girl was killed a few weeks ago in Imbituba, he says suddenly. Did you hear about it?

Índio Mascarenhas and Homero look at him, then at one another, then back at him.

188

The guy strangled her. Then he pulled out her eyes and cut off her lips.

The singer looks at his plastic cup and downs the remaining liquid in a single gulp.

His daughter reappears with the toffee apple and two reais in change.

Keep the change, honey, says Homero. If it's OK with your dad.

It's OK. She knows how to handle money. I give her an allowance. There's just one thing missing.

Thank you, she recites.

What about you, Gaudério's grandson? What brought you to these parts?

I decided I wanted to live by the beach after my dad died. I'm a PE teacher. I'm a running and swimming coach.

Nice, nice . . . this is a good place to practise a sport, isn't it? Mascarenhas smiles without a trace of sarcasm. His watery eyes are childlike and transmit a *naïveté* that contrasts with his figure. He doesn't appear to have noticed the sudden change of subject and small talk that has taken over the conversation.

This is paradise, says Homero. If you want quality of life there's no better place.

The sea is the primordial soup, says Índio Mascarenhas in a loud voice. The source of all life. From the sea we come and to the sea we return.

True, he says, to be polite. Then the two men excuse themselves and say goodbye cordially. Homero says he has matters to see to later that night and Mascarenhas, if he understood properly, is going to take his daughter through the crowd on his shoulders to the front of the main stage so she won't miss the start of the Claus & Vanessa concert.

7

A man in a green-and-black camouflage wetsuit is carrying a bag of equipment out to a yellow boat waiting in the shallow water in front of Baú Rock. Another man is sitting in the boat, also wearing a wetsuit, holding the rudder in one hand and a speargun in the other. He heads down the steps to talk to them. They are leaving to go fishing around the reefs a mile offshore. Although he doesn't have a full set of spearfishing equipment, he asks if he can go with them and they say yes. He goes inside and gets his vulcanized rubber flippers, swimming goggles, a packet of cream-filled biscuits and the harpoon that Bonobo gave him. He rubs sunscreen on his face and pulls on his Speedos and an old long-sleeved T-shirt. He locks the windows of the apartment, picks his way over the rocks and wades out to the boat. The man in the camouflage wetsuit says he'll be cold and lends him a waterproof jacket. The motor wakes up, gurgles and begins to rumble, propelling the boat into the green waves. He asks their names and only now discovers that the one in the camouflage wetsuit, with his local accent and round face, is Matias, Cecina's oldest son. The afternoon sky is heavy with clouds and the wind picks up as they draw closer to Vigia Point. Antenor, Matias's friend from Rio Grande do Sul, with a rock-star quiff and long face, accelerates the boat as fast as it can go. It skips over the ramps formed by the waves, slapping the ocean. He grips the safety ropes tightly and wedges his feet between the floor and the inflatable sides of the boat, feeling the cold water pelt his face. Matias offers him a seasickness tablet. He thanks him but refuses. The town disappears into the distance and it becomes increasingly evident why the bay is considered a refuge from the violence of the open sea, why sailors, shoals of fish and whales converge on that stretch of coast seeking a calm that those on the land take for granted. The waves that seemed large from a distance look mountainous on the open sea and a feeling of abandonment sets in as the continent grows distant. Foam sprays up over the rocky faces of the headland with gusto. Soon the reefs are visible. Few rocks actually break the surface but around them is a large area of smaller waves. Black frigatebirds glide overhead with their narrow wings and forked tail feathers, scrutinizing the ocean and diving into the water like arrows.

Antenor reduces the speed and slowly approaches the area of underwater rocks as he and Matias discuss the best place to anchor. Matias points at a place almost inside the reef. The two of them ready their spearguns, pull on flippers, secure knives in their shin supports and put on snorkels. Matias is the first in and swims a short distance towards the reef, towing the signalling buoy behind him, before going under for the first time. It is one minute and fifteen seconds before he surfaces. Then Antenor jumps out of the boat and swims to the left, looking for a different place to fish, then dives down with the help of twenty-pound diving weights attached to his wetsuit. He watches the two men for a few minutes, feeling the rocking of the boat, then puts on his goggles and swimming flippers, much shorter than the ones used for diving, takes off his shirt, gets his speargun and slips into the cold sea.

When he is close to the rocks he holds his breath, dives under and hears the tremulous symphony of the shellfish, a sound he has heard before when swimming near rocks on some beaches, but never with this intensity. The clattering of the shellfish is frightening, as if billions of pinchers or teeth are chattering and reverberating in hollow caverns. His swimming goggles allow him to see only the closest rocks. The clamour ceases entirely when he raises his head out of the water and not even the murmuring of the ocean and wind disrupt the sudden impression of silence. Two distinct worlds.

In the murky seascape of rocks and corals he sees shellfish and some fish he can't identify. No sign of shoals of fish, much less groupers, which is what they were hoping to find. Matias had told him to look in holes and crevices, where they like to rest. Most groupers nowadays weigh about five pounds, sometimes ten, with a lot of luck fifteen. More than twenty is a trophy. Nothing compared to what his granddad must have caught several decades earlier, when they often weighed sixty or seventy pounds. He dives down a dozen times but doesn't see any holes or caves or groupers. He doesn't see anything that deserves to be the target of a speargun.

He returns to the boat and when he comes up he sees a storm approaching from the south, covering the hills of Ibiraquera and Rosa Beach. Matias and Antenor are still underwater, among the rocks. Their yellow buoys vanish and reappear in the rise and fall of the waves. They don't seem concerned about the leaden clouds that are drawing near, or the wind that is whistling louder and louder. They're the experts. He leaves the speargun in the bottom of the boat and dives down again. He tries to measure the depth at that point. He descends until his ears hurt from the pressure and he can see large yellow rocks at the bottom. They must be some fifteen to twenty feet below the surface. He swims back to the reef. At some points the rocks almost reach the surface and he is able to stand on them.

According to his dad, his granddad was able to hold his breath for three or four minutes, or even more. Another diver had died of a pulmonary embolism trying to match his time. He dives under, swims around the rocks a little, checking the time on his watch, and emerges only when he starts to feel the terrifying throbbing behind his eyes that is brought on by a lack of oxygen. One minute and five seconds. On his next attempt he sees a purple octopus dragging itself along the bottom, stirring up a small cloud of sand before hiding under a rock. The duration of this dive is only forty-eight seconds. He decides to rest for a moment. The wind churns the waves. On his third attempt, he stays down for one minute and six seconds and decides to call it a day. He doesn't have his granddad's lungs.

He returns to the boat, puts on the waterproof jacket in a useless attempt to warm up a little and tries to measure how long his companions are able to hold their breath. One of Matias's dives lasts one minute and forty seconds. He hasn't been there long when Antenor swims back to the boat and climbs in with difficulty. When he goes to help him he sees that his snorkelling mask is full of blood. Antenor takes off the mask and blood streams down his face and neck.

I've burst something, he says, holding his nose. Fuck, it hurts like shit. I think I've got sinusitis.

The bleeding stops and Antenor starts feeling nauseous.

Fuck, fuck, he stammers. I don't feel well.

He opens his packet of strawberry-cream-filled biscuits and offers some to Antenor. Large waves toss the boat about violently. The temperature has plummeted at least ten degrees and the entire horizon has disappeared in the approaching storm. The wind roars and flings fans of spray into the air. The birds are all long gone. Antenor glances uneasily towards the reef.

Matias found a big grouper in a hole and won't come back until he's got it. I know him.

But soon, to their relief, Matias is swimming towards the boat. After climbing in, he tugs on a rope and pulls two copper-coloured groupers out of the water, a large one weighing some eighteen pounds, and a small one of about five and a half. He poses holding the larger of the two by its enormous, scary-looking jaws with both hands and Antenor takes a photograph. The camera's flash lights up the bright red interior of its mouth and rings of sharp little teeth. It starts to rain. Matias pulls a tube of condensed milk out of his bag and starts eating the sugary goo. Antenor starts the motor and the boat tears off towards the bay, fleeing the storm.

A sprint triathlon makes for a lively morning on the third Saturday in June. The sun is shining but a bad-tempered north-easterly makes things tough for the athletes. The main avenue has been cordoned off for the cyclists and runners and in the choppy sea two red buoys mark the triangular swimming circuit. The bicycles are lined up in the transition zone, which has been set up on a cross street a block from the seaside boulevard. Coaches, families, friends and residents form a crowd behind the yellow tape on the pavements of the main avenue to cheer the competitors on. Two of his running students, Sara and Denise, have registered in relay teams for the five-kilometre run. Sara's shins no longer hurt and her friend Denise has visibly lost weight and is running a nine-minute mile, which is considerable progress since her first few runs on the beach. He is going to do the seven-hundred-and-fifty-metre swim for Sara's team. On the bicycle is Douglas, Sara's husband, a cordial man of few words, some ten years older than his wife, hairy and half bald. Douglas has a strong accent from the north zone of Porto Alegre and stays fit by surfing regularly all year round and riding his sprint bike to Highway BR-101 on Sunday mornings.

He knows some of the professional competitors and his most effusive reunion is with Pedro, sponsored by Paquetá Esportes, who can often be seen collecting prizes on podiums and is ranked eleventh in the country. The night before, at the technical meeting in the Hotel Garopaba dining room, the first thing that Pedro asked him was if he was sick. He thought his old training partner looked a little too thin and haggard, not to mention the unruly beard. He assured him he was in good health and, as for the beard, well, he'd got sick of his own face and was conducting an experiment. Pedro got the joke and laughed. They gave each other a tight hug. Pedro had walked over and said, Hi, it's Pedro. The two of them had great respect for one another. They had spent hundreds of hours together running, riding and swimming long distances, encouraging and distracting each other, one setting a faster pace for the other, trying to keep up with the other one's pace, sharing the semi-meditative mental state of prolonged exercise. Pedro is the same age as him, thirty-four, but he knows they both look a little older than that. Too much effort, too much sun, too many free radicals in the blood, along with all the physical and emotional problems that everyone else has and which you carry in the body as glaring or subtle marks, sometimes extremely subtle or even invisible, and even then in some way perceptible from the outside. The body is its own time capsule and its journey is always somewhat public, no matter how hard you try to cover it or hide it behind make-up.

About twenty minutes before the race starts officials communicate that the water is full of jellyfish. The use of wetsuits is allowed at the last minute and the swimmers race to get theirs. When the start gun goes off the athletes run through the sand, leap over the first few waves, dive in and discover that they will need to forge a path through an enormous soup of gelatinous globules the size of footballs. Those who didn't bring wetsuits or didn't have time to get them leave the water with stings. One woman gets a tentacle right in the face and is pulled out of the water screaming by the referees in kayaks.

Pedro is the first out of the water that morning. He is third. Douglas rides well but is no match for the better-trained cyclists and loses part of the team's initial advantage during the twenty-kilometre ride. Sara almost can't finish the race but he runs the last half-mile by her side and she crosses the finish line all red and out of breath. Even so, they place fourth in the relay, right in the middle of the seven teams signed up. An encouraging result. Afterwards both amateur and professional athletes float along smiling, high on a mixture of tiredness, euphoria and relaxation.

Sara and Douglas decide to throw a barbecue for their friends and acquaintances who also entered the race. At Sara's request, he promises to pitch in with his much-advertised seasoned flank steak, *matambre*. The delicacy requires some preparation. Chillies, sweet marjoram, thyme, lime juice, rock salt and at least an hour and a half on the barbecue, rolled up in tinfoil. Douglas climbs on to his bike and rides home on a mission to get the fire started and put the beer on ice. Sara insists on taking him by car to the supermarket to buy the meat and the seasonings, but he says he needs to go home first to shower and change his clothes. She says she'll drive him there too. No matter how many times he repeats that it isn't necessary, she pretends not to hear him. Are we a team or not?

When they walk into his apartment, Sara does what he felt was coming and did nothing to stop. He has barely shut the door when she takes off her running shoes and tracksuit bottoms and stands there in her blue shorts with her hands on her jacket, as if she is about to unzip it.

Whoa. Sara. Hang on.

Fuck me.

I can't.

You can't or you don't want to?

I can't.

Of course you can, she says, walking over to him. Look at me.

He looks.

You can, OK? She pushes him lightly making him fall into a sitting position on the hard yellow sofa. She is about to mount him but he holds her by the waist to stop her.

You'll regret it.

No I won't.

But I will.

You definitely won't.

People walk down the path outside the closed shutters. He presses a finger to his lips asking her to be quiet.

Anyone you know?

I don't know. But everyone sees everything here.

Don't be paranoid.

She bends her head towards him and whispers.

It'll just be once. I've never done this before.

He remains sitting, she remains standing. Her thighs, speckled like chocolate-chip ice cream, try to move forward. She runs one of her hands down from her waist to her leg and raises it to place her foot on the sofa. Her smell floods the dark, moist apartment. He can feel the pulsing of their bodies. Tiny tremors.

Better not.

Well, what are you going to do with that bulge there?

He leans his forehead against the waistband of her shorts and sighs.

That's it, she says.

His mobile phone starts to ring.

Don't answer it.

On the fourth ring he slowly pushes her away and picks up the phone. It is Gonçalo.

Hey, buddy. How's life on the beach?

All good, Gonça. How are things there?

Same old circus as always. Sorry to keep you waiting but I've been swamped and only managed to follow up on that matter in the last few days. I talked to some people in the civil police and the Santa Catarina state court. There's no way you'll find the inquest, if there ever was one. Forget it.

Fuck.

He goes to the window and unlocks the shutters.

However –

Gonçalo makes a dramatic pause. He opens the shutters a crack and sees the sunny beach.

– I consulted the old payrolls and found the name of the police chief who probably went to Garopaba to look into the crime. I did some research on the guy and discovered two things.

He glances over his shoulder. Sara is sitting cross-legged on the sofa, almost in a position of meditation, staring at the sandy-coloured floor tiles with a vague expression. She looks like a robot that has been switched off.

What?

First, the guy's still alive. Second, I know where he lives. In Pato Branco.

Is that here in Santa Catarina?

In Paraná. In the west of the state. Near the border of Santa Catarina. His name is Zenão Bonato. He's a partner in a private security company called Commando. I hope that's a reference to that Schwarzenegger movie. Give him my regards if it is.

But how do I find him?

I've got the company's address and phone number here.

Hold on. Let me get a pen.

He rummages through the wicker basket on the counter for a pen and piece of paper to write on. He still has a hard-on and Sara watches his movements with the same empty expression on her face.

OK, what is it?

He writes down the former police chief's name, address and phone number on a pamphlet for an adventure tour operator specializing in whale watching.

Thanks, Gonça. I can handle it from here.

No problem. I'm here if you need me. Are you busy?

No, why?

Dunno. Are you OK?

I'm great.

Good to hear. OK then. I've got an article to write here. I hope the info's useful. Let me know how you get on.

Will do. See ya.

As soon as he hangs up Sara comes to life again and glares at him with her slanting eyes. She looks like a patient who has been forgotten for hours in a doctor's waiting room.

That was a friend of mine from Porto Alegre.

She doesn't say anything.

Want a glass of water?

No.

She gets up and walks over to him. She puts her face very close, with her nose touching his cheek.

I'm going to have a shower now.

He moves her backwards and to one side with a deliberately mechanical gesture, as if repositioning a mannequin.

Be quick then, she says, and let's go and buy this fucking flank steak, or rump or whatever it is.

Matambre.

He takes a step towards the bathroom but stops that very second, turns and goes to close the shutters, extinguishing the beam of sunlight illuminating the room. When he turns around again Sara is moving in and only stops when her body is flush against his. Fuck it. He has allowed himself to be cornered and now he needs to act accordingly. Sara wraps her arms around his neck. He wedges his hands under her jacket and runs his palms up her warm belly, sticky with sweat. He works his fingers under her top and fondles her small breasts. Sara kisses him timidly. It is more a series of little pecks than a real kiss, not at all the eager kiss that he was expecting, given the circumstances. It's her way of kissing. Half the fun of it is that things are never exactly as you imagine. She kneels and sucks his cock. He holds her by the pony-tail. She stops for a moment and says, Just today, OK? I promise.

Before catching the bus to Florianópolis he stops by the veterinary clinic. Greice is in a good mood and greets him with a kiss on the cheek. He asks how Jander is and she says he is great. What lovely weather we've been having. Come and see your pup. The kennel is behind the clinic and has a dozen cement compartments with barred fronts. Some are open at the top and this is where the animals that need more intensive care are kept. Beta is in one of these, lying on her side on a blanket. There are two small bowls containing water and dog food and the rest of the floor is covered with newspaper. As soon as she sees or smells him she starts trying to move. One of her front paws is bandaged. Parts of her fur have been shaved and are covered with plasters and crusty bits of healing flesh. She has lost a piece of one ear. Greice says her spine wasn't fractured. It was swelling around the spinal cord. She opens the barred door and strokes Beta. Look at this. Greice carefully picks her up and sets her on her paws. Beta stands there but doesn't move.

Her movement's slowly coming back. I still can't say if she'll be able to walk normally. We'll have to see how she goes. But she's a fighter, your dog. I didn't expect this. It's a tough breed.

Greice steps aside and he enters the small space, crouches down and strokes Beta's neck while murmuring in her ear. She's going to walk again, aren't you? I have to make a short trip but I'll be back the day after tomorrow and I'll come and visit you every day, OK?

The vet lays Beta down again.

How much longer will she need to stay here?

About two weeks. At least.

He smiles to himself several times during the ninety-minute bus trip to Florianópolis, thinking about how things go well when you least expect them to. Beta is able to stand. Sara has still been coming to their morning workouts trying hard to act as if nothing happened. The water has been so warm that he has been swimming in just his Speedos. His more dedicated students haven't abandoned the pool even though winter is coming and they are swimming better and better. When he is out and about, he is greeted and waved at by people he doesn't recognize and whenever he can he approaches them and strikes up a conversation until he is able to tell who they are. Nights pass in the blink of an eye and are restorative. The day smells of ozone and the salty sea breeze. The green of the vegetation pulsates on the slopes of the Serra do Mar Range and the mountaintops framed by the bus windows speak of the mystery of unspoiled places. The vibration of the bus is calming and the landscape sliding past on the other side of the glass makes him think about the obvious things that one never thinks about. How it is incredible that all the things around him are actually there. That he is there. That he can perceive them. He feels as if he is stationary and moving at the same time and remembers his parents telling him how they used to drive him around in the car to get him to sleep when he was a baby. Across the aisle, a few seats ahead of his, a girl is asleep leaning against her boyfriend with her foot stretched out in the middle of the aisle and he can see her turquoise-painted toenails, a Mayan sun tattoo on her ankle, the boyfriend's hand caressing the caramel-coloured skin of her calf. The whole composition reminds him of something he once had and which he isn't sure if he misses. He does and he doesn't at the same time. It is less the melancholy memory of an absence and more the comforting evidence that it exists and is still part of the world.

During his two-hour wait at the bus station in Florianópolis he has dinner at a coffee shop, explores the streets adjacent to the bus station on foot and goes to a news-stand to get something to read. A man with a shocking appearance approaches the news-stand at the same time as he does. His whole head is enlarged due to some deformity or elephantiasis, especially his jaw, which is four or five times bigger than that of a normal man. He is fair-haired and is wearing a pair of jeans and a colourfully striped wool jumper. The man peruses the magazines on the stand, taking casual steps from side to side with his hands clasped behind his back in a restful position, seemingly unaware of his effect on the attendant and passersby, who glance away as soon as they set eyes on him. He takes a few good looks at the man's deformed face, while pretending to choose a magazine. Then he picks up the triathlon magazine he intended to buy from the outset, pays and returns to the bus-station waiting area, trying to retain the man's features in his memory for as long as possible, but they slip away as they always do.

Once he is settled in his bus seat, he takes a look at the map of downtown Pato Branco that he printed out from Google Maps at the internet café in Garopaba. The addresses of Zenão Bonato and the hotel that was recommended by the former police chief himself are written in the margins with a few notes to himself. He got the man's mobile number from his security company. Zenão agreed to talk to him without asking many questions. I think I know what you're talking about, he said in a hoarse voice on the telephone. If you really want to come here, come. I'll tell you what I can remember.

The bus makes a lot of stops. He sleeps for much of the twelve-hour ride to Pato Branco, listening to music at a low volume on earphones connected to his phone. He wakes up every time the bus parks in a small town in western Santa Catarina to drop off and pick up passengers. He gets out to go to the bathroom and stretch his legs. He eats some of the worst highway-diner food of his life and dreams about an icy-cold can of Coke until the next stop. It is dawn when he wakes instinctively at the entrance to the town, feeling the curves and bumpy terrain. It is much colder here, due to the distance from the coast and the altitude. It can't be any more than fifty degrees. He opens his backpack with cold hands to pull out his jacket. Fields covered with veils of dew and tiny sleeping farmhouses give way to houses with verandas that increase in density until suddenly, to his surprise, the bus is in an urban centre with wide avenues, shopping arcades and malls. He takes a taxi from the bus station to the hotel. The car climbs steep streets paved with impeccable tarmac. When the young receptionist hands him the key to his room she says ceremoniously that his password is ninety-eight.

What password?

For the sports channel, sir.

He calls Zenão Bonato from the hotel room. He says he'll be busy all day and asks if he doesn't mind postponing their meeting until quite late, perhaps around midnight. He finds it odd but says it isn't a problem. Zenão asks him to meet him at a place called Deliryu's. He jots down the address with the hotel pen and notepad on the bedside table. He thinks it must be the name of a brothel but doesn't have time to ask because Zenão quickly says goodbye and ends the call.

He turns on the TV and types ninety-eight on the control. It's a porn film with a story and right now it's in the story part. He waits for it to get to the interesting bit and jerks off quickly. Then he takes a twenty-minute shower.

His watch says ten o'clock in the morning. He gets dressed, leaves the hotel, walks down a few steep streets and arrives at a large avenue with a wide planted area in the middle that forms an attractive, well-kept square. He doesn't remember seeing such a clean, organized town before. The side streets are almost deserted but the avenues are busy. The town centre is full of modern buildings with more than ten storeys but the flower beds and gardens are like those of a country town. The air smells of carbon monoxide and wet earth. The women are at once both slender and strong. He withdraws some money at an ATM, stops at an internet café to check his emails and walks in the cold wind and midday sun until he is tired. He has a late lunch at an all-you-can-eat buffet and eats so much that he can barely walk. He drags himself back to the hotel, lies on the bed with the heating turned up as high as it can go and the TV on channel ninety-eight, and alternates between snoozing and anticlimactic sessions of self-stimulation. Late in the afternoon he goes out again, heads down to the avenue and walks through the square a little until he finds a café with large windows and a super-sized TV in the outside area. A few spectators are already gathering, some wearing Grêmio jerseys. He enters and asks if they are going to show the Grêmio game. A muscular waiter in a black apron and hat with the name of the establishment written on them says yes. He orders a coffee. The game begins and in the next two hours he drinks a few draught beers and eats a serving of French fries. Atlético Paranaense beats Grêmio 3–0. His teeth are chattering and the thermometer in the square says that it is fifty-two degrees. He sets off walking through the town again, passing in front of bars full of university students, entire blocks without a soul in sight and petrol stations frequented by young people on their way to parties and taxi drivers without customers. It is almost midnight when he returns to the hotel. He doesn't even go up to his room. He asks the tall young man at reception to call him a cab. He shows him the address and asks if he knows the place. The receptionist presses his lips together and raises his eyebrows.

Hmm.

What?

Who told you to go there?

I have a business meeting with someone. He was the one who gave me the address.

Well, if he told you to go there . . . but be careful.

Why?

Mafia. The sort you don't mess with. And the girls there are quick. Real quick. They make off with your money and you don't even know what happened. My dad used to say we should steer clear of three things in life: fast women, slow horses and engineers. I'm giving you the same advice. Just the other day two guests came back early in the morning in a car with the bouncer of the place. With a gun to their heads. They'd spent eighteen hundred reais and didn't have enough cash on them. They'd thought they were going to spend five hundred each and the numbskulls weren't carrying credit cards. They had to drive around with a gun in their ear until six in the morning to withdraw the rest at an ATM.

What a mess.

They'll kill you if they have to. Mafia. Have a good think if you really want to go there.

I just need to talk to the guy. I don't intend to hang around there.

The receptionist makes a face as if to say 'I warned you', holds up the palms of his hands and returns the paper with the address on it. The taxi pulls up at the entrance to the hotel. Inside it smells of wool and the windows are fogged up. The elderly man in a beret behind the steering wheel reacts as if he already knew his passenger's destination.

It's one of the best places around. I can pick you up if you need me to. Here's my card. But be warned. Don't spend what you haven't got.

The blinking neon of Deliryu's Nightclub is a few miles out of town on high ground just off the highway along a gravel driveway. The square, windowless building is surrounded by a pine plantation. The bouncer, a friendly, hulking bald guy in a black suit, weighing some four hundred pounds, bows ceremoniously and informs him that the cover charge is forty reais. He is given a pay card with his name at the top and he enters. The place looks much bigger on the inside than it did from the outside and is almost empty. At the back are the bathrooms and a small stage with a metal post. The floor is swept by colourful circles from a spinning spotlight in the middle of the ceiling and green light beams coming from another mechanism above the stage, which picks out the silhouettes of the hookers, who are in two small groups at the back of the club, leaning on the wall or lounging on sofas, almost hidden in the dim light. Another bouncer, of average stature, wearing jeans and a leather jacket, greets him inside. His grey hair is slicked back with some kind of shiny gel or grease. There are two hookers leaning against the bar and he can see these ones well: a thin, grumpy-looking blonde, who tries to smile when she sees him, and a tall brunette with very white skin and a slightly gothic look, who is talking to a young waiter with a goatee. She is wearing black knee-high boots with metal buckles and is standing on one leg, with the other perched on the round stool. To his right, in an area which has half a dozen booths with tables and sofas, is the only other client in the place, an older man accompanied by a young woman. It can only be Zenão Bonato.

He walks over and introduces himself. Zenão, a mulatto who appears to be about sixty, although he is older than that, motions for him to sit on the adjacent sofa. He looks like a former athlete, someone who has had to maintain a considerable amount of muscle mass his whole life, like a boxer or rower. He is wearing dress trousers, good shoes and a wool blazer. A cigarillo is burning between his fingers and the smoke from his last few puffs forms a dome that spreads lazily around the three of them.

The young woman's legs are draped over her client's. Her black tube dress barely passes her waist and he can see her red knickers. Her long, straight hair looks discoloured and seems to give off a white light. In fact her whole head emanates a slightly ghostly light. He strains to see her better. She is albino.

Guess what her name is? asks Zenão, noting his interest. Ivory! A guttural laugh escapes the old man's throat in long bursts that end in a smoker's wheeze and start up again with full force. It takes some time. While he tries to stop laughing he pours himself another generous shot from the bottle of Natu Nobilis on the table. Ivory mixes a little of the same whisky with an energy drink in her tall glass, sips it with her colourless lips and then analyses it with a pair of grey eyes almost camouflaged in her un-made-up face.

Why did you want to meet me here?

I'm among friends here.

I figured that.

Because I don't know you and I'm not really sure why you wanted to come and see me in person. You didn't strike me as dangerous, but at my age, in my line of work . . . a guy calls you wanting to know about an old case . . . you know how it is.

I can imagine. Don't worry.

And I might as well take the opportunity and have some fun, right? These folks owe me so many favours that I can hide the hedge-hog for free until I die.

While Zenão has another long fit of laughter he notices one of the hookers at the back of the club heading towards their table. She sits next to him without touching him. She is a brunette with large thighs, wet hair and lips cracked with cold. She is drenched in perfume and appears to have stepped out of the shower moments earlier.

Can I keep you company?

I'm just here to have a quick chat with my friend here.

But what fun is that if you're alone? What's your name?

It takes him a few minutes to get rid of her.

Pick one, says Zenão.

What?

Pick one and call her over to sit here. They're going to keep com-ing one by one and when they've all tried they're going to start again. The house is empty.

The waiter sees him signal and comes over to the table.

Ask the girl in boots over at the bar to come here. And I'd like a can of beer.

I'm on it.

The *forró* song that is playing gives way to a Roxette song that he recognizes from his tender youth. He has to raise his voice to be heard and he and Zenão lean in towards one another, sandwiching the albino girl between them. She nibbles on Zenão's ear and then pulls her white hair over her shoulder and occupies herself inspecting it for split ends. Zenão confirms that he was the police chief in Laguna in 1969.

Do you remember a case where a man was stabbed to death in Garopaba at the end of that year? A man who was known as Gaudério?

A female voice sings 'Listen to your heaaart' in his ear and the weight of a body shakes the seat cushion on the sofa. The smell of cinnamon chewing gum reaches his nostrils.

I was hoping you'd call me.

I like your boots. What's your name?

Honey.

Your real name.

That's something you don't ask, handsome.

He stares into her eyes. Blue irises, heavy mascara. Blood-red lipstick. A small mole on her left cheekbone. It is all he can make out in the half-light.

It's Andreia.

Have a seat, Andreia. I'll talk to you properly in a minute. I just need to finish talking to my friend here.

Can I order a drink?

What would you like?

Wine.

Go ahead and order one.

Zenão gives him a little slap on the knee.

Doesn't she look a bit like a young Anjelica Huston?

Who?

Your girl there.

She looks like who?

Anjelica Huston. The actress. You know?

He doesn't but he looks at Andreia and pretends to be considering it.

I think she does a bit. But anyway. At the end of '69.

I remember that story about the guy who was killed in Garopaba. It was one of the weirdest cases I'd ever come across, which is probably why the investigations didn't get very far.

Weird why?

Because there was no body.

My dad told me the same thing. That when he got there he couldn't find out where they'd buried my granddad. There was a beggar's grave with grass growing over it. It didn't look recent.

Come again? Your dad? What are you talking about?

His name was Hélio. He was the one who told me the story.

Ah, his son. From Porto Alegre. That's right, we managed to track him down a few days later. He came. Blond hair, smoked like a chimney.

That's him.

I remember him. But anyway. The mystery is that there was no body when I got there.

Who'd they bury then?

Dunno. Listen. I got a tip-off by telegraph. There were no phones in Garopaba back then. I think they only got phone lines in the mid-70s. Sometimes they'd call the station in Laguna and ask us to come and investigate more serious crimes in the region. Garopaba had been a separate municipality since the early 60s. The municipalities had their own police commissioners, but it was all a bit primitive. I saw the lock-up once, a little guard post with iron bars where they'd hold their criminals. It was near the parish church. The guy would spend a day in the lock-up and then he'd have to pull weeds in the square in the presence of the police chief or officer. I was called in a few times to resolve things there. Murders, violent rapes, arson.

Arson?

Garopaba has a long tradition of arson.

Were there many murders? One local told me no one had ever been killed in Garopaba.

People are killed everywhere. There were lots of problems when the gauchos started moving there. There was an invasion of them overnight. They'd come to camp, surf. Hippies. A lot of them stayed on and the place was overrun with them. They started to get involved in money, property, power. There was even a gaucho killer. His name was Corporal Freitas. He was kept in work for many years until someone took him out too. He was a walking archive.

Andreia nuzzles up to him.

Move closer.

Her breath now smells of sweet wine.

Put your hand on my leg.

He obeys and feels her fishnet tights. Her cold thighs pin his fingers.

So my granddad wasn't the only one.

Far from it. But your granddad's story was different. We got a telegram on a Monday saying a man had been killed the night before. We didn't even get wind of most crimes. There was a lot of local justice. There were hardly any police in the region and people took matters into their own hands. I left Laguna by car on the Tuesday morning. Rain pissing down. There was lightning on the highway, a huge owl hit my windscreen and cracked the glass, and then there was that dirt road, which was atrocious in those days. I arrived in Garopaba town centre after noon and went to talk to people. First they told me that nothing had happened. The town's only policeman didn't know what was going on and I started to realize that the person who'd sent the telegram had done so of their own initiative. Maybe even in secret. No one was expecting a police chief to show up there. But I let them know who was boss and they saw that they weren't going to get rid of me that easily and told me the story about the lights going out at the dance. When they came on again the guy was dead. Gaudério. No suspect, of course. There wasn't a trace of blood in the hall by the time I got there, or the murder weapon, nothing. The body had disappeared. I spent the day trying to find out what I could but there wasn't much to be done. Night fell and I was about to leave when a woman came to talk to me and said she'd sent the telegram.

Who was she?

If I understood right she was your granddad's girlfriend. A local girl, of Azorian descent, quite young, about twenty years old. She hadn't gone to the dance because she'd had stomach cramps but someone had gone to tell her about the commotion in the town and she'd run to the hall to see what had happened. The scene she described didn't make sense. The hall was empty but there was a huge pool of blood on the ground and signs of a fight, overturned tables and chairs, broken glasses. She said there were women crying in the street, with children fanning them. All she understood was that Gaudério had been killed. She was told not to get involved and they dragged her back home.

What was her name?

I forget. Soraia? Sabrina? I think it started with an *S*. But it's a guess. I'm not sure, it's been a long time. She must have loved your granddad. To contact a police chief under those circumstances. I promised her that I'd look for his body. I ordered a search over the next few days and nothing was found. I closed the case.

My dad said there was a grave in the cemetery.

Yes. A few days after wrapping up the case I found your dad because the girl knew he lived in Porto Alegre and that his family was from a small town, Taquara, I think. Was that it? He went to Garopaba and called me that afternoon saying his dad was buried in the cemetery. It can't be, I said. We didn't find a body. Your people didn't, he said, but apparently someone here did. He's in a pauper's grave. I didn't know. I had a look myself some time later and there really was a grave there that people said was Gaudério's. It was a lie, of course. They had to show the man's son something. Truth is, a body was never found. They must have dumped it way out at sea.

Something about this story doesn't gel.

Nothing does. I think there's some mystery there that no one'll ever know. When I got there to investigate the crime it made a really strong impression on me. There was a sinister atmosphere about the place. The locals were nervous. Another thing that the girl who sent the telegram said was that when she got to the hall the people had already left and they were all on the beach, about a hundred yards from there, staring out to sea. I noticed the same thing over the next few days. It wasn't as if they were waiting for a boat or looking for a school of fish, but as if the ocean had turned against them. As if they suddenly wished it wasn't there.

That doesn't make sense.

It doesn't.

Wasn't there an inquiry?

No.

But –

He feels confused and doesn't really know what to ask.

Can I order some more wine? asks Andreia. She massages his neck and he feels her long nails on his skin.

Have you already finished the bottle?

Almost, sexy.

Give me a sip.

She slides the glass over to him and plunges her hand between his legs. The wine is syrupy-sweet and the glass smells of cigarette smoke.

I'm going to order one more, OK? she says as she signals to the waiter.

Don't drink that rotgut, son. Have some of my whisky.

Zenão asks the waiter for another glass. It arrives in an instant with three ice cubes and the former police chief fills it halfway. They clink glasses and he takes a sip of whisky. Meanwhile, the albino girl gets up, climbs over his legs and sits next to Andreia. They start to whisper.

There's something else I want to ask you. I heard there was a rumour going around at the time that Gaudério had killed a girl.

The waiter leaves a new bottle of wine on the table. Zenão answers by raising his head and repositioning himself on the sofa, giving the impression that the conversation has arrived where he wanted it to.

It's true. That was one of the things that came up during my interrogations. You didn't know your granddad, did you? If there was one thing that was clear to me it was that he was a troublemaker. There was an unsolved murder of a girl some months before he was killed. I think the community suspected your granddad and they may have finished him off because of it. Whether it was him or not is another kettle of fish.

Zenão Bonato looks at him sternly.

Understand, son? Sorry, he was your granddad and it can't be easy to hear these things. But that's what happened. I turned a blind eye and went home.

No, it's OK. I'm not even sure why I'm digging all this shit up.

He looks at his glass of whisky and takes a big sip.

But it sucks not being sure about anything. Whether he was a murderer or just an inoffensive brawler. Whether he's in that cemetery or not.

It's normal to want to know. But no one will ever be able to tell you what really happened to him. Some people disappear from this life without saying how or where they're going. They leave a bunch of clues, but they're all false.

Do you think he might have still been alive?

Zenão's eyes spark.

He might have. He might still be. Imagine! But speculation won't get us anywhere.

Zenão gets up slowly, fills both of their glasses again and walks away with a posture that betrays his age, his knees slightly flexed, his back a little hunched. He walks three paces and turns around.

You know how much those bottles of wine cost, don't you?

No. How much?

A hundred and fifty. I'm going to take a piss. Be right back.

He picks up the bottle and examines the label. The wine is called Coração.

So, sexy. Would you like to go somewhere a bit more private?

I can't. I've just spent all my money on wine.

But they take credit cards here.

I'm already going to have to put this on my credit card. And I need everything I've got left to pay the vet's bill, 'cause my dog was run over.

He throws back the rest of his glass of whisky and chews on an ice cube. He is drunk. She isn't moved by the dog story. It doesn't even register with her.

What do you do?

Me? I'm a PE teacher. And a triathlete.

Hmm, an athlete.

Yep. I swim, ride and run. Fuck, that sucks.

He laughs to himself.

Why do you say that? I think it's amazing.

No, that's not what sucks. It's nothing. Ignore me. I have to go.

I love strong men.

He starts to laugh again. He feels a bit desperate, a bit crazy.

How many tattoos do you have, Andreia?

Nine. This one here on my leg is a Chinese or Japanese ideogram that means peace and health, she says unzipping one of her boots halfway. These here, she says, lifting up her top to reveal her pelvis, are roses.

What do the roses stand for?

Nothing. They're just flowers.

What about that one on your shoulder?

It's a Harley-Davidson on a highway. I love motorbikes. Have you ever done a road trip on a bike?

He examines the tattoo at close range but can't understand the drawing.

Where's the bike?

Here, look, she says, twisting her neck around, pointing and speaking as if she were dealing with a child, the motorbike on the highway. There's a curve in the highway. And there's a sign with a skull on it.

Aaah. Now I see it.

And there's this one.

She turns her back to him and lifts up her top again. Written across the small of her back in big letters is: GOD IS DEAD.

That's a strange tattoo.

Cool, isn't it? I love Nietzsche.

Who's Nietzsche again?

A philosopher. He had a huge moustache. A friend of mine posted the line on her Facebook page and I liked it. I read one of his books. *Beyond Good and Evil.*

Never read it.

Wanna hit the bedroom, athlete?

How much is it?

A hundred and fifty.

You cost the same as the wine? That's not right.

She doesn't say anything.

You should cost more than the wine. That's not right.

Zenão Bonato comes back with a cigarillo between his teeth and holds out his hand to the albino girl. Let's have some fun, blondie. Ivory also gets up and a beam of light strikes her head. Her eyelashes are yellow and where her hair is parted he sees that her scalp is a pinkish colour. Then Zenão holds out his other hand. He stands and shakes it.

I don't know if I've been much help.

You have. Thanks for your time.

Careful with the girl. Want a Viagra?

Not today.

Zenão chortles with laughter. His chortling is broken here and there by a swine-like snort, followed by a terrifying wheeze at the end. When he has recovered Zenão leaves with the albino girl in tow and disappears through a door next to the bar where a woman writes something down, hands the girl a key and lets them into a corridor lined with rooms.

He decides to leave too. He pats his wallet in his back pocket. Near the door Andreia wraps her arms around him and pouts. He falls into her blue eyes in a way that he knows is imprudent but the moment of surrender brings him a sense of calm that only he knows how much he needs. She has an almost invisible down on her cheeks. The fine lines that start in the corners of her eyes like river deltas merely emphasize her youth.

I like you, girl.

I've got other tattoos in places that I can only show you without my clothes on.

I like your mole.

She covers her cheek with her fingers as if she is ashamed of it and perhaps she really is. Then she kisses him. Then hugs him. The curve of her white neck gives off a sharp odour of white wine. A farmer of about fifty, wearing a straw hat, walks in. Then two well-dressed young men. They wave at everyone with familiarity. The place gets going late. Girls appear from the back of the dark nightclub and circle around them, two clinging to each man. Andreia asks where he lives and if she is going to see him again. He asks for her phone number but she says she can't give it to him. He offers to give her his own phone number and tells her to call him if she wants to visit the coast. She goes to the bar to get a pen. The bouncer in the leather jacket runs a hand through his slicked-back grey hair and says, That's love. She comes back, writes down his phone number and address, folds the paper and places it in the pocket of her shorts.

Is this your real phone number?

Yep. But you're not going to call me, are you, Andreia?*

---

* 23 June 2008. Worst hangover ever. My driving test is today. [. . .] Before he left I said I was going to show him something that no one could see and took him into the corridor to the dressing room to show him the girls' mural. The girls hang things on it that make them remember why they are working there. There are photos of their kids, a key ring from New York, a lottery ticket. Márcia wants to be an air hostess, so she put a picture of a plane there. Some things are hard to understand: a woman's leather glove, a silver ring with a skull on it, and there's one girl who always pins up a blue butterfly and it stays there till it's all dry and then she always replaces it with another one exactly the same. I don't know where she gets them. I told him that looking at the mural every day helps us feel a little better. Then he asked what my thing was and I was so

Yes I am, but I don't want you to leave now.

She hugs him again. The friendly giant in the suit is watching from the door and says, I've never seen her like that.

Do you think I'm pretty?

Yes.

I'm much better without clothes on. Why don't you want to come to bed with me? They take credit cards here. I know what I'm doing.

How much is it again?

A hundred and fifty.

Are you sure?

Maybe if I talk to them they'll come down to a hundred and twenty.

You don't get it. A hundred and fifty is the price of that disgusting wine.

She thinks a little. Eyes staring straight into his.

Are you giving me a raise?

Tell me what you're worth.

Two hundred. And fifty.

That's your price?

Yep.

---

embarrassed 'cause I'd forgotten to pin something up there. I've never managed to choose the right thing to hang there. I like to look at what the other girls have put there. If they can achieve their goals, so can I. So he took a piece of paper out of his pocket, a pamphlet for a tour company that offers boat rides in the beach town where he lives, and folded it so all you could see was a photo of a beautiful beach, and he told me to hang it there as a reminder to call and visit him sometime. I told him again that I don't mix work with pleasure but I left it there for the time being, to give him a bit of an ego-boost. I think I'll take it down today. [. . .] I don't know what came over me but I asked him to promise never to go back there or to go to that kind of place ever again. Funny thing is, he actually promised. As if! [. . .]

Let's go.

Can I take a bottle of champagne for us?

June ends dry and cold with dead penguins lying all over the sand. It takes days for the dozens of carcasses to be removed. No one touches them, not even the vultures. The plump black-and-white bodies refuse to decompose and look like plush toys forgotten on the beach. Some penguins appear on the rocks, tired and injured, but alive, and are taken away by members of a local animal-welfare group. The birds have the grumpy demeanour of passengers forced to vacate a bus that has broken down on a highway. From his window he sees children throw buckets of water over a penguin that has decided to station itself on Baú Rock, thinking the showers help in some way. The penguin dries itself off by shaking its head and takes two or three steps sideways, resigned, as if hoping they'll leave it in peace in its new position. A young man stops at his window to ask if he has any antiseptic spray and shows him a bloody finger. He and some other volunteers with an environmental NGO were trying to restrain a penguin and he got bitten. The penguin's wing looks broken and they are going to treat it at a clinic in Campo D'Una. They don't know why dead penguins show up on this stretch of coast from time to time. It doesn't happen every year.

The first whales have been spotted down the coast near Ibiraquera. People have seen males leaping out of the water a few miles offshore and the first pregnant females spouting near the beach, which has started attracting scientists, tourists and curious locals.

He continues waking up early and sometimes puts on his wetsuit and goes for a swim. It takes him a little under half an hour to cross the entire bay and when he is really up to it he swims back. The running group is starting to dissolve. Only Denise showed up to the last two lessons. She is ready to enter ten-kilometre races and if she keeps it up she'll be able to do a half-marathon by the end of the year. Sara has stopped coming and answers his text messages saying she's been busy and will have to take a break from running. He is living on his paltry wages from the gym, but the rent is paid for the year and his expenses are minimal. Beta's surgery and treatment have already cost him three thousand reais and he will also have extra bills for her stay at the clinic and her medication.

On the first Saturday in July a game of water volleyball is held in the gym pool. It was an idea he had to bring together students who trained at different times and everyone opted in. They are all there. He bought the net himself and installed it in the shallower part of the pool. The twins, Rayanne and Tayanne, asked for permission to bring a friend and are the first to arrive. Ivana comes and tells him she is not going to play, but ends up being convinced to participate and discovers that she is a good setter. Then Jorge, the rheumatologist, and Tiago, with the enlarged breasts, arrive, followed by Jander and Rigotti, a triathlete who trains with him from time to time. He had asked Débora to call the students who had stopped coming to the pool and some are there, including Amós, the Rastafarian, who is now married to a hippie woman several years older than himself who speaks slowly and coats each gesture and word with a somewhat disturbing tenderness and calm. The gym owner, Saucepan, also participates. Most of the students already know he can't remember their faces and identify themselves as they greet him. There are so many in attendance that they have to form three teams and play sets of ten points in which the winning team remains and the losing team is replaced with the one on the sidelines. He isn't a good player himself and they spend the morning teasing him about his disastrous attempts at bump passes in the water. Afterwards, his younger students decide to dunk him. He spends five minutes trying to get away from them. After the game there is going to be a barbecue at Jander and Greice's house. As he leaves the dressing room Débora approaches him. She says the students love him. You know that, don't you? It makes him bashful and he says she is exaggerating. At the barbecue Jander shows off the power of his sound system, applying several different equalizer settings to Rush and Pink Floyd CDs, and then puts on a DVD of Charlie Brown Jr.'s *MTV Unplugged*. Greice comments once again on how well Beta is doing. He visits her every day now and the vet is more and more confident that she will regain her mobility. Jorge is there with his boyfriend, an American millionaire investor who lives on Silveira Hill and spends half the year in Garopaba and the other half in New York. Everyone has brought meat and the raw steaks wait their turn to be barbecued lined up on a wooden platter, which inspires looks of disgust and vegan preaching from Amós's wife. Only Tracksuit Man and Jander drink heavily, crumpling one can of beer after another. The women have brought red wine. He sticks to soft drinks himself as he doesn't like to drink in front of his younger students. At one point he comes out of the bathroom and finds the group gathered on the veranda in a strange silence. Ivana, the spokeswoman, says that everyone there is happy to have him as their swimming instructor and that they forgive him for never remembering their faces. She says he doesn't need to be ashamed of it because they can tell how much he cares about them and they are all improving and enjoying swimming more and more. She says they all hope he has a happy life in Garopaba because the town welcomes him with open arms and he is already a local. Then she says that they all pitched in and bought him a present. The twins appear carrying a paper bag from a sports shop. Inside is a Nike windbreaker, for running.

That night after the barbecue he goes to Bonobo's bed and breakfast. Sitting around the kitchen table are Altair, Diego from the petrol station and Jaspion, a large young man with long, straight hair, the son of a Korean father and Brazilian mother. Jaspion lives in Rosa and is a knife maker. He sells his knives, with minutely worked blades and handles of ivory, giraffe bones and other highly regulated or prohibited materials, for thousands of dollars to collectors and white-arms enthusiasts all over the world. He lives comfortably with his wife and young daughter in a studio-home near the beach and sells only five or six knives a year. Bonobo's kitchen is hazy with smoke and stinks of Diego's Indonesian cigarettes and Bonobo's crappy cigar. Bonobo asks him how his trip to see the police chief in Pato Branco went. He fidgets a little in his chair to reposition the geriatric nappy, which is uncomfortable in the groin area, and narrates his misadventures in the state of Paraná.

Fuck, says Bonobo. God is dead? I couldn't fuck a chick with that tattooed over her butt.

He replaces two cards and finds himself with three of a kind and a low pair. He doubles the ante. Bonobo folds. Diego folds. Brimming with confidence, Jaspion doubles the ante again, sucking in his top lip, wrinkling his chin, almost smiling, eyes glued to his own cards at all costs. Bluffing, of course. He calls. Jaspion has two high pairs.

Full House.

Fuck, Bonobo, why did you invite this cunt to come and play with us?

Thank you, gentlemen, he says, raking in the matchsticks.

Burning through nine hundred reais in a brothel in Pato Branco is good luck.

It's not luck, he protests in a solemn tone of voice. You have to know how to read your opponents' faces and body language.

A john's luck. It's classic.

Just look at Altair's face. I reckon he's taking a whizz.

I am not.

Are you pissing, man?

No.

But tell me, did the police chief have any light to shed on your granddad?

A little. But I think he was more of a hindrance than a help. I've given up trying to get to the bottom of it. It'd end up driving me crazy. I'm just going to forget about it.

Bonobo deals and says he is going on a retreat at the temple in Encantada the following week. A whole week waking up at four thirty in the morning to stare at the wall and pray. I think you'd like it, swimmer. You should try going on a retreat sometime.

I like staring at walls, but not praying.

Count me out.

Me too.

Why engineers?

Huh?

Nothing, I'm just thinking out loud. The guy at the hotel said fast women, slow horses and *engineers*. Doesn't make any sense.

Shit.

What's wrong, Altair?

Shit, I've got a leak.

Altair gets up and dashes to the bathroom.

Argh, fucking hell.

Life isn't for amateurs.

8

The emaciated dog hobbles over the tiled floor of the pet shop. Her front paws move forward even though one of them is slightly crooked and weak after weeks in plaster. Her back paws can make only short, quick movements that look more like involuntary jerks and sometimes cease all together. Her tail doesn't wag. Nevertheless, she is able to move without any help. She is walking. He and the vet are standing side by side, watching. Beta breathes in the cool air with her mouth shut. One of her ears has a ragged edge and her fur won't grow back over certain scars, but apart from these things she is fine, alive. He lets her walk around a little, then picks her up and puts her down somewhere else, provoking her with a toy duck that was sitting on a shelf. She yelps and gives a few shrill barks. Greice provides him with a list of instructions. Beta may experience some incontinence and will have to be given medication for a period of time. She will need physiotherapy to get some of her movement back. As she is, she won't need a trolley in order to walk but she can't move as she would like to either. The vet teaches him some exercises that he can do with her at home. She says they were very lucky. She is emotional and can't hide it. She uses the word 'miracle'. She takes a while to say goodbye to Beta and smiles that kind of non-stop smile that is an attempt to ward off tears. Before he leaves, he tells her that Beta was his father's dog for fifteen years. She followed him everywhere like a shadow. If necessary she'd lie for hours in front of a restaurant or shop until Dad came out. Dad wasn't the affectionate sort and he never picked her up or let her lie on his lap or anything like that. He had a gesture of affection that I'll never forget. He'd give Beta three or four slaps on the ribs with a force that sometimes seemed excessive. At times it would make her skittle sideways and she'd echo like a small drum. It was obvious that she liked it, something between the two of them. Private codes between close companions always seem somewhat eccentric to anyone looking on. She's got this shrill bark that can be a bit irritating, but she doesn't bark much. She likes kids but she isn't that fond of other dogs. You have to keep an eye on her or she'll lunge at them. She likes to nip at people's heels too. It's her breed, I think, the herding instinct. When he'd drive somewhere not too far from home, Dad liked to let her chase the car instead of taking her in it. He'd go at twenty-five, thirty miles an hour and she'd chase the car to the grocery shop or even as far as Trabalhador Highway, which was a few miles away. When I saw Dad more often and Beta was younger, I'd take her running with me sometimes. She'd run five or six miles with me, without a problem, on a leash. She was really depressed when Dad died. I reckon Beta was what kept him alive for his last ten years. I think caring for a dog helped keep his feet on the ground, gave him a sense of responsibility, the will or obligation to care about something. My mother isn't very fond of her. She calls her a pest. Get that pest out of here.

Greice asks how he intends to get Beta home. He confesses that he hadn't thought about it and calls a taxi. He leaves a cheque for what he still owes Greice and she gives him a packet of dog biscuits as a present. When the taxi arrives he taps Beta on the side and carries her into the car.

Over the next few days, he thinks for the first time about going back to Porto Alegre or moving somewhere else. He starts over-sleeping. He wakes up mid-morning to the sound of the returning fishing boats' motors or the voices of the young people who come to smoke pot on the stairs outside. He spreads honey and sesame oil on a thick slice of wholegrain bread and eats, feeling the salty breeze on his face. When there's a full moon the weather doesn't change until the moon goes into a new phase. Easterly winds bring bad weather. Who taught him these things? He can't remember. He is enthused by winter for reasons he doesn't understand. He likes heating up the soup pan every night, feeling the gust of Arctic air stinging his skin when he unzips his wetsuit after swimming. He feels comfortable in the season that other people hope will pass soon. He feels the constant presence of something undefined that has been long in the coming. Phases like this are the closest thing to unhappiness that he knows. Sometimes he wonders if he is unhappy. But if this is unhappiness, he thinks, life is incredibly merciful. He may not even have come close to the worst but he feels prepared for it.

Viviane once told him about the Greek gods, which she had been reading up on for the Master's in Literature that she was doing when they lived together. Imagine what things would be like if real life was like that. Gods announcing in advance that you're going to win a battle, survive a shipwreck, be reunited with your family, avenge your father's death. Or the opposite, that you're going to be defeated or suffer terrible things for many years before you get what you want, that you're going to lose or even die. And they go into detail, saying exactly how, when and where, and then fly off on the wind and leave the mortal there with the obligation to fulfil or carry out whatever has already been decided up on Olympus. Imagine how awful. And he had replied that he didn't think it was a bad thing. He liked the idea of gods whispering in your ear much of what was yet to happen to you. He doesn't actually believe in it because there is no place in his heart for gods, but he feels as if something equivalent exists in the earthly world, a natural process, some mechanism in the body or mind that senses things that we might later call fate. In his opinion, life is a little like that. We already know a lot about how things are going to turn out. For every surprise there are dozens or hundreds of confirmations of what is more or less expected or sensed and all this predictability tends to go unnoticed. It used to drive Viviane crazy, partly because he didn't have her education or vocabulary and couldn't express himself all that well, and partly because she vehemently disagreed with the idea. Then she'd go on about free choice, people's freedom to choose, to decide what is going to happen based on what they want. She couldn't accept that he didn't view it as naturally as she did. Their discussions could start with a little joke or affectionate provocation and escalate into exasperating fights in which, for lack of arguments and a weak rhetorical arsenal, he had to defend his position with stubbornness or silence.

One morning in early July he takes off his socks and T-shirt, puts on a pair of surf shorts, picks up Beta and heads down the stairs to Baú Rock. The sea is choppy but the waves are weak. The bright sunlight takes the sting out of the cold. He leaves Beta on the edge of the rock and enters the water, treading carefully over the barnacles and algae hidden under the foam. He picks up Beta again, wades further in and lowers her into the cold water. She stares straight ahead, perplexed by the unexpected bath. She is not in the habit of going into the water, much less the sea. The waves frighten her. She instinctively starts paddling with her front paws and a little with her back ones. He encourages her and remains up to his neck in water in solidarity, to feel as cold as she does. As soon as she finds her pace he places a hand under her belly for support. Beta sniffs and sneezes when the water touches her muzzle. They are watched by a flock of vultures that at a given moment take to the air, flapping their magnificent wings. They are ghastly-looking on the ground and beautiful flying. When the cold gets to be too much he takes Beta firmly under his arm, wades out of the water and carries her up the stairs to the apartment, where he wraps her in a towel. Then he gives her a warm shower and dries her patiently and carefully. He heats up a little soup in a small pot, making sure to throw in several decent chunks of meat, and serves it to her in her water bowl. He starts doing this every day, even when it is raining.

A group of tourists in yellow waterproof jackets and orange life vests, cameras dangling from their necks, is boarding a large dinghy anchored in front of one of the fishing sheds. The dinghy makes several trips to transport all of the tourists to a larger vessel that awaits them further out. He watches the operation as he exercises Beta in the water. The vessel revs up its noisy motor and starts moving towards the seagulls bobbing up and down near the fishing boats. The birds spread their wings and skate a little across the surface before they are fully airborne.

Later, after drying and feeding Beta, he locates the travel agency on the main street of the fishing village. Caminho do Sol. Adventure Travel, Hiking, Horseback Riding, Abseiling on Branca Rock, Whale Watching. The small office, with its floor-to-ceiling window, is behind the fishing shed where the tourists had gathered that morning. There is a red motorbike parked outside. A large right-whale vertebra by the door is a draw card for tourists and a reminder that the hunting of these protected animals was once the main economic activity in the region. Vestiges of the old whaling station are everywhere, from historical buildings with mortar made with whale oil to the bones that decorate houses, gardens and bed and breakfasts.

He opens the glass door and for a split second thinks that the girl sitting behind the desk staring at the computer screen with a gourd of maté frozen halfway to her mouth is Dália. Her curly hair is swept back off her face and she is absorbed in her reading, with her head tilting forward a little and her eyes darting back and forth in horizontal sweeps. But she can't be Dália because she is black. She is wearing a white top and a brown-and-orange skirt, which look more like strips of fabric somehow tied to her body than items of clothing. He says, Good afternoon, and she returns the greeting immediately but doesn't take her eyes off the screen until she has quickly finished reading a sentence or paragraph.

Hi, how are you? Sorry, I was just finishing reading something. Have a seat. How can I help you? My name's Jasmim. What's yours?

Her voice is deep and viscous. She tells him that the trip costs one hundred reais and that there are still tickets available for the next morning. One of the crew members is a biologist, who will give them a lesson on right whales during the outing. Environmental protection norms require that tour boats approach the whales no more than three times in a row and stay at least a hundred yards away from the whales at all times, but the whales themselves often become curious and swim over to the boat. If the whales take the initiative it's OK, but we can't guarantee that it's going to happen. The boat will sail down the coast to Ibiraquera, where the whales are this year, passing Ferrugem, Ouvidor, Rosa Beach, the rocky coasts. It's very beautiful. They're predicting a sunny day without clouds tomorrow and the boat leaves at nine in the morning. You have to be there by eight thirty to meet the group, put on your life vest and listen to the instructions. If there's a free spot tomorrow I'm going to go myself. I've only been once.

She sips her maté and finishes with a slurping sound.

Would you like some maté?

Yes please.

She fills the gourd with steaming water from a Thermos.

What were you reading on the computer when I came in?

Oh, it was a post in a blog I follow.

What about?

About how people need idols these days and the difference between myth and idolatry.

What's the difference?

There are actually a thousand definitions of what a myth is, but most of them suggest that a myth contains some sort of truth, no matter how obscure, about the challenges and meanings of life. They are stories that have to do with heroes, people who experience great hardship while striving to achieve an objective. The stories change throughout time but the patterns stay the same. Their strength is timeless. Idolatry has to do with idols, which are the images or representations of divinities. In idolatry, the idol is worshipped as much as or even more than the divinity itself. In other words, idolatry doesn't contain an implicit truth, like a myth, rather, a lie or a falsification. So this guy is saying that idol worship in our generation is really common, but few people value and recognize myths. He says the traditional idea of myth is in decline because of the speed of social transformation, information overload, unchecked individualism, and so on. We're living through a historical moment of transition from myths to idols. Something like that. Anyway, I haven't finished, but it's an interesting read.

Very interesting.

Do you want a ticket?

Yes.

She takes down his name and phone number in a lined notebook.

A protruding vein runs from the back of her hand almost as far up as her elbow. Her fingers look rough. Angular handwriting. Left-handed. Well-kept fingernails but no nail polish. He finishes the maté.

Would you like another one?

Her bottom lip is a little lighter in colour than her top lip. The colour of raw flesh.

No thanks. Do I have to bring anything?

Sunscreen. Camera. We provide water. But you need to pay up front.

Oh. I haven't got any money on me.

She checks her watch.

I close in fifteen minutes. Look, let's do this: come a little earlier tomorrow and bring the money. We won't tell anyone else. Are you from here?

I'm from Porto Alegre but I live here now. Right behind here, in one of the apartments overlooking Baú Rock. Next to the house with the deck.

Wow! A five-star view. What do you do?

I'm a sports instructor: triathlon, swimming, running. That sort of thing.

Cool.

A car pulls up in front of the travel agency. All four doors open at the same time and an entire family starts piling out. A pot-bellied man, who must be the father, enters the agency, murmurs a greeting and stands there waiting to be served. A woman, who must be the mother, stays outside dealing with the hyperactivity of three girls.

He thanks Jasmim, says goodbye and goes home with his heart thumping. He tries to think about something else but can't. Women with flowers for names and curly hair. Myths contain truths of some sort. Something vulnerable in those big eyes staring at the screen.

Patterns of stories that persist throughout time. He can no longer remember her face but he knows he'll find her beautiful again tomorrow. He remembers her shoulders held back, the way her waist and hips fit together, her straight posture in the chair. He's never seen anyone sit so beautifully before. He is in love with her posture. She is too highly educated to put up with him for any length of time. It would be better to not even start. He gets the hundred reais from the kitchen drawer regardless and heads back to the agency, but when he gets there it is already closed.

Back in the days of the São Joaquim de Garopaba Whaling Station, right whales were towed here and cut up at the edge of the beach. The blubber was melted down in furnaces in Imbituba to extract the oil that was used in oil lamps and to give consistency to the mortar used in construction. The parish church, over there on the old square, was built with mortar made from whale oil mixed with sand and ground shells. Their bones were used to make corsets. They were butchered right there in front of Baú Rock, everyone, and the entrails left floating in the water were devoured by sharks.

Your apartment overlooks a whale cemetery, says Jasmim.

He turns to look at the bay that is growing distant and imagines the calm waters crimson with blood and the sky black with a swirl of vultures and seagulls. The boat moves slowly so that Toni, the thin biologist who is their guide, can finish his initial explanation.

In the past, people hunted with iron harpoons. Sometimes a whale could drag a launch for hours until it grew tired and then the whalers would move in for the kill. Then they started using dynamite with the harpoons.

A young man in sunglasses with a Rio accent laughs. Jesus, did they blow up the whales? Literally?

233

They didn't explode them completely. The dynamite wounded them.

They used to harpoon the calves to attract the mothers, Jasmim whispers in his ear. But Toni never says this. You know, family-friendly tourism.

The slaughter took place once or twice a year during the whaling season. The animals come here seeking warmer water in the winter. We might think this water is cold, but for the whales, who live in polar waters, it's warm. The mothers come to give birth to their calves and these beaches are like maternity wards, where they can nurse and protect their young.

Toni pauses.

The butchering of a whale could last for several days and a strong smell would settle over the town.

It stank, says the pilot of the boat, an elderly man with a nervous tic in his eye and a kind of kepi on his head. It wasn't easy to live with.

Elias, our pilot, was a whale hunter, says Toni. He caught the last whale on this coast, didn't you, Elias? In Imbituba, wasn't it?

Yep. In '73. I caught the biggest one too. Seventy-five feet.

The boat rounds Vigia Point and the waves start getting bigger. Excited by the view and stories about exploding harpoons and giant whales, the tourists start talking loudly, filming and taking photographs. All of the male tourists except him are holding still or video cameras. Most of the women and children are also pointing cameras and mobile phones in all directions. The wind is cold, the sky is completely blue and the nine o'clock sun is already stinging his neck. He feels the sweat trickling down his stomach and takes off the waterproof jacket provided by the agency as protection from the salt water that splashes up inside the boat. Jasmim is wearing the yellow jacket and a sarong – patterned with the famous multicoloured ribbons from the church of Nosso Senhor do Bonfim in Salvador – is tied at her waist. The jacket is open a little, revealing a white bikini top with pink flowers. She has perfect white teeth and an auricle piercing in her left ear. She is covered in goose bumps.

OK, everyone. Attention please. Continuing on: the Garopaba Whaling Station was founded in 1795 and was one of many along the coast of Santa Catarina State. Armação Beach, in Florianópolis, for example, also had one. When they realized how lucrative it was, the Portuguese Royal Treasury took over the running of the stations between 1801 and 1816, but they didn't know how to manage them and they ended up being leased again to private citizens. It was the main economic activity in the region. Our historical centre was built to serve the whaling industry. Everything was there: the shore factory, the residences of the administration and workers, the warehouses. Some thirty African slaves worked in the Garopaba Whaling Station.

Do you live here in Garopaba?

I live in Ferrugem. I rent a house there. With a view of the lagoon. I've got a great view too.

What do you do here besides selling tickets to whale-watching excursions?

Jasmim gives a forced little laugh, then turns her head and looks at the ocean.

I'm not sure any more. It's a bit complicated.

Whaling started to drop off in the mid-nineteenth century. It ended officially in 1851. The main causes were the extermination of the whale population and the introduction of petrol. With the advent of kerosene and cement, people no longer needed whale oil. But hunting continued sporadically until the 1970s, despite international treaties that had banned it since the 30s. Here in Brazil it was only legally banned in '86. The right whale came close to extinction.

There are now conservation efforts and we estimate that the population has grown to eight thousand.

I actually came to Garopaba to do research for my Master's.

Really? Master's in what?

Psychology. At the Catholic University of Porto Alegre. My thesis is on quality of life. The title is *Evaluation of the Quality of Life of Young People in the Municipality of Garopaba*.

She sighs.

That *was* the project, at least. But it's complicated. I don't know if I'm going to finish it. My deadline is the end of the year.

The boat accelerates as it follows the walls of rock bordering Ferrugem Beach. Some solitary fishermen tend their rods atop rocks that look impossible to reach by land or sea. Jasmim points upwards.

The Head of the Great Idol. See it? The sphinx at the top of the cliff. There, look. The stone head.

He makes out what looks like a giant skull without a chin at the top of the cliff.

Isn't that natural?

No! It's a prehistoric monument. Archaeologists have already been there and proven that it was sculpted.

Waves that have travelled from afar break on rocks and give up their shape in a final, tired gesture.

The boat passes Ferrugem Beach, Índio Hill, Barra Beach. A fat girl with bleached hair feels queasy and throws up in the bucket that Toni fetches for her just in time. Jasmim gets a glass of water and a seasickness tablet and goes to look after her. The three girls from the family he had seen outside the agency the previous afternoon vie for the attention of their father's camera and one of them almost falls overboard in a moment of exaltation. The boat passes Ouvidor, Vermelha and Rosa beaches. The water is blue and opaque, the avocado green of the hills pulses in the sunlight and the distant sand of the deserted beaches looks immaculate. When the boat arrives at Luz Beach, Elias slows down and Toni points his binoculars towards Ibiraquera. It isn't long before Elias's experienced gaze spots a V-shaped jet of water. Everyone claps and cameras of all kinds are turned on and adjusted. As the boat heads towards the whale, a male leaps out of the water far out at sea but few people see it. Elias slows the boat and circles around looking for the best way to approach the female that is beating the surface of the water with her tail.

She's with a calf, everyone. Don't make any noise and tread carefully on the bottom of the boat. Let's see if she'll come over.

When they are about a hundred yards from the whale Elias turns off the motor. The black hump breaks the surface and disappears again at regular intervals. Mother and baby exhale almost in unison. The calf's blow is weak in comparison and sounds an octave higher than its mother's. It is a distinctly mammalian sound, not to mention somewhat human. Like the sound of a person sighing heavily amplified a thousand times. He feels an immediate connection to the whales and suspects that everyone on board is feeling the same. Only a few whispers dare break the silence. The women can't suppress maternal coos and the children's euphoria gives way to stupor. No illustrated book has prepared them for this. After a more impetuous dive that ends with a wave of her tail, the whale re-emerges in front of the boat and swims over slowly, its curved back appearing and disappearing.

Stay calm, says Toni. She'll swim under the boat. It's normal for them to brush the bottom slightly. The callosities or warts on their backs are a characteristic of the species. The calves are about sixteen feet long and weigh four to five tons when they are born.

What a beautiful animal, he says.

237

Amazing, aren't they? says Jasmim. You really feel something when they come close.

Damn, I left my harpoon and dynamite at home, says the guy from Rio.

The whale exhales some five or six feet from the boat and the tourists gasp in awe. Many of them are watching the scene through electronic visors. The mother's skin is black, smooth and shiny like vinyl and her calf's is wrinkled and grey. They look like they are about to crash into the boat but they dive under at the last minute and pass underneath it. The boat rises up a little and some of the occupants are frightened. The girl who was feeling queasy is lying on the bottom again, staring at the sky with an expression of surrender. Some people step over her in a collective manoeuvre to get to the other side to follow the whale's trajectory. The surface becomes smooth again. Mother and calf reappear and swim away.

This here was a bloodbath for a century and a half and yet they still come back and greet people, says Jasmim. With no instinct for self-preservation, without history, without bitterness. I think it's amazing the way they come so close to the beach to have their young. Last year there were some practically in the surf there in Garopaba, right up in the shallow water. The babies have to learn to breathe outside of the water. It's totally crazy, but that isn't a fish, it's a mammal. When they come up close and blow like that I can feel their lungs and it gives me goose bumps. They're terrestrial animals that returned to the sea. Have you ever seen a whale skeleton? They've got bones like paws in their flippers. Hands and fingers. Sometimes I wonder if this habit of migrating here to be near the beach has to do with a certain nostalgia for the past. Their terrestrial ancestry. Imagine a whale right there in the shallow water, almost on the beach. I wonder what it feels. Maybe it sees the frontier of another world, remote and deadly, as threatening as the ocean is to us. Or maybe it's like coming home. Like returning to the womb. Something enticing. Maybe that's why they get beached for no apparent reason. Because the sea is limitless. That's the terror of the ocean. It is the opposite of the womb. I think the whales experience this terror.

I know who she is, says Bonobo. A black girl with a voice like a singer. She was at a luau over on Ferrugem Beach a month ago. I thought she was a bit aloof. I don't think she took a liking to me. She came and left on her own. By motorbike. I've seen her around three times at the most. I don't think she mixes much. But she's a beauty. Funny you should ask about her because it struck me that you two might hit it off. She made me think about you.

She made me think about me too.

I'll just pretend I didn't hear that.

Sorry.

You in love, swimmer?

Maybe.

Poor guy. I'll be here when you need me.

His mobile phone beeps to announce an incoming call. He says goodbye to Bonobo and answers. It's his mother. She wants to know if she can come and visit him in three weeks' time, on the weekend. Of course you can. You can have my room and I'll sleep in the living room. It's been quite cold but it hasn't rained much. She says she's planning to drive up. Great. We can visit some of the other beaches around here.

The sun has already risen behind the hill but it doesn't seem all that willing to warm up the winter morning. He takes the dog out to do her business on the grass along the seaside trail and then takes her into the water and exercises her for twenty minutes. A boat arrives laden with fish and the fishermen greet him with nods and stare at him from afar. Cecina comes walking down the trail and stops to watch him and Beta up to their necks in water. She says, Good morning, laughs and shakes her head from side to side. She treats him cordially with a smile on her face, without much chitchat, as if he were a harmless lunatic. Back in the apartment he gives Beta a warm shower, has one himself, makes some coffee and sits in the sunlight on Baú Rock, looking at the beach with a steaming cup in his hands and Beta lying beside him. He runs his fingers over his oily, still-wet beard and feels his moustache hairs creeping over his top lip. Beta stands up and lies down again as if trying to show that she's making an effort. She is able to move around with more ease. She is already attempting to run a little but still can't. Light grey downy fur is growing back over the areas shaved by the vet. The missing piece of ear makes her look cute. He still has to lock her in the apartment when he goes to the pool to teach but he always comes straight home after work and takes her out again. Débora gave her a doggy bed as a present. He thought it was unnecessary but Beta likes it and the bed protects her from the cold.

Late in the morning he locks Beta inside and rides his bike down to the fishing village. Another boat has just arrived and a fisherman is filleting hake and flounder on a wooden cutting board. Gulls and vultures are having a jolly time with shark heads, and tabby cats prowl around the sheds in search of something that appeals to their finicky tastes. A blue plastic drum full of fish offal stinks in the sun. Locals are warming themselves in the sun, sitting on the steps of their houses. The Caminho do Sol travel agency is closed. An old man standing in the doorway of the house next door says they are closed on Mondays. He thinks a little, gazing at the office through the window, then leaves. He rides the entire length of the seaside boulevard and the main avenue to the turn-off to Ferrugem. He pedals down the winding road, passing houses and schools, swamps and thick tangles of vegetation, the sparkling lagoon and hillsides studded with large empty houses, grocery shops and cattle farms, looking for any woman who might be Jasmim and any red motorbike with a low cylinder capacity until he gets to the beach, where there are only two women sunbathing and a child digging a channel in the wet sand. He rides back to the entrance to Garopaba, stops at a self-service restaurant and fills a plate with rice, beans and grilled fish. His afternoon shift at the gym drags along at a torturously slow pace. The first chance he gets when the pool is empty he goes to get a juice at the snack bar and Mila asks what's wrong. He doesn't go into detail but asks what she thinks is the best way for a guy to get a woman to like him. The Chilean answers in her melodic mixture of Spanish and Portuguese that she doesn't know but she thinks it's best never to go to any trouble to get someone to like you. Things that require that much effort cause problems later.

He sees Jasmim at dusk the next day after work. She is closing up the agency and treats him with the exact dose of friendliness to insinuate that he is somehow being inconvenient. Her thick, beautiful hair frames her face. When he kisses her cheek in greeting her dry curls brush against his face and he smells her sweat and feels a desire to pull her to him then and there. All he can say are banal things about the weather and work. He wishes he had all the time in the world to rediscover her face but he needs to do it as quickly as possible, preferably without being noticed, or she'll wonder why he's staring at her like a moron. She has old acne marks on her cheeks and an oval scar at the top of her collarbone, near where her trapezoid muscle starts. As she gets her helmet from inside the office and locks the glass door she answers his questions without enthusiasm. Things are very quiet on weekdays, she spends the whole time answering emails sent to the agency's site and scheduling the few customers that show up before Friday afternoon, when business begins to pick up. She climbs on to her motorbike with her pink helmet hanging from her arm and starts to manoeuvre it. It is a worn-out Honda CG 125cc and must have been bought used. She is wearing canvas shorts, black stockings and brown boots. Woman and motorbike roll from the pavement on to the cobbled street swaying like a gangly animal. He manages to ask if she'd like to go out sometime. Have a beer now, perhaps? She says she doesn't drink and drive and steps down on the pedal but the motorbike doesn't start. She is about to try again but puts her foot back down on the ground. She takes her mobile phone out of her shorts and asks what his number is. I have a mission tonight, she says. I'm going to babysit a friend's kids 'cause she's going to the Jack Johnson concert in Florianópolis. But I'll call you when I can and we can have a beer, OK? He thinks it's great. Have fun with the kids. They're gorgeous, she says, but I hope they go to sleep quickly. I'm taking a book and three DVDs. And I'm going to pick up a bucket of ice cream at Gelomel on the way there. Sounds like a good night, Jasmim. She kick-starts the pedal again and the motorbike starts. Bye then. She puts on the helmet, accelerates slowly and disappears to the left on the first street after the bridge.

She doesn't call. The days tick over and he tortures himself for not having asked for her number too. At the same time, he can't bring himself to go to the agency and bother her again and on the two occasions he ends up passing in front of the office window he merely waves from the other side of the glass. She waves back but doesn't call him. He pays extraordinary attention to his mobile phone these days, keeping it at hand with the battery charged at all times, with plenty of credit, and checks the screen constantly for messages and missed calls. He hasn't had any for months and didn't particularly care until now. He wants her to call, to invite him in. He thinks it's too risky to make another move. He sees couples in warm clothes by the beach, drinking maté and reading magazines on the sunny mornings, and imagines himself doing the same with her. He imagines them sleeping together in his bed, lulled by the endless percussion of the waves, made drowsy by the combined heat of their bodies. He fantasizes that they are living together and have a child. The more he chides himself and tries to quell these ideas the more his mind invents them and the greater the contrast between his fantasies and the mornings when he wakes up alone with the same day in front of him and the same routine that he normally appreciates perpetually overshadowed by a feeling of impotence. He feels sick. On the Friday morning he has the silly idea to buy her a present and by that afternoon the silly idea has become an inescapable obsession and at the end of the day he rides around looking for the few shops selling clothes and gifts that are open in midwinter, unable to think of something that she might like. He remembers the bookshop. The sales assistant suggests a handful of bestsellers and there is a shelf of books on Psychology but he doesn't end up buying anything because it would be too easy to get it wrong with a book, to not know which one to choose, besides which, books say or give away too much and she doesn't seem like the kind of woman who reads any old thing. He makes one last attempt at a shop selling Balinese decorations at the entrance to the town. There are small decorative objects for the house and kitchen that are affordable. The girl who serves him guarantees that everything comes straight from artisans on the island of Bali. He finds a stunning bedspread with an intricate green-and-gold pattern that doesn't cost too much and he suddenly realizes what he is doing there and leaves. Back at home, he checks the gym roster and discovers that he is down to work on Saturday. He goes to bed early and the next day is at the pool at eight in the morning but no students show up until the end of his shift at one o'clock. The temperature is below fifty degrees and it looks like it is going to rain. Instead of eating lunch he pulls on his running shoes, shorts and the jacket his students gave him and runs along the beach to Siriú intending to think about Jasmim until he forgets her, to accelerate until he blows his engine, to sweat out his relentless desire to see her. It takes him over an hour to start to tire. At some point he starts to feel peaceful. It never fails. He hears a single crack of thunder without lightning somewhere but it doesn't rain.

It is sunny again on the Sunday morning and he puts Beta to the test in her first long walk since the accident. He carries her to the start of the beach and accompanies her slowly. She has a strange limp. Her fractured front paw is stiff and her back legs are still a little atrophied but she walks quicker than he expected and shows no sign of wanting to give up. On the contrary, she gains confidence. From time to time she wanders close to the water and on more than one occasion he has to rescue her so that she won't be knocked down by a wave washing up on the beach with greater momentum. He can hardly believe it, but Beta seems to have developed a taste for the sea. He walks with her to the start of the beach promenade, sits on the steps that lead down to the sand and strokes her head, thinking he'll let her rest a little, but she takes off in her jerky trot towards the water. He goes after her and by the time he catches up she already has her muzzle in the waves. Hey, crazy girl. He picks her up, returns to the sand, strips down to his black boxer shorts, piles his clothes up on a small dune and wades into the water with Beta under his arm. The waves are stronger here than at the end of the beach but she doesn't seem to mind. It is so cold that it doesn't even feel like cold water, but more like abrasive heat, as if the outer limits of hot and cold temperatures can't be told apart. He keeps both hands under her belly the whole time to help her float but lets her work her paws, and the waves wash lightly over her. Beta, you're a crazy girl, he says through chattering teeth. You think you're a whale now? Do you want to be the world doggy-paddle champion? She sneezes and swims, sneezes and swims. When his limbs start to hurt and tingle he takes her out of the water and dries her with his T-shirt, then puts the rest of his clothes back on and heads home. He is stiff with cold. A short distance from two fishing boats raised up on planks of wood on the beach he hears Jasmim's voice calling his name. She is sitting by herself on a bench on the promenade, drinking maté. Her silhouette is plumped out by a navy-blue padded jacket and a wool scarf wrapped around her neck. She walks over to him.

There were some guys here staring at the water saying that some lunatic was swimming in his underpants with a dog. I stopped to take a look and thought, hmm, I think I know that guy.

It was me.

Don't you feel the cold?

I'm freezing. But this sun's helping a bit.

You're lucky there's no wind.

Wasn't there an excursion today?

No, we didn't have the numbers. Frota, the owner, stayed in the office and I went to church early today. I stopped off here for a maté before going home.

Do you go to church?

On Sundays. I've been going to the chapel on the square there. It's gorgeous. Have you ever been inside?

No.

245

Don't you have a religion?

No. Do you?

Oh, I believe in God. That's all. I was brought up that way. Church on Sundays ever since I was a child. It does me good to pray. The act of going and praying. I know it's irrational. I wish I could stop but I can't.

I wanted to believe at some stage but I couldn't.

It doesn't matter. God doesn't care about that. But I doubt he likes it when people play with life like you do. You're blue. Blue people tend to wake up in hospital with hypothermia. You should get home quickly.

I think I'd rather stay here a bit longer.

She stares at him and despite his best efforts he ends up looking away.

Then have a maté to warm up.

She presses the button on the Thermos and the stream of steaming-hot water gurgles noisily through the maté leaves and into the gourd. Beta was following her own nose, already a distance away, but now she is returning to her owner with her crippled gait. Jasmim hands him the gourd and watches her, intrigued.

What's your dog's name?

Beta.

What's wrong with her?

She was run over. The vet wanted to put her down but I didn't let her and in the end she pulled through. She'll have to have physiotherapy to see if she can walk properly again but I had the idea to put her in the water to exercise. There was a guy that used to come and exercise his pit bull in front of my apartment almost every night. It'd spend hours fetching a plastic bottle from the water. It got me thinking. I know a little about post-op hydrotherapy. It's helpful with

246

spinal injuries and it can't be very different for veterinary purposes. That's what gave me the idea. I think it was a bit of intuition too. And she reacted well. When she was released from the clinic she couldn't even wag her tail. And not only is she improving, but she's taken a liking to water. Did you see her? She's learning how to break through the waves.

He sips the hot maté and his body relaxes a little.

Do you go in the water with her every day?

Yep.

She stares at the dog and doesn't say anything else until he finishes the maté and returns the gourd.

I have to go now. It's really cold. Look, I –

I'll call you next week to arrange something.

I waited for you to call. I don't have any way to write down your number now but if you dial my number –

I'll call you.

I'd like that a lot. Have a good day.

You too. Go and get warm.

She doesn't call but two days later shows up without warning at sunset. They sit in front of his building, looking at the ocean and drinking maté until the last scrap of light is absorbed by the night and then they go inside and continue talking in the living room with the window ajar. She pats Beta and says she misses buying loose yerba maté leaves at the Porto Alegre Public Market. Mixed, you know? Pure leaves with coarsely ground Ximango. She says she isn't hungry but changes her mind when he starts to inspect the cupboards and fridge and announces that he has a packet of chicken nuggets in the freezer. As a child she spent her free afternoons watching the afternoon movie on TV and eating nuggets with ketchup. She repeats that she doesn't drink when she has to ride her motorbike afterwards but she accepts a glass of Chilean red. Jasmim listens to him succinctly narrate his father's recent suicide with scientific interest and says that there are famous cases of people who killed themselves out of boredom or because they were tired, people who were naturally inclined to see death as a pragmatic issue. Live as long as it's worth it, as long as it's useful. She is interested in suicides. People think that those who kill themselves are depressed, have given up or can't take things any more, but there are many kinds of suicide, such as honour suicide, kamikaze suicide, suicide for the benefit of others, suicide because of old age, suicide because of an incurable chronic disease, suicide to prove an intellectual argument or promote an idea, protest suicide. She tells him about the recent case of a young American psychologist who killed himself in the middle of the street and left an almost two-thousand-page suicide note talking about Auschwitz and the rise of a technological God engendered by mankind, a huge philosophical, theological, sociological and scientific argument to give meaning to a bullet through his brain. She read about two hundred pages of it. The whole thing is on the internet. Then he tells her what he knows about his grandfather and she tells him to be careful poking into that kind of old story involving death and mystery because the people of Garopaba are very superstitious and she has had problems with it herself because of a local legend about buried treasure. They say that when someone dreams three times that there is treasure buried in a certain place it's because there is, but if the person who dreamed about it digs up the treasure, they die. Just ask around, there are people who really believe it. They say a guy died last year over in Ouvidor because of it. He dug a hole in the place he had dreamed about, found something and died at home for no apparent reason. She says that these cursed treasures were supposedly buried by Jesuits who were here in the seventeenth century, before the region was colonized, to catechize the Carijó Indians and take them to Rio de Janeiro. Did you know that the town of Tubarão is named after an Indian chief who refused to be converted? He said that God hadn't made him for heaven, but to live on the earth. Tubarão means 'fierce father' in Tupi-Guarani, not 'shark', as it does in Portuguese. It's in the Garopaba history books. I can lend you one. Anyway, people believe that the Jesuits left silver objects buried here and there, gold coins, that kind of thing. Some fifteen years ago they found a kind of vase in the shape of a ram's head buried in Encantada. It was made out of a metal that looked like bronze, and no one could say what it was. Have you ever heard of the Caminho do Rei? There are lots of bed and breakfasts and gated communities named after it these days. It's a trail in the hills that still exists and was used by the Jesuits and colonizers. It had its origins in an indigenous path that came from the Pacific, crossed the whole Inca Empire and ended here on the coast of Santa Catarina. Many legends date back to that era and – he interrupts her and asks what it has to do with her problems. Well, I'd heard of this legend about the buried treasure and the three dreams and maybe for that very reason I ended up dreaming that there was treasure buried under the steps leading up to my front door. The first time was almost a year ago. And more recently I dreamed the same thing again. I thought it was funny and made the mistake of mentioning it to some people in Ferrugem. One day I was at the supermarket buying some things and a really old man came up to me. I knew him by sight: it was old Joaquim, a local who makes fishing nets over by the lagoon. I don't know exactly how old he is, but he looks about eighty. He's blind in one eye, really rickety. He took hold of my arm and asked me about my dreams. He told me that when I dreamed about it for the third time I couldn't dig up the treasure or I'd die. He said to call him and he'd dig it up. At first I was amused but I started to get scared. He was dead serious. Since then he's been keeping an eye on me and I've seen him prowling around my house twice with a young man who looks like a psychopath who must be his grandson or something. He's really sinister. Legends might be harmless but sometimes the people who believe in them aren't. Your granddad's story sounds a bit like that. Don't invest too much energy in these things. Folk tales can bury reality for ever. You'll only be able to reconstruct what really happened up to a certain point. The rest becomes legend. And it's pretty cool, isn't it? Having a granddad who's kind of a local legend. Yes, it is, he agrees. He hadn't thought of it in those terms before. He wishes he could think of other things in her terms too and wants to tell her this but can't find the words. She pauses, eats the last nuggets and sips the wine. He stretches, stares at the intestinal-looking fluorescent light tube on the ceiling and lets the pleasure of listening to her settle for a few seconds. I'm talking too much, she says. Tell me more about yourself. When he mentions that he did the Ironman in Hawaii she gets excited and wants to know everything. What was it like? What's Hawaii like? What do you guys eat during the race? How do you train for it? He shows her his medal and she turns it over carefully, as if it were fragile. She seems shocked by the object. It's just a medal for completing the race, he tries to explain. Even so it's incredible. Have you thought about entering again? No way, those days are over. Don't be silly. You should do it again. Aren't there people who do it at the age of fifty or sixty? Isn't this the perfect place to train for it? I don't know, but people say it's the perfect place to be happy. Jasmim is perplexed by this comment and he has to explain that it is just a joke based on the guarantees of bliss that he has heard from so many people since he arrived. People say that kind of thing a lot, as if they were trying to convince you and themselves of it. She is visibly perturbed and he worries that he has said something really wrong but can't figure out what. Funny you should say that, she finally explains, because it is precisely what my Master's thesis is about. Have you got any more wine? I've got another bottle but it's a crappy label. It'll do. As he removes the cork she tells him that she decided to do her research in Garopaba because she had a theory already formulated that there was a dark side to life in this place. I spent a summer in Ferrugem in my first year of college and just out of curiosity I went to see the Centre for Psychological and Social Assistance here. A woman who worked there told me that the incidence of psychological disturbances and use of psychotropic drugs in the town was astounding. Adolescents addicted to two or three different medications. Mothers using Klonopin to calm three-year-olds. She told me it would be easier to put amphetamines, tranquillizers and antidepressants in the town's water supply once and for all. That stuck with me. I worked up a whole theory about the contrast between the ideology of living in a coastal paradise and the oppressive reality of day-to-day life in the place. The following year I spent two weeks here in the winter holidays and I talked to residents, doctors, social workers. Outsiders think of this as a place to open a bed and breakfast, surf, lead a holistic existence in a natural paradise. But if you talk to the right people you hear about the crack epidemic, drug dealers killing one another. People holding up health clinics to steal packets of Valium. The taboo over homosexuality and all the problems that causes. People suffering a lot in their private lives. The spread of AIDS. It's a serious problem. Lots of fishermen have unprotected sex with one another and then they end up transmitting it to their wives too. Didn't you know about that? It's kept very quiet. It only takes place on the boats, when they spend the night fishing. And in the heart of outlying communities like Campo D'Una, Encantada, some pretty primitive things go on. It's really complicated. I was fascinated by this contrast. I ended up writing my final paper on something else but I designed a Master's project to research the issue of quality of life here and got a scholarship. And I came here with my theory ready. But when I started to do research and conduct interviews I started to realize that things here are pretty normal when you start to crunch the numbers, look at the interviews. Nowadays the Centre for Psychological and Social Assistance has two thousand people on their books and treats about five hundred. That's five per cent of the population. Which is all normal, nothing out of the ordinary. The staff do a really good job and told me the truth. The kinds of problems they see are the same things that happen in Porto Alegre, in São Paulo, in Manaus, or anywhere else. The only difference here is the seasonality of the patients' disorders. They disappear in the summer and flock back fraught with problems in the winter. Summer is euphoria, money. They're too busy to suffer. Winter is boredom, lack of perspective. Cold. That's when it sets in. The cycle is the aggravating factor. Apart from that, Garopaba is the world. I joke with my girlfriends that we're living through the Fucked-Up Era. It's a whole society that's unprepared for suffering or too aware of it. The more we understand and treat it, the more we think we suffer, and, at the same time, other people's suffering starts to seem silly. And who did I think I was, imagining I could see the truth behind appearances? My premise was pretty arrogant. Happiness here is very real, as real as people's suffering. The beauty here is as real as the degradation. I thought I had a secret, you know? But there's no secret. My research deconstructed my personal fiction. That could be the conclusion of my thesis, but I lost my enthusiasm for it somewhere along the way. And now I have only five months to finish it but I wouldn't mind just working in the tourist industry or a shop, you know? They say life seen up close is more interesting. Delving into things. It's always the opposite with me. Everything from up close is so banal. I think I'm kind of sick. But I'm going to stop unloading my problems on you. Sometimes I can't stop talking. I love listening to you, he says. She looks at him with some tenderness for the first time and her lips part with a little smack. I hardly ever let off steam like this. I'm a bit of a loner here. Me too, he says. You're strange. I usually have people figured right from the start but I don't know what to make of you. You don't have ambitions. Your face doesn't tell me anything. It's really weird. I don't know if I like it. She finishes her glass of wine and says she needs to go but she is drunk. You can sleep here if you want. Take the bedroom, I'll stay in the living room. She sighs. No, I'm going home. I shouldn't drive in this state but I'm going to. He walks her to the motorbike, which is parked at the upper entrance to the building. A black cat watches them with gleaming copper eyes from a wall. As she gets settled on the bike he says he's been thinking about her non-stop. She gives him a kiss on the cheek and an affectionate tug on his beard, then puts on her helmet. She pulls out her mobile phone, dials his number and lets it ring a few times. Call me, she says. But you'd better not fall in love with me. I don't know how to really love people. But I like talking to you. Let's see. She turns the key in the ignition and drives away. He heads downstairs and saves her number in his contacts. Then he sends his mother a message asking her to bring five pounds of yerba maté from the Porto Alegre Public Market when she comes, pure leaf mixed with Ximango.

In the morning his throat feels scratchy and his muscles ache. He can't muster the energy to take Beta for a swim and instead falls asleep again listening to her barks of protest. He gets up at midday with the shivers and a runny nose but goes to work anyway. By mid-afternoon he is shaking with a fever and Débora sends him home. He leaves instructions on the whiteboard for the few students who still come to swim on the winter afternoons. He stops at the first pharmacy he sees and buys some cold tablets. The hills are no more than shadows in the grey day. He doesn't see a single person on foot and the few vehicles on the road are all stopped at intersections with their headlights on, unmotivated to drive on or unable to decide which way to go. The town is huddled up with cold in the light rain and he rides quickly home with the wind making his wet clothes even colder. As he passes the fishing village he stops in front of the travel agency and Jasmim comes to the door to talk to him.

Great day for a ride in the rain. Are you trying to prove something?

I'm going home. I'm running a fever, he says sniffing.

I wonder why.

If I'm better by Friday, do you want to go out for some Japanese food?

Go home.

He showers and puts on several layers of clothing. He pours hot water into a mug and adds lime juice, honey and a citrus-fruit tea bag. He swallows a cold tablet and then sips his tea slowly. Beta doesn't even get up from her doggy bed. He blows his nose until his nostrils are raw and his beard is speckled with little white scraps of toilet paper. He cuts slices of ginger and chews on them. Looking out the window, he watches a long-haired man in a sweatshirt and shorts fish with a net from a rock. The net comes back three or four times without any fish. He closes the shutters and window, gets into bed and falls asleep.

He wakes with a start at the sound of someone knocking on the door. Beta barks. He opens it a crack and sees Jasmim closing her umbrella and taking a step forward with plastic bags hanging from her arm. She dumps everything on the table, takes off her wet backpack and glances around like a detective looking for clues.

I heard you need a babysitter.

She places her hand on his forehead. He sneezes to one side and goes to get the roll of toilet paper.

Have you taken your temperature?

No.

Do you have a thermometer?

No.

You're pretty hot. Here, take this to bring down your fever. And I've brought you some vitamin C too. I'll leave the packet here for you.

As he watches the tablet fizz and dissolve in a glass of water she takes a laptop out of her backpack, puts it on the table, opens the lid and goes to plug it into the nearest socket.

Careful 'cause –

Jasmim shrieks and jumps back.

– you'll get a shock. There's a trick to it. Here, let me do it for you.

He plugs the adapter into the socket. She turns on the computer and they both wait rather awkwardly for the system to start up, not really sure what to do. She types in a password, waits a little, slides her finger across the touchpad and clicks a few things. The laptop's weak speakers start to whisper music.

Are you familiar with Kings of Convenience?

No.

It's good. Nice and calm. Have you got a good knife?

What for?

Soup for a dying man.

She turns on the kitchen light and rummages through the cupboards above and below the sink until she finds a large pot. He opens the cutlery drawer and takes out the knife he inherited from his dad.

This is the sharpest.

She gives the pot and the dishes piled up in the sink a quick wash. Then she gets the two plastic bags and starts arranging their contents on the counter. A Styrofoam tray of chicken pieces appears, along with a cabbage, onions, potatoes, carrots, a courgette, half a pumpkin covered with plastic wrap, celery and a tablet of chicken stock.

I think I bought too much, but this is how I like to make soup: throw everything in. Got any garlic?

He lets his aching body collapse on to the sofa and watches Jasmim chop the vegetables, heat water, pan-fry things in the bottom of the large pot. She sings parts of the songs and sometimes sways her head from side to side and dances with her shoulders.

Is this really happening?

What?

Are you cooking in my kitchen?

She comes over, sits near him on the sofa with her knees pulled up and stays there without saying a thing. She bites her thumbnail voraciously, turns her head, stares into his eyes for a minute and goes back to staring at the wall. Her breathing is audible and mingles with the music, the waves and the bubbling of the pot on a low flame.

Take it easy with that fingernail there, you're going to gnaw your finger off.

She laughs, hides her hand under her arm and turns to him.

Look, can we try not to talk about it?

About what?

About me being here. About us meeting and anything else that happens from here on. Let's just try not to talk about it. Let's not ask if it's really happening, what our reasons are, if it's going to be like this or like that, what the other person is thinking. I know I must sound mad, but talking about things messes everything up for me. Talking ruins things. As soon as you give something a name it dies.

She rests her head on his shoulder. Later she serves the soup with bread rolls heated up in the oven and after dinner she shows him photos on her laptop. Her father is a lawyer and state deputy with the Brazilian Communist Party and her mother runs a restaurant in Tristeza, the neighbourhood where she grew up and where her family still lives to this day. There are old photos of a beach house in Tramandaí, a fifteenth-birthday party, a secondary-school volleyball team. He has already told her that his father killed himself and now he tells her that the woman he used to love traded him for his older brother. Sharing intimate details of his life with her seems like the most obvious thing to do and he doesn't even think twice. The desire he feels for her is accompanied by a strong unconscious rapport, a symbiosis that develops regardless of what he thinks or wants. Jasmim is the first person he has ever met who knows what prosopagnosia is. It is the kind of thing she studied at university and reads about on internet sites with an insatiable interest.

So how do you recognize me? she asks.

By your hair, the colour of your skin, your hands, lots of things. Normal people never use hands to recognize other people but I've learned to notice them. After the face, the hands are the most distinguishing aspect of a person. But in your case it isn't necessary. It's really easy to recognize you.

It was meant to be a compliment but she doesn't seem flattered.

Want to know what I think? I think you refuse to ask people if you know them out of spite. And because it gives you an air of mystery.

You're attached to the distance it gives you. You've got this whole self-sufficient, superior thing going on. Like a lion sitting on his throne. And at the same time you're so sweet. You don't make sense.

She plays with his hair until he falls asleep. At one point he wakes up and she is on the other sofa watching a movie on the computer and gnawing on her thumbnail. He falls back asleep, listening to the English dialogue, and when he wakes up again he is lying in his bed. He doesn't remember how he got there. He gets up and finds her sleeping on the sofa, rolled up in a blanket that was in the cupboard. She is lying on her back but rolls on to her side when he enters the living room, perhaps disturbed in the depths of sleep by the sound of his footsteps. She doesn't wake up but changes position several times in a row as if she can't get comfortable. She frowns and makes a cage over her face with her hand as if trying to solve a very serious problem.

A few days later, at Jasmim's house, a rustic two-storey cabin tucked away on a side street just off the road to Ferrugem, surrounded by vegetation, overlooking Garopaba Lagoon, when they sleep together for the first time, he discovers that she is the most agitated sleeper he has ever seen. First she braids her hair so her curls will be intact in the morning and then she spends half an hour tossing and turning as she tries to fall asleep. One leg gets caught in the sheet and she kicks with the other, tugs on it and smoothes it back down over the mattress, moaning and babbling things in a limbo between wakefulness and sleep. She isn't a small woman but her body doesn't seem a big enough theatre for all of the sensations it houses. When she finally falls asleep, the inner narrative of her dreams frees her from outside stimuli. Her body relaxes but when he least expects it she changes position again. Sometimes she talks and he can't tell if she's awake. I can hear frogs. Look. I want to sleep. She opens her eyes briefly, murmurs a word or two, or three notes of a melody, and falls back asleep. The second-floor room of her cabin looks like an attic and becomes impregnated with her earthy, citrusy smell the minute she takes her clothes off, a smell that saturates the bed in seconds and invades everything, but which doesn't survive without her and exits with her when she gets up to go to the bathroom or to make coffee. It leaves no trace of itself and its absence is concrete and instantaneous. When she falls asleep at his place she seems a little more peaceful. Maybe it is the sound of the waves. He falls asleep easily but tries to stay awake so he can watch her sleeping, a desert animal in musty sheets. All he has to do is touch her lightly and she immediately turns and tries to hug him, but almost always misses the target and embraces nothing or a pillow.

The late July days become sunny and the natural light wakes them sometime between eight and nine o'clock in the morning. He and Jasmim go to the beach together on the clear mornings and she sips maté on the sand, watching him take the dog for a swim before work. They are days that pass quickly and he can't remember very well what happened yesterday or imagine a tomorrow very different to today. They almost always come at the same time and rest with their noses and mouths almost touching, breathing in and out in synchrony. She is always cold to the touch, as if her inner heat were dammed up inside. Even when analysed up close, her irises with streaks of coffee and emerald transmit anticipation and indecision.

One morning he wakes up to find her cleaning his apartment from top to bottom, vigorously mopping the floor, with the rugs hanging over windowsills, the abrasive smell of bleach in strange harmony with the sea breeze and the cold, and when he says it isn't necessary, that the apartment is already clean, she ignores his comment as if it were irrelevant. The next night he goes to her house and notices how filthy it is but doesn't say anything.

She likes to be held firmly and fucked hard. He pulls a muscle in his back trying to give her his best and goes down on her so much that he tears his tongue frenulum. She waxes him, promising that he won't regret it and he doesn't. He lies on top of her and presses his chest into her dark, arched back to warm it up. He runs his fingers along her outstretched arm and grips the bouquet of veins and tendons wrapped in the delicate skin of her wrist. What? she asks and he says, Nothing.

One Sunday they go to Florianópolis by motorbike for a double bill at the cinema and a McDonald's at the mall. In one of the films Angelina Jolie is looking for her missing child and in the other Brad Pitt is born old and dies a child. She cries in both. The sun is setting behind the mountains when they take the road back. The motorbike speeds down the highway at over sixty miles an hour in the places where the tarmac is good, and vibrates docilely between his legs. He clings to her tightly as if they are a single body travelling at high speed and daydreams behind the insulation of the helmet. He had thought he'd never fall in love again and was fine with it, believing that once was enough for a whole lifetime, but it is happening again, this feeling a little like a light depression that makes everything that doesn't have to do with the woman he is hugging unimportant. He is bored when he isn't with her and one must either be an adolescent or in love to be bored. He wants her to know it but he made a promise not to talk about these things for now and he is going to honour it.

There is a full moon in the clear night sky and they go down to Ferrugem Beach, where they sit on the steps outside Bar do Zado and admire the blue moonlight reflected by the ocean and the glistening sand. The sand reflects the moonlight in a very particular way and the blue shine has the artificial quality of a night scene in a film. He tells Jasmim about the strange black clouds that he saw or dreamed he'd seen on that same horizon months earlier.

It wasn't a dream. I saw it too.

Really? You were here too?

Yep. That was a Fata Morgana. A mirage.

Later, in the cabin, she turns on her laptop and 3G modem and opens several browser tabs with a definition in Wikipedia and photographs in Google Images. It has to do with layers of hot and cold air trading places over the vast surfaces of deserts and oceans. He leans in towards the screen and doesn't tire of looking at one photograph after another, with his mouth half open. It is exactly what he saw.

He is timing a student who is doing a set of twenty-five swim sprints when his mobile phone vibrates in his pocket. The screen shows Jasmim's name and number.

Hi, what are you doing? Could you come over to my place now?

I'm at the pool. I get off in half an hour. What's up? Is everything OK?

Joaquim showed up at my place with a metal detector and I can't get him to leave.

Who?

That old guy I told you about. The one who thinks there's treasure buried under my house. He's brought that other guy too, and they won't leave. I'm a bit scared.

What's that noise?

It's this fucking contraption they brought with them. Some kind of home-made metal detector. I don't know how to explain it any better, it's too surreal. I've already asked them to leave but it hasn't made any difference.

Stay calm. Don't fight with them. I get off at five and I'll come straight round.

They dug a hole and found some beer cans. They wanted to tear down my front steps but I didn't let them. I'm going to lock myself inside until you get here. Please come quickly.

He hangs up just as Leopoldo, a Buddhist with size-fourteen feet and large, equine lips who moves through the water as if propelled by an outboard motor, touches the edge of the pool and looks up with an expression of panic, wanting to know his time.

What did I do?

Sorry, Buddha, I took a call and got distracted.

You're kidding, he exclaims with his São Paulo accent. His mouth opens in a half-smile and he peers at the poolside chronometer through his misted-up goggles.

It was more or less the same as the last one. One twenty-five. Bend your arm a little more in the water. It's too straight. Ten seconds. On your mark.

Leopoldo turns with a horrendous cry of exhaustion, stares at the lane extending before him in the empty pool and exhales three times, whistling like a pressure cooker.

Get set . . .

Leopoldo positions his feet on the wall underwater, raises his torso out of the water and starts to breathe in.

Go.

Leopoldo sinks under, stretches out his arms and pushes off the wall without hearing the beep of the chronometer. He emerges a few seconds later and the warm pavilion is filled with the din of his kicking. He'd be a champion if he trained more often, but he spends two thirds of the year on travel, fashion and sports photography assignments all over the world for a number of publications. He attends the Buddhist temple in Encantada with Bonobo. After his workout they both shower quickly in the dressing room.

Bonobo's been asking about you. He said he hasn't seen you lately. He wants you to come and see the temple.

Is he still going on about that? I already told him I don't want to.

He thinks you're a Buddhist and you don't know it.

He tried to indoctrinate me. When he got to the part about reincarnation I stopped.

There isn't actually reincarnation per se in Buddhism. Because the concept of rebirth —

That's it, rebirth. Same thing. I've got to fly. My girlfriend's in trouble. You swam well today, Buddha. See you tomorrow.

His dripping beard gets cold in seconds outside. He rides his bike at full speed down the road to Ferrugem and skids to a halt outside Jasmim's cabin before he has even had time to break into a sweat. He can't see anyone on the sloping property but hears monosyllabic complaints, the sound of a shovel digging and an electric drone punctuated by sharp rings. Jasmim opens the door before he can knock, careens down the five steps and falls into his arms.

Thank God you're here. They started digging under the house about twenty minutes ago.

They walk around the right side of the house, where a ramp of tall grass descends as far as the light green rushes at the side of the lagoon. On the way they pass a rectangular hole the size of a kitchen sink, about two feet deep and full of stringy roots, where earlier on the invading duo dug up a couple of beer cans from another era. At the corner of the cabin they come across a wizened old man with a cloudy eye in light brown corduroy trousers, a threadbare grey jacket and a black beret. He is leaning on the ground with a kind of robotic extension attached to his arm, watching a boy of about sixteen dig a hole near the foundations of the house.

Hey. Stop right there. You can't dig here.

It takes them a moment to show signs of attention, but when Joaquim turns his head and sees him the old man gets a fright, loses his balance and stumbles down the slope a few steps. He almost falls and the contraption extending from his arm lets out shrill noises full of static. The boy stops digging, looks at his grandfather or great-grandfather until he is sure he is OK, then turns to face him. The brim of his cap casts a shadow over his face, where there is an expression devoid of feelings or intentions of any kind. It is getting dark.

Who said you could dig here?

The old man looks afraid to speak but eventually blurts out, There's treasure buried there. Did she tell you about the treasure?

It doesn't matter if there's treasure or not! shouts Jasmim. You can't dig around my house without my authorization. It's private property.

With all due respect, you're a tenant. The property belongs to Abreu.

Who's Abreu? he asks.

The owner of the house, says Jasmim. They know each other.

So fucking what? It doesn't matter. You need to leave now.

Joaquim scales the rocky terrain to the position he was in before and readjusts the contraption on his arm.

But let me show you. We found it. It's right here. Just listen to the device.

The device, he sees now, is a home-made metal detector. A circular bobbin is attached to the plywood base together with a tangle of circuits and wires. A cable winds around the metal rod to the other end, where there is a handle and a forearm support, and is connected to a box hanging from a belt around Joaquim's waist that looks like a small car battery with a set of switches and dials on top. He turns a dial, flips a switch and passes the bobbin over the hole in smooth movements. The drone grows more intense and an irritating sound, like a cross between a motorbike horn and a dial tone, goes off at apparently random and ever-more-frenetic intervals, with a hiss of static in the background.

It's here, says Joaquim with a childish smile. From one moment to the next his tone of voice becomes subservient. I've found other treasures with this device. There's something here. But the lady can't dig it up. You know, don't you?

For God's sake, exclaims Jasmim. It's probably just another rusty can, Joaquim. A pen. A nail. I only dreamed it *twice*. It has to be *three*, doesn't it? Right? Doesn't it have to be three times?

The boy starts digging again.

It's not a nail, lady. The signal's real strong here. You'll see. It's for your own good.

A flock of cormorants flies around the lagoon chirping. The only trace of the day is an orange halo behind the hills.

That's enough. Give me that shovel, come on.

Holding his hand out, he starts walking towards the boy, who is unable to abort his movement and rams the shovel into the bottom of the hole one last time. A metallic clang leaves everything in suspense for a long second. Everyone looks at one another. Jasmim raises an eyebrow and takes a deep breath.

OK, Joaquim. Let's see what you've got there.

Joaquim's grandson or great-grandson works perseveringly as the old man rolls a cigarette and passes down instructions. He and Jasmim watch the activity from a distance, lying in the hammock strung between two tree branches at the edge of the neighbouring property, which is overrun with a tangle of vegetation, listening to the growing riot of crickets and toads.

Didn't you dream that the treasure was under the front steps?

Yes, but they wanted to tear down the steps and said that afterwards I'd have to move the position of my front door to pacify the spirits. Imagine. Move the position of my front door! The spirits here are cool. I don't want to upset them.

What are you talking about?

This house is kind of haunted. I was the first person to rent it in ten years. There was no electricity, water, nothing. I fixed everything. In the first few months I kept hearing a woman's laughter and one day I was lying in the hammock over by that tree and I felt a hand stroking my face and heard a woman saying, *Don't be afraid*. I got the hell out of there, of course. I moved the hammock here and nothing has happened since. I don't want to mess any more with these things. I lied to Joaquim and said I'd actually dreamed about that rock there, so they'd dig and then leave once and for all. I didn't know what to do.

Damn Jesuits.

Will you sleep here with me? I'm going to be scared.

I've got to go back. I left the dog there.

Can I sleep at your place then?

Of course.

Did you see how Joaquim got a fright when he saw you? Do you know him?

I've never seen him before.

His eyes just about popped out of his head. He almost rolled into the lagoon.

It is already dark when the old man and boy come walking up the property towards them, Joaquim carrying his home-made device, the boy with the shovel slung across one shoulder and holding a rusty bicycle frame in the other hand.

9

He waits at the top of the steps for his mother to arrive. He expects to see her black Parati but the car that appears around the bend in the road is an older model champagne-coloured Honda Civic. She parks diagonally in his outdoor parking space. He hugs her. It is the first time he has seen her since the funeral. She is wearing red gloves and a beige wool coat. She looks smaller and thinner than he remembered. Before she came, he had decided to tell her about his conversation with his father on the eve of his suicide, but when she called minutes earlier to say she was in town and needed instructions on how to get to his place, his conviction went down the drain. By the time he said goodbye he already knew he'd never be able to tell her. She would torment him for the rest of his life for not having warned the family immediately or done something to stop the tragedy. He can never tell anyone. The only other person capable of understanding the pact was directly involved and placed a pistol under his own chin and fired it, taking care to tilt it to cause as much damage as possible.

Now his mother stands back a little, without taking her hands off his waist, gazes into his eyes and studies him with a smile on her lips. They don't look much alike, but staring at a close relative is a little like staring in the mirror and there must be something of him in his mother's watery black eyes, wide open and earnest. Perhaps it is more a question of faith than recognition, but he sees something of himself in them. She must be seeing her ex-husband in her son's features now. And he knows that she feels relatively young and safe as she looks at him because he doesn't have any way of knowing what has changed in her. The car's radiator fan turns itself off and they realize it was on. His mother takes off her gloves and strokes his beard.

You look good like this. But you're too thin.

I've missed you.

You'd better have.

Is that your boyfriend's car?

Yes. Ronaldo lent it to me because it's an automatic and has a heater. I was nice and warm on the way up and there was hardly any traffic on the road. Want to make your mother a coffee?

The sun is framed by a clearing of clouds and the forecast is for fine weather until Monday. He carries her bag down the steps and she follows him, taking photos of the view of the bay. She looks worried when she reaches the bottom of the steps and sees the front of the apartment.

Isn't there a danger the ocean might come up here?

Of course not, Mother. If the ocean came up as far as my window the whole of Garopaba would be underwater.

He puts her bag in the bedroom and smoothes out a wrinkle in the clean sheet that he has just changed as he explains in a loud voice that she'll be sleeping in his bed and he'll sleep in the living room. She doesn't answer and when he returns to the living room she is sitting on the sofa with her hands together between her knees, dumbfounded, staring at the dog standing on the rug in front of her.

What happened to her?

She was run over. It was nasty. She almost died.

She's limping and missing an ear.

It's just a piece of her ear. She's getting better. If we take her to the beach you'll see. She can already run a little.

How old is this dog?

Fifteen or sixteen. You haven't seen her in ages, have you?

Not since I left your dad.

Beta takes a few steps towards the sofa and his mother draws back.

She remembers you.

Get that pest out of here, please.

He opens the door, puts the dog outside and closes it.

After drinking a black coffee and chatting some more, he takes the key to the Honda and drives her to lunch at a fancy restaurant on a hill overlooking Rosa Beach. It is early for the weekend surfers and the place is still empty. The wood-and-stone building is decorated with furniture made from recycled timber, Indian statuettes, African masks and totems, turtle shells and whale bones. Ballads are playing softly on hidden speakers. They pick a table near the deck with a view of the beach and the lovely Meio Lagoon, where it is said that many people have drowned after getting tangled in the seaweed. In the background enormous waves break and march staunchly across the sand with lacy swathes of foam in tow. His mother is enchanted with the crystal glasses, the votive candles, the sunflowers in test-tube-shaped vases. They order a seafood *moqueca*. The waiter suggests some wines and his mother chooses a South African pinotage. He spots a right whale's spout and points at the blue ocean. His mother puts on her glasses and manages to see the next two spouts, but then the whale disappears. The stew arrives and the penetrating smell of the seasonings and seafood wafts across the table.

This puréed arracacha is really good. Have you been here before?

No. A friend who has a bed and breakfast near by recommended it.

Have you made many friends here?

A few.

I thought you'd become a bit of a hermit.

Life here is normal.

Normal for you. I don't get why you have to hide yourself away in a deserted place like this in the middle of winter when you could be in Porto Alegre, or even São Paulo like your brother. I think you're still upset about your father's death and will end up coming back. But it's your life. You're an adult. I know you like to be on your own. You've been like this ever since you were a child and I've always respected it, but I've never agreed with this lack of motivation to do something with your life. How long are you going to stay here giving swimming lessons to a handful of students? Living alone with that disgusting dog. She won't last long. This isn't a place to make a life for yourself. I've always thought your lack of initiative was your father's fault. He always told me to let you be, let you do what you wanted. Let the kid study P E. Let the kid ride his bike and swim: it's what he likes. You inherited the worst of your father, and it wasn't the booze or the cigars or his lack of respect for me, but this absurd notion that you can live in the middle of nowhere like people did a thousand years ago and that it was an accident that you were born in the twenty-first century in a big city where you can do things, create things, make money, travel the world –

I was born in the twentieth century. So was Dad.

– and study fascinating things and live an interesting, modern life, full of culture, and make the most of it all and have your own family, who will also benefit from it all, and so on. The kind of thing our ancestors thought we were going to do, you know? Your dad never let me get on your case about these things when you were growing up and now you think that letting your beard grow in a tiny summer rental that smells of mould and fish, earning just enough to pay the electricity bill, is a decent life. That's not how I see it. One day you're going to want to get married. You're going to want to make a home for yourself. This new girlfriend of yours is from Porto Alegre, isn't she? Does she want to spend the rest of her life here? I doubt it. Do you think you'll go the distance with her? Do you think you might get married? Have kids? Is there a decent school for them in this place? You told me she's well educated, doing a Master's. She must be ambitious. I've seen it all before, believe me, and things won't turn out well for you. You can spend the rest of your life looking for another Viviane but unless you change your outlook the *same* thing is going to end up happening over and over again –

Only if you give me another son of a bitch for a brother.

– because the problem is that you see life as something to be lived alone unless circumstances force something different on you. I know you don't do it on purpose, it's in your nature, but you need to fight it, darling. And if you want to call your brother something call him something else because I'm no dog.

I didn't mean –

You need to stop hating Dante for what happened. It's not his fault Viviane took an interest in him.

You don't know anything.

And the way you ran off from your father's wake was embarrassing. Why do you have to avoid running into Dante and Viviane if you're as independent and self-assured as you think you are? Do you really think you don't need anyone else? Years ago I actually thought that Dante was the son who was going to have a hard time in life with his dream of being a writer. I still have no idea how he makes a living seeing as his books don't sell much and he never wins the prizes with the big money. I think it's from his speaking engagements. But I know he's living in São Paulo in a great apartment that he managed to buy —

He's got a thirty-year mortgage.

— because he went after his dreams —

And she pays half.

— and objectives while you let your furniture and few belongings go practically for free to the first person who appeared at your apartment in Menino Deus. You granted power of attorney to your lawyer friend so he could wrap things up for you, while you ran away to the beach and burrowed a hole in the sand like an armadillo. How do you know she pays half?

She told me.

When did you talk to her?

She sends me messages on Facebook sometimes.

But you aren't friends on Facebook. I've looked.

You don't have to be a friend to send a private message.

I didn't know you were speaking.

I don't answer her messages. And I closed my account the other day anyway.

I didn't know she pays half.

There are lots of things you don't know.

Dante never told me she pays half.

It's normal. They live together. And I hope you're done because I don't want to talk about this any more. It was good we had this talk 'cause now we don't need to have this talk any more. I couldn't give a fuck what Dante does or doesn't do and I don't care if he's your favourite until the day you die. I came to terms with that a long time ago. Just don't compare me to him. Spare me. *São Paulo?* You always hated São Paulo and now that *they* live there it's the only place a human being could want to live. Look me in the eye and tell me that you think someone like me could –

I'm not comparing you, darling, I just wanted –

I'm fine here. Seriously. I know you don't understand how it's possible. But try. I like living here.

I love you both equally. I don't have a favourite.

It's OK.

I don't.

How are *you*, Mother?

I already told you. I'm really well. I've talked so much since I arrived. I don't know what else to tell you. What do you want to know?

Are you walking? Have you managed to get your triglycerides down?

Yes. Walking and stuffing myself full of omega-3. I got tested last month and the doctor told me my blood is like a little girl's.

What have you got them down to?

Two hundred and a bit.

It's not like a little girl's but it's come down a lot. That's good. Are you working? I know you get a big kick out of this Ronaldo guy but I reckon you should take more interior-decorating assignments to keep busy.

I've been busy with your dad's will and probate.

I thought Dante was looking after almost everything.

Dante's in São Paulo and only comes if it's absolutely necessary. I've been acting on his behalf. By the end of the year you and your brother should get your money. And I'm going to sell his house. I'd like you to give some thought as to what you're going to do with the money. Use it to set yourself up. Get a partner and open a gym in Porto Alegre. Or put a good-sized deposit down on an apartment. Don't give your money away.

Who would I give my money to, Mother?

You know what I'm talking about. You're too generous. Hold on to the money when it comes. Promise your old mother.

Do you miss him?

What are you talking about?

Do you miss Dad?

She turns to stare at the ocean and bites the insides of her cheeks.

I hate to admit it but I do. Now that he's gone I miss the good years. There were lots of them.

That's nice to know. I'm glad.

His mother wants to feel the sand on her feet. They drive down to the south end of the beach, walk to Meio Lagoon and return. They barely speak. The hills are imposing and make them seem small in comparison, while on the other side the ocean flaunts its infinitude. The wind blows his mother's straw hat off twice and he has to chase it over the soft sand. The beauty of the beach erases the last traces of the animosity of lunch.

Jasmim greets them in her cabin in Ferrugem late in the afternoon with coffee, maté and an orange cake cut into little cubes. They give her the yerba maté that his mother brought from the Porto Alegre Public Market. He instructed his mother the night before not to bring up certain topics and the conversation flows without any hitches, propelled by the contrived enthusiasm of his mother, who thinks everything is absolutely wonderful, funny and incredible. It is at times like this that he is most irritated by her, when she is trying to please and there is no trace of the love that underpins her scolding and judgement and eternal comparisons to his older brother. Jasmim hams up the story about the metal detector and his mother laughs until she cries. At one point, which he can hardly believe, they actually discuss a detail of the plot of the nightly soap opera, even though

Jasmim doesn't even own a television set. There are no questions about what it's like for a woman to live alone in a place like this or about future expectations, nor are there any quips about mothers-in-law and grandchildren. He wonders if they could really get along. It is possible. With time.

On the Sunday morning he doesn't take Beta for her swim, in order to avoid upsetting his mother. He thaws out a fish for lunch and opens two beach chairs on the paved area in front of the apartment. Beta barks a lot and he catches his mother pouring hot water from the Thermos on her, but when he confronts her about it she swears it was accidental. The pest passed underneath right when I was going to fill the gourd and I got a fright.

A woman goes past on the footpath and stops in front of them to chat. He only realizes it's Cecina when she starts saying that he's a good tenant, the best she's ever had in the off season, really easygoing, unlike his granddad, who lived here many years ago. He has never talked to Cecina about his grandfather and the inappropriateness of her comment can only be some kind of veiled message, but it is a topic for another time. When Cecina leaves, his mother asks what she meant with that comment about his grandfather.

I haven't got a clue. She's not all there. She's always confusing me with other people who have stayed here before.

Close to midday, he goes inside and sets about seasoning and baking the fish. It is a while before he hears her voice again.

Come and look at this, son.

He goes outside and looks around but can't tell what his mother is referring to.

Over there. A booby fishing. It's a brown booby. Watch.

The bird is gliding between the fishing boats at a height of seventy to ninety feet. It starts its descent in a wide circle, then suddenly changes course, folds itself into an arrow and pierces the water at a right angle. It bobs up seconds later without a fish in its beak and takes flight again, resigned.

If there's one thing I love it's watching these birds that fish by diving. I used to come up to Florianópolis and Bombinhas a lot with my family when I was a teenager and I'd spend hours watching the boobies. My dad knew everything about birds. They have pockets of air in their heads to absorb the impact when they dive. Did you know that? I like it when they stand still on the rocks with their gawky feet and white bellies. They're such show-offs. Dad once told me that someone had found a booby that had plunged into the water with so much force that it had gone beak-first into the mouth of a fish. They pulled the fish out of the water with the booby's head still in its mouth. They had both died at the same time because the booby's head had got stuck and it had drowned. Can you imagine?

He looks at his mother, who keeps watching the booby like an awestruck child, and smiles to himself. He feels a lump in his throat.

A friend of mine would say that their lives were connected.

After lunch they go for ice cream at Gelomel. He suggests they visit another beach but his mother says she is tired and isn't up for another long drive. They head up Antenas Hill in the car to enjoy the view of the town, beaches, dunes and Siriú Lagoon. When it starts growing dark, they go home and make a simple dinner of coffee and sandwiches. His mother asks how he is doing for money.

I'm fine. The money from the car has kept me going and I can live off my wages from the gym no problem. You don't have to worry about me.

Have you got anything you can lend me?

He can't understand why she would need money. She tells him she had plastic surgery.

Where, Mother?

I had a chin tuck. And got rid of the bags under my eyes. You don't want your mother to look like a toad, do you? I know you have no way of knowing the difference, but I look a lot better.

But where did your money go?

I don't know. Everything's really expensive. I lent Dante some money too and he's going to pay me back, but I don't know when. He said he'll only have some money after he finishes his book. Because he has to stop working in order to finish. I've got four instalments left to pay on the surgery.

Now I know how he got to Vietnam last year.

He's going to pay me back.

Doesn't Ronaldo have any money?

He has a bit. But I don't want to ask him. He didn't want me to have the surgery. I think he'd give it to me, but I only want to ask him as a last resort. But if you can't spare anything don't worry. I'm just asking.

I've got almost nothing.

He promises to wire the little savings he has to her the next afternoon and she promises to pay it back as soon as possible. They wake up early on the Monday morning so she can drive back down to Porto Alegre. It is starting to grow light and the lamp post flickers over their heads. He closes the boot, hugs his mother and kisses her on the cheek. He tells her to take it easy on the highway. Before backing out of the driveway, she half opens the window.

I don't mean to meddle, but I don't think the little black girl really likes you.

Jasmim doesn't answer the phone all morning but calls early in the afternoon when he is at work. She is sobbing, out of breath from crying so much.

I need you to come here now.

I can't leave before five. What's wrong?

A new wave of sobs makes it impossible for her to speak.

For Christ's sake, what happened?

Come as soon as you can, OK?

At five thirty he speeds breathlessly down the driveway to her cabin, leans his bike against the fence and only notices that the front steps are gone when he is about to knock. Not only have the steps disappeared, but they have given way to a deep, irregular hole surrounded by clods of damp soil ranging in colour from beige to black. A pick and a spade are lying on the grass. He makes his way around the hole and knocks on the door. Jasmim shouts that it is open and tells him to come in. He places one foot on the threshold, grips the door frame with both hands and enters the cabin with a kind of rock-climbing manoeuvre.

She is prostrate on the ground in muddy jeans and a windbreaker. There is dirt on her hands, in her ponytail and on the tip of her nose. Her eyes are dull and the cheekbones that he sees as if for the first time are glazed with tears. She gives him a pained little smile when she sees him. He turns on the light, kneels and hugs her, asking what has happened. She sighs with relief but her kisses are no more than involuntary reflexes. She points at the kitchen counter and turns her face the opposite way as if something terrible that she'd rather not see is sitting there. He gets up and goes over to the counter. There are two objects. A silver candlestick, the length of a child's recorder, and a kind of iron goblet or chalice with bronze or some other orange-coloured metal on the inside. Both are still covered with dirt.

I'm positive the candlestick is made of silver, says Jasmim in a tired voice behind him.

This goblet here looks like it's bronze on the inside.

I think it's gold.

It can't be.

Jasmim lets out a deep sigh. He puts the objects back on the counter, crouches in front of her and takes her rough, muddy hands in his. She tells him that she asked her neighbour to help her remove the front steps last night. The neighbour noticed that the block of steps was a little loose, worked on it for a while with a sledgehammer, then tied it to the back of his pickup with a rope and accelerated up the driveway to pull it off. Because the travel agency doesn't open on Mondays, she spent the whole day digging with the same tools her neighbour had lent her and already had weary arms, blisters on her hands and an aching body when she hit something strange with the spade. The objects were wrapped in crumbling swathes of fabric and she burst into tears as soon as she brought them inside.

That's incredible. It was right in the spot you'd dreamed about, wasn't it?

Yes, she says, exasperated. Tears snake down her cheeks again like rain on a window. She removes her hands from his and rubs her face, smearing dirt across it like fresh warpaint. *Shit*. What the *fuck* have I done? What am I going to do now?

They must be worth a fortune. I doubt the goblet is made of gold, but if it is —

Fucking hell, don't you get it? I had *another* dream on Saturday.

Now it dawns on him and his only reaction is an exclamatory grunt.

After you and your mother left I lay down to watch a TV series that I'd downloaded and I fell asleep and woke up an hour later right in the middle of the dream. The same one as the other times. Two priests burying something in front of the door of my house and a woman in white watching. And this time there was the old guy with his metal detector and some other bizarre stuff, but it was the same situation.

That's why you're like this? For heaven's sake, Jasmim. It's just a superstition. You dreamed about it again because you'd just told my mother about the legend and the dreams and you got a fright when those guys came over here to dig around in your garden. Sometimes ideas get stuck in our heads and then we dream about them. Don't take it to heart.

It was the *third* time and there really *was* something there. I never thought that —

Get up. Let's get you showered. You're a mess.

I'm going to have to change the position of the door. I'm screwed.

He pulls her up into a standing position.

You've let it get to you. Let's think about what to do with your treasure now. I'm going to fill in the hole in front of your door. Everything's OK.

Will you sleep here tonight?

He needs to go home to make sure the dog has food and water but he knows that this moment is decisive and if he wavers even slightly in his answer it will change everything.

Of course I will.

While she showers, he goes outside to fill in the hole. It takes him a while because the soil is everywhere and the darkness makes it hard to work. An unnatural silence sets in and he hears branches breaking in the nearby woods. A vehicle passing on the road above reassures him. When the hole is full enough not to cause an accident, he calls it a night and goes inside. He locks the door and shutters, takes a shower and makes a sandwich out of whatever he can find in the fridge. Thinking it is probably a good idea to remove the candlestick and goblet from sight, he gets a cardboard box down from the top of the fridge, takes out the blender, puts the objects inside it and hides it under the sink among the cleaning products.

Jasmim is lying on her side under layers of blankets and quilts, knees pulled up to her chest, staring at the wall. She doesn't want to eat. He gets under the blankets with her and tries to soothe her, caressing her body and hair that is now dry and braided. She doesn't want to live in the cabin any more. He says that she can stay with him for a while if she wants and asks if she's thought about staying on in Garopaba in the future. There's still some cheap land in Ambrósio, Pinguirito, Siriú. In two or three years everything's going to double in price but if we start looking now we can find some good land and start building slowly.

Are you inviting me to live with you?

Yes. If you want to.

And what would our house be like? Do you think we could find some land on a hill? I like living on a hill. It doesn't need to be very high up or anything.

They fantasize about the house for a while until her beautiful, monotonous voice grows rubbery and weak and then disappears completely. It is the first time she has fallen asleep next to him without the long preamble of kicking and muttering. He knows that she is mentally and physically exhausted but lets himself believe it is something else.

In the morning he sees her for the last time. He wakes up earlier than usual and shakes her lightly. He whispers in her ear that he needs to go home and asks her to call him as soon as she gets up. She grumbles and nods. He rides home. Beta has piddled on the bathroom floor. He gives her food and water then takes her for a walk on the beach. He lets her go into the water by herself and keeps an eye on her. She is hard-working and her swimming is incredibly efficient. She faces the backwash in the shallows bravely and allows the water to wash over her, shaking her head and blowing the water with her nose. After a few minutes she returns to the sand and comes trotting over with her limited movements, using her front paw for balance only when necessary. Since Jasmim hasn't called by eleven, he tries to call her but she doesn't pick up. He comes to the conclusion that she must have left her mobile phone on silent mode but keeps trying her every ten minutes until he starts getting a message saying that it is out of range or off. He realizes he is late for work. Throughout his entire afternoon shift at the pool he tries to call her and even calls Bonobo to ask him to drive over to her place to see if everything is all right, but Bonobo is at the federal police in Florianópolis getting his passport renewed. At five o'clock he gets on his bike and pedals over to Ferrugem. The cabin is locked and her motorbike is gone. He still can't get through on her mobile.

He drops by the cabin over the next couple of days and sees no sign of her. The neighbours haven't seen her coming or going. On the third day, a new girl appears at the travel-agency counter and says that no one there has the slightest idea what happened to Jasmim but she didn't come to work on the Tuesday, nor did she leave a message, which is pretty strange because she hasn't collected last week's pay. On the fourth day, he goes to the police to file a missing-person report. The police officers say they are going to look into the case informally and initiate a search if she hasn't reappeared within a week. He doesn't know her full name but he gives them the name of her father, who is a state deputy in Porto Alegre, and says that she did some research at the Centre for Psychological and Social Assistance and in municipal health clinics in the region. He also tells them that an old Ferrugem resident by the name of Joaquim was prowling around her cabin recently, but he decides not to mention the legends and treasure for the time being.

On the fifth day, he and Bonobo prise open the shutters on one of the cabin's windows. As far as he can tell with his problematic memory, the inside of the cabin is intact and things are in the same places as they were on the Monday morning when he left her sleeping there alone, the only difference being that the box containing the candlestick and the goblet is gone from the cupboard under the sink. On the sixth day, he stops by there again on his own and finds Joaquim and his grandson or great-grandson snooping around the back of the house. He asks if they know where she is.

I thought *you'd* know that, says Joaquim and points at the window. Somebody broke in.

That was me. Get off this land and don't come back. If I catch either of you here again things are going to get ugly.

You found it, didn't you?

Out of here.

He takes Joaquim by the arm and leads him towards the gate for a few yards. The young man puts his cap on backwards and glares at him as if reinforcing a curse before following the old man and disappearing up the driveway.

On the seventh day Jasmim sends him a text message saying that she is in Porto Alegre, that she needs to think and that she'll call him as soon as she gets back, which should be in the next few days. He texts her back asking if he can call but she doesn't answer. He tries anyway but she doesn't pick up. He calls five times in a row until she turns off her mobile. He goes to the police station and withdraws the missing-person report. She's at her parents' place in Porto Alegre. The officer says it's always like that.

She doesn't call until mid-August. She and a cousin visited the cabin in Ferrugem two days earlier to pack up her things, put everything in a small removal van and hand over the keys to the owner. She is already back in Porto Alegre. She apologizes for not calling and for disappearing without an explanation in the first place. She doesn't want to live in Garopaba any more and doesn't intend to finish her Master's. She was lost for a long time and didn't realize it. She is going to live with her parents for a while until she gets back on her feet and finds a new direction for herself. At one stage she thought she might fall in love with him, but she warned him, didn't she? She doesn't know how to really love someone. She says he's a good guy. Handsome, affectionate and a good guy. She hopes he hasn't fallen in love for real. It's always hard to do what has to be done, to break up with someone nice, even when you're sure it's for the best. She says she felt she had no choice. That morning, after digging up the treasure, she woke up alone and in a panic at around ten o'clock and felt an urgent need to get out of there. The objects were no longer on the counter but when she saw the blender on top of the fridge she figured it out and hunted for the box until she found it under the sink. She put on warm clothes, boots and gloves, attached the cargo box to her motorbike, put the candlestick and goblet inside it, got her handbag and left, determined to rid herself of the objects in the most remote, out-of-the-way place she could get to with the fuel in the tank. She took Highway BR-101 south and the further she sped down the road leaving Garopaba behind, the more she felt that she wouldn't be coming back because she was somehow going to die before she could get rid of the accursed treasure that was like a grenade without a pin in the back of her old motorbike, and in those final moments of clarity that precede death, a clarity brought on by desperation and fatalism, she perceived the size of the farce she had been living for the last few years. She felt as if the years, after she'd turned twenty, had lost the unique personality that they'd had when she was younger and become nothing more than vague references to the passing of time. She didn't want to believe that any more. She didn't want to live on her own in a cabin by a lagoon or keep asking people if they took medicine and were happy and then go and design Excel spreadsheets and graphs and not come to any conclusions. She didn't know what she wanted to do, but it wasn't that. She wasn't like him, who seemed to belong there. She would never belong and had been there long enough to learn this last lesson, the only one still available to her. Before she knew it she was near Criciúma and without thinking too much she decided to take the first exit on her right and keep going as far as she could. The road narrowed and the post-apocalyptic towns on the edge of the BR-101 gave way to simple villages and green farms while the monstrous mountain walls of the Serra Geral loomed ahead. She saw parrots and toucans flying close to the forest and filled her tank in a small town called Timbé do Sul, where the petrol-station attendant suggested that the remote place she was looking for might be at the top of the Serra da Rocinha mountains and that was where she headed after drinking a Coke and eating a packet of Ruffles and turning off her mobile phone, when she saw that he'd sent several messages and tried to call numerous times. If she replied to him at that moment she'd be putting everything at risk. The dirt road was *extremely* steep and *extremely* dangerous and after a few miles in first gear, riding over huge stones and using her legs to stop the bike from plunging into terrifying abysses, praying on the hairpin bends with limited visibility that she wouldn't be hit by a cargo truck lurching down the hill without brakes, she stopped at a kind of natural lookout where she could see everything from the canyon walls and the coastal plains to the ocean itself, took the candlestick and goblet out of the cargo box and hurled them with all her strength, one after the other, into the closest ravine, where the dense forest swallowed them without a sound. Then she continued up the mountainside thinking that maybe now she was free of the curse and by the time she got to the top she didn't believe in legends any more and realized that her terror was of another nature and that the curse had just been something to blame. She could see everything from up high and far away and was free. An afternoon fog was beginning to condense on the canyon slopes, forming prodigious clouds of white vapour that curled and twisted before her eyes and soon threatened to engulf the whole edge of the mountain range. She started up her bike and drove along dirt roads covered in thick gravel. She crossed hills and aqua-green, almost oceanic fields, slightly burned by the frost, feeling cold to the bone, until she came to São José dos Ausentes and then Bom Jesus, where she rented a hotel room for twenty-five reais and collapsed on to the wool bedspread, completely exhausted and happy. The next day she took the paved roads down to Porto Alegre on a beautiful five-hour journey that ended at her parents' house and after a few days of reflection and listening to advice she decided to cut her ties with Garopaba and everything there because she was already a new person and couldn't live there any more, it no longer made sense. She didn't answer him or call because she didn't have the words to explain what was going on and because she thought that perhaps it was better like that. How sad it is to talk about things, to try to explain yourself, try to express yourself. As soon as you name things they die. Does he understand? Does he forgive her? Is everything OK?

He says he doesn't forgive her but he understands and it's OK. She knows where to find him if she wants and he hopes she's very happy. He doesn't see any reason to tell her that he spent ten days suffering as if his life had lost every possibility of happiness and enchantment, drinking until he blacked out and running and swimming until his muscles cramped, but that afterwards everything went back to normal and to be honest he doesn't miss her all that much any more, and her face vanished from his memory fifteen minutes after he left her sleeping that last morning and will never return unless she sends him a photo, which he'd really like, by the way, and truth be told he has already forgotten her in the other sense too, the sense that would make him suffer now, but he ends up telling her all this anyway and she falls silent for a few moments and says, See? You didn't really love me all that much.

Cecina doesn't seem surprised by his visit and invites him in without asking why he is there. They exchange the usual pleasantries. The TV in the living room is showing the midday news and an old man in a vegetative state watches his arrival from a wheelchair next to the sofa, protected from the cold by a wool ski cap and blankets. The smell of fried fish wafts up from the kitchen downstairs.

You've never met my husband, have you?

No. What's his name?

Everyone calls him Quem. His real name is Quirino.

Afternoon, Quirino, he says waving.

The old man's breathing grows laboured.

Please, have a seat. Would you like a coffee?

No thanks, Cecina. I'll be quick. I just want to ask you something. Do you remember that my mother was here a few weeks ago and you talked to her in front of the apartment?

Yes. Very friendly, your mother.

She thought the same about you.

And how's the girlfriend?

She's gone. She went back to Porto Alegre.

For good?

I think so.

Aren't you going to go after her?

No.

Oh dear.

Cecina, I was swimming with my dog this morning over near Baú Rock and —

How's she doing?

She's great. She still walks a little crooked but she's already running around with her tongue out and goes everywhere with me.

She looks like a fish in the water.

She does. And it was precisely as I was taking her for her swim this morning that I looked up at the door to the apartment and remembered that time you stopped to chat with my mother. Something was niggling me and I couldn't work out what it was and then suddenly it came to me. You mentioned my grandfather. Remember?

Did I?

Yes. But I'd never talked about my grandfather to you.

Old Quirino wheezes in his wheelchair.

People are saying that you've been asking around about your grandfather. And, to be honest, if it were up to a lot of people you wouldn't be here any more. Several people have asked me to turn you out. But you gave me a cheque for the whole year. It's become a problem for me.

You said he wasn't easygoing like me, or something to that effect. Did you know him?

No.

But what do you know about him? I know that he died here but besides that everyone tells me different things. I had decided to forget about it but now it's all come back to me and this whole story is driving me crazy.

Are you sick? You didn't have dark circles under your eyes before.

I can't move on with my life as long as I don't know, Cecina. Before he died, my dad told me about my grandfather. He wanted to know and now I want to know. I need to. You have to help me. Of the people who were around back then, you're my only friend. I'm begging you. Please.

Old Quirino starts gurgling saliva. Cecina is silent. She looks at her invalid husband, gets up and disappears down the corridor pushing his wheelchair. She comes back several minutes later and sits on the armchair opposite him again.

I knew your grandfather. Everyone knew him during the time he spent here. But few people knew him well. I was a teenager.

Do you know how he died?

Yes, but I can't tell you.

Why not?

I'm afraid. No one who saw it and is still alive will tell you.

Did you see it?

I did and I pray every day to forget it.

He rests his forehead in his hand and sighs. Cecina goes to fetch a pen and notepad then sits and starts writing something in her slow handwriting to the sound of a hysterical department store advertisement.

Don't tell anyone I told you about her, she says, handing him the paper. Say you found out some other way. My husband's the only one who knows you came here and he can't speak.

He looks at the paper. There is the name of a woman, Santina, a mobile phone number and a street address in Costa do Macacu.

289

She didn't see what happened that day with her own eyes but she knows everything. She's the only person who will tell you.

Who is she?

She was your grandfather's girlfriend.

The dirt road follows the edge of Siriú Lagoon, passes through the communities of Areias do Macacu, Macacu proper and Morro do Fortunato and arrives at Costa do Macacu, a huddle of wood-and-brick houses perched on a partially cleared hill, the slope of which ends at the edge of the lagoon. From the village itself, the hills appear to embrace the lagoon, leaving only a narrow opening through which he can see the creamy sands of Dunas do Siriú, and beyond them the ocean stretches out to the fold of the horizon. Two cows chewing the cud in a small roadside barn look bored with the landscape, and friendly mutts keep an eye from verandas and gates on the traffic of motorbikes and bicycles, protecting their tiny kingdoms. Most of the houses are closed due to the cold, and clusters of children in blue uniforms walk down the middle of the road on their way to school. Beyond the school, there are fewer houses and the steep little road that leads to Santina's house appears on his left. After his arduous ride up the long, winding road to the village, he has to push his bike up this last stretch. The door and windows of the light blue cottage are ajar and he can see several people moving about inside.

He knocks lightly on the door and is greeted in seconds by a young woman with cheeks flushed from the cold, black hair in a ponytail and a wide scar on her jaw. He says he is looking for Santina and she gives him a good look up and down while holding her cardigan closed at chest height. He explains that he tried to phone beforehand but no one answered, and it is an urgent matter. He expects to be interrogated and provide explanations but the woman opens the door and invites him into a dimly lit dining room with one door leading to a corridor and another to the kitchen, from which wafts a strong smell of chicken soup and coriander. The table is set for lunch on a pink tablecloth embroidered with flowers, and an old man and two children are still eating. Near the door to the kitchen a small woman of about sixty in a thick brown wool cardigan is kneading bread dough on a smaller table beneath a large framed portrait of Christ. The young woman nods at her and at the same time the older woman stands, wipes her floury hands on a white tea towel and speaks in a weak, croaky voice.

Come in, son, come in. Have you had lunch?

I have. Are you Santina? I –

Yes, but visitors aren't allowed to just stand there looking at food in this house. Aninha, get another plate, please. Do you like chicken soup?

Santina starts to pull out a chair but stops suddenly, takes a step back and claps her hand to her mouth.

My God, he's the spitting image of Gaudério.

I'm his grandson.

Who's Gaudério, Grandma?

No one moves or says a thing. Santina stands there with her hand over her mouth, eyes bulging. Another woman appears at the kitchen door. The old man swallows what's in his mouth, drops his fork noisily on the plate and turns to look at him.

What're you doing here, kid?

Be quiet, Orestes.

Who's Gaudério, Aunty?

Would you rather I came back some other time? he says.

No, son. It's no problem. Have you eaten? Aninha, the plate.

The woman who answered the door fetches a plate and cutlery

from the kitchen. Santina serves him a glass of Coca-Cola, chicken soup, rice, black beans and a bowl of locally produced manioc flour. As he eats he explains where he lives and where he is from. He says that his father died at the beginning of the year and that his grandfather used to live in Garopaba. He approaches the subject with caution because there are other people at the table and in the kitchen. Santina notices.

Let's talk outside. But finish eating first.

As they leave the house he notices that the breeze has become a strong wind, which is making little waves in the lagoon and buffeting the vegetation. There are no rain clouds in sight. He holds Santina's arm as they walk with short steps towards the dirt road. She points at a place across the street.

I can't walk very far but we can go over there. There's a bench that's protected from the wind by the wall of the school. I don't know if I'll see this year out. I've been on a waiting list for an operation through the public health care system for seven months.

What do you have?

Cancer. It's the second time.

Santina doesn't say where and he doesn't ask. He tries not to hold her arm too tightly. She doesn't weigh a thing.

This place is beautiful. I'd never been up here before. From a distance these hills don't look so big. We see the lagoon and the beach from a completely different angle.

She looks over her shoulder and makes a gesture that takes in the slope behind her house.

See all that there? All that land? Guess who it belongs to.

Your husband?

It's mine. My husband died. The man inside is my brother. Just yesterday a young man from your city showed up here wanting to buy some land on the hill. My grandson took him up and showed it to him. I was asking fifty thousand and he thought it was too much. So I told him it had just gone up to one million. Because that's what it's going to be worth in ten years. It'll be covered in mansions. Take a good look at this nature. Make the most of it because its days are done. I won't live to see it but you will. I just hope my children don't sell it off too cheap and fritter away the money. My neighbour gave a piece of land to each of his children, an awful bunch of no-goods, and they turned around and sold them for a pittance and spent the money on car tyres and drugs. I try to make my children and grandchildren understand what is going to happen here.

He offers to help her sit but she refuses with a wave of her hand.

I'm not that weak. How did you find me?

I've been doing some investigating. I found the police chief. The one you contacted in Laguna.

He didn't find a thing, poor man. They lied to him from start to finish.

Were you my granddad's girlfriend?

Yes. I was very young. I thought he was going to take me away from here as he used to say he would. Love is the heart of desperation.

You didn't go to the dance the night he died, did you?

No. I was at home feeling nauseous. I —

She takes a deep breath and shudders.

Are you OK?

She turns her face in his direction but doesn't look at him. She isn't looking at anything. Her face is wrinkled and tense and her eyes are red.

What did they tell you? That he's a ghost? That he's a demon? That he never dies? Did they tell you he brought a curse on

Garopaba? That he kills young girls to avenge himself? There was no place for Gaudério here but he insisted on staying. What a stubborn man. They said he'd killed José Feliciano's girl but it wasn't him. He swore to me. Nobody knows who did it. But they took the first excuse they could find to get rid of him. Lots of gauchos had started coming here in that decade and people didn't like it. There were lots of fights, lots of disputes. Your granddad always stood up for himself and would threaten people with his knife. Everyone was afraid of him. He was a very big, strong man. He'd disappear underwater to fish. Lots of people said it was a trick. That he was dangerous. He wasn't. He just didn't have a way with people. On the inside he was sweet, very honest. Affectionate. I didn't go to the dance that day because I was feeling dizzy. I was pregnant. He never knew. Maybe if I'd gone they wouldn't have done it to him.

What did they do to him?

I sent the police chief the telegram because I was sure he was just missing. In spite of all the blood. I wanted to see the body. I wanted to find the father of my child.

What did they do to him, Santina?

And then I lost the baby. If I hadn't, it'd be your aunt or uncle.

What did they do to my granddad?

They turned out the lights and stabbed him to death. It was several men at the same time and I know the names of each and every one of them. They tried to cover it up but in time I found out everything. The men who tried to kill him are all dead now. They say they stabbed him more than a hundred times. When the lights came back on his body was lying there. Someone went to get a sheet so they could roll him up and dump him in a grave in the middle of the forest. It took a while and before they were organized he stood up. After lying there for ages. He started to move and then he got up. His knife was still in its sheath at his waist and he pulled it out. They backed away and he stood there looking each one of them in the eye and saying he was going to kill them. Everyone started screaming but no one dared get close enough to finish him off. It wasn't possible that he was still alive. The place looked as if they had butchered a cow there. They drove him towards the beach. He shook his knife at them and said he was coming back to get each one of them. That he'd kill their wives and children. Some people say he shouted things in languages that don't exist. Others say he had fire in his eyes. He stumbled across the sand and into the sea. He swam out into the deep and disappeared. To this day people think he's a ghost. They say that if you mention him he appears and a tragedy happens. They say he's worse than the devil. The fear's been passed on from father to son. Haven't you noticed? When a girl is killed they say it's him. Even when they find the real murderer. It's a belief no one can erase. They say Gaudério's spirit won't rest until he's killed every descendant of those who killed him. They say he'll never stop, even after death. Even the people who knew he was still alive kept the stories going so people would believe he'd died, to help them forget. Shame and fear. That's all.

But didn't he die?

We met three times.

Where did he live?

In the hills.

A house in the hills?

No, in the hills, around about. But he was mad. There wasn't much left of him. It was very sad. Very sad.

But do you think he's still —

I don't know. The last time I saw him was five or six years ago and I decided it was going to be the last. My health isn't up to it. I don't want to see certain things any more. He'd be about ninety now. I wouldn't be surprised. He won't be checking out so soon.

Where did you see him the last time?

Behind here on Freitas Hill. The other two times were in Ouvidor. But he wandered all over the place. In each place they call him something different. In Jaguaruna there's talk about an old man who is sometimes seen around the shell middens and I've always thought it was him.

Santina covers her mouth with the back of her fingers and stares at him until he looks away at the wind-ruffled lagoon.

You're going to look for him, aren't you? I know you are.

I think so, Santina.

I can see it on your face. You're just like him.

So I'm told.

There's a man in Cova Triste who doesn't know how to read or write but he makes up rhyming verses. He dictates and people write them down. One of them goes like this.

> *every old man was once young*
> *every boy will be a man*
> *I pray to God that he may earn*
> *a good name if he can*
> *don't be proud my son*
> *for pride the earth doth spurn*
> *because from dust we come*
> *and to dust we shall return*

PART THREE

10

The car skids in the middle of the interminable drive up to the top of the hill, where the Encantada Buddhist Temple is located. Leopoldo pulls on the handbrake and lowers the volume on the avalanche of distorted electric guitars coming out of the speakers. Staring straight ahead, he focuses for a moment, his lower lip hanging open, and accelerates carefully. It is and it isn't raining. A thick mist is always waiting a little further up but they never reach it. Parts of the steep dirt road are cemented over but even then Leopoldo, who knows the way well, is unable to get out of first gear. They finally reach the highest point of the road and after a brief descent the forest opens to reveal a cleared area of uneven land. On the right is a statue of Buddha and on the left is a flagged driveway up to the temple, a two-storey building with Portuguese roof tiles and wooden walls painted an earthy red. An SUV is parked outside the front steps. It is still before nine o'clock in the morning and the sunlight that manages to filter through the clouds has the flickering, dreamlike whiteness of a spent fluorescent bulb. The Buddha statue still isn't finished and is covered with patches of dark concrete at different stages of drying. The entire statue is over ten feet tall and the Buddha is a little larger than a normal human being. His throne is borne on the backs of lions sculpted in relief on the pedestal. The Buddha is sitting with his legs crossed in the lotus position with one hand in his lap and the other raised, both holding objects that he can't identify. Leopoldo, who has helped build parts of the temple on a number of occasions, goes to talk to two men who are working on a roof structure that is being built next to the statue, while he goes to look for Lama Palden, whom he has arranged to visit.

The floor, walls, ceiling and beams inside the temple are made of wood and painted blood red. Several statues three to four feet tall represent sitting divinities making a range of gestures with their hands and arms or holding swords and other relics. They are painted gold with details in blue, red, green and yellow. In one corner is a shrine with a portrait of a lama. The ceiling is covered with lanterns decorated with scraps of colourful fabric and there are Tibetan inscriptions everywhere. The smells and sounds of the wet forest mingle with the aroma of incense sticks and the squeaking of the floorboards under his feet.

Lama Palden suddenly emerges through a door at the back that opens on to an enclosed courtyard, accompanied by a little girl. Both are blonde and barefoot in spite of the cold. They introduce themselves and Lama Palden doesn't seem to remember that he phoned the day before. As she sends the girl outside he wonders what exactly he has come to ask and how he should do it without sounding ignorant or disrespectful, but before he can say anything she tells him that he is the first to arrive and invites him to place some offerings before the six Buddha statues on the altar in order to earn merit. Lama Palden moves her tall, slender body with elegance. She has on a seed necklace exactly like the one Bonobo wears and a pink cashmere jumper. From time to time her bony feet peek out from beneath the beaded hem of her long, intricately patterned skirt. Her most striking facial feature is her long, narrow chin. Her blue eyes and almost-transparent eyelashes radiate serenity and her physique suggests that she adheres to some kind of radical vegetarianism. Her voice is soft and resonant at the same time. Her sparing use of words seems to be underpinned by a deliberate reverence of silence. She doesn't appear to be happy, much less unhappy. She goes into the courtyard, where she fills a bucket with tap water and returns. Following her instructions, he makes three consecutive greetings by pressing his hands together above his head, then in front of his face and chest, symbolizing spirit, mind and body, and then prostrates himself and touches his forehead to the ground for purification. Lama Palden gives him a few last instructions and withdraws. He uses a plastic jug to carry water from the bucket to fill approximately thirty bowls arranged around the main shrine and a smaller shrine in the corner. He feels like he is being watched by the statues. He hears two other cars pull up outside and devotees start to arrive: three discreet, well-dressed elderly women, two young women who seem slightly crazy, a short-haired Brazilian woman and her long-haired Argentinian boyfriend, a typical middle-aged surfer with prominent veins and faded tattoos on his neck and forearms, and finally six-foot-tall Leopoldo, who greets everyone as he enters.

The service itself consists of sitting cross-legged in front of little wooden prayer-book rests, expelling air through his left nostril, then his right, then both together to symbolize the expulsion of hatred, selfishness and ignorance, listening to Lama Palden talk about the need to avoid the pitfalls of the ego, to observe the mind and to recite a series of prayers and mantras, almost always three times in a row. The mantras are chanted quickly and monotonously, sometimes with small melodic variations, in long sentences that take up all his breath. Between one set of prayers and another the lama asks the devotees to visualize spheres of light coming out of the mouths, throats and hearts of the divinities and penetrating their own. He tries to imagine it, tries to keep up with the mantras as much as possible and to focus on her teachings but it isn't long before his thoughts start to wander.

The trees are dripping outside and someone is walking and knocking things over on the upper floor, maybe the little girl who was with Lama Palden when he arrived. He has been attracted to a series of Buddhist ideas and concepts patiently explained by Bonobo: the impermanence of all things, the illusion of individuality, the vision of a person as nothing more than a fleeting configuration of the unstable components of body and mind, the need to fight the erroneous notion that we are whole, permanent, durable, autonomous and uncon-nected to the flow of all things, so that we may interact with the world with more spontaneity, compassion and detachment, so that we may suffer less and cause less suffering. Many of the ideas that were being explained to him for the first time corresponded with his own intu-itions and convictions, but nothing could be further from the path that had brought him to them than this repetitive reading and group meditation. Even in this moment of prayer and meditation he feels an urge to stop all the talking entirely, eliminate lamas and statues and be alone and silent with a wall or with the horizon or run and swim until the constant awareness of being a person is naturally dissolved by the extreme physical effort and the conversion of all thought into strides, strokes, breathing, heartbeat. He understands what these people are seeking. It is what he and everyone else seeks, but their methods are different and perhaps, he suspects now, incompatible. He begins to grow impatient with the ritual. From a certain point on all he wants is for it to stop.

When it is over he waits for the lama to finish talking to the short-haired woman about Buddhist decorations that are going to be made to sell in the temple so he can ask her the question that brought him here in the first place. He asks how Buddhists can talk about reincarnation if the whole philosophy preaches detachment from any notion of an ego that endures through time. Because for a being to reincarnate — I mean, to be reborn — something of what he was must reappear further down the track or it doesn't make any sense to use the term. Bonobo has told him it's not exactly like that, it isn't beings that are reborn, but states of mind and, truth be told, it's pretty hard to explain, but he sees no difference between a reincarnated spirit and a state of mind reappearing at some point in the future and being attributed to someone who died as if something of the person still existed. He can't find the words he is looking for and knows that his question is starting to border on total incoherence but Lama Palden listens with all her attention until he tires of speaking. Then she says that only meditation can lead to the rational certainty of the existence of karma and rebirth. The path to enlightenment is a training of the mind, analogous to training the body. Only practice reveals the teachings, she says. Truths cannot be understood through a rational, dualistic Western outlook. She also points out that enlightenment eliminates the cycle of rebirth and asks if he would like to know anything else. He stares at her as if he is taking it all in, thanks her repeatedly and says goodbye. She tells him not to miss the coming services, which are every Sunday morning at nine.

Leopoldo agrees to stop by the bed and breakfast to visit Bonobo, who is watching a porn movie at a high volume on the computer in reception and shouts when he sees them walk in.

Captain Ahab! Leopoldo Beefsteak!

I told you not to call me that. I don't like it.

OK, Leopoldo Beefsteak.

You really are an idiot.

You guys call me Bonobo and I don't complain.

But you like it, don't you? It's different. I'm going to make up a bad nickname for you.

Back in Porto Alegre they also used to call me Monkey, Ebola and

303

Velvet Dick. Your choice. But tell me, swimmer, did you talk to the lama?

Yep, we've just come from the temple.

Cool. Wait around. A family from Curitiba is going to check out in about fifteen minutes and then we can fire up some pizzas. Grab some beers from the fridge in the café.

The three of them spend the afternoon drinking and eating at one of the four tables in Bonobo's Café. Leopoldo is a big man but he gets drunk quickly and starts joking about his participation in that morning's service. Bonobo listens to everything, shaking his head, and then tells him off.

You're really something, aren't you, swimmer? Jumping on the lama like that with the whole rebirth thing.

What's the problem? I wanted to know.

What did she say?

To meditate until I understand.

Leopoldo laughs.

I told you, Bonobo, let's not go there.

Man, you're obsessed with this rebirth thing. Turn the page. Why is it so important to you to know if rebirth exists?

It's important to know that it *doesn't* exist. All the rest seems right to me, but that detail spoils everything.

Listen, swimmer. The question of rebirth isn't all that important in the original Buddhism. There was a lot of black magic in Tibet when Buddhism first appeared there and part of the madness stayed on. But it isn't like the Kardec brand of reincarnation. If you understand that a person is just a dynamic agglomeration of states of mind, the idea of a soul that can reincarnate stops making sense. To put it in crude terms so you can understand it, it's these states of mind that are reborn, that continue on and recombine to a certain degree. Just as your body feeds plants and worms if you're buried in the ground. Just as the atoms of your body are stardust.

The atoms of my body might be stardust, but that doesn't mean there are stars in me.

Stop talking like hippies.

Do you get what I'm trying to say, Bonobo? The star is dead, I'm going to die. It doesn't make any difference. The atoms didn't *belong* to the star. My states of mind aren't *mine*. And what the fuck is the *mind* anyway? I think it's just a clever way to believe in a soul. It's the leftovers of permanence that Buddhists keep stashed under their beds.

We've created a monster, Beef.

I warned you. We shouldn't have gone there.

Life can't continue after death. I can't. It'd be ridiculous. If they prove that it does, I'll kill myself.

But in that case it'd be pointless.

You're a piece of work. The most sceptical bastard I've ever met.

No, I'm not. I just don't believe in *any* old thing.

If there was a God he'd be amused by you.

Leopoldo raises a bottle and hiccups.

Here's to the passionate belief that none of this exists.

He and Bonobo join the toast. The three bottlenecks clink together and his bottle shatters, sending beer and glass flying. The trio looks at one other with their arms still outstretched and their shoulders up, unmoving, slowly taking in what has just happened. The bottle broke up in the air instantly but the feeling that he is holding it is slow to disappear.

Some winter days are like summer days and this Monday in early September is one. Clothes lines sag and mattresses sunbathe on lawns and verandas. Those who can, enjoy the sunshine on the beach.

305

Leaders of the two political parties running for election in the town set out early on their rounds to buy votes by giving away bags of cement and paying off motorbike loans. Poor children receive free surfing lessons and eat oranges for breakfast by the beach. He pulls on his wetsuit, lets the dog out and walks across the rock to the ocean. With his first few strokes the freezing water works its way through the neck opening and zipper and down his back and belly but in seconds it is warmed by the heat of his own body and the suit becomes protective and cosy. When he turns his head to the side to breathe, he can see Beta limping across the sand, accompanying his forward movement through the fishing boats. He doesn't know how she does it but she does. On the main avenue a mentally disabled man holding the Olympic Week torch runs slowly beside a guide, followed by an Association for the Handicapped microbus occupied by other disabled people taking part in the relay and two police cars with flashing lights. They are headed for the town of Paulo Lopes, where the torch will be passed along. In Rosa, Bonobo receives a phone call from a friend in a fix whose first thought was to talk to him and if possible see him, if that's OK. In her house in Ferraz, a local woman is talking on Skype with her thirteen-year-old son who lives with his dad in Spain and only comes to visit during the summer. A gardener stumbles across the body of a dog that died of cold two nights ago in the flower bed of a summer house on Rua dos Flamboyants. In an isolated community in the hills of Encantada that lives according to the Mayan calendar a toothache brings a young woman to tears and she can't stop thinking about what her life will be like if the world doesn't end in December of 2012 as predicted. He swims out deep and feels the waves growing larger and the surface growing rougher as he approaches the middle of the bay. The wetsuit attenuates his fear of the ocean but it is still there and looms up as soon as he starts thinking about it. He has the feeling that the ocean *wants* something from him but he can't imagine what that thing might be. Perhaps a piece of information that he has forgotten or doesn't even know he has. The ocean interrogates him and seems on the verge of losing its patience but he usually gets out in time to avoid an attack of fury. In the health clinic the doctor on duty is sewing up the face of a handsome surfer who hurt himself with his surfboard on the rocks in Ferrugem, using plastic surgery stitches to try to preserve his appearance as much as possible while his girlfriend records the procedure with the camera on her mobile phone. A group of young women working in lottery houses, pharmacies and clothing shops exchanges text messages to arrange the details of a secret party with champagne and vibrators that night. A coral snake slithers over the foot of a small-time drug dealer smoking marijuana on Siriú Hill without him noticing. A pyromaniac's car is seized because he was driving without a licence and he decides to set fire to the entire town. In the municipal school a teenage boy wants to talk to the girl he lost his virginity to the night before after the Campinense Club ball but isn't sure of her name. The owner of a coffee shop on the outskirts of town tallies up the weekend's takings and calls his wife to let her know that the new all-you-can-eat pizza service at night has brought them profits in the winter for the first time in three years. In some offices in a small arcade on the main avenue a designer tweaks the vectors on the logo of a surf boutique, a lawyer holds an almost full packet of cigarettes under the bathroom tap until it is drenched and then throws it in the bin, and a Pilates instructor hangs a student upside down on a wall using hooks and belts. He has been swimming without looking ahead for several minutes when he senses something strange. He raises his head and sees what appears to be a rock but which then reveals itself to be the warty black mass of a right whale some thirty to forty yards away. His first reaction is to swim away in panic but he calms down as he observes the unmoving animal. It must be one of the last whales of the season and is incredibly close to the beach, perhaps eighty yards. He sees Beta as a bluish blob with legs in the sand. A handful of humans is admiring the cetacean from the beach. The whale blows and a shiver runs down his spine. Then there is another jet, smaller and higher-pitched, and he realizes that there is a calf near the mother, out of sight, on the other side of her. The whale doesn't seem bothered and he can't tell if she is watching him. Her enormity is intimidating but she gives off a sense of calm and camaraderie. Her back appears and disappears in the waves, reflecting the blue of the sky, and she flaps her flippers out of the water. It occurs to him that the whale is nursing and that the calf is probably a newborn. As he emerges from the water Beta throws herself into the shallow waves to meet him. He plays with her in the sand a little and suddenly everyone around them gasps in admiration. The whale starts beating her tail in the water. A young woman standing near by says with a smile that the whale is happy because of her baby. Each beat of her tail makes a big splash and produces a pleasant boom. The whale starts to swim away and he heads home too, walking slowly with Beta limping behind him. She is already able to walk long distances but still has difficulty running. Over in the direction of the town he sees a column of grey smoke and then another. It is too much smoke to be garbage burning in empty lots. A man is surfing the point break in the south corner of Silveira Beach alone. The sea is calm and the waves are low. There is no one else on the beach and a feeling of solitude suddenly grips the surfer with a mixture of ecstasy and terror. It is a winter day that feels summery. Sitting on his surfboard, he wiggles his toes in the cold water and imagines that there is no world on the other side of the hills. A gull appears out of nowhere and starts flying in circles over his head. It is all white and he wonders if maybe it isn't a gull after all. He can't tell. The circles get smaller and smaller and the surfer is suddenly certain that he is receiving a warning to get out of the water immediately. He has been detecting a series of subtle variations in the sea, invisible phenomena that are hard to describe. The rocky bottom starts to bubble. He paddles with all his strength towards the water's edge, electrified with fear, aiming at a fixed point in the sand. As the surfer runs through the shallows with water up to his knees he finally looks back and sees gigantic waves breaking over the rocky seabed, the waves that he believes would have drowned him.

He spends his entire afternoon shift at the pool thinking about what he is going to say to Saucepan and when it is time he just says that he wants to leave the job, if possible only for a while. Saucepan can't accept it.

Do you want a raise?

That's not why.

Why, then?

I need a bit of time.

When do you want to leave?

Now.

You know that's not how it works. I need a month's notice.

A bald guy with a hugely muscular upper body and skinny legs lets out animal-like grunts as he completes his last few reps in a set of lateral raises, dumps the dumbbells on the wooden floor and paces in circles around the weights room next to reception, panting as he goes. Débora rolls her eyes and goes back to the game she is playing on her mobile phone.

A month is too long for me.

I need at least two weeks to find someone else.

I'll stay another two weeks, then.

OK, but talk to me. What would make you stay?

Nothing, Saucepan. Sorry. But I might be back in a while.

I can't guarantee that you'll have your job back.

I know. When it's time we'll see. Thanks for the opportunity to work here. It's been really important to me.

You'll be missed, man.

Saucepan shrugs and leaves. Débora was listening to everything and now looks at him with her lips pressed together and raised eyebrows.

I hope you have a good reason.

Me too.

Aren't you ever going to shave off that beard? You'd look a lot better without it.

You think so?

Not just me.

I'll give it some thought, then.

Are you OK?

In what sense?

You've been looking a bit down in the dumps lately. I've seen the winter here do a lot of people in.

It's like a summer's day today.

You know what I'm talking about. A guy finds himself on his own without his girl in the cold weather, quits his job, stops going out, no one sees him any more. I don't want you to . . . I dunno.

It's not like that, Deb. I'm fine. Don't worry about me.

If you need anything, talk to me. OK? Anything.

He nods.

Take care, Mystery Face.

I bet the twins invented that one too.

Of course.

I haven't left yet, Débora. I've still got two more weeks. See you tomorrow.

He hesitates a little before leaving and walks around the counter. Débora stands before he gets there and they hug at length without saying anything. Beta walks past the glass door.

Your dog pulled through, didn't she?

She's great. I walked here today, slowly, and she came with me.

I heard she swims out in the deep with you.

She swims a little, yes, but not out in the deep. People exaggerate.

He tells Débora about his early-morning encounter with the whale and she doesn't seem particularly impressed. She touched a whale while surfing at Ferrugem Beach four winters ago and has seen dolphins leap out of the water right before her eyes as they chased a school of mullet. He gives up and says goodbye.

He buys a cheese sandwich from an itinerant vendor in the Silveira Supermarket car park, eats it sitting on the low wall next to the pavement and by the time he starts to head home night has fallen. The Al Capone is open as always and he has a beer sitting at an outdoor table. Janis Joplin is playing softly in the background and he remembers a cassette-tape compilation that he used to listen to on his Walkman on the bus to school. The Rastafarian waiter strokes Beta's neck and looks both ways down the avenue as if something might happen. There is a couple inside and two men at a table outside near his. They all know that this winter night is already over and they'll soon leave. No stranger will talk to him. No one has talked to him lately. He eats the salted peanuts, finishes his beer off quickly and pays the bill.

He has walked just over a block towards the sea when a blackout blots out the town. The main avenue becomes a dark tunnel of cold wind. The stars slowly become visible and his eyes adapt to the light of the new moon, revealing a world of silhouettes. On his way to the beach all he can hear is the sound of Beta's paws clicking on the tarmac. The black ocean snores in the darkness like a large slumbering animal, its waves breaking rhythmically like gentle breathing. Solitary figures go past on the sand, though it is unclear where they are coming from or going to. Gas lanterns light the insides of some of the fishing sheds. He carries Beta up the rickety steps and sets her down again on the footpath. The glow of a cigarette reveals another three or four figures coming in the opposite direction and when they pass him, not far from his apartment, he feels a fist land with full force in his face and falls on to the narrow grassed area between the path and the rocks. His partial vision fails him altogether now and his head throbs. As he tries to get his bearings he hears Beta yelp. He clambers into a standing position and sees the figures crossing the strip of sand between the end of the path and the entrance to the square. A valve of pain opens and he feels his left eye swelling. Beta is leaning against his legs. He squats and pats her. She appears unharmed. She must have been kicked. He almost shouts something and goes after his attacker but the group is gone. They didn't laugh, swear at him or threaten him with anything, but their message was clear.

He wakes up with a black half-moon under his eye but the swelling has been brought down by the previous night's ice pack. Broken blood vessels have tinged the white of his eye red. The pain comes and goes and extends up to his forehead and down to his chin. He goes for his walk on the beach with Beta and watches her enter the water on her own and paddle in the waves for a few minutes. On his way back he finds a fisherman sitting on a mountain of blue-and-white nylon that has been resting on Baú Rock for a few days. The man is strong, with tanned skin, a sparse beard and curly hair and is dressed in a pair of dirty white football shorts and flip-flops. He stops for a moment at the top of the cement steps and watches the man use a reel of nylon twine, a small penknife and a kind of plastic needle to mend the fishing net with the fast, hypnotic movements of an illusionist. The fisherman glances up from his work for just a second and smiles out of the corner of his mouth.

Trip over?

I got a free punch last night.

Who was it?

Couldn't see. It was during the blackout.

I almost didn't recognize you with that beard there.

He studies the fisherman again, looking for a sign that might remind him of his identity, but doesn't find anything. He wants to ask but feels his pride like a hand on his mouth, the pride that Jasmim recognized. The lion on his throne. He misses her. Everything he imagined he'd share with her.

I'm sorry, but do we know each other?

It's Jeremias, the owner of *Poeta*, the boat that was being repaired in front of the rock on his first morning in the apartment. He sits on a step and asks how the fishing season went. Not good, not good, says Jeremias. We get fewer fish every year. It's the anchovy season now but nobody's catching anything. It's tough. There's croakers. The season opens soon and we're hoping to catch a few. All the while continuing to mend his net, he says that the *Poeta*'s motor died in June and will have to be replaced, but he doesn't know where he'll get the money. I'll tell you something. Fishermen like me will last another ten, fifteen years at the most in these parts. The big industrial boats are doing away with the fish. They round them up out at sea and nothin' comes to the coast. There's no money in this any more and the young folk aren't interested. None of my boys or nephews have gone into the trade. Not one. Of everyone here in the village, only three or four fishermen's boys fish. The ones who've got money get degrees, open shops, become dentists. The ones who don't work in tourism or look after summer houses. And there're the ones who hang around and do nothing. Even us fishermen end up havin' to work on the side as bricklayers, waiters, dustbin men, postmen. When the seas are rough and it's rainin' you need five or six men to pull in a net and there aren't enough for the job. All these boats here, he says, pointing with his needle at the boats anchored in the bay, the whole lot'll be runnin' boat tours in ten years' time.

When I first arrived here I read in the paper that the biggest school of croakers in the history of the town was caught here last year. There was a photo of a pile of fish the size of a truck.

Jeremias laughs and shakes his head as if he shouldn't talk about it but reveals that the school of croakers was rounded up out at sea by a large industrial trawler in an illegal manoeuvre during the closed season. The local fishermen found out, put several boats in the water and sailed out to the trawler. There were threats of violence, the trawler's crew got scared and when everyone had calmed down they struck an agreement. Most of the fish brought in were already dead. The trawler kept five tons and the fishermen of Garopaba took the rest. When they arrived it looked as if they had caught those sixty-four tons of croakers with their own nets. The story, he says, just proves that our days are numbered. It's not worth it any more to buy a ton of nylon and pay someone to hand-sew a net. The industrial nets are cheaper. This net I'm mending here is two and a half miles long. It'll take me another three days to finish. In the past the women used to stay at home making nets. Those days are over too. They don't think it's their job. The younger generation doesn't even know how. Ever been to Laguna? The women there still make nets. It's a pleasure to watch. They're so fast you don't even see the needle. It's all over here. Soon there'll be universities and the young folks are going to get degrees and move away as soon as they can. Not to mention the climate. It's a mess. They all sit around arguing about whether or not the climate's changing, but us fishermen know for a fact that it is. In the old days we knew that in October we'd have calm seas, southerly winds, blue skies. It'll be October soon and you'll see the mess. It won't change anything for me. I'm getting on in years. That dog of yours likes the water, doesn't she? She goes out swimming with you. I've seen her.

She does. She was hit by a car and lost a lot of movement in her paws. I taught her to swim and now she's almost recovered.

Is that so? Well I'll be. Never seen anything like it.

She sees her master swimming all the time: I'd say she got it from me.

Must be a family thing.

They exchange a smile.

Sure you don't know who gave you that black eye?

I couldn't see. I think it was the kids who hang around on the rocks.

If you find out or if it happens again you let me know.

OK.

I know everyone.

Thanks.

He gets up and stretches.

See you later, Jeremias. I was going to go for a swim but it's a bit late now. I'm going to have lunch and go to work. Have a good day.

Jeremias nods without taking his eyes off the net and his needle. He works there from dawn to dusk for three days, sitting in the same position, mending his net with his back to the sea, and on the fourth day the net disappears.

He works his last few afternoon shifts at the pool unable to hide the fact that his head is elsewhere. The vigilance with which he usually instructs and corrects his students gives way to a glum lack of focus. Spatula, Saucepan's partner, puts in a rare appearance and tells him that if he has to pretend he's working, he's better off leaving once and for all.

One morning the skeletal, long-nosed postman hands him an envelope that isn't an electricity or phone bill. The first personal correspondence he has received since he's been there is from Jasmim. Inside the envelope is a letter* written in large handwriting and a photograph that she took of the two of them in Ferrugem. They are sitting at a table in Bar do Zado at sunset. She is wearing a white halter top with a yellow-flower print and hoop earrings. He studies her curls tumbling down over her shoulders, the piercing in her left ear, her black skin with its golden sheen, flared nostrils, small eyes, fleshy mouth glistening with lip gloss. There is a certain seriousness in her gaze. Her lips are parted, showing the tips of her white teeth, but her smile is small, as if she were more surprised than happy. He isn't wearing a shirt and has messy hair, a long beard and a broad smile that stretches from ear to ear. At first he thinks she has sent him a picture of herself with another guy, but it can only be him.

* *Hey, fish. You asked for a photo of me, but I'm sending one of the two of us, because I want you to remember your own face too whenever you want to remember mine. You're very good-looking and I reckon you know it. I'm helping my mother out in the restaurant while I decide what to do with my life. The curse of the treasure hasn't caught up with me (I hope!). I'm working on a proposal to try for a Master's in Rio de Janeiro. I'm resigning myself to being alone and hoping it doesn't take you long to find the person you're looking for. I didn't mean to hurt you and I hope you don't hold it against me. I adored being part of your life. I hope Beta is well and running on the beach with you. I like remembering how you took care of her. Put this photo of us somewhere safe. xxx J.*

Every morning he runs barefoot to Siriú or rides to Silveira and swims across the bay, where he sees timid schools of fish in the clear water, the first and only sign of the approaching spring in those weeks of dry, persistent cold. Beta is now allowed out all the time and never ventures far from home except on her early-morning walks, when she limps along the beach with growing boldness and swims through the waves like no Blue Heeler before her. She tags along whenever he goes out on foot and heads back to the vicinity of the apartment only if he stomps on the ground and shoos her away with a short, dry hiss, one of the signs of the new language that is slowly replacing the previous one established over a decade and a half of living with his father. His long, frequent runs along the beach bring him knee pain for the first time in years. He spends his nights in bed in his dark, slightly musty room with the windows and shutters closed, eating pasta or rice and meat straight from the pot, bags of ice on his knees, playing FIFA on PlayStation. He feels hungry all the time and takes to going around with bars of chocolate and packets of biscuits in his pocket. Every time he goes out he feels like he is being watched and he starts to avoid meeting people's gazes. Sleep hits him and passes in a flash. He compares his face in the mirror with the photo of his grandfather and notices that his own beard is already a little longer than his grandfather's. His thinner, more tanned, older-looking face has never appeared more like the one in the photograph and every time he wakes after a lightning-quick night he feels as if he has spent the last few hours dreaming he was his grandfather, wandering the coastal cliffs and hills on sultry afternoons filled with thunder, lightning, drops of rain, water splashing up as the waves break against the rocks, herds of cows trampling trails, grasses rustled by snakes, black birds in flight and ocean winds. The rain arrives quietly. No one gives it much thought and there is no reason to believe it won't leave in a few days as it always does. The last few whales head with their calves for the Antarctic seas and with them the last few winter tourists go too.

The news that he's leaving the gym spreads among the students and he starts receiving invitations to farewell outings and dinners that he politely turns down with lies. After a certain point it doesn't even occur to him to recharge his mobile phone battery.

His brief career as a swimming instructor at Academia Swell comes to an end on an abnormally busy Saturday morning. A lot of locals are out and about despite the fine rain and on his way home he notices that many are carrying small blue or red flags and listening to handheld or car radios. A taxi driver explains that a live election debate is taking place on Rádio Garopaba between the two contenders for mayor: the Progressive Party's candidate, who is up for re-election, and his opponent from the Workers' Party. For weeks all the talk in town has been focused on promises of paved streets and new municipal health clinics, accusations of favouritism and corruption, videos and recordings on the internet showing supposed cases of vote-buying, and a rumour that the current mayor has a new swimming pool paid for with public funds, which hasn't stopped hundreds of his supporters, most born and bred in Garopaba, from flocking to the square waving blue flags with a few colourful umbrellas among them. The Rádio Garopaba headquarters is in an office adjacent to the parish church and the stairs are cordoned off with tape and watched by two guards. A car with a loudspeaker on top blasts out the debate for all to hear and each good reply by a candidate is applauded and celebrated with cries of support and slogans. There are people of all ages, with respectable families and gangs of adolescents moving through the crowd like schools of fish, and tense Party members in dark glasses coordinating things. Wary children watch everything, leaning against cars or sitting on their parents' shoulders, and elderly people look rejuvenated, dashing here and there, cheering with raised fists, reeling somewhat from the overload of stimuli. There is something threatening in the air. Workers' Party activists circulate around the perimeter of the square with red flags and the exchange of threats and cursing is frank and humourless. Politics has got the population worked up, and stories are making the rounds about everything from verbal arguments and fist fights to iron bars and fish knives. Ever since he got punched in the face by strangers he has avoided getting too close to the locals but today it seems that all aggressive impulses are being channelled towards the exaltation of one or another candidate and hatred for his opponent and his opponent's voters. He remains at the edges of the tumult, neutral in his preference and at the same time interested in the growing intensity of the collective frenzy. A few cars inch their way through the alleyways around the square, honking endlessly. Over the loudspeakers the current mayor refutes his adversary's allegation that he is planning to raise property-tax rates and says that during the four years of his administration rates have merely kept pace with inflation. The crowd celebrates his answer with flag-waving, horn-honking and shouting. Girls parade around in heavy make-up with glistening lips, long, straight hair, platform shoes and their best and tightest jeans. A fisherman in tattered clothes doesn't tire of inciting others to shout, The people united will never be defeated! with little success. Many people are drunk and beer cans are inadvertently kicked across the ground. The unexpected arrival of two cars carrying opposition party members creates a stir. Workers' Party members wave red flags out of the windows and try to forge a path through the busy street with their vehicles. The people in the square start chanting, Look who's desperate! Look who's desperate! The din is so great that the debate can no longer be heard. People start plastering the cars with blue stickers. The driver of one car tries to tear a blue flag out of the hand of a voter and a heated argument spreads in waves of shouting, running, pushing and shoving. Parents start ushering their children away but the fight is soon broken up and the crowd parts to let the two cars drive away. They disappear around the first corner. The Workers' Party candidate speaks poorly of the doctors in Garopaba, giving rhetorical ammunition to the current mayor, who wins the debate. The two opponents can soon be seen talking to the local press at the entrance to the church, at the top of the hill, and a few minutes later they start walking down the stairs. The Workers' Party candidate leaves discreetly while the current mayor savours each step and opens his arms like an emperor going to meet his people to the sound of his campaign jingle. He is a large man who looks like an American film star who is murdered in *The Godfather*. As the mayor picks up a child a new fight breaks out between opposing activists on the beach side of the square. He is a certain distance from the centre of the commotion but he is able to see men and women in a scuffle and a man getting knocked to the ground with a leg sweep and getting up again. The police move in quickly and the fight is reduced to small groups backing off while swearing and making threats. In the meantime a rally led by the car with loudspeakers has begun to form. He buys a beer at the coffee shop on the corner of the square and tags behind the cars and pedestrians as they head for the town centre. It isn't long before dozens of cars and hundreds of motorbikes and bicycles form a long serpent that slithers through the narrow streets of the village to the main avenue, passing the health clinic. The intermittent rain slowly drenches the participants. The sounds of car horns, engines revving and exhaust pipes backfiring mix with the repetitive election jingle in an infernal cacophony. The motorbikes

320

lead the way down the main avenue, most with a driver and someone on the back waving a flag. In their wake comes a line of cars, pickups and SUVs packed with people. A toothless man in the back of a pickup that is falling to pieces beats on the roof incessantly with a bicycle wheel. Some people ride on car bonnets and boots. The rally becomes an apocalyptic parade and those who are not involved look on in shock from pavements and front gardens. Men whistle at rain-drenched women leaning out of cars displaying their cleavage while older residents sip maté and smoke, watching everything with a slightly bored expression. Everyone seems about to crash their car, fall off their motorbike or start a fight. He follows the rally for a while, but when the rain gets heavier he decides to call it a day. He stops off for another two beers on his way home and in one tavern he hears that someone tried to stab a rival voter and accidentally clipped a child's arm. Another man brags that he sold his vote to both candidates on the same day and confesses that he still isn't sure who to vote for. When the men at the next table find out that he is from Porto Alegre they ask how the election is going there. He hiccups, says he hasn't got the slightest idea and gets up to pay. Then he returns to the table and quickly looks at each of their faces.

Do I know any of you?

Slowly they say no.

Nice to meet you, then. Goodbye, gentlemen.

He walks back to the village through the trail of silence, flags, exhaust fumes and beer cans left in the wake of the rally. The jingle, the yelling, the engines and horns grow more and more distant until they completely disappear.

II

He waits for the rain to stop for two days but by the third it is evident that it isn't going to let up any time soon. Matches won't light. Droplets of water slide down the sides of the old white refrigerator as if it were in a feverish sweat. The moisture in the air weighs down his greasy hair and the dog's fur. He packs his camping backpack with two changes of clothes, a towel, a bar of soap, a toothbrush, the knife with the armadillo-leather handle, his tightly rolled sleeping bag, two lighters, a small mirror, a bottle of mineral water, a quarter of a wheel of cheese, a salami, two packets of cream-filled biscuits, dried bananas, a few apples and a packet of dry dog food, all in plastic bags. He puts on a tracksuit, his waterproof jacket, his running shoes and a cap. He firmly closes the windows and waits for Beta to come out before locking the door and hiding the key under a rock among some plants alongside the building. He pats Beta's ribs and she wags her tail a little. The winter cold has gone but the sun is unable to force its way through the clouded sky.

After thinking for a moment he decides to head out through Vigia Point. He passes the unoccupied summer mansions on deforested grounds and reaches the headland. The trail grows narrower and steeper as the native vegetation closes in. Where it starts to drop down towards the sea the scrub gives way to bromeliads, cactuses and small coastal bushes capable of withstanding the constant wind and drawing sustenance from the saline soil. Thorny leaves nick the legs of his tracksuit. Beta isn't intimidated and moves at her steady, tenacious pace, disappearing in stretches where the grasses are high. The trail ends at a granite outcrop made dark by the rain and he looks for another, higher way through for Beta. The going is treacherous and he advances one step at a time. His feet slip on smooth rocks and sink ankle-deep into mud. Halfway up the headland he looks down and sees tide pools shielded from the waves by rocks and covered with thick layers of brown foam. He moves cautiously until the slope levels out and the low scrub gives way again to the grass of a large residential subdivision that is for the most part undeveloped. Near the only house standing a man shouts something and starts walking towards him. Beta stiffens and growls. The man stops about thirty feet away, adjusts his straw hat and places his hand on the handle of a large knife hanging from his waist.

You can't come through here. Private property.

I'm taking the trail to Silveira.

You'll have to go back.

I won't walk on your land. I'll go around it.

You can't come in here.

The watchman spits on the ground and points at a row of stone markers in the sand a few yards from the waves.

Is that the perimeter?

Yep.

That's totally illegal.

Not my problem. You'll have to turn back.

No way.

He clicks his tongue to call the dog and starts heading up the next hill. The man comes after him.

Hey. Don't make me —

323

He turns and walks towards the watchman with firm footsteps as he lets the backpack slip off his shoulders. Beta growls again.

Get out of my way and leave me alone or I swear to God I'll kill you here and now.

His backpack drops on to the grass and the watchman takes a step back. He has drawn his knife but is holding it down by his thigh. The two of them study one another for a time, then the watchman leaves without a word.

He puts his backpack on again and resumes his hike. The rain grows heavier and rivulets of water run down the grassy slope between cowpats. Halfway up three bay stallions and a white mare snap out of a contemplative daze and enter a state of alert as he approaches. Their manes have been clipped and their taut bodies look waterproof. He feels a foolish urge to mount them, and one of the stallions stomps its front hoof as if it knows.

On the Ferrugem headland he inspects a few steep trails that lead down through the cliffs and finds a natural shelter covered with cave drawings among the rocks. After carrying Beta down, he spends the first night there, drying off as best he can and curling up in his sleeping bag. He uses a lighter to study the triangular patterns and large circles and diamonds decorating the walls but the drawings remain indecipherable. He can't imagine ancient people trying to represent anything but fish, waves, arrows and celestial bodies but the geometric shapes in the cave don't remind him of any of these. They are codes for other things. The cave is dry and clean except for a green plastic bottle and the waxy remains of a white candle that may have been left there by a solitary fisherman or a hermit. When night falls the darkness is absolute. Waves are breaking near by but they sound further away. Little by little the subterranean rumble and the smell of stagnant seawater make the cavern strangely cosy and he sleeps peacefully.

He continues heading south for a few days. He hikes up and down hills with the sea and cliffs on his left and, on his right, stretching for miles out to the dark green wall of the Tabuleiro Mountains, a landscape of slopes and flatlands where he sees summer homes, deforested subdivisions, islands of native forest, dunes covered with a dark web of grasses, rice plantations, cattle pastures, lagoons and dirt roads. When the rain lets up, from higher vantage points he can see the paved lanes of the highway and roadside communities. The tapestry of vivid contrasts comes to life on the rare occasions that the rain stops and the clouds part enough to allow a few rays of sunlight through. Night falls and the day breaks as always but he goes for days on end without seeing a shadow. There is no thunder or wind. When he comes to beaches, he crosses them quickly and returns as soon as possible to the hills, valleys and headlands. He finds the vestiges of fires and campsites in clearings beside trails beaten by the herds of cattle that roam the slopes looking for places to graze. On the surfaces of some beachside rocks are polished circles and longitudinal grooves used by indigenous peoples to sharpen their instruments thousands of years ago. He walks slowly so Beta can keep up and takes long detours to avoid more difficult stretches. Sometimes he carries her over rocks and sometimes she waits for him to return. She eats her dog food faster than usual and looks surprised when she is done.

When he gets to Ferrugem Beach he takes shelter for a few hours at Bar do Zado. He orders a fried pastry and a Coke and drapes his sleeping bag over one of the tables to let it dry out a little. The incessant rain has even driven away the surfers, and the girl at the cash register asks if he is lost and keeps a watchful eye on him the whole time he is there. On Barra Beach a man in a light purple bathrobe smoking a cigar on the second-floor balcony of his house waves when he passes and he waves back. On the trail to Ouvidor Beach he passes a man in a blue raincoat fishing and finds two arrow tips in a small landslide of sandy soil eroded by the rain. The bed and breakfasts and beach bars in the south corner of Rosa Beach are still closed or undergoing renovations. Concrete mixers, shovels and piles of wood sit idle in flooded, temporarily abandoned building sites. He hasn't seen a soul all day and doesn't think twice before stripping off his clothes and using an open-air shower. He manages to sleep, clean and dry, on the deck of a small shopping complex built over a strip of sand beside the dirt road. In the morning he is awoken by Beta's barking and sees some cars parked near by. A surfer is cursing as he tries to do up the zipper on his wetsuit a little further down the deck. He gets up and offers to help but the pale, red-haired kid takes a few steps back, says it isn't necessary, picks up his colourful surfboard and heads for the water with his zipper still open. The waves are big and every so often he sees a small, courageous figure in a black wetsuit dropping into a wall of water and tearing the surface of a wave. The rain hasn't stopped and the shops haven't opened their doors but the presence of surfers guided by weather reports, who have probably come a long way to make the most of the portentous swell, indicates that it must be Saturday or Sunday. He realizes that he has lost track of the days.

That morning he crosses the next hill and comes out on Luz Beach and then the sandbar at the entrance to Ibiraquera Lagoon. There, a strong, icy wind blows in and he starts to tremble violently with cold. He eats the rest of the food in his backpack and instead of continuing along the beach he takes the dirt road and walks to the first junction. Cars go past from time to time but don't stop. Finally the driver of a white pickup sees him signalling for a lift and pulls over. He greets the man through the crack in the window.

Morning.

Afternoon.

Where are you headed?

To Tubarão. I'm going to get on the interstate.

Hmm.

Where do you want to go?

Garopaba.

I can leave you in Araçatuba.

That'll work. Thanks.

The dog'll have to ride in the back.

I'll ride with her. She might jump out.

The chubby blond man looks straight ahead, with one hand on the gear stick and the other on the steering wheel with a lit cigarette. His skin is a little reddish and he is unshaven. He is wearing a grey knitted jumper, a scarf and beret. The stench of tar wafts through the window. The windscreen wipers squeak against the glass three times.

Ah, what the hell, get in.

He leans across to unlock the passenger door.

With the dog?

He nods and waves them in.

He puts his backpack in the middle seat and settles the dog at his feet.

I'm going to get your car all wet.

Don't worry, it'll dry as soon as the sun comes out.

The pickup rattles on the road dug out by the rain. The driver blows his smoke through a crack in the window and clears his throat from time to time.

Where're you coming from?

Garopaba, actually.

You work here in Ibiraquera?

No, just hiking around a bit.

In the rain?

I left home thinking it was going to stop in two or three days but I'm not so sure it was a good idea.

The flood in Blumenau's looking pretty ugly. A friend of mine works at the Port of Itajaí and said the water hasn't stopped rising.

Really? Flooding?

Haven't you seen it on TV? It's all they've been talking about. They're collecting donations for the flood victims now and the thieving's already started. Not to mention that now they've got an excuse to put off the expansion of the highway for another few years. Every month of delay is worth another ten-bedroom mansion on a hill. In a nature reserve, of course. Contractors, suppliers, everyone's swimming in federal money. It was supposed to be ready in 2008. In the original plan they forgot to include Laguna Bridge, the Morro dos Cavalos Tunnel, a whole bunch of things. Now they're saying it'll be ready in 2010. I'll tell you when it'll be ready. Never. Literally never. When a section of highway is ready another section that was ready two years earlier will need to be rebuilt. The tarmac they're using is like eggshells. The pilfering's never-ending.

Do you use the highway a lot?

All the time. I'm an engineer. I've got two houses under construction here and I came to take a look at them because of all the rain. My clients wanted them ready by December but I told them not to hold their breath.

The headlights of an old truck appear halfway around a bend and the pickup skids and almost slides into a ditch at the side of the road. The engineer curses.

Fucking bastard.

Look what I found when I was walking over the headlands.

He opens the side pocket of his backpack and takes out the two arrow tips.

What're those?

Arrow tips.

The driver flicks his cigarette butt through the crack in the window and takes his eyes off the highway for a second to glance at the two triangular stones that he is holding up in his palm.

Are you sure?

Yep, look at the chipped edges. The stone is smooth, it was polished.

The driver turns his head again but this time doesn't look at the stone, but at him, giving him a quick once-over. The conversation dies. As he gets out he apologizes for having got the seat of his car all wet and offers him one of the arrow tips as a present. The driver thanks him and puts it in his glove box.

He tries to hitch another lift at the side of the road near the turn-off to Araçatuba but no one stops. He is starting to feel hungry so he goes into a diner and orders two meat pasties and a Coke. The girl at the cash register turns her head to the back of the establishment, looking for someone who isn't there, then looks at him.

Have you got money?

Of course I have.

He realizes he is dripping on to the floor and goes to eat in the small covered area outside. He gives half of his second pasty to the dog, pays and starts walking along the edge of the road towards

Garopaba, sticking out his thumb to pickups, trucks and old cars, but no one pulls over and he soon stops looking over his shoulder every time he hears the drone of an engine. Near speed bumps and pedestrian crossings drivers slow down and glance curiously at the bearded man and dog walking in the rain. Chances are he knows some of the people heading for Garopaba but he'd never be able to recognize anyone through the fogged-up windows of a moving vehicle. Just in case, though, he meets every gaze with a smile and a wave. A woman smiles back but doesn't stop and another gives him a piercing look of indifference. One man is about to pull his van over but decides against it mid-manoeuvre and steps on the accelerator. One or two miles later he spots Branca Rock on his left and decides to leave the highway and continue along the dirt road to Encantada.

He is surprised by the abruptness of nightfall and takes shelter in a garage under construction next to an empty house not far off the road. He can see car headlights passing in the distance but all he can hear is the water dripping from the roof and the desperate croaking of toads in the flooded land behind the house. Beta insists on gnawing on one of her back paws, clicking her teeth and panting. He lies down in his sleeping bag but for the first time in days he doesn't feel sleepy. He rolls on to his back, puts his hands behind his head and tries to make out the wooden beams of the roof in the darkness. The cold air has a pleasant smell of wet cement that reminds him of the garage he liked to spend time in as a child. His favourite songs start appearing one after another in his head and he is surprised to discover that they are still intact in his memory. He sings quietly and little by little raises his voice until he is belting it out in the choruses. They are songs that his mother and father used to listen to when he was young. He sees his mother as a young woman singing the sad verses of

'Mucuripe'*, as she trims the pink azaleas and white germanders in the garden of their old house in Ipanema on a Sunday afternoon with the record playing at a high volume in the living room. His father preferred tango and gaucho music and as a result he is able to hum the melody of a few Gardel hits and sing a number of popular folk songs from beginning to end. He sings 'Veterano'†, the 80s classic, in counterpoint to the screeching of the toads and crickets. The louder he sings the warmer his body gets. He has never again heard songs as beautiful as the ones his parents used to listen to. Whatever became of those records? They were divided up when his parents divorced. His father kept his, of that he is sure. No one remembered the records. It upsets him to think that they may have been sold for peanuts or given to Dante. His brother was obsessed with old blues songs in his adolescence and for many years listened to nothing but blues and underground or indie bands that still hadn't found mainstream success. English singers whining that all it does is rain on their heads. And Viviane was the only person he had ever met who liked classical music so much that she frequently went to hear the Porto Alegre Symphony Orchestra and dragged him along to recitals. She knew more about the pieces and composers than the programmes did. To him, it was an ambiguous experience. Sometimes he'd leave the concert hall feeling that he'd been swept away, but he didn't care if he never heard anything like it again. For some reason his ear was unable to retain the music. He didn't have a single word to describe his impressions, couldn't tell the difference between Bach and Mozart and had only a vague notion that there was that famous piece by Beethoven. And yet one piece in particular has never left him. Just

* By Raimundo Fagner & Antônio Carlos Belchior.
† By Leopoldo Rassier.

one, the one Viviane said was her favourite and which she referred to as 'my Chopin nocturne'. That piece *is me*, she used to say. He hums it softly now, most definitely off-key, but the melody resonates in all its lunar placidity, with precise piano notes, in the chamber of his imagination.

The next day he climbs the steep trail up to the top of Branca Rock. He discovers that behind the small escarpment visible from the road is a long wall of rock streaked with lichen. At the top he finds a very beautiful woman in a leotard and tracksuit practising yoga. He puts Beta down after carrying her up the last difficult stretch of trail and looks at the woman, not entirely sure what he is seeing. She is sitting in a strange cross-legged position, completely wet, with her short black hair slicked back on her head. His footsteps finally rouse her from her meditative trance and they stare at one another for a moment, not really understanding the other's presence there. He gets the last two apples from his backpack and they eat them together and talk. She tells him she is on a retreat at a nearby meditation centre and explains that they are sitting on the exact site of one of the biggest energy portals in South America. You can feel it, can't you? The first inhabitants of the region used to speak of a wagon of light that left the lagoon in the south and crossed the sky until it disappeared behind Branca Rock. She shows him the path of the wagon with her pointed finger. Even blurred in the distance by the rain, the landscape is immense. Beyond the highway the swamps and waterlogged fields make everything down below look like it has become a giant lagoon and the dunes and hills of Ferrugem appear as ghostly contours against the phosphorescent grey sky. He says goodbye to the woman, takes the trail back down and continues towards the hills behind Encantada.

The dirt road passes an old sawmill with water-powered wooden gears, and an ox-drawn manioc flour mill. Children in blue-and-white uniforms carrying umbrellas come out of a tiny municipal school and point at him, laughing and whispering shamelessly. The lamp posts end at two wooden houses surrounded by vegetable gardens and pastures fenced off with barbed wire. After this the trail disappears and he doesn't see anyone else for days.

On his second morning lost in these hills he is awoken by warm sunlight. Birds sing and swoop through the air, narrowly missing one another. Colours pulse. There are shadows. He takes off his jacket and T-shirt and feels the sun on the top of his head, nose, shoulders. Lizards with enormous tails warm their blood lying on the rocks, gazing upward like martyrs. He spreads out his clothes and sleeping bag on the rocks, takes the soap and looks for a stream to bathe in. The dog goes with him, snapping at flies, trying to catch them mid-flight. He fills his water bottle and remains naked in the midday sun until he is dry. Half of the sky is blue. Butterflies and cicadas vie for space in the underbrush and the air slowly fills with buzzing in a variety of timbres. Blades of grass sway as crickets land on them. A tiny bush is covered in red wasps that don't look like anything he has seen before in the wild or in photographs or documentaries. He crouches down and watches them for a long while. From time to time they all move a fraction of an inch in perfect synchronicity, reconfiguring their occupation of the bush. He looks around and hasn't a clue where he is. He knows more or less where he came from and where he needs to go from there. A fertile smell wafts up from the moist soil warmed by the sun. Hairy black bumblebees hover in the air, pollinating orchids. The overcast half of the sky starts to encroach on the blue half and he can hear thunder in the distance. He decides to move on and walks along the crest of the hill, picking his way through the vegetation.

In the short space of time between nightfall and the return of the rain he comes across a valley of low scrub covered with a luminous mist of fireflies. He doesn't dare move, as if a single footstep might scare off the thousands of bugs all at once and break the spell. Large raindrops start to fall and the little dots of green light slowly disappear.

He improvises shelter beneath a leafy tree and in the middle of the night is awoken by the dog howling. She is a short distance away and he can't see her. It is the first time he has heard it and he feels strangely guilty, as if he were spying on her in a moment of intimacy. Her howls are long and far apart and there is no answer.

At the end of the next day he realizes that he is walking along the ridge of Freitas Hill. To his left he sees the streets and houses of Paulo Lopes and on his right Costa do Macacu and Siriú Lagoon. Somewhere near by must be the land that Santina's children will inherit. He spends another night out in the open. It no longer bothers him that he is wet and the hunger that has clawed at his stomach over the last few days has disappeared. The following day he continues walking from one hilltop to the next with plodding footsteps, followed by the dog a short distance behind him, avoiding roads and plantations, until he is close to the village centre of Siriú Beach.

He heads down the first trail he finds, stops at the first diner he sees and orders a cheese-and-chicken-heart sandwich. The sound of his own voice echoes in his head and it occurs to him that he hasn't uttered a word since his conversation with the yogi in Encantada. Two young men in baseball caps and baggy jeans are drinking beer and smoking cigarettes at the table next to him, slouched in their plastic chairs. Their dialogue is cryptic but they seem to be talking about a party and a girl who was there. The skinny one talks more and the muscular one listens as he turns the alarm of his car parked outside on and off with his key. The small TV on the wall is showing a dubbed film but the volume is so low it is almost inaudible. The pregnant woman in a white apron and hairnet who takes orders and flips burgers at the same time appears with his sandwich and a tray with napkins and sachets of ketchup and mayonnaise. His contracted stomach can tolerate only half of the sandwich. He leaves the rest on some grass near a post for the dog to eat. A news bulletin interrupts an advertisement and shows scenes of the flood. A river of chocolatey rapids cutting right through a highway. Men rowing boats around an archipelago of roofs. Families camped out in a gymnasium.

He asks the young men for a cigarette. They look at him with blank faces and he asks again. The muscular one gets up, walks over to his table, holds out the packet, waits for him to take a cigarette with his long, mud-caked fingernails and holds out the lighter for him. He thanks him, puffs on the cigarette a few times without inhaling and tosses it half burned into the middle of the puddle-filled road.

Argh! Disgusting shit.

He clears his throat and spits on the pavement. The skinny one lets out a scornful chuckle.

Where'd you come from, nutcase?

He gets up, signals to the waitress, leaves the money on the table, turns his back to the men and walks away talking.

It all started a long, long time ago, he says in a drawn-out, theatrical voice as he walks towards the beach and points at the shadowy mass of the hills. It was a dark . . . stormy night . . .

What a mess, he hears one of them say.

He laughs to himself, checks to make sure Beta is behind him and stomps his way through the puddles until he reaches the sand. Garopaba is on his right, far away and ghostly. He walks to his left until he comes to a seaside hill and takes a trail that soon leaves him on a craggy headland. The waves crash with gusto against the larger rocks, throwing spray high into the air. The rain has dwindled to a drizzle and he looks for a way through for the dog but it is growing more and more difficult. Over the rocks, over the rocks, this is the way, he mutters to himself. He steps from one to another and slowly leaves Siriú behind him. For a long time all he can see is the top of the next rock.

When he finally raises his head to look around he realizes that it is growing dark. He is in the middle of a rocky headland between nothing and nowhere and has already come too far to turn back. He steps on a loose stone and his fall is broken by his backpack but his elbow gets a good whack and he feels the pain travel up his arm to his shoulder like an electric shock. He tests the joint and feels his arm with his other hand. A little blood and some throbbing, nothing to worry about. He lifts the dog on to the larger rocks before scaling them himself. He progresses in this manner until the boulders of granite give way to greenery. He tries to climb the slope but the barrier of bushes is too dense and thorny. He returns to the rocks and shortly before it is pitch black he spots a natural shelter between two large boulders. As he draws closer he discovers that the narrow cavity extends inwards a short way, forming a small, dry grotto. He leaves his backpack inside, makes the dog comfortable and sits at the entrance to his triangular niche as if he were a stone statue placed in the most improbable, absurd place precisely so as not to be seen. The ocean in front of him is a large mass of darkness that is darker than the night, a monster that is both invisible and manifest. He knows he is well above the high-tide mark but is afraid anyway. It is the same kind of irrational fear that slowly grips him when he is swimming alone in deep water. On the other hand, where else could he be safer and more protected? Nothing can touch him here. In a few hours the day will dawn as always and he will be able to leave. No possible surprises tonight. Nothing can happen. Not here.

He strokes Beta, who is warm in spite of everything. Suddenly, without warning, he sees with tremendous clarity something that he has wanted to see for a long time and starts to cry with happiness. He wishes Jasmim were here now, and Viviane, and his mother and father, and even Dante, even the people he wishes he could hate but can't: he wishes they were all here with him now. His dad said it once. You aren't capable of hating anything, kid. It can't do you any good. But that's life, Dad, he answers now staring into the darkness. That's life. He feels lighter and lighter as he thinks these things and falls asleep leaning against the rock.

It takes him the whole of the next morning to get over the rocks and pick his way around a gorge. The next trail crosses the hill through thick vegetation. It is overgrown with grass and bushes and he moves forward almost chest-deep in the dark green tangle, hewing a path for the dog, who comes limping behind. Little by little his legs grow accustomed to the squelchy mud that has replaced the slippery solidity of the rocks. He mutters to himself from time to time. At the top of the hill the trail comes out above a village and a long beach. The residents watch him from the doors and windows of their houses that sit in a cluster of alleyways at the foot of the hill.

He sees people with bags full of fruit and vegetables leaving an old bus parked at the side of a sandy road. He enters the bus through the back door. In the place of seats are boxes and crates of market produce and some women with cloth shopping bags are chatting in the middle of the aisle as they smell pineapples, squeeze mangoes and inspect heads of lettuce. He looks around and the profusion of colours and sweet aromas makes him dizzy. Other customers have already entered behind him and he is forced to go with the flow towards the front door. In the closed environment he realizes that he is wheezing and a little feverish. He gets a bunch of ripe bananas, a pear and two oranges. The woman behind him knocks over a box of beetroots, which roll across the floor, and he helps her pick them up. A plump old man with white hair sitting in the driver's seat weighs the customers' choices on a pair of scales and takes their money. He places his items in the crate for weighing and rummages through the outside pocket of his wet backpack until he finds his last two coins.

Is this enough?

There's a bit left over.

Keep the change.

The tabby cat on the wooden deck of an isolated beachfront bar is unperturbed by their presence. He pulls a stool up to a table and eats the fruit, gazing at the steep beach pummelled by heavy rain. He starts talking to himself and the dog and realizes that he shouldn't stay still for too long or he won't be able to continue. He stands, takes the steps down to the sand and walks along the beach to the next hill.

The stormy seas have excavated the dune leading over to the next beach, exposing stone steps that are so regular they look man-made. On the other side a long series of dunes and clumps of coastal scrub hugs the contour of a beach that extends almost as far as the eye can see. He advances at a firm, slow pace, staring into the distance, lightly buffeted by the wind blowing from the ocean. He passes the skeleton of a porpoise or a right whale calf, with a crocodilian skull poking out of the waterlogged sand and a long row of half-buried vertebrae. He can't imagine what a day without rain is like any more.

In the middle of the afternoon he arrives at the mouth of a river that flows slowly and mightily like lava towards the sea, dragging tree branches from distant mountains. On the other side is a village and a few fishermen are attempting a risky crossing on narrow rafts. One of them, wearing a heavy-duty raincoat, agrees to transport him to the other side and asks where he is from, where he is going, and if he needs any help. He gives each question a great deal of thought as if he hasn't understood it and is trying to come up with an answer only to be polite. I've come from there, he says pointing. I'm hiking around. Following the hills. I'm fine, thanks. Bringing me across the river is already a big help, he says, as his hand is crushed in a goodbye handshake. The fisherman then watches the hirsute figure walk away with the dog limping behind him until he disappears down the trail to the next beach, and the other fishermen come over one by one wanting to know what that was all about.

The trail goes around the first hill, following the river, and leads to a small beach occupied by a herd of cattle. The cows wander among the rocks, calves behind them, and the bulls raise their heads to watch him pass. Beta starts to bark and part of the herd stirs and trots quickly towards the back of the beach, gathering near a small cascade formed by run-off water from the hill. There are two closed fishing sheds, one of which has a sign above the door with the name of a bar that must only open in summer. The trail continues over the next hill and comes out on a deserted beach walled in by an inaccessible green slope. As he is crossing this beach the lightning starts. The claps of thunder take a long time to arrive after each flash but are slow to pass. He tries to pick up his pace but can only go at the same speed. He doesn't have the strength to go any faster and is afraid he'll give out entirely if he goes any slower.

After crossing the deserted beach he climbs to the top of a grassy slope and is surprised by the sight of a large valley running parallel to the sea that extends as far as he can see until it is swallowed by the grey mist of the rain. The trail forks off and he chooses to follow the crest of the hill that separates the valley from the sea because the approaching night will be stormy and the trees on that side look like they might offer a little shelter. Night must be falling, though he can't tell for sure and he walks as quickly as he can. The trunks and branches of the pines on the edge of the cliff have grown curved due to the incessant wind and look as if they want to jump down to the bottom of the valley in search of some respite. The horizontal rain whips the right side of his face.

Further in, the low, dense treetops neutralize the storm's thrashing, shut out some of the cold and make everything a little quieter. He is looking for a sheltered spot to spend the night when he hears a baby crying. He tries to find a plausible explanation, like the bleating of a sheep or the creaking of a tree trunk swayed by the wind, but it isn't the kind of sound that is easily mistaken and the second time he hears it he is sure. He looks around thinking of hauntings and improbable phenomena. Can a sound be carried so far by the wind? A little further along he catches sight of something yellow among the trees. He approaches cautiously, afraid of what he might find.

The yellow tarpaulin has been pulled taut and tied to the trees on a slant so the water will run off it. It serves as a roof for a small igloo-shaped tent. The baby's crying is coming from inside it and the light of what is probably a gas lantern projects the silhouettes of two people against the green nylon of the tent. He shouts hello and claps his hands to attract their attention. The door is unzipped. A head of long black hair with Coke-bottle glasses pokes out.

The couple are called Jarbas and Valquíria but he prefers to be called Duck and she goes by Val. The baby is thirteen months old and is called Ítalo. They are from Santa Cruz do Sul and live most of the year in an eco-village. Duck comes out of the tent and squats next to him in the small area protected by the tarpaulin, hugging his knees with his arms. He is very thin and his glasses enlarge his eyes like magnifying lenses. His mane of unruly black curls frames his face like a cluster of flowers. Val leans out a little to say hi and take a good look at the visitor. She has thin lips, thick eyebrows, short, straight hair and a pinkish mark high on her left cheek. Neither of them smiles at any point. Even after days or weeks of non-stop rain their campground is dry, which must mean that Duck and Val set up camp there some time ago, before the rain started. The slightly sloping terrain helps with drainage. They have dug ditches around the tent and set up a small gas-operated camp stove. In the corner are a black umbrella and a few plastic bags of garbage. Duck lights the stove, puts a teapot on to boil and starts preparing a gourd of maté. The baby wails endlessly and appears to have been wailing for a long time but his parents seem to be able to tune out or ignore their protective instincts and remain immune to his shrieks.

Have you been camping here long?

Almost a month. We came when Ítalo turned one.

I got a fright when I heard him crying.

He's got a fever.

Have you given him any medicine?

We took him to the medical clinic in Pinheira yesterday, says Val. They gave him some medicine.

They both speak very slowly and pause for so long before answering anything that he gets the impression they aren't going to respond.

What are you doing here?

What do you mean?

Why are you camping here in this rain?

Why are you walking through the hills in this rain?

I didn't know it was going to rain until the end of time when I left home.

We didn't know either when we came here to camp.

Val hands a small roll of tinfoil to her companion, who starts to break up the marijuana in a small, round grinder.

Where are we?

Neither of them replies for a long time. Duck closes the joint and Val uses an interval in the baby's wailing to ask, In what sense?

In what sense what?

You asked where we are.

I want to know what place this is.

We're in the valley.

Don't you know the valley?

No. What's it near?

Pinheira's that way, over the hill, about twenty minutes from here, says Duck, pointing in slow motion as he licks the cigarette paper.

It's hard to talk to you guys. You talk really slowly.

They don't answer. Val backs into the tent and then emerges holding a roughly built cradle with the baby in it, rolled up in blankets. Hanging from the handle is a decoration that looks like a spider's web.

What's that?

A dreamcatcher.

To catch bad dreams?

She nods.

The Native American Indians used to put them on their cradles, says Duck. The good dreams pass through this hole in the middle, but the bad ones get caught in the web and are undone by the sunlight. And this feather in the middle represents the air and breathing.

The baby looks at the feather swinging in the breeze and learns that air exists, how it works, understands that it is important for him, says Val.

The baby screams so loudly that he chokes.

Is it normal for him to cry like that?

It's the fever. He'll get some fresh air now and will stop for a bit.

What does he eat?

Val gives her first smile and looks out of the corner of her eyes, amused.

I still breastfeed him. And we give him a bit of baby food.

I make it myself, says Duck, holding in his first puff on the joint and offering it to him.

No thanks.

Daddy's mush. Right, pal?

Val takes the joint.

Isn't the smoke bad for him?

No.

A flash of lightning reveals everything and hides it again before he can see anything properly. The thunder makes a dramatic pause before rumbling in. The rain grows heavier. The teapot starts to whistle on the stove. He glances around for Beta but doesn't see her.

Are you looking for something?

My dog. She was just here.

He whistles and calls her name. Beta appears and keeps a distance.

Put her under here with us, says Duck.

She'll shake and get everything wet.

We'll dry her off. Val, get that dirty towel I hung from the tarp.

He calls to Beta until she is convinced she is welcome and wraps her in the towel when she starts to shake. Then he dries her carefully, talking to her in a low voice, while Duck prepares the maté and the marijuana smoke fills the covered area, mixing with the smells of manure, milk, baby poo and tarpaulin. Duck discards the first infusion and fills the gourd again with boiling water.

There you go, wild man. You're shaking with cold. Maté made with rainwater to resuscitate you.

They drink maté and eat Brazil nuts, admiring the night and the lightning. Little Ítalo calms down somewhat and his mother puts the cot back in the tent.

You can sleep under here if you want. But we don't have a camping mattress and the blanket got wet.

I don't want to be a bother.

You won't be.

OK then. I've got a sleeping bag. Thanks.

He takes his damp sleeping bag out of his backpack and partially unrolls it in the small free space under the tarpaulin.

Where're you headed?

Nowhere special. But I think I'm going to start heading home tomorrow.

How many days have you been walking?

I'm not exactly sure. About ten, I think.

I think it's more.

Do you think I'll be able to get a lift to Garopaba from Pinheira?

Definitely. Tomorrow morning I'm going to head down the valley to wash Ítalo's nappies. Come with me and I'll show you the way. It isn't far. You just have to be careful not to take the wrong trail. There are several that go through the hills and lead nowhere, or to the old man's cave.

Old man's cave?

There's an old man who lives in a cave.

Where?

On the other side of the valley.

344

How do you get there?

He doesn't accept visitors. And he's not always there. At least that's what they say. I've never been. No one goes there.

But how do you get there?

It's in the middle of the forest between two trails. One of them leads through the bottom of the valley and the other one goes to the top of the hill. It's almost impossible to see the entrance until you're really close. I've taken the lower trail. There's a barbed-wire fence and from there you can see the cave. The fishermen in Pinheira say he's two hundred years old and they sometimes leave fish and flour on the trail for him. He must have some kind of contagious disease because they always say not to get too close.

He starts rolling up his sleeping bag.

Can you show me how to get to the lower trail?

You want to go there now?

Yep.

I'll show you in the morning. It's too dark now. You won't be able to see a thing.

I'm going now. Will you show me or not?

I'm not going out walking through the dark forest in this rain.

Let him go, mumbles Val inside the tent. The baby starts wailing again.

He hasn't rolled up his sleeping bag properly and now it won't go back in its plastic bag.

I'm going to leave this here. Is that OK? I'll come back for it afterwards.

Mate, no one ever goes there. There's got to be a reason. I reckon the whole story about an old man is just some fisherman's tale. I just mentioned it for the sake of it.

If he wants to go, let him go, says Val, sounding irritated.

Can you at least point me in the direction of the right trail?

Only if you tell me why you're in such a hurry.

I think the old man in the cave is my granddad.

Jarbas, come here.

Duck pushes his glasses up with the tip of his finger, adjusts the position of his head to see him better, then responds to Val's request and stoops to go into the tent. There is something turtle-like about him. The door is zipped closed. Another clap of lightning brings home the unexpected yet obvious realization that to the couple he is a frightening figure who appeared in the night without warning and that their hospitality may only be an indication that they are scared. He hears whispering behind the baby's crying and the noise of the rain. He can't wait to leave. Duck comes out and explains how to find the lower trail that leads to the cave. He needs to stay on the trail he was on before he saw the tent, take it downhill to a miniature beach where there is an old fishing shed, cross the creek that runs through the bottom of the valley and turn left instead of following the main trail. After walking for a while along the foot of the hill, he will see another trail. He will come to a barbed-wire fence on his right and a little further along there will be a kind of gate that actually looks more like barbed wire rolled around some stakes. That's where they say it is.

He thanks him for the shelter and the maté and apologizes for not being able to offer anything in return. Duck leans forward and whispers.

Don't say anything 'cause I don't want Val to know. If we see you again and she accuses you of stealing this, don't deny it.

Duck hands him a battery-operated torch.

I can't accept this.

Bring it back to me later tonight or tomorrow.

I owe you one.

Sure you don't want to go first thing in the morning?

I've got to go now.

He shakes Duck's hand and calls Beta, who is already sleeping. He covers his head with his hood and leaves. The rain is thick and warm. His feet sink into the mud. He uses the torch to find his way out of the woods and guide him along the trail that soon disappears down a slope covered with low grasses. Beyond the light of the torch the darkness is complete but a sense of his bearings gives him an approximate notion of where the trees, rocks, valley, abyss and ocean are. Occasional flashes of lightning offer snapshots of the diluvial landscape.

The valley ends in the miniature beach of rocks that Duck told him about. All the rain has turned the creek into a small river and it takes him a while to find a place to cross. He wades the two to three yards from one side to the other, through the current, with the water above his waist, torch in his mouth, hugging the dog to his chest. The most accessible path through the other side of the valley must be obvious during the day but requires careful exploration in the dark. He retraces his steps and gets his bearings again every time he finds a steep slope or dense forest blocking his way. When he is beginning to suspect that he is searching in vain he sees the barbed-wire fence. He continues groping the fence with his right hand for a few minutes until he comes to the rusty gate of barbed wire. A quick inspection with the torch reveals that it is easier to open than he had thought. He releases one of the stakes from a loop of nylon rope and the gate lies down docilely on the drenched ground.

For a few yards the path is no more than an almost indistinguishable opening in the middle of dense forest. Then suddenly a carefully tended dirt trail becomes visible in the beam of the torch. The grass on either side appears to have been trimmed recently and the surface is firm and smooth even after weeks of rain. It starts to climb the slope, snaking around rocks, which at one point form a continuous wall on his left. He passes his hand along the slimy stone, leaning into its comforting solidity. Beta stays at his heel, sniffing. He realizes that the wild vegetation has begun to show signs of landscaping. He notices strips of well-tended grass and bromeliads fastened with wire to the trunks of trees that bend over the trail like arches.

A natural staircase, with steps moulded by roots, appears and after another abrupt curve around a rock he comes face to face with a large rectangular aquarium at the side of the trail. He approaches it and points the torch. Inside the glass box are several stone, clay and ceramic chips arranged as if they were in a museum display case. The curved lines of many of the fragments suggest that they are pieces of statues, vases or old plates. Some have inscriptions in unknown characters or patterns of triangles and diamonds. In one corner of the aquarium are half a dozen arrow tips similar to the ones he found in his first few days of walking. The lid of the aquarium is well sealed and the very white sand at the bottom preserves a dryness that seems extinct in the world.

A little further along the trail is suddenly interrupted by a large boulder. Looking closer, he sees that there is a low passage under the boulder, low enough to force a man to stoop. Around this opening is a small bamboo portal. He stands there listening for a time, but all he hears is rain. He turns off the torch. A very tenuous, almost undetectable light leaks through the opening. He stoops and enters.

He stands up inside a kind of rocky antechamber weakly lit by the same light he could see from the trail. On his right is a natural opening invaded by the branches of a tree and partially covered with a wavy sheet of asbestos. A narrow vertical opening leads to another section of the cave. He turns on the torch and shines it around a little. At the back is a large turtle shell.

The dog finally decides to enter and, after adjusting to her new surroundings for a few moments, starts to growl. He shines the torch on the opening, turns and passes through it with two sideways steps.

The old man is facing him, watching, sitting on what appears to be an old rocking chair covered with sheepskins, his arms lying on the armrests. The light of a gas lantern hanging on a rock wall imme-diately reveals the size of the cave but hides its details in the shadows. The old man's grey beard hangs halfway down his chest. He still has a few strands of white hair on the sides of his head. He has a broad face, narrow nose and deep-set eyes. He is a tall man who has shrunk. His faded and tattered trousers, waistcoat and wool jacket must have been elegant when new. The intensity of his cadaver-like figure is reinforced by the presence of a young mulatto woman, who can't be any more than twenty years old, sitting on a stool close to him, slightly behind the rocking chair. She is wearing a kind of knitted robe in a sandy tone and a diamond tiara that can only be a plastic imitation of the real thing. One of her arms is resting lightly on the old man's shoulder. The two of them stare at the intruder with the same stony gleam in their eyes.

Good evening, he says, pushing back his hood.

The old man turns his head a little like a curious dog and wrinkles his forehead. His bushy eyebrows are grey like his beard and his skin looks like a leather bag with centuries of use.

The woman's eyes widen suddenly and she looks frightened. She whispers something in the old man's ear and he raises his right hand to the height of her face, requesting silence. Then he whispers some-thing in her ear. She gets up, takes a few steps to a dark recess towards the back of the cave and speaks to someone.

349

The roof of the cave is an enormous slab of slanting rock that is some ten feet at its highest point and almost touches the ground at its lowest. The cave is dry and warm and there is a blue tarpaulin sealing an upper corner. Near him, an upright log serves as a table for a perfect sphere of granite about the size of a football. A flash of lightning reveals two openings, one on his right that leads into the forest, and another behind him, which he figures is the direction of the valley and ocean, but the two or three flares of light that are gone in an instant are not enough for him to identify the third person that the woman just spoke to. The cave dwelling has a clean, mineral smell. He can't detect the smell of people living there. A puddle of water is forming at his feet.

I'm sorry, I'm getting everything wet.

The old man leans forward slightly and summons him closer with his index finger. The rocking chair creaks. He can hear Beta growling in the antechamber. She must be afraid to squeeze through the opening.

He walks three steps closer to the old man. Behind him and the mulatto woman, a girl of about thirteen, with white skin, tangled black hair and a feral look, gets up. She stares at him with uneducated eyes as she listens to instructions muttered by the woman. In the recess from which she has just risen, he can now see another girl, blonde and bigger than the first, curled up on a bed of mats and cushions. She has just woken up and rubs her eyes, trying to understand what is going on. The mulatto woman returns to exactly the same position on the stool by the old man, her smooth arm touching his shoulder like a dancing partner's. Her nails are manicured. The wild-looking girl who has just risen goes further back into the cave to a tiny kitchen, where there are shelves laden with jars and tins and a hotplate perched over a wood-fired oven of stone. The orange-and-

350

violet embers are still lightly pulsing. She places a teapot on the hotplate.

What do you want with me? says the old man.

It is his father's voice.

I just wanted to meet you.

Have you come to take me away?

No, I've just come to see you. I'm your grandson.

Are you, now? The old man gives an amused snort. How interesting.

He leaves the torch turned off on the log next to the sphere of granite and starts taking off his backpack. The old man tenses.

I'm just going to get something out.

He rummages around until he finds the little mirror. It is cracked all over and the image he sees of his own face is a completely disfigured mosaic. The old man laughs again, more heartily this time, as he runs his hand over his face and beard, trying in vain to remember what he looks like.

I've doubted my image in the mirror, the old man says, but this is the first time my image has doubted itself.

The old man looks serious again. His bare, gnarly feet tap the hard earth floor a few times. The wild girl brings a clay mug of some kind of tea and hands it to the mulatto woman, who in turn places it in the hands of the old man. He noisily sips a little of the hot liquid and hands the mug back to the mulatto woman.

He puts the broken mirror back in his backpack, pulls out his wallet, opens it and takes out the photograph of his grandfather. The beard is grey, the man is smaller, shrunk to half his size, but it can only be him. He hands the photograph to the old man. In the meantime, the dog has finally decided to squeeze through the opening. She faces the rocking chair and starts to growl.

351

The old man doesn't notice the dog. He has stopped laughing and is staring at the photograph. His eyes jump a few times from the picture to the face of the younger man in front of him and his expression slowly transforms into something more perplexed and threatening. He finally places the photo on his lap and signals for him to come even closer.

He approaches. The mulatto woman gets up from her stool and takes a step backwards.

The old man raises his skeletal hand to his face and he notices that his little finger and ring finger are missing. His remaining fingers are soft and warm and they trace his cheeks, nose and eyes. The old man draws his hand back and looks confused.

Are you real?

Yes. I'm your grandson.

The old man rubs his eyes, squeezes the tip of his own nose between his thumb and forefinger and tries to look again, incredulous. He starts breathing heavily through his nose.

You didn't even know you had a grandson, did you?

You shouldn't be here.

The mulatto woman takes another step back.

I've been trying to discover what happened to you for months, Granddad. Everyone thinks you're dead. I met Santina.

This isn't right. You shouldn't be here.

The old man fidgets a little in his chair and shakes his head, repeating no, no.

The girl who was lying down sits up and looks around in alarm. Her face has some kind of deformity that is hard to make out in the dark. The mulatto woman crouches and makes the two girls lie down again.

The dog barks once, twice, three times and only now does the old man notice her.

Dad died at the beginning of the year. Your son.

Out.

Fine, I just –

The old man gets up from his chair and seems to unfold into a man twice as big. His right hand hangs nervously, a short distance from his body, holding a knife. The mulatto woman hugs the two girls and watches the scene over her shoulder.

There's no need for that. I'm leaving.

The old man quickly reaches to one side and turns out the gas lantern.

He manages to grab his arm in the dark but feels the knife nick his waist. He hears Beta lunge at the old man's leg. He shouts for him to stop but it is obvious that he won't. The girls all scream at the same time and then play dead. He and the old man fall on to the rocking chair and then the kitchen shelves. The embers in the stove are the only source of light in the cave and he tries to push his grandfather in that direction. The old man doesn't make a sound, just keeps his bony body tensed and keeps attacking tirelessly like a banana spider trying to catch its prey so it can fill it with venom. He manages to shove him on to the hotplate, breaking free of his clutches for long enough to charge towards what he believes to be an exit. He gropes the walls of rock but can't find the opening he came through. A sliver of lightning illuminates the other two openings in the cave and he throws himself through the closest one. He finds himself on a small promontory, which must offer a view of the valley during the day but is now no more than a parapet to nothing. Afraid the old man will come after him and attack him at any second, he takes off running

353

and tripping down the slope without seeing anything in his path until he runs into the fence and jabs his hands and thighs on the barbed wire. He cries out in pain and is relieved at the same time because from there he can run to the bottom of the valley, to the creek, to the beach.

After putting some more distance between himself and the cave, which makes him feel a little safer, he stops to get the knife with the armadillo-leather handle out of his backpack but realizes that he's left the backpack behind along with the dog. Her name sticks in his throat. Calling out will reveal his whereabouts. The adrenalin is slowly metabolized and his instinct to flee is replaced with paralysis. He wants to go back to find Beta but doesn't know where he is any more. The sound of the sea reverberates against the walls of the valley. He touches the place where he felt the knife tear his skin, on the right side of his stomach, and has the impression that it hasn't done too much damage. But it hurts. He starts walking, heedless of the direction, so as not to stay still while he tries to decide what to do, and slips down a small bank and falls into the creek. The direction of the small current allows him to deduce the approximate location of the sea and the sides of the valley. The couple in the tent has a gas lantern. They must have a knife, another torch, maybe even a mobile phone. He clambers up the slope, praying for more lightning, tugged at by reason on one side and fear on the other. He has the constant impression that the dog has caught up with him and it is only now, as he reaches the trees on the ridge, that his companion's absence starts to sink in. Finally he works up the courage to shout.

Beta!

He shouts a few times with his hands on either side of his mouth. His calls are lost in the invisible valley.

He keeps looking for the tent among the trees. He can see better with his eyes closed, as if surprised at night by a blackout in his own home. The baby's crying has stopped, or maybe he isn't where he thinks he is. He calls the couple's names but there is no reply. The trees start to thin and he picks up his pace in the hope of finding some reference point under the open sky.

A flash of lightning illuminates the cliff, his foot stepping into the void and a stormy sea that is chaos itself extending out on all sides. When everything goes dark again he is still beginning to fall and it is only in the middle of the descent that he realizes what is happening. He thanks the lightning. He almost died unseeing, like a blind man. Or perhaps the vanity of death knows no limits, he thinks, and even to the blind it reveals itself at the last instant so that they'll think about it as it happens. On his way down the vision of the vortex of waves and foam that will swallow him is emblazoned in his mind with hyperreal clarity, the ocean that he so adores showing its most private and destructive facet, revealed to few men. When he is about to hit the water he closes his eyes tightly, as one inevitably does when diving.

In the water there is no indication of the ferocity he had glimpsed on the surface. His body is already decelerating when he arrives at the slippery smooth rocks on the sea floor and he becomes aware that he is suspended in the muffled murmur of the cold sea, softly rocked by the current. He had learned from his older brother how to duck under the big waves to get past the wave break. No matter how big the wave, Dante had taught him, dive down close to the ocean floor and swim towards it as fast as possible. The wave will suck you under it and you'll come out the other side when it breaks. If you try to swim back it'll come crashing down on your head. If you try to dive into it too near the surface it'll pick you up and toss you into the blender. You'll break your back or get sliced up by the corals. His brother was already a good surfer as a kid but he didn't like surfboards himself. He preferred swimming. The first thing he does now, instinctively, before trying to return to the surface, is study the forces of the water until he can say with some certainty in what direction the waves are breaking. He swims a few strokes in the opposite direction to the waves, comes up for air and returns to the bottom, trying to avoid being dashed against the rocky headland.

The bottom is silence. The water is protective and slows time.

But the surface is hell. Trails of foam appear on all sides, covering his head, and salt water runs down his throat. He grows breathless freeing himself of the running shoes and jacket that are restricting his movements. He can't see the moon or stars or anything else that might help him get his bearings. His body is lifted up to the crest of waves and then sucked down to the bottom of troughs and he can't make much out beyond this rise and fall. The clash around him involves familiar natural forces but there is no easily perceived arena for it. He is an insignificant piece of meat, adrift.

The first flash of lightning after the fall doesn't illuminate anything besides a large uniform cloud that covers the entire dome of the sky and contrasts with the black horizon. He needs to choose a direction and swim parallel to the coast until he comes to a beach. The salt stings his eyes. The strength of his arms seems useless against the violence of the waves but he knows it isn't true and that if he takes the right current and swims in the right direction he'll be able to get away from the headland and make it to the sand, even though it may take hours. For the first time he is calm enough to detect the cold that is working its way deeper and deeper into his body. He needs to establish the right pace, which will keep his body warm and allow him to continue swimming for however long is necessary.

Terror rises in him when he imagines reefs and sea creatures or entertains the idea that he might be swimming in the wrong direction, moving away from the beach with firm, regular strokes, into an overwhelming vastness from which there will be no return.

The rest of the time he focuses on swimming, breathing, signs which might help him keep going in a straight line that will take him somewhere. He reaches a point where he doesn't believe he is in any more of a predicament than the other times he has swum long distances in Olympic swimming pools or participated in ocean races with hundreds of other athletes. It all feels quite familiar, like those two miles of the Tapes Open Water Swim that he completed with cramps in his thigh, or the hypothermia he had in the middle of the bike ride that almost got him eliminated from the Ironman in Florianópolis. There's a right cadence for every race and an athlete must pace himself and pay attention to style, the path of his strokes, the rhythm of his kicking and, above all, focus and stay focused on the swimming until his mind and body are one, which enables him to become one with the water and there is no longer any need to focus. Everything he has experienced previously seems to have prepared him for this. It is the race he has trained for his entire life. The imagination can be an ally at times like this. He imagines competitors beside and directly behind him. Only the best swimmers in the world. The leader, whom he wants to pass, is kicking his legs right in front of him. All he has to do is swim in his wake. His mind believes it and his made-up opponent becomes real in no time, a man of flesh and blood who feels the same cold and the same weariness, a companion. He can almost touch his feet with his fingertips. And when this particular fantasy dissipates, he imagines other things. That he is being chased by giant sharks or leviathans the likes of which no one has ever seen before. That if he pauses or slows his pace he will be zapped by lightning. That he is leaving death behind. That a quiet, loving woman is waiting for him on the sand of the beach, a woman who doesn't look like anyone he has ever been with but has nothing extraordinary about her. She greets him without surprise, lets him lie his head on her sand-covered thighs to rest for as long as he requires and says that they need one another, that they will always want to fulfil each other's wishes, and will be able to, without exception. He can tell she is speaking the truth. She brushes his temples with her fingertips and asks what he wants. He babbles that he doesn't want much, just that her legs be warm to the touch in the winter and cool in the summer, and that they have a runny-nosed little girl who scrapes her knees as she tears around the house, and that there be a view of a lagoon that turns golden in the late afternoon, even if from afar. Above all that she remain warm when he is cold. That's all. Then it's her turn. Tell me what you want. She tells him and he says yes to everything and asks what else, what else? It is an interminable list of things and promising her each of them brings him infinite pleasure, no matter what they are. He gives her everything, one thing for each stroke of his arms, begging her not to stop, obtaining from this the strength he needs.

12

Someone shakes him.

Hey! Hey!

He opens his salt-sealed eyes with difficulty and is blinded by the light. The person helps him lift his torso.

Sit up, man.

He shades his eyes with his hand and sees a muscular man crouching in front of him, dripping with sweat, barefoot, wearing only shorts.

Are you OK?

He is gripped by a fit of convulsive coughing, almost vomiting, but nothing comes out. It doesn't last long and as soon as it is over he tries to get up but can't and falls back into a sitting position. He looks to both sides and all he sees are two strips of white sand blazing in the sun. Behind the man is a light blue sea of docile waves.

What're you doing here? What happened to you?

What beach is this?

Siriú.

The Siriú next to Garopaba?

Is there another one?

He starts laughing and coughing.

Would you like me to call someone?

No, no, he says, pulling himself together. Help me up?

The man grabs him under his arms and sets him on his feet.

Have you seen a dog around?

No. What happened to you? Did you drink and go for a swim?

I fell in.

You look like Tom Hanks in that movie, man.

It's stopped raining.

It'll be back soon. It's been raining for almost a month.

What day is it today?

Wednesday.

I mean the date.

I think it's the fifteenth.

Of what month?

October.

The man puts his hands on his waist, glances to both sides, then stares at him with a tilted head and squinting eyes.

Man, you need help. Stay here. I'm going to call someone.

He shakes his head and makes a gesture to say it isn't necessary. His eyes have adjusted to the sunlight and now he can see the houses on Siriú Hill to his left, and, to his right, in the distance, Garopaba, stretching all the way to Vigia Point. His tongue is swollen and salty in his mouth, plastered with thick saliva. He feels a twinge of hot pain near his waist and groans. He lifts up his wet T-shirt and sees a white cut in the middle of a reddish oval.

Did you hurt yourself? Do you remember what happened?

More or less.

Did someone attack you?

It was nothing.

His arms are covered in scratches and his trousers are torn at his thighs. He runs his hands over his face, hair and beard.

You haven't got anything on your face, says the man.

What about you? What're you doing here?

Running. I'm training for a test to be a lifeguard. It's part of a course.

When is it?

In December. It's best to run barefoot in the sand to get used to it.

He puts his hand on the wound on his stomach and starts to get up but falls back in a sitting position again, breathing noisily through his nose. He swallows saliva as a reflex but his mouth is dry.

You wouldn't happen to have any water there, would you?

Nope.

No problem. Have a good run.

The man watches him without moving.

You can go, thanks.

You sure?

Yup.

Wait here and I'll give you a hand on my way back. Or I can let someone know in Garopaba. Is there someone who can come and pick you up?

It's not necessary.

Take it easy with the bottle. It'll do you in.

The man walks backwards a few steps, then turns and runs along the sand towards Siriú.

He crosses his legs and sits there a while, feeling the sun on the top of his head. He doesn't remember arriving at the beach but is able to recall vivid fragments of the whole previous night. It seems rather like a dream, like the Fata Morgana that Jasmim saw too. He remembers Beta and a sudden sigh, deep and long, is born in the middle of his chest and leaves his mouth with a sticky smack of saliva. He needs to go back to look for her but he won't be strong enough for a few days and deep down he doesn't really believe that she is alive or can be found. But he'll go anyway. Judging from the height of the sun it must be about nine o'clock in the morning. He can almost hear the sand drying in the dunes behind him. The tide is high. He still has a white cotton sock on one foot. He has to place both hands on the ground in order to lift his hips and stand up. He starts walking very slowly towards Garopaba. His joints all hurt. He is halfway down the beach when he hears someone shout behind him. It is the same man who woke him up, running back along the sand.

I got this for you in Siriú.

He accepts the bottle of mineral water without stopping walking. He tries to twist the top off but can't.

Here, let me.

The man takes the bottle, opens it and returns it. He takes a series of short gulps. They walk along side by side.

Thanks.

Are you going to make it, Tom Hanks? Are you?

Yep. Especially now, with this water here to save me.

Want me to help you?

No, man, finish your run. I'll make it. I just can't stop.

Put your arm here.

The man offers him his shoulder for support and puts his arm around his waist. They walk together, slowly.

Stop by the health clinic when you get there. You don't look well.

It'll pass.

They walk together for more than half an hour. The sun has disappeared again behind thick clouds by the time they arrive at the Garopaba Beach promenade.

I can make it on my own from here, man.

Don't you want to go to the health clinic?

I want to stop off at home first. I live over there, overlooking Baú

Rock. See? In the ground-floor apartment. Thanks for the help and sorry I spoiled your workout.

Forget it.

Is there a swimming test also to be a lifeguard?

Yep.

What's your swimming like?

Pretty lousy. That's my problem.

Stop by my place in a few days' time and I'll give you some tips to help you improve. I'm a swimming instructor.

Seriously?

Seriously. Don't forget. Lifeguards have to swim well.

OK, you're on. See you later, Tom Hanks!

The man leaves and starts running back towards Siriú again. He continues on his own along the small stretch that remains, eyes trained on his front door. People arriving for lunch at the restaurants on the seafront observe him from afar and take a while to look away. Some fishermen working on their beached boats stop what they are doing to watch him go past. He gives the ones who stare at him longer a quick wave of the hand and gets almost imperceptible nods of the head in return.

His legs shake on the crumbling steps up to Baú Rock. The water at the end of the bay is incredibly smooth and calm. He enters the dark corridor between the buildings and retrieves the key hidden among the plants. Beta's absence screams in the silence of the musty living room. He opens the windows and the light comes in. The humidity is scandalous. Droplets of water slide down the walls and the sides of appliances and into puddles on the tiled floor.

He goes into the bathroom, looks at himself in the mirror and sees an old man. He has spent his whole life seeing his face for the first time in his reflection but now it is different. He can see the contours of his skull behind his forehead and cheekbones. His eyes are sunken in their orbits. His skin looks burned in spite of the weeks with no sunlight. His long beard is full of sand. He doesn't remember what he looked like before but he knows it wasn't like this. He understands now what his grandfather saw. A ghost, a younger version of himself. Something that shouldn't have been there.

He takes off his wet clothes and sees his bones trying to poke through his shoulders, his prominent collarbones and ribs. He is covered in scratches but nothing looks serious. The cut at his waist isn't deep.

He goes into the kitchen and drinks water from the tap in short gulps. Some fruit and vegetables have withered or rotted in the fridge. There is a half-full tub of caramelized condensed milk. He rams a spoon into it and devours it in seconds. He wolfs down the rest of a jar of honey with a packet of biscuits that was in the cupboard. After eating, he returns to the bathroom and takes a long shower on the highest setting. His tiredness crashes over him in the warm water and he can barely stay on his feet. He has to sit on the toilet to dry off. Then he rolls himself in every available blanket and quilt and collapses on the bed, thinking that he needs to buy more food. And a toothbrush and toothpaste. And an umbrella.

For two days he spends more time asleep than awake and goes out only to withdraw money and buy some food at the grocery shop in the village centre. He knows the name, location and function of every muscle in the human body and knows exactly which ones are hurting at any given time. They all hurt. His face hurts. But the pain is normal. The kind of pain an athlete gets used to. It is always raining when he gets out of bed and the few boats that haven't been brought in are always anchored in the same place. The long waves roll up to the doors of the fishing sheds, one after another. The muddy water that washes down the creeks, ditches and dirt roads invades the green sea, forming large coffee-coloured streaks across the entire murky bay.

Cecina appears on the second day holding a flowery umbrella. He invites her in but she stays in the doorway with a concerned smile.

You're sick, boy. I told you you were sick.

He coughs before answering.

I'm fine, Cecina.

You're sick. You look like a dead fish. Go to the health clinic.

I will, don't worry.

Where's the dog?

I lost her, Cecina.

Oh dear.

I know. It's really hard.

She lowers her voice.

Did you talk to Santina?

I did. She told me everything. Or her version at least.

There is no other version. Now you can stop going around asking about it. That's also why I helped you. To see if you'd get some sense into you and stop.

I've stopped, Cecina. The subject is dead and buried. I owe you a lot. Thank you for helping me.

She looks at him as if he were a pickpocket offering to help her cross the street.

You disappeared for a while there.

I went on a trip.

A trip where, for heaven's sake? Everything's under water.

I went to Porto Alegre to resolve a few things. Paperwork to do with my late father, that kind of thing.

Cecina turns her face a little and doesn't look very convinced. He can imagine what she is thinking. As predicted, all it took was the arrival of winter for the enthusiastic young PE teacher who only wanted to live a simple life in front of the beach, and who could prove his good intentions with a cheque for thousands of reais, to become a sick, filthy, evasive liar. Drugs, no doubt. She is relieved to have received a year's rent in advance.

Did the rain do much damage here, Cecina?

Not too much. Just holes in the streets. The road to Ferrugem was blocked for a couple of days but they've fixed it. The real problem for us here is that the retaining wall on Cavalos Hill fell again and closed off access to the highway. Did you hear about it? My nephew who's studying vet science in Florianópolis has been stuck there for two days. Things are pretty ugly in Blumenau and Itajaí. According to yesterday's *Diário Catarinense*, the death toll is already sixty-eight. I imagine there's many more. They just haven't found the bodies. And I saw on TV that volunteers have been stealing donations. It's a tragedy. I've never seen so much rain in my more than sixty years of life.

How awful. At least Garopaba was spared.

We're blessed here.

And who won the election?

There's going to be a second round. No one got an absolute majority. Weren't you here?

No. I'm a bit out of the loop.

She glances inside the apartment.

Someone stopped by here looking for you a few days ago.

Man or woman?

Man. All he gave me was a nickname. He was fairly dark-skinned, bald. You're not caught up in drugs, are you?

Bonobo?

I think that was it.

What did he want?

He was asking after you. I said I hadn't seen you for several days.

He's a friend. I'll give him a call. Thanks, Cecina.

After Cecina says goodbye he gets his black umbrella and goes to the supermarket again to buy a credit voucher for his mobile phone. Halfway there he realizes he's still walking slowly, at the pace he kept so that Beta could keep up with him. He glances over his shoulder all the time, as if by a miracle she might reappear, limping along behind him. Something clutches at his stomach. What he feels isn't exactly pain, but a kind of revulsion, as if his guts were disgusted at themselves. At the supermarket and in the doorways of some houses the fishermen and their wives return his greetings as if merely respecting an enemy. He has done nothing to these people but he understands that his mere presence is an unpleasant spectre. He is sick of it and feels a deep sadness. His grandfather must have felt the same sadness, only a thousand times greater. The origin of his superhuman strength.

When he gets home, he plugs his mobile into the charger, takes a hot shower and makes a ham-and-cheese omelette. Ever since he woke up on the sand of Siriú, he has felt cold to the bone and nothing seems to warm him up. His tracksuit trousers and two wool jumpers aren't enough. His fits of ragged coughing are becoming more frequent. He rolls himself up in the blanket, sits on the sofa and dials a number on his mobile.

Bonobo.

Swimmer.

He invites his friend over to his place for a drink and a chat but he is in Porto Alegre. Bonobo confirms that he stopped by the apartment a few days earlier to say that he had decided to visit his sick father after something he had said the day they met at Altair's kiosk. He says he finally met his nine-year-old half-sister for the first time and went to the neighbourhood where he grew up to see his blood sister, whom he hadn't seen in over a year. Bonobo found his father in a fragile state after surviving an aortic rupture. He'd had the incredible luck to be showing a plot of land to a cardiologist when he'd felt sharp pains in his chest and gone into a cold sweat. The cardiologist had detected irregular rhythms in his heartbeat, phoned a colleague and sent him to hospital by taxi. He was operated on in time. Nevertheless, the damage was extensive and he was very weak. Bonobo's dad's new wife begged him not to broach any potentially stressful subjects, which could be lethal, so their conversation was a little stiff and certain things were left unsaid. At any rate, they forgave one another and joked around a little. He hadn't seen his father in five years.

But you were right about what you said over in the kiosk, says Bonobo. I'm glad I came. I see myself in the old man. I almost wound up as big a prick as him. But now he's there with his new family, more laid-back, retired, living off all the land he bought in the south zone of the city. His wife and little girl love him. And I'm out of the rut I was in and have a bed and breakfast near the beach. I think I surprised him as much as he surprised me. He and I might've gone to the grave without ever knowing the whole story. I don't know if that makes sense to you.

It does.

How are things at your end? You haven't been answering your phone. Your landlady said you'd disappeared.

I discovered more or less what happened to my granddad and I found him, still alive, in a cave over near Pinheira.

No way.

He was missing two fingers on his right hand just like Dad said.

Are you sure you didn't dream it? It sounds like a dream.

I'll tell you more when you get back. I'm almost out of credit. To be honest, I'm calling to ask a favour. I lost Beta up in the hills. I want to go back to look for her.

Which hills?

Behind Pinheira Beach. It's a long story, but I need to go back and look for her. I doubt I'll find her, but I won't be able to rest until I've tried. I feel like total shit. She was Dad's dog. And, you know, before he died he asked me to have her put down.

I get it.

I screwed everything up.

Take it easy, man. We'll find her.

It's killing me. I thought we could go to Pinheira together in Lockjaw and you could give me a hand. I'm not really well enough to go on my own. We can look for her for a couple of days, spend a night there. When do you get back?

In three days.

Shit. Any chance you could come back tomorrow?

I can't. But if you wait for me, I'll go with you. I owe you one.

I'll wait. Thanks, man.

I'll go straight to your place when I get back.

I've missed you, man.

You too. Hang in there.

Same to you.

He can barely get out of bed on Saturday morning. His cough has worsened considerably over the last few days and now he is starting to experience chest pain and shivers. The rain stops at dusk, the sea becomes calm and a flaming sunset appears and disappears in an

369

instant as if it has walked through the wrong door. His wheezing is noisy in the silence of the night and he is thinking about dragging himself off to the health clinic when he hears Beta yelping.

It must have been another dog. Or just in his head. But Beta yelps again, this time insistently. The sound is distant and despairing and seems to be coming from the beach, the hills and the walls of the apartment all at once. He pulls on his trainers, opens the door and stands outside. His shivers worsen and run through his body like electric shocks. He wonders if he is mad or delirious with fever. He hears the yelping again. This time he is almost certain that it is coming from the beach or the seaside boulevard.

He follows the path to Baú Rock without bothering to close the door, arms folded over his chest, listening carefully. He heads down to the beach promenade and is walking in front of the brightly lit, empty restaurants when he hears the barking again, frenetic and incessant. He crosses the street, ignoring an oncoming car, which flashes its headlights and honks twice. The barking is coming from a small bar with outside tables that is famous in summer for its caipirinhas made with bergamot leaves and a dash of curaçao and which only opens occasionally in the off-season, when it is frequented by locals. There are two barmen and another three men sitting at a small wooden table on the pavement. One of the barmen has served him on two or three other occasions, a middle-aged man with an accent from the Brazil–Uruguay border, a moustache, greying side whiskers and goatee, skin wrinkled from the sun and a body hypertrophied from decades of weightlifting. A blender is roaring away at top speed, Sublime is playing at a low volume somewhere behind the counter and someone is smoking marijuana. No one greets him but they all stop what they are doing for a moment, emphasizing the hostility that has just filled the air. One of the men leaning against the counter

370

turns to face the street and starts drumming heavily on the slats of varnished wood on the façade of the bar.

Beta is barking loudly and incessantly but it takes him a while to locate her in the driveway beside the bar behind a low wooden gate. She is tied by the neck with a red rag or item of clothing to the pipe of an outdoor tap. Her protuberant ribs and cloudy eyes explain why she hasn't been able to pull the pipe away. When she smells him near by and finally sees him her barks grow louder, more broken and sharper, like howls. The improvised cloth collar is strangling her.

He climbs over the gate, kneels next to her and focuses all his attention on undoing the knot in the cloth, without wasting time trying to pat or calm her. She stops barking but keeps trying to raise her front paws and lick his face. The gate opens with a creak.

Leave the dog alone, kid.

The knot is as hard as cement.

I said leave her alone.

A kick in the ribs throws him against the wall between the driveway and a closed shopping arcade. Beta starts barking wildly again. He tries to get up but gets another kick in the stomach, just above his inflamed cut. This time he cries out in pain.

Who do you think you are, coming in like this and taking my dog, you piece of shit?

He starts to get up again, expecting the next blow, but this time his attacker decides to watch the spectacle of the man slowly picking himself up off the ground. He is a local, unshaven, with an animal-like ignorance in his eyes. His blond surfer's hair is poking out from under his red-and-white baseball cap and covers his neck and ears. He is tall and fills his baggy jacket and trousers well. A hard man to take down.

Do we know each other?

371

Are you retarded?

I'm serious, I forget people.

The other men in the bar come over, forming an attentive audience on the pavement. One of them opens the gate and enters. The moustached barman hasn't bothered to come out from behind the counter and can't see anything. Beta snarls. The local kicks her and then immobilizes her with the makeshift collar.

Course, we know each other, arsehole. And if you don't get out of here right now you won't forget me again, believe me.

The dog's mine and you know it.

I don't know anything about that. I found her wandering along without a collar on the edge of the beach.

You're the dickhead who was after Dália, aren't you?

The local gives a little snort of amazement and takes a step forward, letting go of Beta.

What was that?

You've got a shark tattoo or something like that on your leg, haven't you? I recognized you by your girly voice.

Jesus, this guy's really asking for it.

He glances around and sees faces hungry for violence. Beta is sitting between him and the local, tired and confused, hungry and strangled, oblivious to the nature of the dispute. The animal his father loved more than anything. On his left, in the distance, a delicate veil of daylight glimmers on the horizon over the ocean. More or less here, on this same stretch of beach, his grandfather sank into the night sea and never returned, after rising up from a pool of blood as a whole town looked on, riddled with a hundred stab wounds, the living-dead going home. Right there where the waves are now breaking, grinning white smiles in the darkness. In the icy-cold water that helped Beta walk again. Beta, the old dog that everyone had given up on. Maybe that is what his father had feared. Not dying easily. Not dying ever.

The dog's mine and everyone here knows it. You've all seen me with her ever since I arrived. I'm taking her back and I'll be off now.

He bends over to start undoing the knot and receives a kick in the side of the face. There is a crack and he feels tooth fragments on his tongue. Beta barks desperately. He and his attacker quickly end up on the pavement and the group of locals starts in on him, from all sides. He manages to land a couple of punches but he can no longer see a thing. Someone grabs him by the hair. His head is smashed a single time against the hood of a car and blood stops up his nose and fills his mouth. A flying kick in the back brings him down in the middle of the road. He pulls his knees towards his chest as they continue to attack him, unable to react now. He hears Beta barking until it is over.

A car stops in the middle of the street and its headlights reveal the silhouettes of those who have been watching from a safe distance. More and more people arrive. He manages to sit on the kerb and realizes that he has been kicked right across the street to the beach promenade. He keeps his mouth closed and is afraid to open it, as if something vital might leak out.

Get him out of here, someone says.

Take him down to the sand.

Several hands pick him up by the arms and legs. He is carried for a time and then gently placed on the cold, hard sand, as if they now want to be careful not to hurt him. He lies there, his breathing heavy and bubbling with blood.

Sit him up.

Someone helps him sit and he wavers like a gymnast making a concerted effort to keep his balance.

Can you make it home?

I need to get my dog.

Go home.

They leave and his sight slowly returns. He is sitting facing the sea with the wall of the promenade at his back. Two men come down the nearest set of steps and approach him.

How are you?

Need some help?

He needs to go to hospital.

Do you want to go to hospital?

Where do you live?

He's having trouble talking.

I'm going to call the police.

Stay here with him.

One of the men crouches down next to him and asks him the occasional question, but he isn't listening. All he can hear is Beta's tireless, surreal barking. She managed to make it back. Starving. Limping. She made it all the way back through the hills.

He starts to get up. It takes him a while but he manages. He stands there for a few minutes, coughing and steadying his feet on the ground. The man looking after him holds his arm and tells him to stay still, but he pulls his arm away and looks at him with an expression that makes words unnecessary, because the man doesn't touch him again. He takes a few tentative steps. He can walk.

He stumbles across the sand to the steps, climbs them, walks a little way along the promenade and starts back across the street towards the bar and Beta's barking. He wipes the blood from his eyes with his sleeves and has another little fit of coughing. Those who are still standing around talking about the fight stop talking and stare at him. Someone in the bar points across the street and everyone else turns to look. He stops two paces away from the pavement.

Five men are sitting at one of the tables. The moustached bartender is behind the counter drying cups with a white tea towel.
Everyone stares and no one says a thing. He has already forgotten
what they look like and glances from one to another, feeling the
blood running into his eyes, blinking without stopping and frowning
with his swollen face. Four of the five are wearing baseball caps, three
are blond, and he can't take in any more than that. He places his hand
around his chin and runs it all the way down to the tip of his
blood-drenched beard, which drips into a small puddle on the white
paving stones.

Which one of you was it that took my dog?

You're kidding.

He's in a state of shock.

He takes a step closer and runs his tongue over his teeth, feeling
two crushed molars and a loose canine.

I forget people's faces. Now, who was it?

It was me.

Ah, right.

Still not happy, jerk?

Can I take my dog now?

Give him the dog, for Christ's sake, says the bartender with the
moustache.

The dog's mine, says the local.

Then I want to know if you're man enough to fight without the
help of your girlfriends here.

What?

He repeats himself, trying to pronounce each syllable clearly with
his bitten tongue and cut lips.

I don't kick dead dogs. Go home, motherfucker.

He spits all the blood in his mouth at the guy, who sits there frozen for a few seconds, wipes himself off, gets up and turns to his companions.

Wait here.

He takes a few steps back into the middle of the street and waits for the local to come. He raises his fists up to fight but receives three punches in the face in rapid succession and falls to the ground.

Someone tries to help him up but he waves everyone away and stands up again. He knows that if he takes just one more punch it'll all be over. He goes down to the beach and signals to the local again.

This time the local hesitates, feeling sorry for him. He watches him come down the steps looking disgruntled, visibly annoyed to still be fighting a broken opponent. Or maybe he is scared. Maybe he remembers certain stories about things that happened in decades past, right there. Things that his parents and grandparents refuse to talk about.

He sets one foot in the sand. The strong light from the lamp posts on the promenade give the sad scene with its audience of twenty or thirty people the contours of a spectacle. The two of them study one another and he takes advantage of the local's hesitation and bored stance to kick sand in his face. The local reels back, rubbing his eyes, and as soon as he takes his hands away from his face he gets a blow square in the nose. They start blindly throwing punches, a few of which hit their target, until he manages to grab the local between the legs with one hand and his throat with the other at the same time. He can feel the guy's crushed testicles and windpipe squashed between his fingers. The local's legs grow weak. They topple on to the sand together but he doesn't let go. He keeps squeezing and sees the local's numb, terrified face start to turn red and then blue.

Only a bullet in the head'll get rid of me now, motherfucker.

People start trying to separate them, first pulling at them, then with punches and kicks, but he doesn't let go until he recognizes the voice of a woman who has been shouting at him for some time.

Look at me! she says. Let him go. Look at me!

He lets go. After a long, apparently lifeless, pause, the man starts to cough and choke on the sand and is rescued by his friends.

He sinks his fingers into her curly hair.

Dália. I can't see you properly.

My God! Get up, come on.

What're you doing here?

Me? I came for a fucking caipirinha! And I find you two mauling each other on the beach like animals. You need to go to the health clinic. Jesus, your forehead's really hot. Come here.

Hang on. Just a minute.

He gets up and staggers over to the gate with everyone looking on. He goes into the driveway and kneels in front of Beta.

There, Beta girl. Everything's OK now.

He can't undo the knot with his fingers. A man comes over and holds out an open penknife.

This'll help, champ.

Thanks.

That's the dog that swims in the sea, isn't it? And you're the guy with the beard who swims with her. I can see you guys from my front veranda.

He cuts the collar off and pats Beta's ribs. Dália comes over and scratches Beta's back.

Get up, you nutcase. The police'll be here soon. Let's try to get to the hospital beforehand, otherwise it'll take a while.

Soon.

You're not thinking right.

He staggers out of the gate and over to the bar with Beta behind him. He has a coughing fit before he is able to order.

I'll have two of those caipirinhas with bergamot leaves.

You serious?

One for me and one for the lady here. And a bit of ice in a plastic bag, please, if it's no trouble. Are those motherfuckers still here?

They're over there on the other side of the street. I've seen you here before, haven't I? I remember the beard.

I think so. But my beard didn't used to be so long.

They're going to shave it off at the hospital.

That's OK, it's about time it came off.

The barman hands him a plastic bag of ice cubes and starts slicing limes. Dália sits down next to him, covers his whole face with the bag of ice wrapped in a tea towel and presses on it. When she removes the compress a minute later blue and red lights are licking the wooden façade of the bar.

I feel a bit dizzy, Dália. I might pass out.

The barman brings the caipirinhas to the table and puts his hands on his hips.

Where are you from again? You're not from here.

He's Gaudério's grandson, someone says.

The nurse handing him a glass of water is wearing a name tag that says 'Natália' and her uniform reminds him of a scene from a porno movie he watched over and over on the internet a few years back until he got sick of it. All that is missing is the hat with the red cross on it. She has blonde hair, a big nose and eyes the colour of a swimming pool. With an accent from western Santa Catarina, she asks if he knows what his name is and where he is. He thinks about it. He doesn't know. He is in the São José Regional Hospital, Natália tells him, and he was brought in by a woman called Dália, who said she was his friend and left a few hours after checking him in. The same woman phoned in that morning to give the hospital his full name and ID number. He thinks about that too. He doesn't remember a thing, much less having spoken to Dália recently. Natália and Dália, he stammers. Dália, Natália. The nurse grins and squints at him as if assessing how lucid he is. He turns his head with difficulty on the soft pillow and sees hospital-green curtains around him, his own body wrapped in a pink blanket like the ones that used to cover the cosy sofas and armchairs in his grandmother's living room, and pieces of the metal frames of the other beds in the room. The dog? he asks. What have they done with my dog? Natália remembers that the woman said to tell him that the dog was fine and not to worry. She's at her mother's place or something like that. Another nurse, very thin, with a name tag that says 'Maila', appears and she and Natália celebrate his waking as if they have known one another for a long time. He asks how long he has been there and Maila smiles and says it's been almost twenty-four hours. Natália goes off to check on another patient and Maila goes to look for the doctor. He feels stitches and bandages on his face when he wrinkles it. His jaw and neck feel cool, a sign that his beard has been shaved off. There is a needle in the back of his right hand hooking him up to a saline drip or something of the sort. A woman in an adjacent bed has an intermittent hacking cough. The doctor, whose shaved head makes him look like an undergraduate student, says he was transferred by ambulance from the health clinic in Garopaba the night before with hypothermia, hypoglycaemia, dehydration and bacterial pneumonia, which is being treated with intravenous antibiotics. He has a fractured nose and rib, and cuts and abrasions on his face. The doctor asks if he has had a drowning incident or inhaled a lot of water in the last few days

379

and he replies that yes, he took in a lot of seawater, a great amount, about four days ago. He can see that the doctor is thinking about something else much more serious. He discusses something with Maila in a low voice and hurries down the corridor.

Dália shows up the next day with Pablito. She brings the key to his apartment, his mobile phone and battery charger, a slightly musty change of clothes, two books of crossword puzzles, the most recent issues of *Playboy* and *O2* magazines, and a Tupperware pot containing slices of chocolate cake. She says she came with him in the ambulance and left only when the doctor assured her that everything was going to be fine. He wouldn't wake up for anything and she didn't know what was going on and thought he was going to die. She had never felt anyone so hot with fever. Beta is in her back yard, being looked after by her mother, who said to tell him that she had already seen it all in dreams and tried to warn him, but he hadn't wanted to listen. She stopped by his apartment that morning and found the door locked, but went to find Cecina, explained the situation and got a spare key so she could go and get his ID and some clean clothes. Cecina, who had found the door open and apartment empty, asked if he had a drug problem. Later in the afternoon, Dália picked up Pablo from school and came to São José by bus to visit him. Pablito offers to let him play his Nintendo DS a little. Can I hang on to it until I'm released? I'll give it back in a few days. Pablito hugs his video game and shakes his head, and he says he is only joking. He asks Dália about her contractor boyfriend from Florianópolis and she says they're getting married in March. She is going to move to Florianópolis with her mother at the beginning of December. When the invitations are ready I'll send you one. Great, he says. I've always dreamed of standing up in the middle of a wedding and saying I object to this marriage. She holds his hand and he squeezes hers back. Thank you, Dália. I don't deserve any of this. Yes you do, she says.

When he wakes up the next morning, Bonobo is sitting next to his bed, talking to the nurse. Would you like to take some time off and spend a few days hanging out at a bed and breakfast in Rosa? Have you ever thought about being a model? Natália's mouth is half open and she looks both shocked and intrigued by the figure in front of her, but she turns back to her patient as soon as she sees that he has woken. As she takes his temperature, Bonobo tells him that he tried to visit the day before but Lockjaw broke down halfway there and he had to have her towed to Paulo Lopes, where he left her at a garage. Today he got a lift with a girl who was going to Curitiba. You're looking uglier than me, swimmer. I already know the name of the dickhead who did this to you. They say he's at home, can't walk and his neck is black. How can a guy go and steal your dog like that? In times past I would've finished the job for you. I'd have ripped his balls off and thrown 'em to the sharks, but nowadays I only plant kindness and compassion. And anyway, no one else'll ever give you a hard time in this town. Someone told Altair about the fight and Altair told me. People are saying your attackers left you unconscious on the sand but you got up and went after the guy. Wish I'd seen it. It's a bummer that it happened, but I wish I'd seen it. Natália takes his temperature and writes it on a spreadsheet. Don't you have those thermometers that you stick up the patient's arse, Nati? He prefers that sort. Natália makes a face, excuses herself and leaves. Man, what a babe, says Bonobo. Don't you think? I've never seen anything like her. Get her number before you leave. When the effect of Natália's presence wears off, Bonobo asks, What's this story about you meeting your granddad? He thinks for a moment and then says that he has come to the conclusion that it was just a dream or that he was delirious with fever. Not only does he lie, but he embellishes. I went off hiking through the hills in the rain and got sick. I didn't look after myself and came down with a fever, drinking and going out of my mind at home. Beta disappeared and I didn't even notice. I had hallucinations. I was pretty confused when we spoke on the phone. This whole story of my granddad is over for me now. I know I told you that before but this time I'm serious. Bonobo places a hand on his shoulder. Everyone who comes here goes out of their mind a little in their first winter here, swimmer. It's a rite of passage. I hope you make it through. I hope you stay. You're my brother now. Remember that. If you need something, we're brothers. Bonobo leans backwards and looks serious again. I know I still owe you that money but I'll only be able to pay you back after the holidays. Money only flows here in the summer, as you know. I've got big plans for the bed and breakfast. This summer looks promising. There's always a way. I've got plans to expand and diversify the products and services we offer. I want to target two kinds of customer: those who sympathize with Eastern religions; and hipsters. Two strong behavioural trends for the coming decade, thus, two strong consumer trends. Spiritual materialism and ironic consumerism. Zen tourism and self-conscious meta-tourism. The first is right up my alley. It'll be easy. Talks and courses in Buddhism, meditation sessions before breakfast included in the daily rates, a small shrine, a whole programme of activities that feels like a game and makes guests feel that they're fulfilling stages towards spiritual enlightenment, letting go of the material world and attaining happiness for themselves and others. A list of activities that they score points for and which lead to rewards. They'll take home some kind of certificate. And there's always going to be something under construction on the premises so people can volunteer to help. It's kind of bad karma, but I've got bills to pay. The hipsters are a bit harder. They need to feel that they're doing something authentic, but it can't be truly authentic. The atmosphere needs to be retro and a little anti-establishment, but without these terms ever being mentioned. Hipster guests aren't tourists. They're authentic, alternative individuals consciously acting like tourists in touristy settings, which turns the spiritual poverty of silly commercial tourism into something cool with the wave of a magic wand. The good old long weekend at the beach repackaged as a fetish. We'll offer authentic package deals with an old-fashioned flavour. I'll have to work out how to exploit it. At any rate, I'm going to go ahead and get a gramophone and set up a charity shop in the front foyer. I've worked it all out on PowerPoint. I'll show you later. If you grow a 70s-style moustache you can be my concierge. Whaddya think, swimmer? Interested?

A delegation from the gym comes to visit on his third day in hospital. Débora, Mila, the twins, Jander and Greice arrive with flowers and a bag of home-made ginger sweets from Celma, who couldn't make it because she is at a reiki conference in São Paulo. They name themselves to spare him the trouble of recognizing them. Débora cries when she sees the state he is in but tells him not to mind her, it's nothing, she cries easily. Jander and Greice ask about Beta and are relieved to hear that she is being looked after by someone he trusts and offer the kennel if he needs it. That dog's a miracle, says Greice. Rayanne and Tayanne say that the new swimming instructor isn't as nice as him. I mean, he's nice, says one of them – though he can no longer remember which – but he doesn't teach us. He just tells us what to do. When we say we've finished warming up, he points at the whiteboard and says, OK, now you can kick your legs. We finish kicking our legs, he says, OK, now do your sets. He just repeats everything that's on the whiteboard. Whenever I ask if

I'm swimming correctly he says yes but he doesn't even look. We miss you. It's no fun without someone correcting us, encouraging us and getting on our case all the time. He says that maybe the new instructor is right. Maybe you're swimming so well that you don't need someone to correct you all the time. You just need to synchronize your arms and legs well, lengthen your strokes, feel that you are moving, gliding through the water. And work hard, of course, to get better and better. I think you're ready, girls. Look, says one twin. That's what we're talking about. Get better quickly and come back to the pool, says the other. Is there any chance you'll come back? I don't know, he says. Ask Débora there. The secretary shrugs and says they'll have to ask Saucepan. When they leave, he is assailed by memories of old friends, faceless figures who are recognizable from shared experiences, and fantasizes about visits and reunions until his daydreaming is interrupted by Natália, who brings him a little cup of pills and asks if it is true that the friend who came to visit yesterday has a bed and breakfast in Rosa.

He stays in hospital for eleven days.

The morning he is released he uses the money that Dália brought him to catch a bus to the Florianópolis bus station, where he has lunch and buys a ticket to Garopaba. When he arrives, he goes straight to Dália's house, although she is still at work in Imbituba. Beta prances about when she sees him and Dália's mother says that she gave her a lot of food so she'd regain her weight. She starts relaying another dream she had about him, but he stops her and says he already knows. This time a woman with black hair comes out of a swamp with a child. She stares at him in silence. That's what you dreamed, right? She nods. You shouldn't waste your time dreaming about me, ma'am. He downs the last sip of coffee, thanks her for everything several times and congratulates her on her daughter's engagement. He promises to return to pay her back for the dog food.

He passes through the middle of the fishing village at dusk, Beta close at heel, with fresh nicks on his face from the nurse who shaved him that morning. He goes into the supermarket and spends the rest of the money in his pocket on bread, butter, coffee, a bunch of bananas and a credit voucher for his mobile phone. Several locals are out on the pavements and on the verandas of their homes after the day of sun. Clothes and pillows are being taken in from windows, fences and clothes lines. The air is filled with the smells of the salty breeze, fish gravy and corn cakes coming out of the oven. The ocean looks like a stained-glass window in motion, as if the light of the setting sun were coming from underwater and the beach were the inside of a church, but the water smells of oil and sewage. And there, perched on the hill, is the apartment he wanted so badly to live in and did. He opens the shutters to let air into the living room and stays there in the dark until the street light in front of his window comes on and casts its light inside. He doesn't feel like he is returning home. Jasmim was wrong about that. He doesn't belong here. There are two possible places for a person. Family is one. The other is the whole world. Sometimes it isn't easy to figure out which one we are in.

After a night of sleep like any other he wakes up on 30 October 2008 in a dirty, mould-infested apartment, with no money and no job, but with no fear either. He phones a laundry service and arranges to have them pick up his dirty clothes. He phones Saucepan, who tells him that at the moment there is no way he can have his old job as swimming instructor back. The new instructor is doing well and he has no reason to replace him. Besides which, it wouldn't be fair to the guy. The number of people using the pool has actually picked up

385

a little. He tells Saucepan that it's not a problem and congratulates him on the success of the gym. Then he goes out for lunch and stops at an ATM to withdraw the last of his savings. He phones Sara and asks if she thinks Douglas would agree to fix his teeth and let him pay the following month, presuming he doesn't know anything about the day of the barbecue, etc. She calls him back a few minutes later with an appointment time. Back at the apartment, he starts cleaning. He is scrubbing the floor with bleach when he hears someone clapping to get his attention outside the window. He doesn't recognize the strong, tanned young man smiling at him.

Good afternoon.

Afternoon. Who are you?

Don't you remember me, Tom Hanks?

He invites the man in.

All I can offer you is cold water.

No problem. I stopped by here a few days ago to see if you'd survived but the windows were shut. Are you OK?

I'm still a bit weak. I spent a few days in the hospital. I had a bad bout of pneumonia.

Do you remember what happened that day on the beach?

Yep. I fell off a headland near Pinheira in the middle of the storm and swam all night trying to get to a beach.

And you ended up on Siriú? From Pinheira to Siriú?

I guess so. I must have caught a current.

Beta comes through the door and goes to drink water from her bowl.

So that's the dog you went to get back from the guy.

You hear about it?

Everyone heard about it. They told me not to come and see you.

Huh? Why?

I dunno. People invent stories.

What stories?

The man raises his eyebrows.

Forget it, he says. Tell me something, when's that course for life-guards that you told me about?

End of November. It runs for three weeks. There's a theoretical component and a practical one. The problem's the practical component. They put you through the wringer.

But if you pass you'll have work all summer?

It starts just before Christmas and goes until Carnival, at least.

How much does it pay?

It's pretty good. A hundred reais a day. Even counting days off, you bring in over two thousand a month. Did you mean what you said? About giving me a hand with my swimming?

I meant it. But I want to do the course too. Where do you sign up?

At the fire department. Over in Palhocinha.

Great. Just give me a few more days 'cause I'm still a bit weak, but we can start next week. Meet me here at eight in the morning, even if it's raining, if there's a north-easterly blowing, whatever. What's your name?

Aírton. Are you going to charge me for it?

Absolutely not. Take down my phone number.

After Aírton leaves and the laundry lady stops by to pick up his clothes, he takes Beta for a walk along the beach and is still thinking about the course for lifeguards when he remembers a story that was born, lived a long life and died in his own mind, or at least was dead until now, a story that he had started imagining for no apparent reason when he was about twelve or thirteen and continued imagining until the end of his adolescence. It was just a sketch or daydream that never came to a conclusion worthy of the name but which always began in the same manner. He'd be sitting on the beach looking out to sea when he'd see someone waving for help out in the deep water. After swimming past the surf he'd discover that the person drowning was a girl his age, a girl who gradually got older as he imagined the scene year after year. He would pull her out of the sea and she'd cough up water and lie on the sand, weary and breathless. Sometimes she'd be wearing clothes, other times she'd be in a bikini. Her skin was always very white, her hair always black, straight and long. Her eyes were blue. She wasn't anyone he knew or came to know. After recovering enough to stand up and walk, she'd thank him with a hug or just a word and a look and she'd run off down the beach without looking back, her thin arms swinging, until she disappeared along a path through the dunes. Months would go by, sometimes years. He imagined he was older than he was. These futures varied but in all of them he'd find the girl again and she'd be in a terrible state. She had suffered at the hands of men or had become an addict of some sort. A suicide. A wandering orphan. She'd end up crying. Her hair would stick to her cheeks streaked with tears. The slightly older version of himself that was now the protagonist of the story had spent months or years looking for the girl, imagining who she was, how she had come to be out in the deep, where she had gone after disappearing down the beach, and now she reappeared and he loved her. It was that simple. Nothing easier than loving a nameless girl who was a mere idea, delivered to him by fate, vulnerable and sensuous, ready to be rescued, run away and reappear. But she hated him. Sometimes she accused him of saving her against her will. Why did you pull me out of the water? You shouldn't have. More often she would accuse him of abandoning her. How could you have abandoned me? How could you have let me go? But I saved you, he'd argue. She'd shake her head, saying no. Why didn't you ask my name? Why didn't you hold my hand? Why didn't you come running after me? Why did you let me go? You didn't want me. And to him it all seemed terribly unfair. How was he supposed to have known? He'd done what had to be done. He'd done everything that could have been done. How unfair it was that she could look back after so long and accuse him of not having done something differently at the time. Didn't she remember running off without a word? Sometimes there was a sexual tension in this conflict, sometimes he felt sheer desperation. It ended in that, in the intrinsic unfairness of the act of looking back, of daring to imagine a past different to the one that had brought him to precisely where he was now. He imagined variations on this story for years on end. In all of them he ended up alone. It never occurred to him to tell it to someone, write it down, draw it. Why this story? Why any story? Where had it come from and where had it been all this time?

13

He sees a pair of grey-green eyes above fleshy cheeks with dimples that frame a pearly, expectant smile. Light olive skin and thick, peeling lips almost the same colour, just a little rosier. He knows the nose ring in one of the nostrils and the small scar right in the middle of the forehead but he is unable to retrieve the entire face from memory. Long black hair tumbling over the shoulders. His eyes take in every quadrant of this face in the space of a breath and he could swear he's never seen this woman before in his life but he suddenly knows who she is. Something tells him. He thought about her a few days ago and always knew she would come some day. At the same instant in which he recognizes her, she gets a fright and her smile gives way to a pained expression.

Shit! What happened to you?

I got a little roughed up in a fight, he says smiling.

You never were the brawling sort.

Some guys stole my dog. Beta. I went to get her back and they didn't like it.

She tilts her head and narrows her eyes as if she doesn't believe him. They stare at one another for a while. He feels his body swaying softly to the rhythm of his racing heartbeat and sees Viviane's chest inflating and emptying like a bellows. Organs working to feed brains at the peak of activity, almost paralysed by the millions of things to be said.

Did you recognize my face when you opened the door?

No. But I recognized you.

How?

You know how.

She nods and tries to blow away some hairs that are falling over her face. He realizes that both of her hands are occupied with some kind of frame wrapped in brown paper and tied with string.

Even after all this time?

Guess so.

Well, *I* almost didn't recognize *you*. You're so thin.

I know. There are several reasons. Among which pneumonia.

Pneumonia? You never used to get sick. Just colds.

I got water in my lungs.

How did that happen?

I fell off the top of a headland and had to swim all night to get to a beach.

You can't be serious.

You look beautiful. You seem happy. I look at your photos sometimes.

Are you going to let me in?

She is wearing a military-looking burgundy coat with large pockets and a belt of the same colour at the waist. Black jeans and boots adorned with metallic buckles. Everything looks expensive and elegant, different to the little summer dresses and department store tracksuits that clothe the image of her that inhabits his memory. She takes a few steps into the living room and looks around. Her tall figure in the morning light looks like something straight out of a fashion magazine and contrasts with the second-hand furniture of the apartment.

Your mother told me you were living in front of the beach but I imagined something different. This is practically in the water. What an incredible view. You could just about swim out the door, couldn't you?

It's what I do almost every day. Have a seat. I'll make us some coffee.

She leans the frame against the arm of the smaller sofa and sits. He fills the kettle with tap water.

When did you get here?

Last night. I got to Florianópolis in the afternoon and rented a car. I got a room in a bed and breakfast in front of the beach. It's so cheap in the off-season! The room's really nice. I think I'm the only guest.

You came alone, didn't you?

Yes.

He goes through four matches trying to light the stove.

I wanted to call to let you know I was coming but your mother said your phone had been off or out of range for several days, and you closed your Facebook account too. Though you never did answer my messages anyway. Did you even see them? I sent you some text messages too but you didn't answer. In the end I decided to come anyway because I'd already scheduled the time off from work and I wasn't going to have another opportunity so soon. I hope it's not a problem. I don't want to be a bother.

No problem. I've been a bit out of touch with the world.

You never answered any of my messages. I came to the conclusion you didn't want to have any contact with me. But I came anyway. Because, after all, I know how things work with you. If I were to wait for a reply . . .

It's nice to see you. I think –

He considers what to say as he spoons coffee into the filter.

– I read your messages for a while, but I dunno, Viv. I didn't really feel like chatting on Facebook. It's not that I didn't want to talk to you.

No, I understand.

It was great to open the door and see you. Really great. It's nice to see you in person.

I've been worried about you. Everyone has. Especially after all this rain, the flooding. And then you up and disappear all of a sudden. Was there a lot of damage here?

Not here.

I kept seeing all those people dying on TV. They say it was the biggest flood in the history of Santa Catarina. There was all that construction work on the highway. I'm glad it didn't affect you.

He hears Beta's paws as she comes out of the bedroom.

Beta, look who came to visit us. Someone you know.

Beta comes limping into the living room. She looks at Viviane and sniffs the air, but doesn't approach her.

She got hit by a car but she's OK now.

Viviane snaps her fingers and makes some sounds without much conviction to call Beta, but the dog just stands there in the middle of the room, out of reach. The two of them stare in silence at Beta, who in turn stares at nothing. Everything is frozen for a few seconds. The kettle starts to whistle.

So how are you holding up?

I'm fine. They messed up my face a bit. The worst thing was the pneumonia, but I'm over it.

After your dad's death, I mean.

Oh. I'm OK. I miss him. But that's to be expected.

I wanted to go to his funeral but I'd just started my new job and couldn't get the time off.

You told me on the phone. You don't have to justify yourself. Everything's OK, really. What's done is done. Keeping Beta has helped me deal with it. Sometimes I remember him and I feel sad, but

393

we didn't even visit each other all that often, you know? He was in pretty poor health. But he had a good heart. After he killed himself I think that became clearer. He was good for everyone in his own twisted way. We never wanted for anything, if you think about it. I remember him holding me by the scruff of the neck and giving me advice. He'd hold on tight and start telling me some home truths. Dad always knew what he was doing. He made quick decisions and never went back on them. He made a decision.

Dante was really upset. He can't accept it.

That's his problem.

He goes back into the kitchen and pours the boiling water into the filter.

Dante was also upset that he didn't see you at the funeral. You left early, didn't you? You missed each other.

We didn't miss each other. I left before he got there on purpose. Dante can fuck himself. And I don't want to talk about him right now.

The hiatus in the conversation is filled by the smell of coffee and the sound of the waves crashing into the rocks near the window. He returns with two coffee mugs, gives one to Viviane and sits on the other sofa. She is so beautiful. His coffee-making hasn't kept him with his back turned long enough for him to forget her face. When they lived together he used to play a secret game where he would test how long he could remember the face of the woman he loved or try to look at her often enough so as not to forget her for an entire morning or a whole day. In the beginning it was easy, then it grew harder and at some point he lost the will to try, but seeing her again now, after more than two years, the game makes sense again. He decides to put it in practice. He won't lose sight of her. He won't let her face escape his memory until she leaves again. When she walks out the door he will hold her face in his memory at the same time as he remembers how they met at the pool where he was teaching, she in a black bathing suit and blue swimming cap, swimming clumsily with her tall, strong body, stopping at the edge of the pool to breathe and chat, letting her guard down for an invitation to go out for a beer. The house brimming with books where she lived with her rich parents before she moved in with him in a horrible apartment in Cidade Baixa, surrounded by noisy bars and schizophrenic neighbours. Her face will start to fade but the memories of what they did together won't. The first time they went to the seaside together and camped in a deserted campsite at Christmas. Her coming out of the water in the middle of the deserted beach shaking with cold, covered in goose bumps, and not noticing the blood running down her thighs and cringing with shame when he told her. Lying on her back on top of him in the damp, stuffy inside of the tent, having little convulsions after she came. Them looking at themselves in the mirror together. Their bodies were so beautiful it was agonizing. She used to say that the human body was fortunate. It didn't make much sense, but it was what she said, as if 'fortunate' were a synonym for 'beautiful' or something of the sort. He never corrected her. The one who was right about words was her, always her. He didn't read books and she didn't watch him compete but it didn't seem to matter. It will take a few minutes for her face to disappear. Then all that will be left is a blur. It doesn't matter what he feels for someone, it always happens. But he won't allow it to happen as long as she is in his apartment. He makes the most of her being there. One, two, three, go.

Tell me about yourself. How's life in São Paulo?

I'm well. Really well. We've bought an adorable apartment in Pinheiros. One of those old ones with high ceilings that you've got to be on a waiting list to get. I went to all the small estate agents in the neighbourhood, where the agents are really old and only know how to use fax machines, and I left a description of what I wanted and asked them to call me when something appeared. The owner of this apartment had health problems and went to live with one of her children and they put it on the market. The agent called me the same day and told me to go and see it because it'd be gone in a week. We were so lucky. I spent ages freelancing, making contacts, and then at the beginning of this year I got a job working in the children's book department of a publishing house, which I love. I get to work with writers, translators, *amazing* illustrators. I went to Flip in July. Have you heard of it? It's a literary festival that takes place in Paraty. The programme includes Flipinha, which covers children's literature. I worked my backside off but it was great fun. Dante went with me. He might even be invited to be a guest speaker next time round, if he manages to finish his book by the end of the year. Noll was there, a writer I like a lot. We had some great chats with Verissimo. He talked a lot! He always struck me as so shy that I used to think he was mute.

Verissimo's the one who does those cartoon strips with snakes, right?

That's him. And I'm writing a weekly column about books and the publishing industry for a newspaper's website, and sometimes they ask me to do reviews too. The cultural life in São Paulo is something else. Porto Alegre isn't bad, but in São Paulo it's endless. It's a bit scary even. It's a city that doesn't seem to let a person feel good when they're isolated, even if their isolation is voluntary, if they want a breather. For example, I don't know if you'd feel good there long term. It's an aggressive place for introspective sorts. There's a bewildering range of wonderful things to do, see and eat all the time, and there's a kind of cosmic ether of interesting people, power and money that inflates ambitions and makes you feel a little guilty to stay home with your phone off reading *Harry Potter* or thinking about life and eating chocolate, you know? By the way, changing the subject, did you see that Obama won?

Who?

Obama. He was elected. I saw it last night on TV in the restaurant. He won. The first black president of the United States. 'Yes we can.' I wanted to download his speech on my iPhone but there's no 3G coverage here. I bought an iPhone! Look. Have you seen one? It's Apple's mobile phone. A friend brought it for me.

What are you talking about, Viv?

You know who Obama is, don't you? For heaven's sake.

Of course I do. Wittgenstein's friend.

The old inside joke gets a chuckle out of her. Shortly after they met, back when Viviane was still studying journalism at the Federal University and taking some optional classes in Philosophy in her free time, she tried to impart to him all of the enthusiasm she felt for the *Tractatus Logico-Philosophicus*, which she had read after a teacher talked about it in class. It ended in an argument. After that he'd jokingly evoke the philosopher's name whenever she started ranting on a subject that he couldn't follow either because he lacked the cultural references or wasn't up to date with it. Part of the joke was hearing her out patiently and even encouraging her to go on, only to make some kind of reference to Wittgenstein at the end, which meant he'd been completely lost for some time.

I know who Obama is. I just didn't know he'd won the election yesterday and I don't know why you're talking about your new mobile phone now.

You asked about São Paulo and I started talking and I don't know where I was going with it, sorry. I'm a bit nervous. You think it's easy for me to be here?

No, of course not. I don't really know what to say either.

397

She takes a sip of coffee and indicates the package with her chin.

I brought you a present.

Can I open it now?

She nods. He stands, goes to get a serrated knife from the kitchen, takes the package and sits on the sofa with it. He cuts the string and tears off the brown paper, to reveal a large framed portrait.

It's your dad, says Viviane, taking care to let him know before he finds himself faced with the cruel challenge of identifying the person in the portrait.

He finishes unwrapping it. It is an enlarged black-and-white photograph, almost a metre high. Every pore, eyelash and wrinkle shamelessly offers itself up for examination. His father is smiling in the head-and-shoulders shot, wearing a white dress shirt. There are blurry plants and houses in the background. He can't tell where the photo was taken.

I took this photo of him when we went to Jaguarão to go shopping at the border. Remember? I think it was the first time we travelled somewhere with him. He was going to buy whisky and cigars and we hitched a lift. You bought those Ray-Bans.

I remember.

I was still using that old camera back then. The one I used for photography at college. I've still got all the negatives.

I remember.

He stares at the photo with a lump in his throat.

Do you like it?

Yes. I do. A lot.

I thought you must have lots of photos of him but this one's nice and there's this great place near home that does these enlargements really well.

It's amazing. I don't even know what to say, Viv. Thanks.

I hope you like it.

He takes his eyes off the photo and sees Viviane's eyes shining. She is sitting on the sofa with her hands clasped together, fingers squashing other fingers, insecure and glowing like a woman who has just declared that she is in love. He sets the portrait down on the sofa and almost leaps to his feet, where he finds her standing too.

I knocked over the mug, she whispers in his ear.

Leave it.

Coffee stains.

It doesn't matter.

They stand there hugging until a feeling similar to sleepiness loosens their limbs and they step back. His heart is skittering. He picks up the mug that fell on the rug and she announces that she is going to the bathroom. The seagulls screech as they fly over the bay in insane circles as two boats return to the beach after a night of fishing. Beta perks up her ears, stands and heads outside.

The bathroom door is unlocked. Viviane walks past him, goes over to the window and stands there, staring at the ocean. He sits on the sofa again and remembers her face as he gazes at her long legs and black hair that spills halfway down her back and looks like it is in motion even when it isn't, some hairdresser's magic. He needs to get her to turn around. The blurring will start if he gives it a chance.

Did you come here just to see how I was or have you got something to tell me?

She turns.

I'm pregnant. You're going to be an uncle.

How long have you known?

For two months. I'm fifteen weeks along. It's a boy.

Congratulations. I'm happy for you.

Are you really?

Of course, Viv. You're happy, aren't you? You wanted this.

I did.

Then I'm happy too. I'm able to see it independently of everything else. I knew it was going to happen. I knew one day you'd come to me to tell me this. Remember that little piece of paper you signed for me?

What piece of paper?

Before you went to São Paulo to live with him. We were still together. In that café in Moinhos de Vento.

I don't remember any pieces of paper.

You dated and signed a piece of paper and I wrote something on it.

I don't know what you're talking about.

He gets up, goes to the wardrobe in the bedroom and rummages through the contents of a box until he finds the folded piece of paper. He hesitates for a moment. Part of him doesn't want to show her and would rather tear it up, throw it in the bin and change the subject. But another part remembers that nothing can be erased. You can't pretend that something doesn't exist.

He goes back into the living room and hands it to Viviane. She reads it quickly and looks up with an expression of confusion and disappointment.

Is this a joke? I didn't know what you had written here.

But you remember that you dated and signed it, don't you?

Now I do, but what the fuck? If you knew that we were going to break up, if you knew that one day I'd show up to tell you I was pregnant, why didn't you say so then? Why didn't you do something?

I did everything I could. Maybe it feels like nothing to you, but I did everything I could. It wasn't a lot. There wasn't a lot I could do. I knew it wouldn't make any difference.

She walks over, hands the paper back to him and sits on the sofa.

I really don't like this. What did you do it for? Seriously, what was your intention? To be able to say 'I told you so' or 'I knew it' or something like that? Does it make you somehow superior to me? Superior to your brother? Do you know everything that's going to happen to everyone? Who do you think you are?

No. That's not it. I think I wrote it down more to assure myself that I wasn't crazy. So that when it happened I'd know that I really had seen what was to come. And that there was nothing I could have done. Or you.

Or Dante.

Dante too.

But why did you let me go, then? Why didn't you try to keep me in Porto Alegre? Why didn't you come with me?

You know the story as well as I do, Viv.

No I don't. You're the one who knows everything. Help me out here, because I don't get it. I don't know how you see things. I don't know what you're doing now.

Dante decides to move to São Paulo and a month later you get a work offer there. You'd dreamed of it for a long time, to get you out of that suffocating little backwater, as you used to say, like a house with a low ceiling that forced you to stoop. And you were right. For someone like you, Porto Alegre is small. I couldn't go with you at the time because I was training for the Ironman in Hawaii. Which was my *dream*. There was no way I could just stop and move to *São Paulo* out of the blue. Then Dante goes and gets a huge apartment somewhere or other and invites us to go and live with him in the beginning and you ask me if I'd mind if you went on ahead. If I'd *mind*. Which was the same as asking my permission. I think that was when I saw everything. It was pretty easy to see. Everything that was taking shape at that moment in time, forgetting the little stories we make up in our heads, our desires, the things we'd like to happen, just looking at reality, every single thing had a consequence. It wasn't a puzzle. Because I knew Dante liked you.

Did he ever tell you that?

No, but he's my brother. And I could see how much you admired him. Especially after he published his book. Or the second or the third, I don't know. The one that did well. I read that crap. I recognized everyone in it. Friends of mine were characters in it. The only part of our adolescence that he didn't devour with his fanciful imagination was me. He had the decency to leave me out. All the rest is there. And he calls it fiction.

Well, technically —

But it doesn't matter. I know you loved me, Viv, but I also know that sometimes you thought I was a thick athlete, uncultured. Which is what I am. A nice guy, a good person, but not an intellectual. Big dick, small mind. When we met you were only twenty-one and that was all you wanted. But it got stale. Maybe if I'd been a bit more open-minded. If I'd read the books you'd given me and liked them. If I'd changed over time. If I'd taken an interest in your world. If I'd been a little more like someone I wasn't. Imagine if I was a *writer*.

Don't say that. You're making light of what I felt for you. What I still feel.

No, I'm not. I know what you felt for me. I *felt* what you felt for me. I know that in a way you've never stopped loving me. But am I wrong? Wasn't that what was going on when you asked me if I minded?

You're exaggerating.

Maybe. But I'm exaggerating something real.

She looks at him with an expression not of anger, but of animal ferocity, of self-defence, and a single tear escapes her left eye, plops on her cheek and falls to the ground as she asks the next question.

So why'd you say you *didn't* mind if I went? If you already knew it was going to happen?

Don't cry, Viv.

I'm not going to cry. Tell me *why*.

Because I was going to lose you anyway. The only question was how. If I'd held on to you, today I'd be the guy who held you back. And I would have.

Oh, thanks a lot. You're so nice. What a sacrifice. You thought it best to keep quiet and let me go so you could be the victim. The victim with his ridiculous piece of paper saying *I knew it*.

I'm not the victim. There's no such thing.

Maybe I wouldn't have gone if you'd insisted that I stay.

Don't fool yourself.

She shakes her head and blows air through her nostrils.

So you knew everything. Well *I* didn't. I didn't predict that any of it was going to happen. I just fell in love with him. I had no way of knowing that my life was going to become a poor remake of *Jules et Jim*. You could have told me if you already knew. I'd have prepared myself better. Can I have a glass of water?

He goes into the kitchen and comes back with her water. She drinks it all and holds the glass in both hands so tightly that her knuckles turn yellow and he is afraid the glass might break.

I should have told you this as soon as I came. Now it's going to be harder. But I'll say it. I came to ask if you'd be the godfather.

He takes his eyes off the glass and looks at her. She gives him a little smile.

I don't think you saw *that one* coming, did you?

Does he want it too?

It was his idea.

And do you think it's a good one?

I do.

It sounds completely absurd to me.

Whatever. It's time we put this all behind us. All this resentment. Your father died and you guys weren't even able to give each other a hug at his funeral. Your mother pretends it doesn't matter but she's afraid to broach the subject with you. Dante's afraid too, but he's suffered a lot as a result of all this and he misses you. Everyone's hurting like hell and it isn't necessary. *It isn't worth it*. But I'm not afraid to ask you. Because think about it. It's perfect. Precisely because it sounds absurd. It's our child. Your nephew. Let's take the opportunity to move on. We're young but we're grown up. We can still do the right thing and live everything that we still have in front of us without any bitterness. It's a question of family. We're a family. I know how much that means to you. Have you thought about it like that?

Stop.

You know I'm right. It's your resentment that's stopping you from accepting.

I understand what you're saying. But I can't.

You can't?

I can't accept.

You're turning down our invitation to be your nephew's god-father. Really?

Look. I understand what you're saying. Imagining it, it really is perfect. But it's impossible. I can't pretend it's possible. I can't forgive him just like that. You're out of your minds.

Why can't you forgive him?

Isn't it obvious?

Are you really that petty? I forgive you for letting me go and writing a little note to yourself instead of talking to me. Are you incapable of forgiving?

I don't want your forgiveness.

I forgive you anyway.

Well I don't accept it. I refuse to be forgiven.

Ha! Incredible. This is too good to be true.

I can live with whatever I've done wrong. Nothing disappears just because we decide it should, or because we want it to. No one can take back any harm I've done to others. It helps us become better people. Forgiving is like pretending it doesn't exist. But life is the result of what we've done. It doesn't make sense to act as if nothing has happened.

That's not forgiveness! You're mad! To forgive someone is to free them of blame. And, in doing so, you free yourself too. It's not pretending it never happened. It's an act of charity, a white flag. It's a choice you make. It takes courage, but it's worth it.

It's not a choice. There's no such thing as choice.

No?

No, not really.

OK then, but then why the resentment? Why be resentful if no one has any choice in anything? If we only obey fate, no one can be held responsible for their actions. Right? Everything I did, everything you did and everything your brother did is all just destiny. There's nothing to forgive because no one is to blame.

But that's how it is. No one chooses anything but we're responsible anyway. That's just how it is. I can't explain why. I don't have the words for it. Maybe you do.

I do, but what you're saying doesn't make sense. It's absurd. Either there is free will or there isn't. If human beings are free agents, if we have choices, we are responsible for them. If there's no free will, if the universe is predetermined by the laws of nature and everything is just the result of what has gone before, then no one is to blame for what they do. Neither resentment nor forgiveness make any sense.

Wittgenstein.

Don't give me that Wittgenstein crap! You know what I'm talking about. I know you're more intelligent than you like to admit in your fits of woe-is-me.

So what are the two alternatives again?

Free will and determinism.

I don't think it's that simple.

There's nothing simple about it.

What I mean is that both alternatives seem wrong. Or both are right at the same time. Two right answers to a wrong question.

Jesus Christ. What's the right question, then?

I don't know.

This is a replay of every maddening argument we've ever had. The topic changes but the script is always the same. No one wins.

I know that there are no choices but that nevertheless we have to live as if there were. That's all.

I think it's my turn to say 'Wittgenstein'. Am I allowed to?

That's why forgiveness doesn't make any sense. Forgiveness is cowardice. What takes courage is to keep on loving and having friendships and doing the right thing by others without pretending that you can erase things, without forgiving or accepting forgiveness. You said Dante's upset because Dad killed himself. What for? I think what he did was fucked up and I don't forgive him for what he did, but he told me he had no choice but to kill himself and now I understand that in a way he really didn't. I'm not angry at anyone. Why would I be? He was good to us all until that moment. When we look back it's all inevitable.

Your dad told you he was going to kill himself?

He doesn't answer and she covers her mouth with her hand.

Viv, no part of me is capable of forgiving my brother for what he did. It's not that I want to but can't. I don't *want* to. It'd be *wrong*. Deep down, he didn't choose to do it, just as no one chooses anything, but it doesn't exempt him from the responsibility for inviting you there knowing that I couldn't go, for having gone ahead with things, nor does it exempt you from the responsibility for having gone and for leaving me for him. And I'm not exempted from my responsibility for letting you go, for not helping you to be happy, for having become the guy that you ended up having no choice but to leave. It all works together and is a part of our lives now. At some point you guys decided that your feelings for each other justified hurting my feelings. You didn't decide out of choice, because you didn't have a choice, but Porto Alegre wasn't an option, I wasn't an option, you guys were in love in São Paulo where everything is an option, but the decision is there, it exists in the world like a stone, like a knife, the decision is *here*, it exists *now*, it's something that happened and had consequences like any decision, any gesture, anything you do or say whether you believe it's your own free will or not. You guys decided that the life you wanted to have together from that point on was more important than any mark that it might leave on me and you went ahead with it. And it's OK. I can put myself in your place. I don't think I'd have done the same thing, but I can imagine it and understand it. But have the courage to stand by it now. I'll love you for ever and I would still defend my brother's life in any way I could if it were ever in danger. But I don't want to see him and I won't be your child's godfather.

I'm sorry for coming here.

She gets up and straightens her clothes.

You don't need to leave.

Yes I do.

But she doesn't leave immediately. She stands there a while, staring out of the window at the sunny ocean.

Viv.

You're happy here, aren't you?

Me? Yes. I think so.

I actually believe you. When they told me you'd come here, they said you were running away, or traumatized by what your dad did. I tell everyone it's not true. I must be the only person who gets that that's not it. There's nowhere else you'd rather be right now.

Maybe. I don't know.

I feel like shaking you, slapping you in the *face* for your coldness, your arrogance, your vanity, for God's sake. The *vanity* of thinking you don't need anyone, of believing you shouldn't forgive or be forgiven. But it's not like that from your point of view, is it? You're happy. I can see in your eyes the loneliness I've brought you. I know you never feel alone. It's just because I'm here now. Tomorrow everything will be fine again. I'm going to head back early. I'll change my ticket this afternoon at the airport. You don't need to say anything. I know how much you love me. It exists somewhere. It's safe. I won't come back here again. If you want to visit us one day, the doors will always be open. I'm due mid-April. OK? He'll be your nephew. If you don't have the dignity, the courage to come and see him, maybe one day he'll come looking for you, when he's old enough. Because that's how you like it, isn't it? When people come to you.

He chokes trying to say something.

I'm going now. Don't worry. Things happened as you predicted they would, didn't they? But it'll be quicker than you imagined. It's already over.

Acknowledgements

The verse extract quoted at the end of Chapter 9 is by Manoel Brandão de Souza and was taken from the book *História de Garopaba* (*The History of Garopaba*), by Manoel Valentim.

I would like to say a special thanks to my friend and open-water swimming companion Mário Martins da Silva Jr, for his limitless wisdom and generosity, and to my father, Gilson Galera, who told me the story that gave rise to all the rest.